THE SILENT VALLEY

Also by Carey Cleaver

The Wild Rose of Meath

THE SILENT VALLEY

Carey Cleaver

HEADLINE

First published in Great Britain in 1996 by
HEADLINE BOOK PUBLISHING

10 9 8 7 6 5 4 3 2 1

British Library Cataloguing in Publication Data

Cleaver, Carey
Silent Valley
I. Title
823.914 [F]

ISBN 0-7472-1452-2

Typeset by
CBS, Felixstowe, Suffolk

Printed and bound in Great Britain by
Mackays of Chatham PLC, Chatham, Kent

HEADLINE BOOK PUBLISHING
A division of Hodder Headline PLC
338 Euston Road
London NW1 3BH

For my editor Cate Paterson
who was such a joy to work with
and who steered me so expertly
through the maze

ACKNOWLEDGEMENTS

To my cousin Kathleen Owen for helping me with my research and Alan Tate my friend who knows about boats, cars and planes.

CHAPTER 1

Ballycash, 1951

Father Patrick Mulligan was holding his newspaper in one hand and guiding his cream cracker and cheese to his questing mouth with the other. A plump, grey-haired man, he was wont to describe himself as being 'past my middle years and well on the way to senility', adding with an impish grin, 'And I'm short on patience and long on temper.'

On the other hand, Kitty O'Hara, his housekeeper, although a bit tart at times, had the patience of a saint, even if she did drive him mad with her bossiness. He looked over at her as she busied herself at the big kitchen range. She could still look handsome if she took her hair out of the severe bun and let it swing a bit. He spoke to her back. 'I still say that Mourne is old enough and sensible enough to be told about the circumstances of her birth.'

Kitty turned. Every day for the past month the man had been going on about this subject but she remained adamant, and when she spoke, her tone was crisp and decisive. 'And I say she is happier not knowing the truth.'

With a sigh of impatience, Patrick put down his paper. 'You can't pass it off that easily, Kitty. You know that can't be the way of it. We have got to tell her. We owe it to her – and besides, there are the articles that were with her. She should have them; they can't lie in my safe for ever.'

'Can they not?' said Kitty with bitterness. 'If it wasn't for those gifts she'd not have to know anything. Give them to charity, why don't you?' She made her way to the scullery and called back over her shoulder. 'Do what you like. We've been going on about this for the past year and I know that Gerry agrees with you – I'll bring your milk drink to you in your study then I'm off to my bed.'

'Are you not waiting for Mourne to come in?'

'You'll still be up,' she called out, and thought, You will still be

1

sipping the milk with the brandy you have tipped into it for added flavour.

'I'll have another word with Gerry,' Father Patrick replied. He hated these arguments with Kitty.

Later, settling himself further into the deep, comfortable armchair with the warm milk drink by his side, he leaned back and closed his eyes.

The study was a large, untidy room, with a huge open fireplace and a high surround; it was here, on the high mantel, that he hid his brandy. The carpet was worn and threadbare in places, but it only added to the genteel decadence of the room. There was no woman's touch here – no flowers or ornaments or fancy cushions. A man could lean back into his chair, content in the knowledge that there would be nothing pushing into his spine and trying to make its way out the other side.

He reflected on the problem of Kitty's daughter, Mourne, as he sipped the mellow drink. Since she had been adopted by Kitty and Charlie, she had lived the life of Riley; nothing was too good for the girl who had come into their lives so unexpectedly and under such adverse conditions, and even that crusty old bachelor Gerry Owen thought the sun rose and shone on her. It was understandable that Kitty didn't want to rock the boat, but the girl was approaching her twenty-first birthday and she had a right to know of her past so that she could put her future into perspective. It was a pity that Charlie had died so suddenly; he would have been able to see the sense of it all.

There was a tap on the door and the girl who had been occupying his thoughts walked in, a smile already lighting up the lovely green eyes. She was slightly built, with a wealth of rich auburn hair that flowed over her shoulders like a cape. She tossed it back as she crossed the room to drop a kiss on the top of his head. He sighed. It was the kind of indifferent kiss that he himself might place on a baby's head at baptism – a kiss that gave nothing away, unlike the jammy ones she used to plant all over his face as she told him that she loved him.

'Did you have a good evening?'

'Not bad,' Mourne O'Hara giggled. 'Eddie Moran made a right cod of himself as ever. He can't hold a note as you well know, so he went about the stage declaiming the words like a Shakespearean actor.'

'That must have confused people, seeing as it was a concert.' Patrick smiled up at her, his eyes feasting on her beauty and vitality.

Half the young men in the town were after her, and she would have none of them.

She yawned and said sleepily, 'Well! I'm off to bed. Goodnight, Father Patrick.'

He watched her leave the room, her slight frame looking even more slight and vulnerable in the soft guarded light shed by the standard lamp. She turned and blew him a kiss, and when she had gone he reached for the brandy and tipped a bit more into what remained of his now cold milk. Sure Kitty would never know, and he needed to settle his mind for sleep.

The following morning, Mourne lay in bed with the sheet tossed aside, the better to feel the gentle summer breeze whisper its way across her hot body. She stared out at the sky where the same gentle breeze was sending a couple of wayward clouds scudding before it, and sighed with pleasure. She had enjoyed herself last night. It had been a real gas. She had particularly enjoyed the company of the new lad who had recently joined. He had come to live in Ballycash just a few weeks ago, and he was proving to be an asset to the little theatre group they all belonged to which was run by the church. She frowned. She hoped he wasn't reading anything into the friendship, though. She was still raw from the break-up with Anthony Rice.

Eventually, she rose and crossed to the window and pulled the buttercup-yellow curtains aside to see if the Maguire twins were trying to strangle the cat, which was setting up a terrible yowl: they were.

'Why are you trying to strangle that poor unfortunate animal?' she called out.

The twins, startled, dropped the poor thing, who darted off like the clappers. 'We were only tryin' to love it,' said Noreen, the eldest by ten minutes.

'God help the fella who gets you when you are old enough. You should try a little tenderness for God's sake – what are you doing in our garden, anyway?'

Cassie, the younger of the two, and the cheekiest, looked surprised. 'It's the graveyard!'

'It may have a few hundred souls lying in it but it's the only garden we have unless you count the strip at the front,' said Mourne. 'Get off home and help your mam with some housework.' The words were stern but her voice hid a smile. She thought the twins were great.

'It must be embarrassing to live in a graveyard,' said Cassie, adding:

3

'You shouldn't live with Father Mulligan if you wanted a garden.'

'We don't live with Father Mulligan, you cheeky scallion. If I was dressed I'd be down there after you.' They ran off and Mourne moved towards the tiny basin to rinse her face and hands.

'Mourne O'Hara, have you died in your sleep up there? Your breakfast is fast congealing. Get yourself over to the kitchen this minute.'

She smiled as she heard the door shut downstairs. Her mam could frighten the socks off a saint, but she was as soft as butter underneath.

Over in the kitchen, Father Patrick was reading the Sunday paper, his glasses halfway down his nose.

'You look like Mr Pickwick, with those glasses at half mast,' Kitty observed, mildly.

Ignoring the remark, Patrick glanced up. 'You have a right mouth on you. I heard you from here guldering at Mourne. Let her sleep on; she can go to second Mass.'

'She wasn't asleep. I heard her telling the Maguire twins off. They were after Morpheus again.'

'That cat can look after himself. In a fight to the death I'd put my money on him any day against the twins. The trouble is, he's always sleeping, so they can creep up on him, but I tell you, I've seen him in action and those two are no match for him.'

There was the sound of a door slamming and the noise of running feet on the flagstones and Mourne entered, smiled at her mother, and kissed the top of Father Mulligan's head as usual.

'Will you stop that! I'll swear that's one of the reasons my bald spot is getting bigger.'

'Worry less about your bald spot and more about your weight,' Mourne laughed.

'Don't be so cheeky.' Kitty frowned at her daughter, and Father Patrick looked smug at the telling-off she got.

When she had gone Patrick continued to sit at the table, idly drumming his fingers, deep in thought. He would discuss the business of telling Mourne about her birth with Gerry – after all, he was her godfather – he should take some responsibility for the decision. Up to now Gerry had refused to take sides, but it would not do. It would not do at all. He shook his head slowly.

'Are you shaking your head for a good reason, or have you developed some malady?' Kitty asked. 'I've been watching you in the mirror over the sink.'

4

'Ach! I'm just mulling something over in my mind. Get on with your work. I'm off to put on my vestments.'

Later, during lunch, Patrick was aware of Kitty's silence as he steadily applied himself to the food on his plate. Over his spectacles he watched her rigid back as she moved about. He shook his head sadly. Why wouldn't she see the sense of it? He would have to go ahead on his own – at least she had agreed that he could.

Mourne O'Hara walked into the room and regarded the pair of them. 'Have you two had a row?'

'Certainly not! A difference of opinion, but not a row. And you are late sitting down at the table. I'm well into my lunch.'

'It was my turn to clear up the vestry. I got delayed, I'm sorry.' Her mother was standing by the big, black-leaded range, stirring frantically at the custard inside the pot like one of the witches in *Macbeth*, a look of irritation on her face, and Father Patrick was wearing his weary look. They *have* had a row, Mourne thought. The atmosphere was thick with tension. She sat down and pulled the plate of food towards her and stared down at it. 'Mam, do I have to eat *all* this? You've enough on this plate to feed the forty thousand.'

'It'll put flesh on your bones,' said Kitty, crossly. 'I don't know why I bother – you should be thankful it is there for you.'

Father Patrick looked slyly at Mourne and smiled.

'And you can take that smile off your face, Patrick Mulligan.'

Patrick started. The woman had eyes in the back of her head. He glared at her back as he left the room. Kitty must really be feeling at odds with him. It was rare for her to refer to him as Patrick Mulligan and not Father Patrick.

When she had finished, Mourne joined her mother in the scullery. She put her plate down on the worktop and said gently, 'You're cross about something.'

Kitty turned. 'Take not a bit of notice. That man would drive a saint to drink when he sets his mind to it, but I still think the world of him. By the time you come back I'll have recovered – sure aren't we all entitled to a drop of bile now and again.' But she was thoughtful as she washed the dishes and cleaned up the debris. If Charlie hadn't died they would still be living as a family in their cottage down the road, but he had fallen, suddenly and tragically, under the wheels of a runaway tractor and they had been left – the three-year-old Mourne and herself – to get on with life the best they could without him. It had seemed sensible to accept Father Mulligan's suggestion that they

5

move into the annexe next to the parochial house. It had once been used to house the newly ordained priests who were allotted a parish to study the running of it, but around the time Charlie had died the practice had ceased, and those priests who still came occasionally were invited to stay in the main house.

Eventually, Father Patrick had suggested that it would be a better idea if they all ate their meals together to save doubling up on cooking. 'Besides,' he added, 'I hate eating alone.'

Father Patrick's bolt-hole was his study and apart from a bit of dusting, Kitty was warned not to move an article of furniture or stamp her personality on it. It was his room and he wanted it to stay that way. The bargain was struck.

As the years passed, Kitty and Mourne spent most of the time in the big warm kitchen of the parochial house and went over to the annexe only to bathe, change their clothes and sleep. The arrangement worked very well and they were now a family unit in an odd kind of way. There weren't many of her own family left now. There was a cousin in Dundrum, and his son who married a girl from round Ardglass way, that was all. Her cousin was not in the best of health and the distance had meant that over the years, meetings had diminished in frequency.

Kitty's nose suddenly wrinkled in distaste. There had been a smell around for a couple of days – only today it seemed stronger. She swept a look round for the umpteenth time and was about to give up as she had done the other times when she spied a mass lying on the floor in the recess under the sink. She pulled the heap out, tentatively, with the brush handle to examine it. It was Mourne's old duffle coat. She inspected the odorous orange-brown stain. Cow clap! The silly girl had slipped in cow clap – probably when out walking with O'Rourke. She must have left it there to be washed and forgotten to mention it. God! She had better ring to cancel the plumber's visit. Galvanized into action, Kitty got rid of the ripe-smelling bundle and spent the next hour aerating the kitchen. At least, she thought in amusement, finding the coat had taken her mind off her troubles for a bit.

Gerry Owen was coming to dinner. Father Patrick took himself into his study for Kitty was driving him to drink. 'It isn't the Pope we're expecting,' he grumbled. 'Gerry has had to bear with our lack of sophistication these many years past; sure where is the point of all this fuss? You're running around like a demented banshee, touching this

6

and twitching that and shifting glasses on the dining-room table an inch to the right and then back again.'

Kitty glared at him as he went out of the room and winced as he slammed the door.

'You've not an ounce of breeding beneath your cassock,' she called after him, aware that he had not heard a word but feeling better for letting out her frustration.

In his study Father Patrick poured himself a nip of brandy. It hadn't escaped his notice that Mourne had taken herself off to her room out of the way. The craft of the madam had to be applauded, he thought, as he settled down in the deep armchair to sip his drink and gather his thoughts.

The door opened slowly and he raised his head to find Kitty O'Hara staring disapprovingly at the glass in his hand. He rose hastily.

'Did you not hear the bell?' she asked. Gerry was hovering behind her.

'I did not. Now, will you show my friend in and then get on with the meal while we have our talk.' He walked forward to greet Gerry. 'I'm glad to see you. Living in a house with only two women for company has its drawbacks. When that woman cooks she has the hands of an angel, but her tongue has been programmed by the devil himself.' He motioned Gerry to a chair. 'Have a brandy.'

'Before dinner?'

'What does it matter when? It won't taste any different – besides, I like to flaunt Madam's authority.'

Gerry laughed. 'Patrick Mulligan, you think the sun rises and sets on her so don't tell me different.'

Patrick chuckled. 'The day you let her know, you are a dead man. I'd never be able to hold forth again.'

Gerry took the proffered drink and sank back into his chair with a tired sigh. The only doctor for miles around, he had to work hard and social occasions such as this were like gold-dust. 'I love these chairs of yours. I declare they are wide enough to fit the arse of Finn Ma Coll.' He took a sip of his drink and swallowed with enjoyment before asking, 'What's this invitation in aid of?'

'Can I not invite you for a meal without some devious purpose?'

'Not in the middle of the week. There has to be a reason.'

'Well, there is!' Patrick glanced towards the door and leaning forward, said, 'I've been having a few arguments with Kitty as to whether or not it is time to tell Mourne about the circumstances

7

surrounding her birth. I want you to help me convince her it is the right thing to do.'

Gerry had known Patrick Mulligan since they were boys, attending the school run by the Christian Brothers and driving everyone mad with their antics. No one was more shocked than he when Patrick had decided to enter the priesthood. It had been a rare turnabout, as it had long been assumed that they would both study medicine. Gerry, however, had found himself travelling to England alone, whilst Patrick had joined a seminary.

Having spent years as a surgeon at St Angela's in London, Gerry had returned to his home village to take up general practice in Tullybra and the surrounding areas. It was thirty years since he and Patrick had resumed their old friendship, and it was as much for that friendship as for his expertise that he had been called in to help when Mourne was born. He looked over at Patrick, now.

'I am not going to get involved,' he said slowly, at last. 'We've been through this before and I haven't changed my mind. I got her to hospital and I am her godfather but the responsibility is yours and Kitty's.' He smiled. 'I hope that doesn't mean that I've forfeited a good meal?'

Ignoring the attempt at humour, Patrick said, 'This has caused me a few sleepless nights and Kitty and I are not dealing well with each other because of it, but I feel in my heart that I'm doing the right thing.'

'Then do it!'

'Will Kitty – will either of them – ever forgive me?'

The door opened and Mourne poked her head round. 'Dinner is on the table and Mam says do you think she doesn't know that you are drinking your heads off in here?'

Patrick motioned Gerry ahead of him, and as he passed Mourne he said, 'I want a word with you tomorrow after we've had supper.' There, he'd done it! There was no going back.

Mourne closed the door and followed the two men to the dining-room, her brows creased in a frown. She wondered what the word was to be about – and what a strange time to mention it. For some reason she couldn't fathom she felt uneasy, and during the meal she found her appetite had fled.

Later as she helped her mam wash the dishes she brought the subject up. 'This atmosphere between you and Father Patrick that has been around just lately – has it anything to do with the fact that I've been asked to see him in his study tomorrow evening?'

Kitty stopped what she was doing and faced her daughter. Her heart was banging away inside her as she said, 'When did he ask you this?'

'When I went to fetch Uncle Gerry and him for dinner.'

'I see!' And Kitty did see. She had wondered why Gerry had been invited for a meal in the middle of the week. 'It was an odd moment to ask you to see him,' was all she said.

'That's what I thought. Have you any idea what it's all about?'

'I have my suspicions. I intend to have a word, but it isn't anything to worry about. I shall be there when you have your meeting tomorrow.' She would make certain she was, she thought, grimly.

When Gerry had departed and Mourne had gone over to the annexe to her bed, Kitty tackled Father Patrick.

'Were you going to mention to me that you had arranged to speak to Mourne in your study tomorrow evening?'

Patrick gave a tired sigh. 'It was my reason for coming into the kitchen. My first thought was that I should go to my bed and deal with it tomorrow morning, but I had a feeling that Mourne might have mentioned it to you.'

'Of course she did. She was surprised at your timing and was worried that she had done something to upset you.'

He nodded. 'My timing was off, but I – we – have been dithering about too long and if I hadn't tackled Mourne tonight, I would have gone on for yet another year with the problem hanging over me.'

Kitty's face softened. She knew that he had been put in a difficult position by her own attitude. She looked at the tired face under its thatch of grey hair and laid her hand on his shoulder. 'You're doing what you think is best. I'm sorry that I haven't been able to see eye to eye with you.' She paused. 'I'm frightened that Mourne might be changed by this knowledge – that she might be hurt.'

'We have to take the chance.' Patrick patted her shoulder. 'Away to your bed. The decision is made now, whatever happens. Who knows: Mourne might surprise us and shrug the whole thing off.'

Patrick stared out of the casement window and surveyed the wide street that ran through the small market town of Ballycash, as he awaited the arrival of Kitty and Mourne. To still his nervousness, he assessed the view that had met his eyes for more years than he cared to remember and observed the gentle, sleepy town with a new awareness.

It was lined on one side by a row of shops, and on the other, by

9

houses and pubs and the Castle Hotel. He marvelled now at the conformity of the buildings and the stark simplicity of the architecture, which gave the town a certain air of elegance. The shops included the pharmacy run by Tom McCarty and Barry Grant's emporium, with its oak counters and the wide stairs leading to the upper floor which housed the shoe department.

Barry's shop was the most important one in the street and set incongruously alongside it was the fishmonger's – a thorn in Barry's side because of the reek of fish that pervaded his shop on a hot day and put customers off trying on clothes. Halfway along was the surgery, topped by the sign that said *Gerald Owen MD* without mentioning the string of letters he could add to it after he had passed his gynae and surgical fellowships. The man was too modest, thought Patrick, and smiled fondly. Gerry could have been anything he wanted, but he had elected to return to his home town and set up a practice, thereby earning a pittance compared to what he could have had if he had stayed over the water and taken a consultant's post at St Angela's.

Slap bang in the middle of the market square was the market house, where the stalls were stored when the traders had finished for the day, and where the monthly dances were held at great risk to life and limb as the Irish dancing sessions made the rafters jump and the floor groan with the weight of bodies. The place should be condemned, or designated a listed building with restricted use.

His thoughts were interrupted by the arrival of Kitty and Mourne. He turned and motioned them to a seat before going over to a cupboard and removing a strong but basic wooden box – the kind that held many pounds of fruit for retail. Placing it on the coffee-table he seated himself and stared at it.

Mourne arched her eyebrows at her mother who returned her look but didn't smile in response. She felt a trickle of nervousness go up her spine as she watched Father Patrick put his hand in his pocket to draw out an envelope which was yellowed with age. He handed it to her and she took it.

'I would like you to read this. It will help you understand better what I am about to tell you.'

There was silence in the room while Mourne read the fading words instructing Father Patrick to go up on to the mountain where he would find a box containing something precious. He was to tell no one. At exactly three o'clock he was to be at the east side of the reservoir up in the Silent Valley where he would find the box beneath a large

10

boulder . . . At last she put the letter down and looked at the two people who had been there for her all her life. Kitty was staring at her hands which were tightly clenched in her lap. Father Patrick was looking straight ahead. 'I don't understand,' she said, with a puzzled frown.

Patrick nodded towards the box. 'I have a story to relate to you which involves you, and that box plays a major part in it. It is the box which is mentioned in the letter – the box in which you were placed following your birth . . .'

Kitty made a sound and stared down at her hands. Mourne sat back in her chair, her face pale and anxious as Father Patrick told of the day he had found the note on the mat when he had returned from Mass; of how he had gone up on to the mountain as instructed and found the box under the boulder, just as the note said.

As he spoke of the tiny baby only hours old, wrapped in a hand-knitted vest and covered in sweet grasses, Mourne continued to sit with her head bowed. There were no tears, but a stricken look sometimes betrayed the turmoil and anguish beneath as Father Patrick explained how he had run down the mountain road, angry with himself for not being more fit. He explained how he had taken the precious bundle to his friend Gerry to be examined, before rushing to the hospital at Downpatrick.

Mourne felt as though the blood in her veins was slowly turning to ice, for the room seemed suddenly cold. Did they not realize how they were wounding her? They were attacking the one thing she had been sure of – the stability that had always been there in her life.

Her face grew more pale as the tale unfolded. Thoughts and feelings jostled and contradicted each other in her mind. She had difficulty concentrating on what Father Patrick was saying.

'Two weeks later you were transferred to a hospital in Belfast before being placed in a children's home. The police tried in vain to trace your parents and eventually you were put up for adoption. It was all done very discreetly so that no stigma would be attached . . .'

'Tell me one thing,' Mourne whispered. 'How did I arrive here?'

Kitty, who until that point had continued to sit with shoulders hunched and eyes looking down into her lap, gave a shuddering sigh and spoke. 'Charlie and I had been on the adoption waiting-list for two years, and because Father Patrick had found you I used to visit regularly. The lady almoner and I got to know one another very well, and knowing that I had grown to love you she put our name forward.

We brought you home when you were six months old . . .' Her voice trembled and she fell silent.

Mourne tried hard to escape the blanket of numb incomprehension that surrounded her brain but at last, in a voice that was still little more than a whisper, she asked, 'How many people know of this?' She could hardly bear to look at her mother. She felt strangely angry with her. She knew she was being unfair – she should be grateful for all the love and care that had been centred on her over the years – but an inner resentment had begun to build up against the woman she had known for twenty years as Mam. She should have been told about this when she was young enough to adjust.

'Only four people knew – and now, since Charlie's death, only three.' Kitty's voice grew stronger. 'Everyone knew that Charlie and I were on the waiting-list for adoption and not an eyelid was batted nor an eyebrow lifted. All who knew us were delighted.'

'What about the newspapers? Wasn't the find mentioned?' This was a bad dream! Mourne thought, in horror.

Father Patrick spoke. 'Don't look so tragic, Mourne – nothing has changed. You heard me say it was all done very discreetly. The adoption papers were not signed for nearly two years lest anyone came looking – but no one did. As far as anyone else is concerned, Kitty and Charlie got you fair and square when they moved to the head of the list.'

How insensitive he is, Mourne thought. Nothing has changed? You stupid man! Everything has changed. My whole outlook – my life. She raised her eyes to his face and stared at him in silence.

A sob broke from Kitty. 'Charlie adored you till the day he died when you were only three years old. Sure he had no time with you at all, and he loved you so much.'

Momentarily forgetting her own distress, Mourne crossed to her mother and put an arm round her shoulder. 'Don't cry, Mam. You'll have us all at it. You did your best. I just – I just wish you had told me years ago. It comes harder now. As a child I might have had time to adjust – now I'm going to have trouble coming to terms with this.' Although she spoke the words quietly, she actually wanted to scream out at them both.

Father Patrick gave a small cough. 'Kitty! Away into the kitchen and make us all a cup of tea. I'll show Mourne what is in the box and when you come back we'll discuss the best way forward.'

When her mother had left the room, Mourne sank further into the chair and let the tears flow. 'I don't think I can take any more. I have just had my life turned over,' she said, miserably.

'There is no more to take,' Patrick said, softly. 'I need to show you what was in the box with you. If it hadn't been for the contents, I doubt if you would ever have needed to know the full truth. But they are yours. They were left for you by whoever gave birth to you up there on the mountain, so I have a duty to see that you have them.' Unwrapping the object he was holding, he handed it to her.

Mourne gasped as she stroked the delicately carved cross bearing the figure of Christ. 'It's so beautiful.'

'Whoever carved that cross had a loving and artistic heart,' Patrick said. 'I think the person who left that with you loved you very much, and was broken-hearted at having to leave you.' He drew out a smaller parcel. Weighing it in his hand, he continued. 'This also was found with you.'

Mourne unwrapped the cloth to find a small box covered in faded green velvet. She stared at the contents – a beautiful, most exquisitely fashioned emerald ring which caught the light. 'This must be worth a fortune!' she said, but her voice had gone flat again.

'I would imagine so,' Patrick nodded.

At that moment, Kitty appeared with the tray and her eyes met his. He signalled that all seemed well.

'Isn't that the most beautiful ring? It is the colour of your eyes,' said Kitty. 'That is your dowry.'

Mourne didn't answer, but continued to stare at the ring. Her heart had turned cold.

'I would like to hang the cross above my bed,' she said quietly. 'The ring you can keep. I don't want it.' She handed it back to Father Patrick, and walked out of the room.

'She's upset,' said Patrick, looking calmly into Kitty's frantic eyes. 'I'll hold on to it until she comes to terms with all this. I'm glad it's done, and we can now get back on course with our lives.'

Upstairs in the annexe Mourne was lying on her bed, white-faced and with her eyes puffy with sobbing. However events were creamed over, the fact remained. She had been abandoned in a bloody wooden box on a mountainside, rejected by her mother, unwanted by her unknown father. Her chest was hurting and her eyes felt raw from all the tears she had shed. She rose and crossed to the tiny wash-basin. In the mirror she saw a bloated-faced stranger with wild hair and eyes that had lost their lustre. She leaned forward to splash cold water over her skin and when she was done she undressed and crept under the sheet. The night was hot and clammy, and she lay still so as not to generate any more heat. Eventually the tumult in her subsided and her mind began to clear. The crying was over. She had a life to lead and she was determined that she was going forward. No one would ever know just how deeply she had been affected by the disclosures – she would put a brave face on it – but never again would she allow herself to get into a position where she would suffer the indignity of rejection. She never wanted to feel such pain as this again.

CHAPTER 2

The morning hadn't begun well. She had mislaid two sets of notes and valuable time was lost while she located them. The two patients waiting for their notes to be recovered were not happy at missing their turn.

Mourne apologized, but Dora Cummings, who was nursing a crying baby, wasn't to be appeased. She glared at Mourne, her pale blue eyes snapping with annoyance. 'It's bad enough having to visit the doctor with a young baby, without having to lose your turn,' she said.

Towards the end of the morning she discovered she had run out of tea, and she had to shut the reception area and ring in to let Gerry know that she would be out of the surgery for a while.

'What is the matter with you, Mourne? Try and get yourself together, girl.'

'I'm sorry. I won't be long. There are only two people left to see.'

'Hurry up then!' Gerry, having had to deal with Mrs Cummings and her wailing child, felt irritated by it all. He liked things to run smoothly, and fractious children came low on his list of things to like, particularly when they had a high-pitched cry that bit into his brain.

Mourne made her way across the market square to Cullen's grocery store, pleased to get out of the surgery for a few minutes. All morning she hadn't been able to get rid of the depression that had settled on her last night. She put her hand on the latch. This was always a pleasant moment and she wanted to savour it, now, more than ever. As she entered, the breeze stirred the tin cans and the tin mugs and other items that hung on cup hooks from the roof of the shop, causing a musical jingle like the tiny chiming bells of a Tibetan monastery.

She smiled as she always did at the happy jingle-jangle. Her nose twitched as she revelled in the smell of the strong Irish cheeses sitting on the counter in their butter-muslin overcoats, waiting for Jack Cullen's

15

sharp knife to release yet more of the tangy aroma. As a child she would sneak in behind customers just to stand there and listen to the tinklings and smell those cheeses and the freshly cooked hams carried, still hot, to the counter. She would put her nose against the big shiny oak counter and inhale the aroma of years of grease and polish, and accept the bag of sweets that Mr Cullen handed her, amazed that he should give her a bag of sweets for nothing, unaware that her mam had paid for them with the rest of her shopping. In the light of what she had just learned, these memories seemed more precious now.

'For the second time, Mourne O'Hara – what can I do for you?'

'Oh, sorry, Mr Cullen; this place always brings back my childhood to me. As soon as I hear those tin cans playing their music it sets me back to those wonderful days.'

'Sure you aren't much past your childhood now,' Jack Cullen smiled. Mourne had always been an odd little thing. He could remember her skulking behind the big flour bins on many occasions with a moony look on her face till he gently showed her out. She had grown up into a real beauty, with those amazing green eyes and that creamy complexion.

'Can I sell you anything?' he inquired, gently.

'I'd like a half a pound of tea and a pound of mixed biscuits, please.'

As he prepared the order Mourne explained that she was in everyone's bad books because she had mislaid two sets of notes.

'I wouldn't let that worry you,' Jack said, tapping the bag of tea on the counter to settle it before tucking the stiff paper into its flap; 'such things happen.'

'You're right there, Mr Cullen. Life is too short for such trivial worries.' Mourne took the purchases with a quick smile and made her way back to the surgery, aware of her hypocrisy but determined that no one was going to know just how much the past twenty-four hours had hurt. She might have been abandoned, but she was still Mourne O'Hara and she was going to hold her head high. She wanted no one's pity. If the smile had to be pasted on to her face at times, then so be it.

The last patient had gone, so she set the kettle on to boil and tapped on the office door.

'Come in.'

She looked apologetically at the tired figure writing at the desk and said, 'I'm sorry about the mix-up this morning. I had something on my mind and I put the notes down and couldn't think where.'

Gerry Owen looked up. He regretted his earlier surliness. Mourne was a good receptionist; neat, tidy and efficient, and he shouldn't have been short with her on the rare occasion she made a mistake. He motioned her to a chair.

'I have the kettle on for the tea before you go on your rounds.'

'Forget the tea. It can wait. Tell me what's worrying you.'

'Oh! Nothing important,' said Mourne, hurriedly. 'I just built something up in my mind and I lost track of where I was.'

'Well! If I can help to ease your mind, I'll be happy to listen.' Gerry glanced at his watch. 'I have half an hour before my first visit.'

Mourne hesitated. 'Father Patrick told me about finding me on the mountain,' she said, at last.

Gerry had suspected something of the sort. 'And you are feeling angry and hurt and confused.' It was not a question, more a statement of fact.

'Something like that.'

He sighed. 'I warned Patrick that you might take it hard . . .'

'Merciful God, how else was I going to take it? I've spent over twenty years cocooned within the circle of a loving family, and in one evening the stability of my life has vanished because of a wooden box found on a mountain that had me inside.'

Gerry's pen tapped the desk as he regarded the girl before him. 'You are talking a load of taradiddle. Ask yourself in a quieter, saner moment, what has changed? What happened did so a long time ago and your life has been one of loving care ever since. Knowing that you were left in a wooden box, probably with your young mother crying buckets at the decision she had to make, should have no bearing on how things are with you now.'

'How I am now is that I know I was abandoned on a mountain by my real mother.' Mourne's cry of pain struck him to the heart, but he met her tearful gaze stolidly. 'Talk sense,' he said, quietly. 'When you have got over the histrionics, you can just sit quietly and try to put yourself in that young woman's position. Perhaps, with your intelligence, and in these more enlightened times, you could have come up with a different solution, but twenty years ago it was a different kettle of fish altogether. That young mother had no choice. All that has altered is the fact that you now know what we have known all these years – and not a bit of difference has it made to the way we all feel about your place in our hearts and our lives.' Gerry gathered up his papers. 'Away and get my tea. I'm dying of druth and in that respect,

17

hell all has changed. If you want the rest of the day off to go home and sulk or die then let me know – personally, I think you owe Kitty O'Hara and Patrick Mulligan your heartfelt thanks for the love they have showered on you.'

Mourne rose, her face pink with annoyance. Not even this normally sensitive man could understand the feelings that were affecting her life.

Gerry looked thoughtful as she returned with the tea. When she set it down, he spoke. 'I'm going along to see old Charlie Cavanagh – he's dyin' as you know. I'd like you to come along. I think you would be a comfort to Sarah.'

Mourne wasn't surprised at the suggestion. She had gone on such an errand with him on other occasions. 'If you think it will help.'

'I know it will. I had a message to say that he's fading; Sarah will be beside herself.'

'Shouldn't we get started?'

'There isn't anything will keep Charlie's soul from flying off when it is ready. I'll have time to finish my tea.'

When he had finished his examination, Gerry gently folded the sheet up under Charlie's chin. He looked more rested now, in death, than he had done for the past months while the cancer had been eating into his bones with such devastating effect. Never had a man looked so tortured, and never had a man looked into his soul as Charlie had done and prepared himself for this moment.

'When it happens,' Charlie had said, a short time ago, 'will you be sure and see that Sarah has someone with her at the telling. I need to know that she'll be all right.'

'Don't you worry, Charlie,' he'd promised. 'And I'll make certain she is all right in other ways as well.'

Charlie had smiled that lopsided smile of his. 'Sarah will join me sooner rather than maybe – I know that. I just want my passing to be gentle for her.'

When Gerry re-entered the tiny overheated kitchen he nodded to Mourne and she moved to Sarah. He sat on her other side and took the veined hand into his. 'Sarah,' he said softly. 'The light has gone from his eyes. He is at peace. He told me some time ago that I was to tell you not to fret, because when it happens he will be out of pain and soaring like a dove, and he will be waiting for you.'

Sarah grasped the hands on both sides of her. 'I knew the moment his soul left his body,' she said, quietly. 'I felt a sudden stillness and peace within me and I knew his pain had gone.'

Perhaps this would be a lesson for Mourne on how to cope with life and death, Gerry thought. The dignity of the old was sometimes awesome at moments such as these. He followed Mourne to the door and touched her arm. 'I'll drop in on Maggie Cullen and ask her to do the evening surgery for you. You can take the rest of the day off,' he said, quietly.

'I'm fine! Really . . .'

'Do as you are bid.'

Mourne slipped home for her bicycle, and with the sandwiches in her pocket together with the orangeade she had whipped into Cullen's shop to buy, she set off along the coast road to the point where it turned up the mountain towards the Silent Valley. There had been no question in her mind as to what she would do with her unexpected freedom – she was going to visit the spot where she had been found.

The first bit of the ascent was easy, but she knew that the next lap would be difficult by bike as the road was more scree than anything. However, so desperate was her need to locate the large boulder under whose overhang she had been discovered, she considered the journey worth the effort.

Unfortunately the hot sunny days that had recently made life pleasant had chosen today to change; the sky was slightly overcast. Earlier, she had dithered about fetching a jacket, but after assessing the situation had decided that the few scudding clouds posed no threat; now, however, the dull sound of thunder in the far distance made her stop. The sky looked threatening towards Belfast, but after a moment's hesitation she walked on.

Suddenly without warning the rain came down on her; soft Irish rain that gentled its way through her clothes and did more damage than a hefty downpour because of its insidious nature and the lightness of its descent. Before long she was soaked to the skin and there was little she could do about it; she was too far up the mountain now. The day was humid so she felt more clammy than cold, but the thunder was getting closer and she began to panic. She had always been frightened of thunder and lightning. She hurried on. She would find shelter under the overhang.

By now her hair was plastered to her head, assisting the drainage of water into her blouse, and a frightening brattle of thunder made her jump. It was followed by a flash of lightning which lit up the sky, causing her to cry out in fear. 'Take hold of yourself, Mourne O'Hara,' she said aloud, but the noise from another brattle drowned the words. Terrified by now, she reached the spot at last and gratefully crawled beneath the shelf of the enormous boulder. She stared at the ground between folded knees and tried to feel a sense of belonging, but all she felt was wet and hungry. The sandwiches were sodden and she was now too chilly to want the orangeade.

She was about thirty yards from the perimeter wall surrounding the reservoir and could hear the rain pattering down into the deep well of water as she shivered under her temporary shelter. Eventually, a mist started to form as the day heated up again and the rain began to taper off. A deep sense of loneliness filled her as she waited for the drops to cease, and she had a desire to race back down the mountain to where she had left her bike. This area was not called the Silent Valley without reason. There was an eeriness about the place where no birds sang. The silence seeped into her with the damp.

She ran her hand along the surface under the rock, straining to feel at one with it, but the granite cut her hand, and she stared at the scrape and realized how unyielding her beloved mountain could be. Shivering, she folded her arms round her knees for comfort, huddling them to her out of the light rain that still fell. She knew she should start walking to keep warm but she was scared.

At last the thunder rumbled off across the Devil's Bit, the chunk of ridge that folklore said the devil had bitten out of the mountain in frustration when St Patrick chased him out of Ireland. This mist was slowly clearing and her watch showed that she had been up here for over an hour. It was now four o'clock; her mam would be worried. Her clothes were still wet and uncomfortable, but she ignored the fine drizzle and set off down the mountain. She wondered if it had been worth making the trip. Would she be able to put it all to the back of her mind and get on with her life?

When the hands of the clock reached five, Kitty O'Hara dried her hands and walked purposefully towards the telephone. She rarely made use of the instrument, but she was concerned about Mourne's non-appearance. The surgery was only a few hundred yards away, and if she had intended going somewhere Kitty felt sure she would have let her know. There was no answer and she remembered that the surgery didn't open until six o'clock on a Friday evening. She rang Gerry.

He answered grumpily. 'Sure I don't know where she has gone, Kitty. You have wakened me from a well-earned doze. What do I know about Mourne's movements?'

'It's tipping down with rain,' she persisted, 'and she isn't home. She has never gone anywhere or done anything without telling me first.'

'Is that so? Well I think that it's time she did her own thing without having to plan her day and tell you of it, Kitty. The girl will be twenty-one years old next birthday – I think you should let go.'

Kitty told him crossly that she never interfered with Mourne's arrangements – all she asked was to be kept informed for the sake of domestic continuity and order. She slammed the phone down. There were times when she felt at odds with Gerry. She resented the respect that her daughter had for his advice and the way she hung on his every word – where had the girl got to? She went to the door for the fifth time and looked up and down the busy street. It was market day and the place was thick with the smell of cows and pigs and the cries of the livestock auctioneer. There was much to-ing and fro-ing between the many stalls, in spite of the rain, and she looked enviously at the crowds of people wandering around with nothing better to do than pay out good money for shoddy goods; she wished she had the time and the money for such activities.

By five-thirty she was frantic. She stopped what she was doing in the kitchen for she was making a hash of everything. What with the sudden rain and the thunder and lightning and Mourne missing, she was at her wits' end. Mourne had always been afraid of thunder and lightning and she suspected she was holed up till it passed. She stared up the street again; the crowds showed little sign of thinning in spite of the weather. The only difference to any other market day was the show of umbrellas. Barry Grant was doing a good trade, judging by the number walking in and out of his shop, but there, he always did on market day. They came up in their droves from Newcastle.

She had been indoors only a few minutes when she heard the scrape against the wall that told her Mourne's bike had just been set against it. She hurried into the kitchen so that she would be facing the door as her daughter entered, and gasped at the sight of the bedraggled figure she cut. 'In the name of God, Mourne, your clothes are sticking to your back. Did you not have the wit to take shelter?'

'There wasn't any around when the storm struck and by the time I found some I was already well soaked.' Mourne sank wearily into a chair.

21

'I'll run a bath for you. Get out of those clothes immediately or you'll end up with pneumonia.' Kitty shooed her upstairs and followed. Mourne looked a sad little figure, and ill, she thought. Explanations could wait. She would ask Gerry to visit.

Mourne sank gratefully on to her soft mattress and pulled the bedclothes up over her. She felt her lids grow heavy, and the last thought before she succumbed to sleep was the story she would tell her mother. She had no intention of confessing that she had gone to the spot where Father Mulligan had found her all those years ago.

When Gerry examined her later, he ordered her to stay in bed. 'It's just as well I have Maggie Cullen to fall back on,' he said severely, but his hands were soft on her as he stroked a strand of hair back from her face. 'I don't want to see you till you really feel well enough.' He left the room with Kitty following.

'She'll live!' he said sternly. 'I don't think we should question where she went to, to get in such a state.'

'You mean – you think she might have . . .?'

'I don't know! but it is her business. Just make sure she has all she needs to help her get well again. If she wants to talk about it, she will.' He paused. 'Where's Patrick?'

'He's been away at a meeting since morning. He should be home shortly,' said Kitty, and thought, He's never here when he's needed. He's always on hand for the ills of others, but when something like this happens he's not around. Ashamed at the errant thought, she smiled weakly. 'He's always on the go. The man is a saint – did you want him for anything special?'

'No, no. I was just wondering – I know how fond of the girl he is and I wanted to reassure him.'

'Try reassuring me: I'm her mother.' Kitty looked at him in alarm. 'Is there any danger?'

'God, no! I didn't mean to worry you, Kitty. She'll be fine. She might be under the weather for a while as I'm sure she has caught a bad chill, but the medicine I've given you for her will go a long way to help, and with your good care there's no cause for concern.'

A few days later, standing by the huge kitchen table shredding beans, Kitty looked up at the clock above the mantelpiece. It was three o'clock in the afternoon. She laid down her knife and crossed to the big range to set the kettle on for a cup of tea. She would take one up to Mourne. Now that she was on the mend she might feel like talking. She wouldn't press the matter – she had promised Gerry that she wouldn't, but she felt uneasy about the idea that Mourne felt she should visit 'that place' so soon after she had been told about the history of her birth.

Kitty tapped gently on the door and entered the room. Mourne was lying against the pillow looking pale, but her eyes were clearer. She placed the steaming cup on the table by the side of the bed. 'I thought you might like a cup of tea and then perhaps you might feel like rising – maybe sit in the sun for a while.'

Mourne smiled. 'I'd like that, Mam.'

'The Maguire twins are about; are you sure you can handle them? They're no better for the holiday they've just spent with their aunt,' Kitty warned.

Mourne smiled. 'I adore the rascals. They won't worry me.'

'All right then, I'll put the cane chair out. If they appear then give me a shout – I don't want that pair goin' on and settin' you back.'

'I've only had a feverish cold,' Mourne said, but she was glad of the assistance her mam gave her as she made her shaky way downstairs and out into the tiny strip of grass between the back door and the stone wall that divided them from the graveyard.

True to form, the twins arrived from nowhere and sat themselves on the wall above her.

'I heard tell you nearly died,' said Noreen as she pushed her way out of reach of her younger sister Cassie, who was looking sulky.

Mourne laughed. 'Hardly! I just had a chest cold.'

Cassie looked disappointed and fell deeper into her sulk. 'I've never been to a funeral,' she said. 'I would have been allowed to go to yours because you aren't family.'

'I'm sorry to disappoint you, I know just how you must feel.' Mourne held her side as her laughter caught at her chest, making her splutter and cough.

Kitty, hearing the bout of coughing, appeared at the door.

The twins looked on as she thumped Mourne on the back, and offered some advice. 'Put her head between her legs,' suggested Cassie.

'Stupid! That's for being sick,' said Noreen, calmly.

Cassie glared at her. 'You think you know everything.'

'Why don't you go and sulk somewhere else, Miss Cassie Do Little.'

Cassie, with a yell, started to attack her sister, until Kitty grasped them both by the arms and swung them off the wall. 'Get off that wall, the pair of you,' she said, furiously. 'You're trespassing anyway.'

23

'Sure we only came to cheer Mourne up,' Noreen said.

'Well! You're making a right mess of it.'

'But they weren't doing any harm,' said Mourne. 'I started choking because I was laughing so much. Let them stay, Mam: I'm enjoying their company.'

Kitty glared at the twins. 'If I hear one complaint I'll tan the hides off you.' She turned to Mourne. 'I hope you know what you're doing. I've said it before and I'll repeat it now. Those two were spawned by the devil.' With those words, she made her way back to the kitchen.

'What is the matter with you two, anyway?' inquired Mourne.

'Noreen says I'm a bloody nuisance and she wishes she didn't have a twin sister.'

'That's a bad word to use,' Mourne remarked.

'It's all right. Sure we aren't old enough to go to confession yet, so we can say it without having to tell Father Mulligan.'

'I might tell.'

'No you won't.' The twins spoke in unison, nodding their heads. 'Mam says you're one of nature's ladies.'

Startled, Mourne said, 'Good heavens! Did she really say that?'

They nodded. 'M'da was saying that he never knew you to get into half the trouble some of the others got into when he was your teacher, and that was when Mam said it.'

'Good heavens!' said Mourne again, and added, 'You're always going about together. I thought that was how you wanted it.'

'Noreen's in love with Paddy Toner. She gets mad if I'm there and he kisses her.'

Mourne could barely contain her mirth. 'You don't share everything, then?'

'I only kissed him once, at the school party – and I don't want him to kiss me again. That isn't why I don't want her with me all the time.'

'Then what is the reason?'

'I'm nearly seven—'

'So am I,' Cassie interrupted.

'I'm older than you – I should get to do things without you,' said Noreen.

'But you don't want to.'

'I would if you weren't always there.'

Mourne, aware that a rare old fight was brewing, and in an effort to avert it, leaned back and said, weakly, 'I feel ill.'

'Now see what we've done!' cried the twins together.

24

Mourne hid a smile. They were back on course again. The twins normally did just about everything together – including speaking.

'That's better,' she said. 'I can enjoy your company more when you aren't squabbling. I really am too ill for squabbling twins.'

'Are you certain sure you're not dying?'

'I'm afraid not.'

'Well! Maybe next time. We have to go home now,' said Noreen.

'We lit a candle for the repose of your soul,' said Cassie, bitterly. 'We used our sweet money and it was all for nothing.' They jumped down from the wall and ran off as Mourne let out another peal of laughter which made her ribs hurt again. She rose slowly and made her way into the kitchen. Her mother was peeling vegetables. She sat down, facing her. 'At what age do we lose our ability to be honest and forthcoming?' she said, with a sigh.

Kitty put down the knife. 'What have those two been saying?'

'They thought I was dying. They were very disappointed that they wouldn't be going to their first funeral.'

'That wasn't a nice remark to make.'

Mourne giggled. 'Worse! Cassie was miffed that they had used up their sweet money to light a candle for the repose of my soul, and that it was for nothing.'

'The devils.'

'Don't you see, Mam? They say what's in their minds because they are children and don't yet know the meaning of hypocrisy.'

'You can't go around telling everybody what you really think about them,' said Kitty, appalled.

'No! I suppose not,' Mourne said thoughtfully. 'Honesty is a luxury enjoyed by the very young before they are taught the meaning of tact.'

'Since we are discussing honesty,' suggested Kitty, 'perhaps you'll tell me where you got to the other day – it must have been quite a way for you to get in that state.'

Mourne was silent. Kitty folded her arms lightly against her chest and waited.

'I went up into the Silent Valley – to the rock,' said Mourne at last, her voice little more than a whisper.

'And?'

'Nothing, Mam! The only feeling I had was that I wanted to be home, here, with you. I wanted so badly to be in touch with my past, but I felt nothing – just fear of the storm.'

Kitty stretched her hand out. 'I know it isn't a button of good telling

25

you to forget your origins, not now, but remember that to Father Patrick and me, you are the best thing that ever happened in our lives. You can be secure in our love.'

'I know that, but it hurts deep inside to know that I was rejected by my mother.'

'You were not,' said Kitty, firmly. 'Nor were you abandoned. Didn't you hear Father Patrick say that he could sense another presence, as though there was someone there watching over you – and remember the note stated the exact time for him to be at the rock. There was a desperate reason for that mother to do what she did and we mustn't be quick to condemn her. She – and whoever helped her – made certain that you were left in good hands. To me that speaks of love.'

Mourne sighed. 'I expect I'll come to terms with it in time.' She rose.

'Are you feeling well enough to eat with us downstairs this evening?'

'Yes. I really feel much better. I'm sure I could go back to work soon.'

'You'll go back after the weekend and not before,' Gerry informed her when he came to see her. 'I'll brook no argument.'

Kitty warned Father Patrick that Mourne was still upset.

'I wouldn't have expected otherwise. We must give her time.'

'That's what she said,' Kitty frowned. 'We did the right thing, didn't we?'

'There was no alternative. She would never have forgiven us if she had found out any other way.'

'How could she have found out?' asked Kitty.

'We couldn't take any chances.' Father Patrick ruffled his newspaper. The matter is closed as far as he is concerned, thought Kitty, as she prepared the table for supper.

Mourne was pleased to get back to work. She was even more pleased when she found the small vase of flowers that Gerry had put in the tiny reception area.

'Don't make a fuss,' he said, embarrassed. 'I just thought it would make a change to have a nice scent instead of the musty, dusty smell that pervades the place at times.'

Mourne hugged him. 'I'm not fussing; I just want to thank you for a lovely gesture.'

'Well, so you've said it – and stop hugging me in public and get on with your work.' With a hasty look towards the one patient in the waiting room, he went to his office. The madam does it for sheer devilment, he thought, but was secretly delighted.

The patients told her they were glad to see her well again, and altogether she felt a little buzz inside at the kindness shown by everyone. Tara, her friend from schooldays, popped in to see her as she'd just returned from a holiday in Dublin.

'Never mind my holiday – how are you feeling?' she asked, as Mourne started to question her.

'I'm fine, really. It was just a feverish cold that went straight to my chest. I was in no danger of dying.'

Tara looked at her watch. 'Look! I have to go. Meet me at the coffee bar in Newcastle at seven. I'll give you my news then.'

Although the morning had not been a busy one, Mourne felt tired, and at the end of the afternoon her grey look of exhaustion prompted her mother to remark that she was mad to be trotting off to Newcastle with Tara Foley. Kitty didn't entirely approve of Tara, who had a reputation for being a flirt and too fond of dancing and careering around in cars. 'I'll never understand what you see in that friendship.'

Mourne sighed. 'I've told you. We get along well together. Tara fits me into her life and doesn't expect me to hare around to dance halls or go on her jaunts around the countryside with her other friends in fast cars. She knows I'm not keen on it and she doesn't expect it of me.' This was only one of many conversations she'd had with her mam on the same topic. Mam couldn't understand that Tara and she had their own way of dealing with a relationship which they both considered important.

Later, when they had settled into one of the booths with their coffee and doughnuts, Tara spoke of her holiday, bubbling with enthusiasm.

'I've never been to Dublin,' Mourne remarked.

'It's a really exciting place,' Tara enthused. 'On the only two wet days of the holiday we did the round of the galleries and the museum, and on the other days we did the beach and took some boat trips round the bay. There was never a shortage of things to do.'

'Did you meet anyone?' As soon as she saw the pink blush creep across Tara's face Mourne knew she had hit a nerve. 'You did! I can tell by your face.'

Tara launched excitedly into her meeting with John Joseph Garrity and how they had known *immediately* that they were attracted to each other. 'We met on board the boat; he was with two friends and he

27

tripped over my beach bag when they were making their way to the front.'

'You probably put it there to trip him up,' Mourne laughed.

'With my mother sitting beside me like a Spanish duenna? Not at all. I hadn't even noticed him till he caught hold of my arm to balance himself.' Tara smiled at the memory.

'How could you decide you liked each other on such short notice?'

'Wait till it happens to you,' Tara said. 'When we looked at each other it was all there.'

'How did you get to meet him again?'

'He slipped me a note saying he would be going to the art gallery the next day at two o'clock if I would like to meet him.'

'That was a bit forward of you, wasn't it?' Mourne was intrigued by the romance of it all.

'It's called love at first sight.' Tara gave a theatrical sigh and grinned.

'Have you arranged to see him again?'

'Indeed I have. He lives in Belfast and as soon as he arrives home he's going to contact me.'

This would make a few hearts drop, Mourne thought. Tara was very popular with boys. Much as she wished her well, she felt a trifle downhearted herself at the thought that Tara might become heavily involved with Jay-Jay, as she called him. Her consolation was that Jay-Jay lived in Belfast. Tara said they would only be able to see each other at weekends – and then only every three weeks because his father would let him have one of the cars for his own use just once a month. 'His father says he's in business to make money and not to supply Jay-Jay with a free set of wheels to burn up the miles and wear out the tyres,' Tara groaned.

The following evening after surgery, Mourne rushed home to bathe and change. Uncle Gerry had invited them all to dinner. She loved going to Gerry's: it was a large ramble of a house full of rooms that were furnished but never used. Several times over the years Mourne had stayed there when the parochial house had been overrun with young priests whom the Bishop had sent to Father Patrick for induction and Mrs Haggerty, his housekeeper, had treated Mam and herself like royalty.

Gerry Owen had many times made up his mind to leave the house and find himself a little cottage, but had always changed his mind. This was his family home, full of memories and furnished by his lovely mother, who had died when he was in the middle of his medical training. He'd felt at the time as though his heart had been cut out of him.

Later, his sister Maraid and her young son David had come to live with him and stayed for years after her husband had left her, and for those years the house had echoed with the sound of children's voices and later, the clink of glasses and murmur of conversation as more and more of Maraid's friends visited. Now the rooms that had vibrated with noise and the stairs that had groaned under the weight of visitors were underused, and the house seemed, at times, disturbingly quiet. David had gone over to England to do his medical training.

'You'll not leave this place now,' Patrick remarked to Gerry while they sipped a glass of sherry. Kitty and Mourne had gone into the kitchen to chat with Doreen Haggerty.

'I did seriously think about it recently, and I even went to an agent to have it valued. But you are right – it's too much a part of me. Besides, I've had some good news.' A large smile spread over his face.

'What good news?'

'I'll tell you after dinner. It's why you are all here. I have an announcement to make.'

'You're the great one for making a man hang on. How am I going to enjoy my meal if I'm kept guessing?'

'The day you turn your nose up at food, Patrick Mulligan, is the day the divil will come riding up that road on horseback to claim you – so don't give me any of your old buck, there's a good lad.'

Mrs Haggerty had sent Mourne in to tell them to get themselves into the dining room before everything went cold. 'She said to tell you that she had rung the bell and forgotten that you were both as deaf as posts when you got together.' Mourne delivered the message with a grin.

When they had all settled in the big comfortable study after the meal, with drinks in their hands, Gerry crossed to the fireplace. 'There's nothing like a good fireplace to make a decent announcement,' he said with a wicked look towards Patrick.

'If you don't make this announcement soon I'll personally throttle you. You've kept me waiting long enough.'

Mourne and Kitty looked at each other in surprise. Something was going on between these two.

'I'm going to retire!' Gerry announced, grandly.

There was silence. Everyone looked stunned.

'Who will run the show if you do? We can't be having some new

29

young upstart who doesn't know us and doesn't give a tap how we tick.' It was Patrick who spoke the words.

'That's the beauty of it – you won't have to. If everything goes to plan David will take over. He's coming over in four weeks' time to spend a fortnight with me to see how the practice works. I'm hoping to persuade him to take the practice on, but it has to look as if the decision was his own.'

'Sure why would the man give up a lucrative career in surgery to spend his days in a backwater of a place like Ballycash?' asked Patrick.

'He'll answer that when he has made his mind up. He has his reasons for going this far along the way. I can only say that when I met him at the seminar I attended a few weeks ago in London he jumped at the chance of a visit.' Gerry took a gulp of his brandy. 'I seriously think I have a chance of winning him over to the idea.'

As the two men continued to discuss the issue, Mourne's own thoughts were busy. She remembered David McNeill very well, although he hadn't been back home in twelve years. As an eight-year-old she had idolized the handsome youth, and she recalled her distress when she heard he was going to England to study. She had spent nights of terror thinking about the possibility of his being killed in war-torn England. Each time the news broadcaster reported on the heavy bombing she had cried for days afterwards. She had an old, secret snapshot of them sitting together on the wall down by the brook: she, with her mass of auburn hair blowing in the breeze and he, a tall young man with gentle grey eyes and a steady smile. They had heard of his career prowess from Uncle Gerry, so she knew that he was at this moment up for promotion for the post of senior registrar in surgery. Her heart flipped. She wondered what the thirty-year-old David looked like now, and whether he had changed much from the youth she had had a crush on all those years ago. Of one thing she was certain – he was not married.

CHAPTER 3

David McNeill lowered his tall form into an armchair. He frowned as he pondered the problem that was uppermost in his mind. At some stage this evening he had to break the news to Rosemary that he was going to Ireland for two weeks when he was supposed to be attending a family wedding with her. Anyway, he reflected, a wedding was not the ideal place for an important first meeting with her parents. The idea, when she had first put it to him, had not appealed and he had told her so.

'Why not?' she had demanded.

He had tried to make her see his point. 'Too much going on. How can I get to know your family with so many people around? It would be a better idea to meet them privately.'

But Rosemary could see no problem. 'Besides,' she'd insisted, 'I've already booked the same holiday dates as you so that we can spend a couple of days with them after the wedding.'

Irritated though he'd been at her high-handed assumption that he would fall in with her plans, he had bit on the retort he had been about to make about not consulting him. He loathed rows, but the situation had changed since then. A recent telephone conversation he'd had with his uncle had worried him. He suspected he was not a well man, and if his uncle needed his help he couldn't let the old man down – besides, he had put an interesting proposition to him and it would be an opportunity to explore it further. He glanced hurriedly at his watch and shot out of the chair. He was meeting Rosemary in fifteen minutes and he hadn't changed.

Rosemary was staring at her watch as he drew up and he sighed as he caught her look of impatience by the light of the tall lamp at the front door of the nurses' home. There were times when he wondered why he hadn't fallen in love with a simple country girl instead of a theatre sister who walked and talked and behaved always with the confidence of one who was used to giving orders. Sometimes, he thought ruefully, he had to fight to hold his corner. His eyes softened, however, as she came towards him. She was a beautiful girl, and on the whole she was quite patient with him and his complete disregard for neatness and order. The truth was, *he* had enough of order and control in his professional life and he guessed it was his way of rebelling. Rosemary, on the other hand, carried her professionalism into every corner of her life. She hated chaos of any sort. It was something they would have to come to terms with when they married, when, she had warned him, she was going to make life hell for him if he didn't conform. She had laughed as she said it, and he had laughed with her. He loved her enough to try, anyway.

'Sorry I'm late,' he apologized.

'Did something come up?'

To say something had was tempting, but after a short hesitation David glanced sideways at her profile. 'I just forgot the time,' he said slowly.

'Will you never change, David?'

The long-suffering sigh she uttered jarred on him. There were fleeting occasions, and this was one of them, when her perfectionism made him grit his teeth and wonder if he could ever meet her expectations, but then she would smile and her face would make his heart jolt with its loveliness, and the pert nose would turn up endearingly. He would watch her at work, dealing with people with tact and charm, and have a great desire to hold her in his arms at an inappropriate moment.

They had reached the restaurant where they were to dine by the time he had formulated a reply, but since she didn't seem to be expecting one, he concentrated on parking the car instead. He had already decided he would break his news to her after they had ordered dessert, although Rosemary, always conscious of social etiquette, was unlikely to make a scene. She would wait till a more private moment before tackling the issue. His assumption proved correct. What he hadn't bargained on was the coldness of her manner when he broke the news as he bade her goodnight at the door of the nurses' home.

'You knew we were going to my cousin's wedding that weekend – how could you, David!' Her tones could have chilled soup.

'I'm sorry, but my uncle needs me and—'

Rosemary's anger spilled out. 'You really are a nuisance, David,' she said, her voice blistering with venom.

David, in an effort to control the situation, put his hand placatingly on her shoulder but she shrugged it off.

'You go to Ireland. I'll just have to make something up to explain your absence.'

'Just tell them the truth.'

'Goodnight, David!' Rosemary yanked open the door and went in.

David sighed heavily and made his way back to the car.

The days passed slowly for Mourne as she awaited David's visit. She spoke to Gerry about him. 'You don't suppose David will change his mind, do you? There was nothing definite about his decision, after all.'

'What do you mean, nothing definite? Sure didn't he phone me back to tell me that he was making all the arrangements. What put that idea into your mind?' Gerry looked at her over the top of his glasses.

'He would be mad to bury himself in a village such as Ballycash when he's got used to all the sophistication and the excitement of London.'

'Rubbish. I made the move in the same direction and I've never regretted it. Anyway, he doesn't know the *real* reason why I've invited him over.' Gerry paused and looked thoughtful. 'The boy is a brilliant surgeon but he has not the equipment and the backing for the job he's expected to do. He's tired of the rat race, judging by what he was saying when I was over at the Royal College seminar last month. I have a feeling that working here might appeal to him if the package is presented in the right way. Don't you let on that I have any other motive than to show him what I have going over here,' Gerry warned her.

Mourne looked horrified. 'Uncle Gerry! Are you being devious?'

'As devious as I can get,' he said, with an exaggerated smirk.

'Well, I think you should have been honest with David. What harm would it have done to put your proposition to him in the first place?'

'For the very reason you just mentioned. He has it all. He is up for promotion and he has a good lifestyle over there. He'll hardly jump at my proposition even if he *is* a bit disillusioned about his situation. I needed to get him over to let him see what he's missing. If he doesn't like it here I'll not take offence, but at least he'll have seen both sides of the coin before choosing heads or tails.' Gerry rose. 'Mind what I said, now, not a *word*.'

Mourne followed him and watched as he searched for some notes. 'Do you think he will remember me?'

'Probably not. You were only eight years old when he left.'

'I hope he won't be disappointed.'

Having found what he had been searching for, Gerry turned and looked into the green eyes, unspoilt by flecks of any other colour. He wondered if Mourne was as naïve about her looks as she seemed. With those eyes and her glorious auburn hair she was what young men dream of. She'd turn the head of a saint. 'Away and look at yourself in the mirror and don't talk daft. David is a man of discernment – he'll think his ship has come in when he claps eyes on you.'

Mourne laughed. 'You're biased,' she said, and thought, He really doesn't look well. Just lately his normally ruddy complexion has paled.

'And you are fishin' for compliments. Away off home, you article. I saw Kitty coming out of Doran's shop so you will be having fish tonight.' He smirked as she groaned. He knew she hated fish. She used to say she wished she had been reared as a Protestant so that she didn't have to fast from meat on Fridays.

Mourne didn't fare any better with Father Patrick when she asked him if he thought that Uncle Gerry was looking his age just lately. 'He looks pale and he seems to be walking more slowly,' she said, 'and he keeps getting his notes mixed up.'

'I can't comment on the notes,' said Patrick, 'but I saw Gerry walking up the road towards Molly's brae and he was striding along twirling his walking-stick around in the style of Charlie Chaplin, so he can't be that bad.' He rustled his newspaper in the hope that Mourne would take the hint. In fact, he too had a suspicion that there was something going on. He had noticed the sudden pallor of Gerry's face. He looked as though he was at death's door when he'd last seen him. If he didn't know any better he would have sworn that Gerry had doused his face in talcum powder. Added to which, Tom Tarney had been asking him if he knew why Dr Owen hadn't been in for his monthly trim. Patrick folded his newspaper. It wasn't any of his business. All would be revealed in good time, of that he was certain. He rose. 'I'm away into my study,' he said to Kitty who had all the while been sitting listening to them and had been of no help at all.

On Sunday, after lunch, Mourne took a walk up to the river that wound its way around the lower reaches of Slieve Donard on its way to the sea. She felt restless and edgy and hoped the gentle gurgling waters would ease her troubled spirit. Just lately she had begun to think about her past, and try as she might, she couldn't rid her mind of the feeling that it set her apart from her contemporaries. Even Tara, who was the most amiable and least discerning of people, had remarked just recently that there was something different about her – which made Mourne realize that she was not keeping up such a good pretence as she'd hoped.

As she approached the little wooden bridge spanning the river, she smiled at the sight of the Maguire twins' frilly-knickered bottoms in full view as they leaned precariously over the rail, throwing small stones into the waters below.

A voice hailed her. 'Hello there, Mourne. Come down here and talk to me.'

Mourne looked towards the bank on the other side of the road just beneath the rail, and smiled at Rena Maguire as she scrambled down to her.

'I heard tell you've been ill lately. I'm glad to see you looking well again,' said Rena, patting the bank beside her.

Mourne sat down. 'I'm fine now. I suppose the twins told you.'

'They did! And I threatened them with annihilation if they bothered you. They can be a pair of blatherskites when they like. Children have no thought past their own desires.'

'To tell you the truth, they did me good. They made me laugh so much I nearly choked.'

'They think the world of you, you know,' said Rena. 'You have such patience with them.'

Mourne laughed and told Rena how they had been miffed at being done out of attending their first funeral.

Rena gasped and held her hand to her face. 'Oh God! they didn't . . . What am I going to do with that pair? I dread them going up into the new class. Mr Doyle won't know what hit him.'

They were laughing so helplessly the twins looked up from their task, and seeing Mourne, leapt down the bank towards her.

'Will you come and paddle with us,' they cried in unison. 'Mam won't. She says she's too old for such things.'

Mourne raised her eyebrows at Rena. She couldn't be more than ten years older than herself. 'You're as old as you feel,' she laughed. 'Let's take our shoes off and have a go.'

Rena hesitated, smiled suddenly and said, 'God! Why not? But I'll kill the pair of you if you let on to a soul. A married woman with two horrific children such as you two should have more sense.' But her eyes had taken on a glint and she tore off her shoes and beat them all to the water.

'Look at Mam!' the twins squealed in delight, and taking Mourne by the hand they hauled her down the bank.

Afterwards, Mourne and Rena lay back and soaked up the late spring sunshine. The twins had gone exploring, with Rena's admonition ringing in their ears that they would be in dire trouble if they went too far or got up to any devilment.

When they had been gone some time, Rena sat up again, and, shading her eyes from the sun, looked around anxiously. They were at the other side of the bridge plopping stones into the water. Satisfied, she was about to lie down again when she saw a sudden tear seep beneath Mourne's eyelid.

'Mourne,' she said, softly. 'Is there anything the matter? I couldn't help noticing as you came towards me earlier that you looked unhappy, and now . . .'

Mourne sat up abruptly, wiping her fingers across her eyes. 'The sun is stronger than I thought,' she lied. She didn't know Rena all that well. She had already left school when Mourne was still a junior. It was only because of her interest in the twins that they had recently formed a sort of casual friendship.

Rena looked embarrassed. 'I didn't mean to pry.'

Mourne relented. 'There isn't anything wrong that time won't change,' she said, quietly.

'If that's how it is.' Rena put out her hand. 'But if you need someone to confide in, you know I'm here.'

The urge to confide in Rena was great, but determined as she was to put the recent disclosures to the back of her mind and get on with her life, Mourne squashed the feeling and gave a tiny smile. She must be strong. This conversation with Rena should not be happening. She was failing in her resolve to try and plan her life so that the past would one day be obliterated. She stood up. 'Don't worry about me, Rena. We all have our gloomy days and you and the twins have managed to brighten mine up. I feel a lot happier just having spent this short time with you.'

'Now that we've broken the ice perhaps you and I could begin to get to know each other better,' Rena suggested gently. She wasn't convinced by the sudden cheerful manner that Mourne had put on and she was certain that one day she might need someone she could talk to.

Mourne smiled, and this time the smile was warm. 'I'd like that very much,' she said, and with a last wave towards the twins she set off home.

She arrived at the surgery earlier than usual that Monday morning. She wanted to get everything ready and under control well ahead of schedule, for Uncle Gerry had phoned the parochial house to say that David had arrived.

She couldn't contain her restlessness. Several times she went to the door to see if there was a sign of Uncle Gerry's car, chiding herself for her foolishness. It wasn't going to make them arrive any quicker. Taking a deep breath to calm herself, she began to put the notes in order and when that was done, she sat and waited with impatience.

Mrs Harris, the third patient on her list, arrived and duly seated herself and Mourne, not wishing to chat, pulled her chair further away from the reception window and began to fiddle with the laboratory results which were already filed in order of importance.

At last the door opened and Gerry came towards the reception area. Mourne watched his progress with disappointment – he was alone. She handed him the medical notes she'd prepared, controlling the desire to ask where David was and hoping the disappointment wasn't showing on her face. 'There are only twelve patients today,' she said brightly.

Gerry observed the empty surgery. 'And by the look of it they're all going to be late. Where is everybody?' He poked his head out through the hatch. 'Do you know something we don't? Mrs Harris?'

Mrs Harris looked up in surprise. 'About what?'

'About' – Gerry scanned the list – 'where the hell my first two patients are. You are third on the list.'

'Depends who they are. I saw Jimmy Dolan and Phil McCann going into the chemist.'

'That's one of them,' said Gerry. 'He was second on the list, but seeing as you're already here, I'll see you first and the others can wait.' He ushered Mrs Harris into his consulting room and before following her, he turned and spoke to Mourne. 'Are you not interested to know where David is?'

He was smirking and to teach him a lesson Mourne, with pink cheeks, said haughtily, 'I've no doubt you'll tell me before the end of the morning surgery – meanwhile I'll get on with my work.'

'He's parking his car,' he grinned.

Mourne's heart leapt. She had feared that he wasn't going to turn up on the first day and she had been disappointed, although she would never let Uncle Gerry know, for he'd be taking the rise out of her for the rest of the day. Jimmy Dolan hurried in and knocked on the tiny window. Mourne looked at him crossly. 'You're late for your appointment,' she said, accusingly.

'Only by a few minutes.' He looked round the surgery. 'I can't see that it has made a tap of difference anyway. There's no one else here.'

'Mrs Harris has gone in before you, now.'

'Oh God! That means I'll be here for another half-hour. I made the appointment early so I could be out and away back to work. Mr McCrory isn't happy that I needed to be away in the first place. I promised I'd be at my machine by ten o'clock.'

'Well! I'm sorry about that. I don't think Mrs Harris will be too long.' Mourne returned to her own work and only looked up when the door opened again and a tall figure filled the space, blocking out the morning sunlight. Her heart jumped as he walked towards the reception office and entered, smiling.

'This can't be Mourne O'Hara. She of the lank ginger hair and the face hidden beneath a hundred freckles.'

Mourne blushed and held out her hand. 'Hello David.'

'Is that all you can do?' David pulled her towards him and planted a kiss on her cheek and gave her a bear hug. 'What changes a few years can make,' he said, holding her at arm's length.

'I was never covered in freckles,' Mourne cried. 'And I did not have ginger hair. It has always been auburn.' She felt a sense of exhilaration as she looked up at the good-looking man now smiling at her affectionately. 'However, I notice you have lost your boyish weediness, so there have been changes all round.'

David grinned and at that moment the telephone rang. Mourne lifted the receiver and listened. She turned to him. 'It's himself. He says he brought you over here to give him a hand and to see how things are done, and will you get in there quick or you go back on the next plane.'

'I'll see you later,' David said.

The rest of the morning seemed to pass slowly. When she'd brought their coffee in during a lull, Mourne found uncle and nephew with their heads together, studying a handwritten note. She set the cups down and smiled at David. 'Don't let him work you hard. He looks mild and milky but he's changed over the years, and he demands his pound of flesh and gets crotchety if he's not satisfied. You have to be strong.'

'You have the life of Riley working here with me.' Gerry leaned back in his chair and looked up at her. 'We are making out a list of times when David will be with me. For the rest of the time he will be doing more interesting things – it is his holiday after all. I want you to come in as soon as the last patient goes so that we can discuss the plans with you.'

Mourne looked at them in surprise. 'What do I have to do with your plans?'

'That will be made clear, later. Meanwhile away and get on with whatever you're doing.'

Mourne gave David a see-what-I-mean look and returned to the reception area. She was curious to know what they were plotting, her mind wasn't on what she was doing, so it was no surprise when the last patient ticked her off for forgetting to give him his prescription. She apologized sweetly and gave it to him and began to tidy the notes and sort out tomorrow's list. She was almost finished when the phone rang. It was Uncle Gerry, instructing her to leave what she was doing and get herself into the consulting room. She placed the pile of notes in their elastic band in the 'Tomorrow' tray and did so.

'Would you like something to drink? The kettle's just boiled.'

Gerry shook his head wearily. He looked tired. Mourne hoped that he would have some success in persuading David to take over from him. He was nearly seventy. He had earned his retirement. Besides, the idea of David staying on appealed to her. She pulled another chair to the desk.

When she was seated, Gerry spoke. 'I've been going through the routine with David and this is the plan we've come up with.' He paused. 'David will work with me every morning for the first week and for the second week he will take over for three mornings while I have a break. With you out there to keep things on track I don't see any difficulty. During the second week he will run two of my evening surgeries so that I won't have to get my locum in when I go to the two meetings that I have scheduled. Altogether, I'll be having a bit of a rest – for which I'm grateful to David.' Gerry held up his hand as David made to speak. 'It has to be said, David, that you are giving up part of your holiday to help me, and I'm grateful.' So soulful did he look when he said it that Mourne looked at him suspiciously and then chided herself for her thoughts.

'Where do I come in?' she asked.

'As David is over here on holiday he would like to visit a few places, so your job, as a way of saying thank you, is to show him around – take him to areas of outstanding beauty and all that.'

'I take it you'll be running the place on your own then,' Mourne said.

'No I will not, you sarcastic article – I've already arranged with Maggie Cullen to fill in and she was very willing.'

'She never mentioned it.'

'Which is possible, seeing as I asked her only an hour ago.'

'But—'

'But me no buts. Have you any objection to swanning around the countryside at my expense?'

'None at all,' said Mourne crisply. 'But it would have helped if I'd been asked.' It was very high-handed of them both not to include her in the initial discussions.

Gerry leaned back. 'You're working for me. I don't normally send out signals before I ask you to perform a duty – however, if you have any problems, then I'll switch the arrangement round and Maggie can do the careering about in David's hired car.' He softened as he watched her face. 'You're right! I should have asked. Are you willing to do this or not?'

'I'm more than willing.' She turned to David. 'I really didn't mean to imply that going around with you would be a chore. Indeed it will not be, but I have to hold my own here or I'd go under.' Mourne smiled. 'When do we start?'

'Tomorrow!' announced David. 'Now we've sorted things out I would like to enjoy myself – that's if you won't be too tired to gallivant around after a morning's work.'

'Of course she won't,' said Gerry, rising. 'Maggie won't mind clearing up anything that's left over – she told me – so Mourne needn't worry if she hasn't finished.' He walked to the door to retrieve his jacket and Mourne and David exchanged a smile and Mourne slowly shook her head. 'The man will never change,' she said. 'I tell you, you'll have to hold your own here; he's been the boss for too many years and he'll put every word in your mouth for you.'

'I'd better get going, I'm doing his rounds with him. Will I see you tonight?'

'I suppose it depends on whether or not Uncle Gerry lets you off the leash,' said Mourne.

'I'll get him to pop over with me to see Uncle Patrick. Leave it to me to—'

'Are you coming or not, David?' Gerry put his head round the door. David winked at Mourne and hurried out.

Mourne learned quite a bit about David and his lifestyle that evening as she sat quietly in the big study where she had joined the men after she and Mam had done the washing-up. She knew she was privileged because normally, unless there was to be a family conference, Father Patrick entertained his friends alone. She and Mam had much the same arrangement in that they entertained their friends over in the annexe.

She was suddenly aware that they were discussing David's career and, sitting almost unnoticed, she hung on every word.

'Why don't you do something about the situation?' Uncle Gerry was saying.

'Don't think I haven't tried: several of us have made enemies by our persistence, in fact, but Professor Roberts is against change and—'

'I know that old blirt well,' Gerry cut in. 'I trained with him and he was a right eejut then. How the hell he got where he is I'll never know.'

'He's a clever surgeon,' David said. 'It's just that he's so entrenched in old methods he will not see further than his own nose. Every time we try for some of the latest machinery and ask for funding to go on courses to learn the newest techniques, he rattles on about lack of money. He just cannot understand that unless we keep up we will get nowhere. As he sees it, he's so far managed to cure and heal and operate with the equipment on hand very successfully.'

'The man is a menace – he should be retired.'

David said, 'Hospital superintendents are being replaced – mostly by natural wastage – so I think that he'll retire soon and St Angela's will be under the new system. We've managed to replace two of our anaesthetic machines because the others were becoming dangerous.' He grinned. 'It's like driving a Rolls-Royce instead of a Wolseley. Vincent Carstairs, my anaesthetist, had to go on a short course to learn how to handle it, and it certainly makes his job easier.'

'What about your promotion?' asked Father Patrick. 'Is it time to congratulate you?'

'Yes and no!' David said, ruefully. 'I got pipped for the general surgery but I was recommended for the senior registrar's post in gynaecology.'

'And?'

'I accepted it, of course, but I'm more interested in general surgery. I find gynae too restricting. The other reason is that the theatre sister who works on the general side is extremely efficient and I would hate to lose her – we make a good team.'

Mourne felt a tiny pang. She didn't like the way David's voice had softened slightly as he mentioned this woman. She continued to listen quietly as he spoke of the rapport between them and she sighed. He had a life away from them and she felt suddenly jealous of it. Perhaps if she hadn't dropped the idea of becoming a trained nurse, she would have been able to meet him on his own ground. As a doctor's receptionist she was only on the very outer edge of the knowledge and expertise this other woman possessed; indeed, the *very* outer edge.

Gerry, being nearest to Mourne, heard the sigh. He turned to her. 'You must be bored stiff.'

'Oh no, no, I most certainly am not bored. Please don't worry. It's been an insight into David's life.' She reddened and stood up. 'Anyway, I must go and see Mam. She will want a hand with things.'

'Don't go yet,' said Gerry. 'David will want to discuss plans for tomorrow and I have to know about time, etcetera, so that I can work my way round it. For all I know he'll be taking you off somewhere distant and Mrs Haggerty will need to know about meals.'

'Don't be nosy, Gerry,' grinned Patrick. 'They'll let you and Mrs Haggerty know if they're to be away for meals.'

David spoke. 'I thought we might start nearer home and spend the day in Newcastle. I'd like to see how it has changed – if that's all right with you, Mourne.' He looked at her. Tomorrow he would make it their special day.

They headed towards the bottom of the high dunes which bordered the Slieve Donard Hotel, a popular Victorian redbrick building which sat solidly on the high ground above.

Mourne flattened the pale golden sand as best she could and covered it with a rug, whilst David found some pieces of driftwood on which to place the canvas bag containing the food. They were both old hands at this. 'It was all part of the fun when we were young to eat dry sand in our sandwiches,' David remarked, 'but I like my sandwiches sand-free these days.'

'A sign of ageing,' Mourne laughed, but she was careful to ensure that the sand was well tamped down so that the rug lay flat and clean.

It was a wonderful hot, sunny day and the water, having had the benefit of several hours of the morning heat, was tepid. They swam and floated and dunked each other, laughing, and with high spirits enjoyed their renewed friendship. They spoke of their ambitions and dreams and explored rock pools, and when they tired of talking and exploring, they played the game they had played as children, which was to start at the bottom of a huge sandy dune and try to reach the top without sliding back down the deep, loose sand. Mourne was sorry when the day ended and they had to head for home.

'Will I see you this evening?' David asked, as they packed up.

'No, I'm afraid not. It's my evening for supervising the youth club.'

'I could help.'

Mourne hesitated. 'I'd rather you didn't,' she said. 'I would find it difficult if you were there watching me.' She reddened. 'I sound rude, but I do have a problem with keeping control and with you there, I'd go to pieces.' She looked at him pleadingly.

'I understand. I'll see you at the surgery tomorrow.'

Next day David tentatively said that he would like to go fishing on Strangford Lough, and suggested that if she felt she wouldn't enjoy such a day then perhaps they could meet that evening.

'Would you prefer to go alone? I won't mind,' Mourne said.

'I'd rather you were with me. I enjoy your company, but fishing isn't something most girls enjoy.'

'And I'm one of them.' Mourne grinned. 'But it beats a day behind the reception desk. I'll be very happy to lie on the bank and read and enjoy the sun.'

'Are there any good restaurants near by?'

'I don't know. I've only been once, when I was younger. I think it would be wise to bring our own. There might be a café but I couldn't guarantee quality.'

David looked into the amazing green eyes smiling up at him. She was more obliging than his Rosemary, but then, she was more naïve. She was a real beauty, and he wondered if there was a man in the background. There had been no mention of one but surely the men around here weren't blind.

'Packed lunch it is then. If it's anything like yesterday's then I'm more than satisfied with the arrangement.' He smiled at her.

Later that evening David dropped her off and hurried away. He was dining out with Uncle Gerry, and they had arrived back later than they'd meant to but the day had been so enjoyable, time had flown past. Mourne let herself in. The house was strangely silent. Her mother would normally be in the kitchen preparing dinner. Puzzled, Mourne placed her canvas bag on the floor and went into the kitchen. It was empty. She caught sight of a note on the mantelpiece and took it down. It explained much. Her mother had been called away as her cousin Pat had been rushed to Downpatrick hospital with a heart attack. Could she start the meal. She would find all she needed. The vegetables were on the sink waiting to be prepared and there was a piece of steak ready for the frying.

She groaned. Father Patrick was so fussy about his steak. He liked it rare 'but not so rare that the blood is oozing, but not so cooked that I can't see the beast has not been drained of it.' Her mam could cook it to perfection but even she, in the early days, had fallen foul of his bad humour when it wasn't to his liking. She looked at her watch. Six o'clock! Mr Rice the butcher never closed on time if he could squeeze another customer in – she'd have time to get some liver. Father Patrick liked liver and onions. She could manage that. The steak could do for tomorrow.

She had just finished cooking the meal and was ready to dish up when she heard the sound of the front door opening. A quick glance at the clock told her that Father Patrick, a man of habit, was dead on time.

She called out to him. 'Dinner's ready for the table.'

Patrick walked in and glared at her. 'Am I imagining things or can I smell liver?'

'You like liver,' said Mourne defensively, and seeing the look in his eye she tilted her chin and continued. 'Father Patrick, you had a choice of badly cooked steak and me in a state of trepidation, or a well-cooked liver and onion dish with me smiling at you as you enjoyed it.'

'I was promised steak. I was looking forward to my steak. I am a sorely disappointed man and not a happy one therefore.'

'You'll have your steak tomorrow. Meanwhile,' said Mourne, with concealed amusement, her lip trembling like a leaf in a stiff breeze, 'liver it will have to be, followed by a sulk in your study.'

'You're a bad article with no respect for your elders,' Patrick grumbled, before sitting down to tackle the meal with gusto.

David phoned at ten o'clock to make arrangements for the following day. As he outlined his plans, Mourne listened and then gave a little gasp.

'Something wrong?'

'Oh David! I'm sorry. I've got a long-standing arrangement to go out walking with an old friend. I can't let him down at such short notice.'

Him? So she did have a boyfriend. Somehow he felt disappointed.

'That's that then,' David said. 'I hope your boyfriend isn't too mad at you for spending time with me.'

'My boyfriend? Oh, no! It isn't a young man. I go walking with Mr O'Rourke once a month and—'

'Not O'Rourke and his dog O'Malley?'

'You know him?'

'Since boyhood. My mother gave him O'Malley when he was only a tiny pup. I'm surprised he's still alive – that was nearly twelve years ago.'

Mourne laughed in delight. 'He's still going strong.' She hesitated and then spoke again. 'Mr O'Rourke is a very reclusive man but perhaps as you know him from boyhood he might . . .'

'He'll not mind a bit, I promise. Is he still living along the Bryansford road?'

'Er – no! He lives off the beaten track, in a stone cottage on the lower reaches of the mountain. He has shut himself away for years. Once a week he joins his friends round the stove in Cullen's stores, but the rest of the time he keeps away from people.'

'How did you get so close?'

'O'Malley likes me.' Mourne laughed. 'It's as simple as that, and I think Mr O'Rourke enjoys a bit of company on his walks. I met him a few times when I was out walking on the hills and we started off from there.'

There was silence, and then David spoke again. 'I'd like to come. If O'Rourke objects then I'll disappear.'

The man standing outside the cottage door was of gargantuan build. He wore a short coat of indeterminate age, and on his head of iron-grey hair a green woollen cap was pulled down over his ears, for in spite of the warmth of the day there was a stiff breeze. Over his shoulder was slung a large canvas bag. He adjusted the straps of the bag and called out in a loud voice: 'Come O'Malley! It's time to go trout-tickling.' At the magic words a huge dog appeared in the doorway, his ears pricked up and his tail wagging furiously. His eyes looked up at O'Rourke in excited anticipation. He was a handsome dog but, like O'Rourke's coat, was of indeterminate breed.

Mourne and David had just rounded the corner of the high hedge and had witnessed the scene and before O'Rourke caught sight of them, Mourne called out, causing him to stop in his tracks. He frowned and remained silent.

'Mr O'Rourke, I hope you don't mind me bringing David along. I realize you're not keen on—'

David put his hand on her arm. 'Do you remember me? David McNeill. I pressured Mourne into taking me along as I wanted to meet you again. You were kind to me when I was a young lad.'

They waited. O'Rourke didn't reply as he cradled the dog's head in his huge palm. 'Come O'Malley. It's time to tickle the trout,' he said at last, and regarded the two young people. 'Come if you want. If it was anyone but you, young David McNeill, I'd have sent you packing, but a son of Maraid Owen is welcome here. She was a fine young woman and I thought the world of her.' Without another word he set off in the wake of O'Malley who was giving great yelps of sheer joy.

Mourne ran ahead to catch up with the big dog so that the two men could talk and get to know each other again. The renegade O'Malley, his tail wagging and his rear end stuck out of a bush, was barking excitedly. 'Come out of there O'Malley,' said Mourne fiercely, but O'Malley was oblivious to all but the fact that there was a rabbit in there. He wriggled further into the bush and sniffed around the spot where he had seen the puff of a tail disappear, and so busy was Mourne in her effort to pull him from the bush, she was unaware that the two men had now passed her, deep in conversation.

'I seldom go down into the village,' O'Rourke was explaining. 'Once a month I have a jar with the lads and a chat, but for the most part I prefer my own company. For me nothing can compare with the quiet of the hilly night and walking the paths with O'Malley. I have my cottage, I have my beloved mountain, and I have my dog – sure what more does a man need.' Realizing that Mourne hadn't caught up, he turned, and weighing up the situation he let out a gulder of a shout. 'O'Malley! I am impatient to be gone. Didn't I tell you, it's trout today, rabbits tomorrow. Get your priorities right, boy.' For emphasis, O'Rourke went back and smashed the bracken with his boot and watched in satisfaction as O'Malley hurriedly backed out and sidled up to him with a look of apology in his dark, dog eyes.

Mourne joined the men. 'That dog of yours is almost human,' she laughed.

'He's a dog a man can talk to, which I do most of the time.' O'Rourke's eyes crinkled. 'It's either that or I start talkin' to the wall. By now he has a fair idea of what I'm on about and he knows when I mean business.'

Mourne walked along, listening to their discussion about lifestyles and careers. She had never known O'Rourke to talk so much. She was pleased that the two men were getting on so well.

They walked until they came to a stile leading to a meadow luscious with buttercups. 'Up and over boy!' roared O'Rourke, and O'Malley, with a quick scramble and a skid, was over and racing joyfully towards a group of mournful-eyed cows who followed his progress with obvious concern. They formed a protective ring as the big dog waltzed and sidestepped at a safe distance, barking with great ferociousness. O'Rourke whistled him back, and with one parting volley O'Malley bounded away.

When they reached the riverbank O'Rourke put his finger to his lips for silence and motioned Mourne and David to their positions. No command was necessary for O'Malley; he was an old hand at this. He flopped down on his belly and pushed his head forward till his chin rested on his front paws. O'Rourke crept up beside him, silently removing his coat and bag as he did so. Kneeling down on the bank, he leaned forward and quietly slid his arm and hand into the river till the water lapped his rolled-up sleeve. Mourne and David held their breath. David looked on in wonder at the big man's dexterity. He could see, just behind a large boulder, a dark shadow. The big man's hand slid forward as he moved his fingers to and fro rhythmically until, with a forward sweeping movement, he guided his hand towards the boulder. Gently, insistently, his finger continued to move, backward and forward, backward and forward.

O'Malley panted quietly. He knew O'Rourke would eventually get the fish. David's heart was pounding with excitement as the fish began to move as though hypnotized towards the hand that was still stirring the water gently. He could have sworn there was a look of bliss on its face as it lay on its side whilst O'Rourke tickled its belly. The trout slowly rolled over. Obviously this was the moment they had been waiting for. With one quick pounce, the net which had been firmly clasped in O'Rourke's left hand was down with a mighty swoop. Up in the air went the fish and with a soft thud it landed on the bank.

This was the signal for O'Malley to start barking, all tension momentarily released. David felt his own tension drain away and he looked over at Mourne, who was lying with her eyes closed and her face to the sky. He felt the heat of the day permeate his body in delicious waves and he too rolled over on to his back.

Mourne, on the other hand, was feeling restless. She had been trout-tickling before, but this time she hadn't enjoyed it. Perhaps it was the look of delight on David's face as the fish was caught. Men had the hunting instinct in their genes for ever and she wished that David's pleasure had been for her and not for the sport.

O'Rourke had moved further downstream to another boulder so David, with a sigh of contentment, wriggled towards Mourne and touched her. She opened her eyes, and he was lost in their green depths. The prickles on his neck stood up and his heart began to hammer in his chest. 'Why don't we go for a walk?' he suggested, suddenly, and let go of her arms to stand up. Another moment and he would have made a fool of himself.

Mourne rose and went quietly to where O'Rourke was lying and whispered their intentions to him. He nodded and continued with his task. Walking back to David she smiled at him and said, brightly, 'Off we go.' Her heart was aching. She had noticed how abruptly David had turned from her, and she had realized when she looked into his eyes that she loved him.

CHAPTER 4

During the second week of his holiday David asked if they could visit Belfast. Mourne was surprised. 'I'd have thought you would have seen enough of cities,' she said.

'Ah! But there are cities and there are cities. Belfast is unique. It has Stormont and the River Lagan, and the city hall – and besides, I haven't been to Belfast since I was a small boy. I'd want to recapture the feeling I had then of bustle and throbbing life. I want to stand on the bridge over the Lagan and smell the fishy breeze and see the tall cranes of the Harland and Wolff shipyard . . .'

'This is the small boy coming out in you?' Mourne laughed. 'Sure London Bridge would seem more romantic than lookin' down into the murky grey waters of the Lagan.'

'I won't have you spoil my illusions,' David said, sternly, but his eyes twinkled. 'We'll wander round the town and have lunch at a hotel and listen to the Belfast accent, which is worth the trip in itself, and walk down past the town hall and feed the birds.'

Later, as they stood on the large, busy pavement and leaned over the bridge and stared into the depths of the river, Mourne glanced at David's face. He was so obviously enjoying himself she wanted to hug him to her. He was again the little boy who had come here with his mother to see the ships being built and watch the screeching gulls swooping for food. Later, as he had promised, they had an excellent lunch and afterwards made their way to view Stormont; an elegantly impressive, neoclassical mansion, with beautiful lawns and walks. They visited the cornmarket and strolled around the narrow alleyways of the Entries. David suggested going for a drink in White's Tavern, but Mourne was hesitant, so they went along to one of the little cafés near by instead.

She went to bed that night, tired out but content – David had kissed her goodnight. It had only been a small peck on the cheek and if analysed, it would be considered a social kiss to say thank you, but she hugged the sensation to her as she settled down to sleep. As she drifted off she felt a nagging conviction that she was heading for trouble by letting her feelings run away with her, and the thought that she might be running the risk of another rejection preyed heavy on her mind.

Two days before he was due to go back, David said, 'I've trailed you here, there and everywhere and not once have you stated a preference, so today is Mourne O'Hara's day. Is there anywhere special you would like us to visit?'

Afterwards, when she had time to ponder, Mourne wondered what had possessed her to say what she did, but when David had made his suggestion, she had hesitated for only a second and then said, 'I'd like to go up into the Silent Valley.'

'The Silent Valley? That's quite a climb.'

'It's a long climb, but the ascent is fairly easy and the views are worth it. We could take a packed lunch.' Mourne, already regretting her impulses, wavered. 'Perhaps it isn't a good idea. This is your second to last day and there must be other places you'd prefer to see . . .'

'Of course we'll go,' David grinned. 'I'm not having you tell people I was too soft to make the climb.' He looked at her curiously. She was an odd little thing. He recalled her reluctance to go into a pub during their visit to Belfast, and yet she had no compunction about spending time on a lonely mountain with him.

He had to admit later that the climb had been worth every bone-shuddering, lung-gasping effort. He had never been up this far before. As a boy, his great loves had been fishing and swimming and later, as he got older, chasing girls. The mountain, hauntingly beautiful though it was, had no appeal for a tearabout like himself in those early days.

They had reached an enormous boulder before Mourne stopped. He unstrapped the haversack from his shoulders and sat down. 'I take it we're resting awhile,' he gasped.

'This is as far as we go,' Mourne said, and added, 'You're seriously out of condition, David McNeill.'

David nodded and grinned. 'Why here?' he inquired. 'I would have thought you might want to test me further.'

It was some time before Mourne answered and when she did so, he

50

was arrested in the act of disgorging the contents of the haversack by the sadness in her voice.

'I felt a need to show you where I was probably born.'

David looked around. 'What? I don't understand.'

'I was found underneath that rock,' said Mourne, with quiet bitterness.

David, recognizing the unspoken hurt that was in her, remained silent. So! She'd had a reason for bringing him here. Suspecting that she needed a listener, not a questioner, he leaned against the huge rock and waited.

When she had finished telling her story, he gently reached out and took her hand in his. 'As far as I'm concerned, and indeed everyone who knows you, you were adopted by Kitty and Charlie O'Hara from an orphanage.'

'I can't shake off the feeling that I was abandoned . . . that my mother didn't want me . . . that I was an encumbrance to be discarded. I feel such a terrible sense of rejection.' Mourne's voice broke. 'How could a mother do such a thing?'

David waited till she had composed herself before saying, 'There were obviously circumstances we know nothing about. Look at the way it was organized. You weren't abandoned, Mourne – and certainly not rejected. Everything possible was done to ensure that you were found. Instructions were clearly given. You said yourself that Father Patrick had the strong feeling someone was keeping watch.'

'That's another thing! I've sometimes had the feeling that I *am* being watched.' She leaned against the rock beside him. 'Uncle Gerry suspects that my mother might have been a young tinker or gypsy girl who would have been severely punished if her condition had been discovered. He says he's seen caravans in the area during the winter months and that the cross resembles one he once saw being carved, by a gypsy.'

David held her away from him and looked into the beautiful eyes, now bright with unshed tears. 'My uncle's talking sense. Put this behind you and carry on with life.'

'It's easier to say than do. I will *always* wonder why I was left there.'

'Is that why you were called Mourne? It's such an unusual name for a Catholic child. We are mostly named after saints.' David was trying to stabilize the situation.

Mourne smiled wanly at him. 'Actually, my name is Catherine Mourne O'Hara.'

51

'Why did you want me to know all this? It really doesn't make any difference to how I feel about you,' David said.

Mourne wanted to ask him just how he did feel about her. She longed to hear him say he found her attractive, but she smiled tremulously and said, 'I don't know why – it was a sudden impulse. Can we have lunch now? I'm absolutely starving.'

She wasn't seeing David that evening as he was taking the surgery for Gerry, so she retired to her room early. Once there she took out the box that held the emerald ring and stared at it for a long time before replacing it. Looking up at the exquisitely fashioned crucifix which hung above her bed, she blessed herself. 'Oh Lord, please help me to be generous in my thinking towards my mother and help me to forgive,' she said aloud, and making the sign of the cross on her lips she put the case containing the beautiful ring into the drawer. She had never attempted to put it on her finger. Something about the ring repelled her. She found herself wondering who had given her mother such an expensive ring and for what reason.

David, having arrived back in England, was not looking forward to his first meeting with Rosemary. The issue of him going to Ireland had not been satisfactorily resolved. He didn't know if she would throw his ring at him or just give him a blasting in that tidy way she had.

He threw his jacket on to the bed and left his case where it was before tackling the pile of letters and circulars he'd lifted from the mat. They were mostly from medical equipment firms, with one or two invitations to functions or meetings. There was nothing from Rosemary. He would phone her: that way if things got sticky, he had a good chance of reasoning with her. She was always more amenable on the phone. Rosemary would find it difficult to have a row with a voice floating somewhere in the ether. As far as she was concerned there was no point in rowing into space. Face-to-face contact in an argument gave her the advantage.

She was out. He breathed a sigh of relief. He wasn't in the right frame of mind for an altercation – and now he could say with truth that he had tried to contact her. Meanwhile, he craved a leisurely soak in a hot bath. He put the water heater on and made his way into the living room to pour himself a drink.

Later, as he lay back enjoying the warmth and relaxation, he let his mind drift. His uncle had lost no time in trying to persuade him to take over his practice. The idea was an appealing one. Things were not going well for him at St Angela's. He grew more frustrated as the weeks passed – that was the downside. The upside was that he loved surgery; he was good at it, and this fact would have to be taken seriously into consideration in any future plans he made regarding his professional life.

His uncle had given him a time limit. 'I have someone waiting in the wings,' he had said. David suspected this was a ploy to get him to make a hasty decision. The old boy was a dab hand at getting what he wanted: he was a very shrewd manipulator.

However, the offer was one that he didn't want to reject out of hand. Having spent the last two weeks in Ballycash he had come to realize how much he missed his old home, and he had enjoyed working in a country practice more than he had thought he would. He frowned and sipped his drink. Was it a good enough reason to turn his life around and give up the job he loved? There had to be a stronger pull – some sort of challenge. Having spent the past year in the cut and thrust of surgery, he couldn't see himself settling down to diagnosing mumps and delivering babies. The new system was beginning to take off, and in spite of his frustration at the short-sightedness of management, his blood surged at the new techniques that were now being used as a result of the mistakes and discoveries made on the battlefield during the war and later improved upon. Instruments and equipment were becoming more sophisticated as the months passed, and an exciting new era in surgery was beginning.

His thoughts turned to Mourne. He had been entranced by her loveliness – a fact that caused him some disquiet. The last time he had seen her she had been a skinny eight-year-old with masses of freckles and a pair of amazing eyes. When he had held her close to him, there on the mountain, something inside had stirred. He rose to refill his glass in an effort to calm his feelings and bring his thoughts back to the present. It helped that the doorbell rang; he answered it.

Rosemary stood there, a bottle of wine in one hand and a bunch of flowers in the other. 'The wine is for you – the flowers are for me, to brighten up the room.' She held her face up for a kiss and before he could put his arms round her she had passed him on the way to the kitchen for a vase. Bossy as ever, but at least she had forgiven him his transgressions, he thought, in amusement.

'I'm just going to dress,' he called to her. 'Help yourself to a drink.'

When he came out, Rosemary was standing by the window. She came towards him, smiling, so he put his arms round her and kissed

53

her gently. 'I've missed you,' he said, and was rewarded by a passionate response. 'You're not angry with me any more, then?' he inquired, surprised at the fervour of the kiss.

Rosemary shook her head as he drew her down on to the sofa beside him. 'The wedding was boring anyway and I came back the next day.'

'What about your holiday? You were going to spend it up there with your parents.'

'Not without you I wasn't.' She sat up. 'Actually, I spent the first week with a friend and the second week we decided we would up sticks and go off to Spain.'

David's eyebrows rose. It was uncharacteristic of Rosemary to do anything on impulse.

'It was Maureen's idea. I was so mad at you, I went along with it. We had a lovely time too. How about you?'

'It wasn't meant to be a holiday, exactly.'

'There must have been moments. The old boy wouldn't have kept you to the grindstone, surely? He was ill, not dying.'

Irritated by the patronizing way she spoke of his uncle, but unwilling to fan the flames of a possible row, he said coolly: 'I managed to enjoy myself when I wasn't helping out. It was wonderful to visit old haunts and meet up with old friends.' He thought it wise not to mention Mourne's part in his enjoyment or that she had been the largest part of it.

'Is your uncle feeling better?'

'What? Oh yes, much better.' He hid a smile. He and Father Patrick had sussed out that Gerry had been applying the talc a bit liberally to his normally ruddy face to simulate pallor. He had also been limping a lot too, but the game was up when David observed him walking normally when he thought he was not being observed. It hadn't taken Father Patrick and him long to work out that something more was going on than met the eye. Towards the end of the visit, Gerry had stopped walking slowly and his colour had returned to normal. Father Patrick had remarked how much better he looked since David's arrival, and wasn't it wonderful what a good haircut could do for a man's looks.

Gerry had glared at him and told him that he'd had it cut for his nephew's last night in Ireland. 'I couldn't be seen dining out with you all looking like a tramp.'

Father Patrick and he had smiled at each other over his uncle's head and Gerry, catching sight of them, had laughed and confessed that he'd been putting on an act in the hope that David would feel pity for him and see his way to agreeing to run the practice.

Realizing that Rosemary was looking at him curiously, David smiled at her and concentrated his mind on the present.

'You wouldn't consider working over there, would you?' she inquired, her eyes raking him warily.

David laughed and pulled her to her feet. 'Enough of this. Let's go out for a meal.' He hastily kissed her and handed her her handbag and gloves, thereby avoiding giving an answer.

Mourne hadn't seen her friend Tara for a while as Tara had been spending much of her time with her new boyfriend, Jay-Jay. If *he* wasn't journeying to Ballycash to see her then she was visiting him in Belfast. While David was home Mourne hadn't really minded, for Tara phoned her often to keep her informed of the progress of the romance, but now that David had gone back to England she was feeling restless and slightly depressed at the sudden lack of excitement in her life since his departure. Not even the Maguire twins with their uniquely distorted, childish philosophy could raise her spirits. So it was with a feeling of relief that she answered the phone to hear Tara asking her to come to Belfast on her next trip.

'Sure I couldn't go with you. I'd be playing gooseberry,' but her voice sounded hopeful.

'Will you listen for a minute – I haven't finished,' Tara said, and continued after a pause. 'There's a concert on at the Ulster Hall that Jay-Jay wants to go to and I asked him if you could come as well as you like classical music—'

'Are you mad or what?' Mourne cried. 'You can't stand the classics. The nearest you get is "Hear my Song, Violetta."'

'You needn't go on. I'm doing it for love.' Tara burst out laughing. 'They say you do anything for love, but if anyone had told me that I would be prepared to sit through two whole hours of dirge, I'd have laughed in their faces.'

'You can't go pretending you like it,' Mourne cried. 'You'll come a cropper when Jay-Jay finds out that he married a culshie and not the sophisticated concert-goer you're presenting yourself to be.'

'Sure it will be too late then,' laughed Tara. 'I'll have him hooked.'

'That's terrible. He should know the truth.'

'Ach away! He's not goin' to fall out of love with me just because I don't know a sonata from a cantata.' Tara giggled helplessly. 'I'll have caught him with my apple pie and my apple scones by then.'

Mourne laughed with her. 'Well! I do like classical music, so I don't know why I'm trying to make you see sense if it will ruin the invitation.'

'Great girl!' There was a pause. 'By the way, you're going to be partnering Jay-Jay's friend Eamon Leeson. He's tall as a long drink of water so wear your high heels.' Before Mourne could answer the phone went dead.

When she told Mam about the invitation she didn't mention that she had been paired up with Jay-Jay's friend. There was no point causing waves.

'Am I missing something here or have my ears gone? I thought you just said that Tara had invited you to go to a classical concert.'

'I did.'

'There has to be a reason. That girl can only recognize dance music.'

Mourne laughed. 'I think she's trying to impress her boyfriend.'

'That's devious!' Kitty put down her sewing. 'It never works, you know. Two people who are seriously thinking of marrying should be honest with each other. There has to be a common interest in most things if they're to be well matched, otherwise the marriage will wither and die the death.'

'Oh Mam! Tara's pretty open about who she is and what she's like. She just lied a little on this one thing.'

'Mourne O'Hara! You can't lie a *little*. A lie is a lie. Tara would be better telling the truth. I don't suppose this young fella will drop her like a brick just because she isn't a classical fan. Where are the girl's wits?'

'I've told her this, but it's too late now so there's no point going further with it. I'd like to go.'

'Well at least *you'll* enjoy it.'

Mourne smiled inwardly. So would Tara. With her box of chocolates and Jay-Jay's arm round her she would be in seventh heaven. She wondered about herself, although putting up with a boy she had never met was a better option than not going at all. She just hoped the maligned Eamon was the outgoing sort. She wasn't too good at conversing with comparative strangers in whom she hadn't the slightest interest.

She needn't have worried. The concert was as good as it was cracked up to be and although Eamon Leeson towered over her even in her high heels, and her feet were killing her as they walked to the restaurant for dinner, Mourne was enjoying the tall man's company. He was a bit of a laugh and had her in stitches as he related some of the things the bold Jay-Jay and himself had got up to in their time.

'I suppose you miss going around with him now that he's going out with Tara,' Mourne said.

'Not at all! I get a rest. We were always going somewhere or other – the man is never still – and there were times when all I wanted to do was go fishing, but Jay-Jay hates sitting on damp riverbanks so I usually end up trailing him.'

'Why don't you put your foot down?'

'I'm too easygoing and good-natured,' Eamon grinned. 'Besides, I manage to get a few days' fishing in, so why ruin a beautiful friendship.'

They had reached the restaurant as he finished speaking. Tara turned to Mourne and told her she was going to the cloakroom. Mourne nodded and followed her while the two men sorted out the table.

'Well?' asked Tara as they washed their hands. 'How are you getting along with the long leek?'

Mourne frowned. 'Is there any need to keep calling Eamon names? I think he's a lovely person. We're getting on great.'

Tara looked at her friend in the mirror. Mourne's pretty face was pink and cross. 'You like him!' Tara said, with satisfaction. 'There! I told Jay-Jay I thought you would. Isn't this great? We'll be able to make up foursomes now and again.'

Mourne stared at her in horror. 'Now just a holy minute. I like him – but not enough to spend my days running up and down to Belfast to see him.'

'He can come up to Ballycash with Jay-Jay.'

'No! I like him – who wouldn't, he's a really nice lad – but I'll never like him enough to encourage him to get serious, and inviting him up to Ballycash would send out the wrong message.'

'But you don't—'

'No I don't – whatever you were going to suggest. The idea is not a workable one under the circumstances so don't you go making sly remarks along those lines during dinner.' Mourne finished wiping her hands and waited for Tara.

'I think you're being silly,' Tara pouted at her.

'Just remember what I've said,' Mourne whispered as they approached the table.

'We've ordered some wine and the waiter will be back for our food order,' said Jay-Jay. He had caught the frown on Mourne's face and raised an eyebrow at Tara, who shook her head slightly. He hoped Mourne was enjoying herself. She and Eamon appeared to be getting along well. He sneaked a glance at the girl as she bent her head over the menu. She was a real stunner. He had been prepared for her to be unusual, for Tara went on about her non-stop at times, but at his first meeting with this paragon he could see what Tara meant. She was deep, that one, but although she was quieter than his Tara she had an easy way with her and conversing was not a problem – not that it would be with the big fella, he could talk a donkey blind, but things could have been sticky if she had put on airs. Tara had warned him that Mourne was on a higher plane than most of her friends: however, in his book she was all right, and from what Eamon had said while the two girls were in the cloakroom, the same went for him.

Just as they were about to set off home, Eamon drew Mourne aside. 'I've really enjoyed our evening. Would you mind if I came up to Ballycash next time Jay-Jay goes to see Tara? The summer's nearly at an end and it would be nice to go to the beach or walk up Slieve Donard.'

Mourne's heart sank. She had feared this. 'I've enjoyed your company, Eamon,' she said, with hesitation. 'But I—'

Eamon put his finger on her lips. 'I know what you're worried about. You think I might be trying to start off a romance.' He shook his head. 'I'm just getting over a break-up and all I need now is someone to have some fun with to help me over a bad patch. I like your style, and knowing that nothing would happen between us I did just wonder if we could get together as friends.'

'And you won't expect more?' Mourne needed to know that she was in control.

'Hand on heart,' he smiled. 'I haven't got over Kate yet. I'm certainly not ready for a new relationship this soon.'

'Don't you think you're risking complete rejection by coming up to see me? After all, who knows, she might change her mind.'

'She won't. I couldn't be more certain.' His eyes pleaded with her.

'All right,' Mourne said. 'Just so long as we've the understanding. I'd enjoy the company. I don't have many young men running after me – unlike Tara.' She laughed and then said, 'If you like you can bring your fishing gear sometimes and I'll take you to some good rivers I know.'

Eamon was delighted. 'I knew there had to be a good reason why I liked you. At last I've found a girl who will come fishing with me.'

'Don't let it go to your head. Our arrangement still stands.'

'Amen!' he grinned.

Later, on their way home, she told Tara that she had agreed to see Eamon again.

Tara frowned. 'Did he tell you about his girlfriend?'

'Yes, but that's fine. I did warn him that he might never get her back if she finds out about him coming to see me, but he shrugged it off.'

'Which is not surprising. He has as much chance of getting her back as he has of catching carp in the local river – she got married two weeks ago.'

The following week Mourne had a letter from David. In it he said that he was actually missing her – not to mention the few freckles that he'd discovered she still possessed. *I'll never forget our days together,* he wrote. *You made my two weeks in Ballycash worth the trip and who knows, I may see you all sooner than you think.*

She read on, her heart beating fast, and when she reached the end of the two-page missive she lay back on her pillow. What did he mean – sooner than you think? She read the letter again, searching for a clue but couldn't find one. The rest of the letter just dealt with the things they had done and how he had enjoyed working at the surgery, although things had been a bit quiet and slow compared to his work at St Angela's. She put the letter away as her mother called her name. Breakfast was on the table. She glanced at her watch, wondering if she had time to draft a reply before she went to the surgery, but she hadn't, and she tore downstairs and across to the big kitchen. Father Patrick had already eaten and gone on a visit to a sick parishioner, so she gulped down her food hastily as her mam tackled the washing-up.

During the morning she had only half her mind on her work and twice she found herself in trouble. First with Uncle Gerry, who was demanding where his mug of tea was as he was dying of thirst with all the talking and advice he was giving, and then with Pigsticker Riley who, as usual, wanted his treatment in a hurry before he ended up getting the sack.

Mourne sighed. 'Every time you come you tell me this, Pigsticker,' she said. 'I'm only the hired help. Have it out with himself in there. I can only go at the pace he dictates.'

'You just brought him in his tea. Could you not have waited till I had my turn. I think the man drinks it through a straw, he takes that long to get it down him.'

Mourne sat down on her tall stool and watched him return to his seat before phoning in to Gerry to tell him that Pigsticker was getting het up.

'Tell the old fool he can find a new doctor,' said Gerry, adding, 'if he can.' He smiled to himself as he put the phone down and took another slurp of the strong tea. He had the monopoly. There was nothing Pigsticker could do but put up with the delay. Anyway, the man had a new complaint every time he came. He was as sour as his father had been, God rest his soul.

A few minutes later Mourne poked her head round the door. 'Are you ready yet? There are a few restless feet shifting around in there.' She nodded towards the waiting room.

Gerry grinned. 'Tough!' was all he said, but he handed her the cup.

'I have to take the flak,' Mourne grumbled.

'For which I'm paying you a fortune.'

'I wonder why I'm finding it hard to exist, then,' she said cheekily. 'My mother would no doubt like to see me set up home for myself, but I can't afford it.' She moved to the door and went through, ignoring his laugh.

Mourne motioned to Pigsticker. 'You can go in now – and I'd thank you not to upset him. He isn't in the best of moods as it is.'

Eamon came up to see her that weekend. It was hard to imagine that they had met only once before, they got on so well together. They sat on the beach, and she laughed at his droll comments which were funny and apt without being hurtful. Later, when they had afternoon tea at the ice-cream parlour and tea rooms run by an aunt of Tara's, they had a discussion about the state of things in the six years since the war ended. Eamon thought there was an air of decadence around. 'I disapprove of the latest desecration of a man's last stronghold – the pub. It's all right for older women to have a drink in the snug, but nowadays more and more women are brazenly standing up with the men – certainly in the bigger towns like Belfast.' He sounded so indignant, Mourne laughed.

She defended their right to do so, however. 'I wouldn't have the nerve myself,' she said, 'but why should women be hidden away in a stuffy little room with thick frosted glass separating the sexes, while the men socialize in a large room with good lighting and music?'

They argued the toss about this and other issues and both said, at the end of the day, that they had enjoyed themselves and they must do it again. Mourne saw him off before taking the bus back to Ballycash. She was pleased for Tara that she had been invited to meet Jay-Jay's parents, although it had meant that Eamon had to come up by train. Much as she knew she would have enjoyed their company, she felt that she and Eamon had really got to know each other better on this first visit.

Over the following weekends, their friendship flourished as they took walks along the lower reaches of the mountain and went fishing in the rivers that she suggested. Those days were the best. She was content to lie on the bank and enjoy the late summer sun and read a book, while he quietly pursued his hobby. She knew that he was appreciative of her silence, and the knowledge that he was enjoying himself gave her a great deal of quiet pleasure. Sometimes she left him sitting on his canvas stool and went for a long leisurely walk alone, and it was at these times that her mind was full of David. She hadn't heard from him since she had replied to his letter. She had hoped he would keep in touch now that they had met again. She tried to convince herself that he had such a busy schedule he didn't find time to correspond, but she knew she was deceiving herself and that it was more likely he had a girlfriend or two: a country clod of an Irish girl like herself held no allure for a sophisticated young surgeon who was surrounded by knowledgeable, beautiful women all the time.

Towards the middle of September when she and Eamon were out walking, shushing the early leaf fall with their feet, Mourne realized that he was quieter than usual. There was a slight frown creasing his forehead and now and then he would glance quickly at her and away again. They had just spent the afternoon exploring the area in and around Kilkeel, including half an hour at Greencastle fort situated on a point of land at the mouth of Carlingford Lough. Tara and Jay-Jay had gone off to climb to the top to photograph the view up the mouth of the lough while she and Eamon made their way down.

'You're very quiet,' she remarked, and stopped, forcing him to do likewise.

Eamon hesitated. 'Let's sit down here for a moment. I want to talk to you.' He looked hastily up towards the fort.

'They won't be coming down just yet,' Mourne said. 'Tell me what's wrong.'

'Nothing is wrong. It's not that – it's just – just . . .'

'What?'

Eamon gave a long sigh. 'You remember when we first made arrangements to meet we said that it would be as friends?'

Mourne gave him a startled look. God! he wasn't going to tell her he wanted to go further after all! 'Yes?' she said, nervously.

Eamon cleared his throat. 'I – I've met someone – a girl I used to know well, but we lost touch when I fell for Kate. We – er – find that we – that we – have a lot in common. I'm getting quite serious about her and I think she likes me. It means that I can't come up again to see you. It wouldn't be fair to her – to Shelagh.' He looked so miserable, Mourne laughed.

'Good Lord, is that all? For one minute I thought you were going to tell me you were getting serious about our relationship – that wouldn't do at all.' She squeezed his arm. 'I can't tell you how pleased I am for you. I shall miss you, of course, but I'm sure I'll settle into a routine again.' She smiled. 'We both knew it could happen.'

Eamon sighed with relief. 'Maybe I could bring Shelagh up to meet you one day?'

'I don't think that would be a good idea, somehow,' Mourne said, cautiously. 'If she's in love with you, the last thing she'll want is to meet someone with whom you have spent a lot of time.'

'I'll explain the situation to her,' said Eamon.

Mourne laughed again. 'Trust me. It wouldn't be worth the risk. Look! We used each other for the same ends. We've had a lovely few weeks, and they were lovely weeks because we weren't under any romantic pressure. It won't work that way with you and Shelagh – there would be tension and possible suspicion. It might spoil things. Let's just meet as friends of Tara and Jay-Jay.'

'What's happened to Eamon?' Kitty eyed her daughter shrewdly. She had noticed that she hadn't been going out so much just lately, and she hadn't had the usual news about what the pair of them had been up to. She had liked that young man. He was always polite and thoughtful with Mourne, and Kitty had quickly taken to the soft-spoken youth. Anyone who could lift her daughter out of herself and make her laugh was fine in her eyes.

'We won't be seeing each other any more.' Mourne had her nose in a book and didn't look up.

'In the name of God, Mourne O'Hara, is there no one in this land good enough for you? He seemed a fine lad. Why isn't he up to scratch?'

Mourne placed her book on the table. 'It wasn't that kind of relationship,' she said. 'He was a very good friend, that's all.' And I set the rules, she thought, with satisfaction.

As though she hadn't heard, Kitty continued, 'I despair of you. There was Anthony Rice whose father owns shops everywhere and who could buy and sell the rest of us. The son thought the world of you. He drove you around the countryside in a luxury sports car and bought you presents like every day was Christmas Day *and* escorted you to the annual golf club ball – something that doesn't come the way of many young girls—'

'Mam!' Mourne interrupted, horrified. 'Are you telling me that because he had money I should have encouraged him?'

'Don't you be giving me any of your lip, my girl,' said Kitty, glaring at her daughter. 'I'm making comparisons, that's all. What I'm saying is that you don't encourage them if they're charming and loaded with money and you don't encourage them if they're charming and haven't a penny to bless themselves with – what kind of man *will* suit you? You're going to be twenty-one soon and there have been more young men after you than I can count on my fingers and toes and you've sent them all packing. Do you not want to marry and settle down?' Kitty put her hand on her hip. 'Just what was wrong with Anthony Rice, anyway? One minute he was God's gift and the next minute he was out on his ear. I liked him.'

So did I, Mourne thought – until he drank himself silly on the night of the golf club ball and on the way home nearly raped me. Of course he was abjectly apologetic the next time they'd met. He'd blamed the drink. 'I promise you, Mourne, it'll never happen again.'

'You can be sure of that, Anthony Rice,' she had retorted, 'because you won't have the chance.'

'What am I going to tell the father? He was hoping that you would one day become one of the family. He'll go spare.'

That had made her laugh. 'I'd not be marrying your father. Why should he care?'

'He thinks we're a great match,' Anthony had said miserably. 'I don't normally behave like that. Give me another chance.'

She had thought about it but turned down the offer. 'Do you know the saying "What's in you when you're sober comes out when you're drunk"?' Mourne had looked him straight in the eye. 'I could never trust you.'

Mourne brought her mind back to the present. 'Answer me!' Kitty was saying.

'He was fine, Mam, but I didn't like him enough to want to marry him. Anyway! he didn't ask me.' She put her book under her arm and rose to go.

'You probably didn't give him the chance,' Kitty said crossly and slapped the dishcloth down on the sink as she watched her daughter leave the room.

The following days passed lazily in their usual fashion. Work at the surgery didn't alter in its form and evenings were spent watching her mother sew and knit with intense concentration as she listened to the radio. The Maguire twins continued to be Mourne's chief source of amusement.

She was glad when the day came round for her visit to Mr O'Rourke. Just lately she had found herself wishing her life away. She wished she had taken up the place at the hospital to study for her state registration – she wished she hadn't been so hasty in throwing in the towel with Anthony Rice – and she wondered if her mother was right when she said that she didn't encourage any of the young men who had shown some interest. She wished she could have been as outgoing and popular as Tara. She sighed as she approached the cottage where she could see Mr O'Rourke sitting on a huge boulder. Here she was, a young woman barely out of her teens, walking towards a man of indeterminate age who was her only trusted male friend. There had to be something wrong with her when all she had to look forward to was a walk in the pale autumn sunshine with an elderly man and his dog.

O'Rourke tapped his pipe out on the boulder and watched her approach. His world was now muted with the gold tints of autumn, and the leaves that lay at his feet were like a magical carpet. He lifted one of them and idly stroked it in his palm, feeling its slight crispness with pleasure. He called O'Malley who promptly hared round the corner of the cottage to scud to a halt amid the leaves. He gazed at O'Rourke with that special look that said 'adventure'.

'You are a rogue, O'Malley, but a lovable one. Away you go, but keep your distance from the cows. Magee says the milk yield is down because you scare the divil out of them.' O'Rourke looked more closely as Mourne neared. The beautiful eyes were downcast as she stepped across the stile which straddled the last wall between them and the set of her shoulders told him there was some problem on her mind.

'What's lying so heavy on your mind that you walk with bent shoulders and eyes that should be raised to the beauty around, and not steadily fixed on your feet – that are doing nothing more than bringing

64

you closer to your destination?' O'Rourke asked gently as they walked. They were on their way towards the woods to gather fir cones for Christmas decorations as they had done since Mourne had been a young schoolgirl confiding her dreams and aspirations to him. Now she looked as though there were no more dreams, and her aspirations had dried up.

Mourne didn't answer immediately and O'Rourke, wisely, didn't press her. He helped her over the ditch instead and was rewarded by a weak smile.

'Take no notice of me, Mr O'Rourke,' she said at last. 'It's been a boring old week and I'm craving a bit of excitement.' She had hardly spoken the words when there was the sound of galloping hoofs and a horse and rider came pell-mell towards them from the direction of the woods. The rider was trying hard to control the large horse and as he tore past to jump the ditch, the horse's flank caught Mourne a blow on the shoulder. With a cry of pain she fell and O'Rourke, his big fist already raised at the fleeing figure, dropped his arm and knelt beside her.

'This is not what I meant when I said what I did about excitement,' she gasped, and grimaced with pain.

O'Rourke helped her to rise and they were so busy neither realized that the rider and his horse had returned.

'Look! I'm terribly sorry about this. My horse bolted. Some bloody great dog shot out from behind a bush and scared the life out of him.'

O'Rourke, about to tear a strip off the stranger, stilled his tongue. 'That was probably my dog, O'Malley,' he said, instead.

The man had alighted and was looking at Mourne. 'These things happen,' he said, and added, 'Can I help? I think you may have dislocated that shoulder.' His gaze travelled over the girl with appreciation. She was the most attractive woman he had seen for a long time. Attractive and classy – not many like that around these parts – and those green eyes looking up at him threatened to throw him into confusion.

Mourne looked up into the dark, brooding eyes and felt her heart miss a beat. 'Mr O'Rourke will . . . will . . . er . . . see to me,' she said, and added hastily, 'but thank you.'

As though brought out of a trance, O'Rourke put his arm round her waist and they set off, Mourne's face creased with pain as she tried to hold the shoulder still with her other hand. Of O'Malley there was not a sign.

The tall dark man with the riveting eyes that had made Mourne stumble over her words gazed after them with a thoughtful look. That girl had potential. She could very well fit in with the plans he had been making just recently. Idly stroking Bantry he continued to watch the slowly receding figures. 'She would do very well indeed,' he said aloud, his voice almost purring with satisfaction. He became more certain by the minute that she was just what he was looking for. He must find out who she was. She must live locally. Putting his foot in the stirrup, he hoisted himself into the saddle, his long legs holding close to the animal's belly and his back relaxed but straight, his dark eyes staring ahead and his mind working on plans for the lovely girl he had just encountered . . .

CHAPTER 5

Mourne was washing her hair when Kitty called up that Gerry was on the phone and could she have a word with him.

'Will you tell him I'll ring him back? I'm in the middle of washing my hair.'

'Didn't Gerry tell you that you were not to do anything to stretch the ligaments in that shoulder?' Kitty raced up the stairs to find Mourne about to towel her hair dry.

'It's been a week since I hurt it, Mam. I can do things gently now, and besides, I'm goin' back to work on Monday.' She wrapped the towel round her head. 'I might as well answer the phone now,' she said.

Kitty's hand flew to her mouth. 'The phone. He'll still be hangin' on wondering what's keepin' us.' They hurried down the stairs and across to the main house. Mourne took up the phone and spoke.

'Were you off to Timbuctoo or what? I have work to do. We can't all skive off.' Gerry sounded testy.

Mourne apologized. 'I was washing my hair. Anyway, what did you want me for? You can't be ringing me up to tell me off for something I've not done, seeing as I've not been at work for a week,' she joked, in an effort to lighten his mood.

There was a pause, then Gerry spoke again. 'How do you fancy partnering me to the Christmas dinner and dance at the golf club?'

'Are you stuck for choice then?' Mourne laughed, but excitement ran through her. It had been a week now since her injury and she was fed up sitting around. She was looking forward to getting back to work, and this was an added bonus.

Gerry laughed. 'Cheeky article. The truth is I have a big surprise up my sleeve and I want to drop it into your lap and capitalize on the outcome by doing it in a big way.'

Mourne's heart surged. 'What is the surprise?' she asked.

There was a noise at the other end of the phone. 'In the name of God have your wits gone? How can it be a surprise if I tell you now?'

'Whenever you tell me it will be a surprise. Why not now?'

'I told you. I want to do it at the ball. Now! Do you want to come or not? I'll have no trouble finding someone else.'

'I'd love to come!'

'It'll mean wearing an evening dress. Will Kitty run to buying you one?'

'I've already got one. I went to the ball last year with Anthony Rice and his parents.'

'Good! We'll discuss it more when I see you on Monday.' Gerry paused. 'You will be ready to come back, won't you?'

'I've been up to the hospital for a last check and all's well.'

'It's a pity you had to go to hospital. The truth is I've lost my expertise in such matters as reducing a dislocation – now if that nephew of mine had been here he could have sorted it out at the surgery. I wish I could convince him that he could change things here to suit his needs and so make a move into general practice worth while.'

'Is he not interested then?' Mourne couldn't keep the disappointment from her voice. A fact which was not lost on Gerry.

'The ship isn't lost till it hits the ocean floor. Anyway I haven't given up yet. At this moment I have work to do. I can't keep up the crack with you all day. I'll see you Monday – and see you square things with your mam.' The phone line went dead.

The following Friday Mourne kept an appointment for tea with Rena Maguire. Since she had met her that day down by the brook they had become friends. The twins were at school and they had the afternoon to themselves.

'I heard about your accident. How's the shoulder now?' Rena asked as they made their way into the tiny kitchen where she set the kettle to boil.

'It's almost better. I'm not allowed to swing the cat,' Mourne laughed, 'but I can do most things. Uncle Gerry fusses round me at work – he won't let me reach up for notes on the higher shelves – but he's gone back to his old ways of ordering me about and is running me off my feet.'

'He's very fond of you.'

'He's invited me to the Christmas ball at the golf club,' said Mourne, with excitement.

'You lucky thing,' said Rena, enviously. 'Have you something nice to wear?'

They took their tea into the tiny sitting room and settled themselves. 'I'll wear the same dress I wore last year. It doesn't matter a toss to me if everyone recognizes it. I can't ask Mam to buy me another one. I don't suppose anyone noticed me, anyway.'

'Who did you go with last year?'

'I went with Anthony Rice.' Mourne looked away.

'B'God you must have been noticed then,' Rena laughed. 'Anyone who's seen out with young Anthony Rice couldn't escape notice – him being the most eligible bachelor around for miles.' Rena looked curiously at Mourne. 'Did you go around with him, then?'

Mourne shrugged. 'For a while, but I didn't want to carry on.'

'You fool!' Rena said. 'The man's made of money – at least his father is – you'd have been set up for life.'

'Oh! Never mind him. I have a problem . . .' Mourne put her cup down. 'I don't know what to wear over the dress. Last year I wore my tweed coat and nearly died of embarrassment when I got out of the car and stood with everyone else at the cloakroom. They all had grand shawls and jackets and fur coats and—'

'I've a cloak I could lend you,' Rena said thoughtfully. 'It all depends on the colour of your dress?' Her voice rose on a question mark.

'It's a cream dress with a halter neckline. Just a long slim tube of a thing – no flounces – rather plain, but it'll do again this year even if the fashions have changed. Beggars can't be choosers,' Mourne sighed.

Rena rose. 'I'll fetch it. I've a feeling it'll be absolutely the thing.'

She came back a few minutes later with the cloak folded over her arm. She studied Mourne for a moment before saying with controlled excitement, 'This is the perfect colour for you, with those eyes.' She unfolded the cloak – a lovely shade of green and made of crushed velvet – which caught the light as she held it up.

Mourne gasped. 'It's lovely.' She took it from Rena and threw it over her shoulders, tying the drawstring at the neck and turning the collar down so that it lay flat against her neck. She twirled round and glanced at herself in the mirror. 'I like it! D'you think it'll do?'

'Of course it will. I tell you, it has a look of class about it, and with the cream dress and that copper-coloured hair of yours it'll look grand.'

'Thanks, Rena.' Mourne giggled. 'You don't think I look like the wicked queen in *Snow White and the Seven Dwarfs*?'

'You look no such thing!' Rena scoffed, and took it off her to wrap it up. 'I want to know everything that happens. I wish I was going with you. I bet it'll be a right shindy.'

'Things do get a bit boisterous.' Mourne laughed. 'Mam has no idea or I wouldn't be allowed to go.'

'What! Not even with Dr Owen?'

'Well, no! I was thinking of the time I went with Anthony Rice, actually. She wouldn't mind this time even if she did know what they all get up to.' Mourne paused thoughtfully. 'It's a bit high-spirited. Nothing more. But you can understand that most of Mam's generation would find it all a bit naughty.'

'So! You're stepping up into a different class in society,' Rena teased. To her, Mourne had always seemed different from the other young people of her age.

'I haven't the money or the contacts to step up,' Mourne laughed. 'It was always a surprise to me that Anthony Rice took a notion for me: he must have been mad, as we've nothing at all in common.'

He could do worse, Rena thought. She finished wrapping up the cape and placed it on the chair. 'Would you like another drop of tea?' she asked, and poured it out when Mourne nodded.

Later, as Mourne gave her a showing of the cape, Kitty stood with folded arms and watched her daughter waltzing round the big kitchen with the cape twirling out round her and the russet hair whirling round her face as she danced about. She caught her breath at the loveliness of her daughter – and with not an ounce of pride in her – until at last she stopped twirling and looked at her with her wide anxious eyes.

'What do you think, Mam. Will I pass muster?'

Kitty swallowed. 'You'll do!' she said, but with a smile. 'Now put it away in your room and come and help me with the meal. Your head'll be gettin' too big for you with all this.'

'I'll need a pair of shoes and a bag,' Mourne said, later. 'I'll go into Newcastle on Saturday and look around.'

'What's wrong with Hughie Grant's shop?'

'There's more choice in Newcastle, and besides, it's a bit more interesting there.'

'Please yourself. Do you want me to go in with you?'

Mourne shook her head. 'Not unless you want a day out?'

'I wish I had the time for such luxuries,' Kitty said. 'I have the church to clean and the brasses to do.' She smiled at her daughter.

'Anyway! I daresay you'll do better on your own.'

Mourne was enjoying her day. She had managed to find a pair of shoes but had difficulty matching them up with a handbag. She persisted, and eventually found one in a little shop with the unlikely name of the Peggy Arcade. It wasn't what she would have chosen, given the time and better shops, but the little clutch bag was only a slightly deeper shade than the shoes, so with luck no one would notice the mismatch.

Realizing she was hungry, Mourne made her way towards the best of the many tea shops along the high street. She entered, glad of the warmth, for her hands, even in the gloves she was wearing, were cold. In the last few days of November the mild autumn weather had turned and the real cold snap of winter was upon them at last.

John McCrory, passing the tea shop, glanced casually through the window and watched Mourne take her seat in a corner near a heater. His eyes narrowed. He couldn't believe his luck: he'd wondered if he would see her again. Since that day when he had met her with O'Rourke she hadn't been far from his thoughts. His first impulse when they had parted was to ask her where she lived, but he had quickly decided that the move would not be a good one. That old cod O'Rourke would have seen him off with a few choice words. And now here was the opportunity he needed to renew the acquaintance. He would have to handle the meeting with care if his future plans were to come off. He suspected that this girl would not be an easy target.

He waited till she had ordered and then entered the tea rooms. A fussy waitress came towards him but he waved her away as she indicated a table on the other side and walked towards a table near the girl. The waitress followed.

'I'm sorry sir. I'm afraid that table has been reserved.'

'Then unreserve it,' said John McCrory, haughtily. But the waitress was made of sterner stuff.

'I'm sorry sir, I'm afraid I can't do that. This table was reserved for three o'clock and it is now five minutes to that time.'

'Look, you stupid girl. The solution is simple. The table you were going to show me to is still vacant – use that one for God's sake, and stop making such a fuss about nothing.'

Mourne, busy with the menu, was only vaguely aware of the altercation near by, but she raised her head when she heard the waitress raise her voice and say, 'No!' forcefully. She frowned. The tall figure of the man seemed familiar. He turned and their eyes met, and she recognized him as the man who had knocked her over when she had been out walking with O'Rourke. He came towards her.

'So. I've found you!' he smiled. 'I was hoping that one day we'd meet so that I could apologize. I felt very bad about your accident . . . may I join you?' He held out his hand. 'John McCrory.'

Mourne nodded uncertainly. 'I remember.' She wasn't sure if she wanted him to join her but how could she tell him she'd rather eat alone, without sounding rude? She waited till he had seated himself before speaking. 'It wasn't your fault,' she said. 'It was one of those fate things. Mr O'Rourke and I happened to be in the wrong place at the wrong time.'

'Nevertheless, I felt badly about it. I hope you're feeling better . . . You hurt your shoulder, didn't you?'

'It was dislocated. I had it set that day, and it's fine now.' She giggled and he smiled in response. Watching her now, he was more convinced than ever that she was the answer to the problem that had been on his mind for some time.

'I've had a few days off work because of it, so you did me a favour. Once it was set it wasn't painful any more but my boss told me to take the time off to allow the shoulder to settle back.'

He grinned. 'So you owe me! How about letting me buy tea?'

'That isn't a fair trade,' said Mourne, but he called the waitress over and gave his order, ignoring her objection.

'Do you live in Newcastle?' he asked, as they waited for tea to arrive.

'I live in Ballycash,' said Mourne. She felt shy. This man was more sophisticated than the lads she had grown up with – unless she counted Anthony Rice – and she found herself unusually disturbed by his presence. 'And you?' she inquired, trying to control the tiny tremble in her voice.

'I live just this side of Kilkeel.'

'That's quite a way from where you were riding. I haven't seen you riding around the outskirts of Tullybra before.'

'I ride far afield quite often,' John said. 'Although, I must admit, it's usually in the other direction. However I have in fact ridden the area around O'Rourke's domain once or twice – I just haven't had the good fortune to meet you until now.'

Tea arrived at that point and there was a pause while the waitress set things down. When she had gone they busied themselves buttering scones and pouring tea.

'Did O'Rourke not mention that he knew me?' John asked, with studied carelessness.

Mourne's brow creased. 'No, he didn't! I wonder why?'

'I'll tell you why – he disapproves of me.' John McCrory watched the effect his words had on the girl, through half-closed lids.

Startled, Mourne said, 'Good heavens, why?'

He grinned. 'He thinks I'm a thoroughgoing rascal of the first order – and before you say "Why" again, I'll tell you. I'm a gambler, and for reasons best known to himself, O'Rourke despises gamblers. He thinks I should spend more time looking after my business and less time at the tables.'

Mourne looked at him in astonishment. 'How well does Mr O'Rourke know you? Surely it isn't his business how you conduct yourself.' She was amazed at the revelation. She had known Mr O'Rourke for a number of years and she had always respected his complete disinterest in anyone else's life. His philosophy was that man manufactured his own destruction – or his own salvation. The choice belongs to the individual. They were his very words.

'Never mind O'Rourke. Let's talk about us.' John held out his hand. 'We'll start again. I'm John McCrory. I own the canning factory in Kilkeel. I dabble in other things as well – but I'm better known for being the owner of the factory.'

Mourne shook his hand. 'Mourne O'Hara, doctor's receptionist.' She smiled. 'I have no other claim to fame. I live with my mother who's the housekeeper to the parish priest and I'm a sore trial to both of them at times, so they tell me.'

John McCrory smiled at the quip. He was disappointed to hear that she was the daughter of a housekeeper and his first thought was that it might set his plans back but when he sneaked a look while she was eating and saw the dainty way she dealt with the meal, he decided that all might yet be well. Time would tell.

'Did you have a successful morning's shopping?'

'Pretty successful,' Mourne said. 'I've been buying shoes to go with my evening dress – I'm going to the annual dinner and dance at the golf club.'

'You're a member?' There was no mistaking the surprise in his voice.

Mourne shook her head; her eyes held amusement. 'No! I'm going with Uncle Gerry – er – with Dr Owen. He's—'

'I know Gerry Owen . . . he's your uncle?'

'Not really. He's my godfather, but I've always called him Uncle.'

'I'm a member of the club. I've met him there on many occasions,' John said. Things were looking up. If the girl had Gerry Owen for godfather and she had been to the golf club dance before, then she was used to moving in the right circles. He dabbed his mouth with his napkin and began to fold it, his long, slim fingers delicately smoothing the edges. 'I shall be going to the ball. I hope you'll keep a dance for me,' he smiled.

'I will indeed.' Mourne laughed. 'I don't think there'll be a line of men digging a path to my side – I expect poor Uncle Gerry will be glad to get me off his hands so he can sit down somewhere to smoke a crafty cigar.'

They shook hands as they parted at the door and she thanked him for tea. 'I'll see you next Saturday, at the dance.'

John McCrory studied her departure. She walked with a long elegant stride, her head back and shoulders straight. She looked good. He hadn't made a mistake. She was the one! He turned and re-entered the tea rooms and crossed to the cashier. 'May I use your phone?' He clicked his teeth with impatience as she looked uncertain. 'I'll pay extra . . . don't worry.'

As the cashier walked away to stand against the wall, he dialled Benny Allen's number and waited impatiently for him to answer. He had lied. He never attended the annual dance. He had better things to do, such as pay a visit to his club in Belfast for a night with the cards, but on Saturday he would make an exception. He hoped there was a ticket left. Even if there wasn't, Benny owed him a few favours.

When Mourne walked into the large, crowded room she did so with her head high and an easy confidence about her. She knew she looked the part. Her mother never lied when asked for an opinion, and her idea of a compliment ran on the lines of a gruff 'Ye'll do,' which meant that Mourne would stand up to examination. Tonight, however, she had looked at her and sighed. 'You look like a grand lady. There isn't a one there at the dance that won't think the same.' Coming from Mam, this meant that she had nothing to worry about; she could hold her own.

Gerry guided her to the bar, weaving a path through the crowds with dexterity, and as they went Mourne was aware of the looks of those she passed. She smiled to herself. The dress was having its second outing but it was making an impression all the same.

'Did you see the way the men were eyeing you?' Gerry murmured. Mourne nodded happily. 'And the women,' she said.

'Smug article that you are,' Gerry grinned. He took hold of her arm and led her to a quiet corner. 'Hopefully, now that I've fulfilled my role by escorting you here, you'll oblige me by taking on all offers for a dance so that I can sit out and sup my brandy.'

'That reminds me! What's the surprise you promised me?' Mourne, aware that a rather attractive man was watching her, swept her hair back with a flourish of her wrist and faced Gerry.

'I haven't forgotten. Just bide your time, my girl.' His voice was definite but his eyes, when the girl by his side wasn't looking his way, scoured the room. He was just a mite worried that his surprise might not materialize. If it didn't, he thought grimly, a certain head would roll.

The dancing had begun so they made their way to the huge ballroom. 'At least we can breathe in here,' Gerry said, thankfully. 'The drinkers will all be standing in the bar. There'll be a right crush in there.'

Mourne was soon drafted on to the floor and he leaned against the wall and watched her movements as she and her partner waltzed around the room. She's no dancer, he thought with amusement, but her movements were stylish and fluent enough to pass muster. Anyway! The young man she was dancing with seemed more interested in the conversation they were having.

It was a good half-hour later before his worry was eased and he waved to the young man who had just entered the ballroom. 'I thought you'd let me down,' he grumbled. 'I opened my big mouth and told Mourne I had a surprise waiting for her, and when you hadn't arrived I was getting a bit concerned as to how I could explain myself.'

'My plane was delayed and when I got to Belfast I had difficulty getting transport.' David, having just caught sight of Mourne dancing, turned to his uncle. 'Is that stunning creature just dancing past my young friend Mourne O'Hara?'

Gerry smiled gleefully. 'Indeed it is – and she hasn't stopped dancing since we arrived. Her feet must be feeling the pinch.'

'Who's she dancing with?' David scowled. 'He looks full of himself.'

'And well he might!' Gerry observed. 'That's John McCrory. He owns the canning factory down at Kilkeel – he's made of money.'

'Does that make him eligible? He might be a right con man. He has hard eyes.'

Gerry grinned. 'Sure what has it to do with you? If Mourne takes a notion for him she'll be set up for life.'

Realizing that Mourne had caught sight of him, David gave a wave and was slightly mollified by the look of annoyance thrown in his direction by her partner. However, his own eyes darkened when Mourne, dragging her partner by the hand, came over to stand before him.

'Is this the surprise?' she asked Gerry delightedly, as she hugged David. John McCrory looked on silently, and shook hands when he was introduced to David. David, deciding to behave in a civilized manner, smiled at him. 'I'm surprised we haven't met before,' he said.

'I spent my youth at boarding school,' John explained. 'You were probably away doing your thing in England by the time I arrived back to take over from my father. Mourne tells me you did your medical training across the water.'

Gerry looked on as the two men conversed. They were like a pair of gladiators. Polite though the conversation appeared on the surface, there was an underlying air of distrust and dislike. He decided it was time to intervene because he had noticed that Mourne had looked from one to the other with slight puzzlement.

'Why don't you take Mourne on to the floor for this dance?' he suggested to David. 'Your man here looks as though a glass of liquid is needed to cool his throat. Dancing's a hot business.' Gerry smiled encouragingly at the dark-eyed young man facing him with raised eyebrows. 'What do you say?'

Already Mourne and David had started towards the dance floor, so John McCrory had no option but to follow the older man towards the bar, but his mood had suddenly turned black and he had to concentrate on what the other man was saying and try to look as though he was interested, but he was furious at the skilful way the old bugger had manipulated the situation. To make matters worse, three dances later Mourne was still partnering the old fool's nephew and looking pleased about it. Deep down he knew that he had lost the evening, and, seeing no way of regaining the advantage without seeming doltish, he decided to cut his losses and say goodnight.

Mourne and David had stopped dancing and were so deep in conversation, neither had noticed the other man's departure. Gerry, seeing that he had no further role to play, retired to the bar again.

'Are you telling me that you're going to take a six-month sabbatical and you intend to spend it working with Uncle Gerry?' Mourne asked.

David nodded. 'I'm over for a couple of days to make the arrangements.'

'Correct me if I'm wrong,' she paused. 'But isn't a sabbatical supposed to be a period of rest – repose – from one's labours? A time to recharge your mental and physical batteries?'

David grinned. 'Correct!'

'Then why are you coming over to Ireland to work for your uncle? The work of a country doctor is not what I'd call taking a rest.'

'But it is, in a way. I'm feeling quite stressed at the moment. I don't know where I want to go; I need a change from hospital work and all the frustrations that have beset me lately, so when Gerry proposed the idea some weeks ago I said I would give it some thought, and here I am.' David raised his arms and set them down on his knees again by way of emphasis. 'I'd like to think that you would look forward to working with me,' he grinned.

Mourne looked at him thoughtfully. 'I don't know what you're like to work with. You might be a right slave-driver. When you were over for the two weeks during the summer you were only having a dabble. You could be a different person when you're working under pressure.'

'Greater faith hath no woman.' David rose. 'The dance is nearly over. Let's have one more. I'm sure you'll get used to the idea.'

'Oh, I like the idea,' said Mourne. 'When do you intend to begin this sabbatical, and come to that – what happens afterwards?'

'If I find I like working as a country doctor I would seriously consider taking over the practice, eventually,' David said.

'You knew all along what he was up to, didn't you!'

'I did, indeed!'

They were silent during the last waltz, both busy with their own thoughts. David was enjoying the closer proximity of her soft body. The last waltz was always slow and lazy and intimate and he didn't want anything to intrude upon the moment. He felt his pulse stirring at every turn they took as the lissom body swung towards him with the movements of the dance. He could get to like this. He tried to push the thought of Rosemary from his mind.

Mourne's thoughts were on another tack altogether. She suddenly noticed that John McCrory was missing and wondered what had happened to him. Her conscience smote her as she realized that she hadn't given him another look since David had arrived. She stumbled, and David looked curiously at her as she blushed. She tried to concentrate on the dance but found her thoughts wandering again. She thought she could be happy about a relationship with John. He was good company and he wasn't a threat to her. David, however, was

77

another matter; her feelings for him were much stronger. The crush she'd had on him all those years ago had very rapidly turned into a much deeper feeling and it frightened her with its intensity, but she was determined she would not give way to it: the overwhelming fear of being hurt was alive and raw in her. Where relationships were concerned, she had to be in control. It was the only way she could protect herself. To be rejected again would destroy her. She must never become involved emotionally. Never!

'When do you intend starting at the practice?' Mourne kept her voice even, although her heart was pounding in her chest as she waited for his reply.

'Probably April. There will be quite a bit of preparation. I've projects to finish and there are long-term patients who will need to have some continuity organized for their care. Also, there will have to be an induction period for my successor' . . . he paused . . . 'and then there are facets of my social life to sort out . . .' God! Rosemary would hit the roof. He had to work out a way to handle her – play the time element down a bit.

Gerry was waiting for them. 'I thought you'd got lost.' He stole a look at Mourne. Her pretty face had a kind of squashed look about it – as though she had just suffered a disappointment. He studied his nephew. David was looking thoughtful. Hell's bells! He hoped they hadn't had a row.

The weeks following Christmas were harsh – so harsh that Mourne hadn't been able to visit O'Rourke and O'Malley. She crossed the street to Cullen's stores during a lull from a busy surgery session to see if he had been able to get down for his monthly visit. His friends were sitting round the stove playing cards and she frowned as she entered the shop and saw them all heavily engrossed in their game. They were at the far end where the stove sat like a squat black beast in the middle of the floor by the hardware counter, well away from the front door and the groceries.

Tom Dillon, a large man with a shaggy white beard, glanced up at her as she stopped by him.

'Has anyone heard if Mr O'Rourke is all right?' Mourne asked, worriedly. 'I'm told the snow and ice is pretty bad up towards his place.'

'Don't worry, girl,' said Tom, and slapped a winning hand down on the rickety table at which they all sat. 'I went up there the other day and he is well shut in, and his place is warm and there's food aplenty. I brought some fresh bread and some milk.'

'What's happened to the goat he keeps for milking?'

'She died . . . got caught up on the bluff when the worst of the snow came, and she fell over. I got the word from Barry Todd, the shepherd, so I took the food and milk up there – O'Rourke's a holy terror if he has to go without his mug of strong tea. I figured if I didn't get up to him, he might try coming down the valley and he's not that quick on his feet these days, and I was afear'd he'd end up in a drift somewhere. Anyways, he has all his orders now and is warm and fed. In two days' time I'll take some more groceries up to him. Don't you worry now – I'll tell him you were asking after him.'

Relieved, Mourne thanked him. 'And will you tell him I'll be up as soon as the drifts are less and the weather lets up a bit?'

Tom nodded. 'I will, and don't you be trying to make it up there until it's safe to do so or I'll be in dead trouble with himself. He thinks the world of you. I'm certain he'll know you're thinking of him.'

When Mourne returned to the surgery, Gerry accosted her. He was wanting his tea and wondered where she had skived off to.

'I was worried about Mr O'Rourke. I haven't seen him for some weeks and I heard the snow was pretty bad up past the Bryansford road area.'

'Oh aye! But O'Rourke has lived up that way for a good few winters,' said Gerry crisply. 'He has all his orders up there and the man is sensible enough to know when to stay put—'

'He ran out of milk.'

'What has that to do with the words of wisdom I've just uttered? He'll hardly put himself in danger for the sake of a drop of milk. He has plenty of water – and I doubt if he'll starve.'

'Biddy – his goat – fell over the bluff and died. Mr Dillon knew that he would go mad without his drop of tea so he took some milk up to him, so you see he has a weakness – and the desire for a mug of milky tea could have been the death of him. Mr Dillon knew that he would have taken the risk and made his way down to buy some.'

Mourne didn't wait for his answer but went into the tiny kitchen to put the kettle on. Gerry followed her.

'You're very fond of O'Rourke, aren't you?' He leaned against the row of cupboards and regarded her rigid back. 'I'm sorry if I sounded a bit brusque. I didn't mean it that way. I really do think that O'Rourke can look after himself. God knows the poor man has been doing it these last twenty-five years since Maura died.'

Mourne turned. 'I never knew he was ever married,' she said, in wonder. 'I just assumed that he'd always lived like that – a bit of a hermit I suppose.'

The kettle boiled and she turned to make the tea. Gerry carried on where he'd left off, and she poured the tea and listened.

'He married Maura McKenna, whose father was the head gamekeeper for the Anglesy estates. O'Rourke was his assistant. The day they married I remember well, for I was fifteen years old at the time and madly in love with the twenty-year-old Maura. I thought I'd never forgive Finbar O'Rourke for stealing her away . . .'

'Finbar?' Mourne gasped.

Gerry grinned. 'Don't go lettin' on that you know. It's why he's always referred to as O'Rourke. There would be holy murder if anyone from the old days referred to Finbar O'Rourke by that name. The last time it was used was when the priest at the time said the words, "Will you, Finbar O'Rourke take Maura" . . . There wasn't a dry eye in the church – and it wasn't for crying. O'Rourke swore on that day that if he ever heard the name Finbar mentioned again, the perpetrator would end up in hospital with a hefty bill for treatment.'

'I never knew. I've always called him Mr O'Rourke. I often thought how rude it was to refer to him as just O'Rourke.'

'It was a kindness, you'll agree – and his own wish.'

'Well! I'll continue to call him Mr O'Rourke. I'm easy with that,' Mourne said, and handed Gerry the mug of strong tea.

'I'll take this into my room. I've a lot of notes to write up. If Mr Black rings, tell him to hang on for a bit . . . I'll be a little late for my visit. The man will ring as soon as the hand of the clock goes past the hour. He has no patience.'

John McCrory was in a foul mood. His mechanic had reported sick and the bloody sealing machine had chosen this day to pack in. No one else knew how to fix it and he'd had to ring for someone from the factory at Ardglass to come over. It was going to be some time before he arrived, and time meant money. He scowled at his secretary as she broke the further bad news to him that four of the floor packers were ill and he jumped to his feet and brushed past her, his mouth tight with fury. Someone up there had it in for him.

He strode into the large building which housed the machinery and marched up to the foreman, who was standing by the tiny office with a clipboard clutched to his chest, giving orders to some of the packers.

'What the hell is going on here, Molloy? Mrs Frost tells me there are four people going off sick. Is it not enough that my mechanic is off – now I'm losing four of the workforce. They only have the bellyache for Christ's sake . . . Give them a dollop of something and get them back to work.'

'It isn't as simple as that, Mr McCrory.' James Molloy gave a nervous cough. John McCrory could be a right bully if the occasion warranted. Nobody's job was safe, and his own was always in the balance because there were at least three people waiting to step into his shoes – as McCrory went to great pains to remind him on many occasions.

'Why isn't it that simple?'

'I'm certain they have food poisoning—'

'What!' John McCrory glared at the man facing him. For once he didn't delight in the sight of the man practically falling apart at his tone. He was too aware of the seriousness of the situation.

'I'm afraid so, Mr McCrory. Eight of them went out for a meal last night and four have had to go home. The other four are also feeling a bit queasy so they might go down with it as well – although so far they are holding up.'

'I don't care. Just get things moving – output must be kept up. Your job could be on the line here, Molloy. It's your responsibility to keep production going. Deal with the matter how you will, but remember that however many have to be laid off, at the end of the day I want results – even if it means you have to man a machine yourself – so for a start you can use the men who are waiting for the sealing machine to be fixed. The mechanic won't be here for three hours and a lot of cans can be sorted and packed in that time – so get on to it!'

James Molloy stared after the retreating figure, anger showing on his face. The man was the biggest bastard out and if there was any chance of a job somewhere else he wouldn't work for him one moment longer than necessary – and that went for many of the workers – but work was scarce around these parts and the money was good here, so they all had to bite their lips and keep going. James called the four men who normally worked the sealing machine and set them to work on the packing line. They scowled, but knowing that there was little James could do about the situation they did as they were told. Where was the point in making a fuss? They needed the work and on that basis John McCrory had them by the balls.

81

John McCrory's day ended as badly as it had begun. The emergency mechanic didn't arrive till well after midday, by which time the other four workers had succumbed to their stomach problems and that put the work further behind. There was a stack of defrosted fish which had to be thrown out which meant a fair loss in revenue, and John McCrory had every intention of making someone pay for the day's mishaps. For a start those people who had gone sick would have their pay docked. He would find a way to do it so that it wouldn't be brought before the union. He mulled things round in his mind for some time and then smiled to himself. There would be no bonus at Easter. Bonuses were given at the boss's discretion for work well done, and he'd never thought the idea was a good one anyway. His father had started it years ago as an incentive to work hard, but then, he had been a stupid old fool who put more store in people than he did in banking profits – a terrible way to run a business – and it had taken John all his time since his father died to get production up by handling the staff more firmly.

When he arrived home he called his housekeeper to the sitting room. He wasn't keen on her but she was an excellent cook. Anyway, he was stuck with her, thanks to his father. It helped that she didn't live in, so he could invite all his friends for a night's gambling with the cards and no one was the wiser.

'Mrs Flannigan, I won't be here for a meal. I'm going into Belfast for the evening to meet up with some friends.' John McCrory avoided the woman's eyes. He knew that she was well aware he was going to his gambling club and the last thing he wanted was a lecture. Only this woman could give him one. She had been with the family since before he had been born, and because of her length of service she felt she had special privileges. She was the one person who could intimidate him. She always referred to him as he grew up as Mr John and when, shortly following his father's death, he had remonstrated with her and asked if she would in future refer to him as 'Sir' or 'Mr McCrory' when he entertained, she had laughed.

'I skelped your ass for you when you were younger and prior to that I changed your nappy and washed your nether regions, so I know every inch of that body of yours. You were Mr John to me then and you are Mr John to me now. If you want it any other way then let me know and I'll let you terminate my employment.'

John glared at her. The bloody woman knew she had him – and all because of his father. John had realized, with fury, after the reading of the will, that he was stuck with her, for one of the clauses in the will stated that should Mrs Flannigan be asked to leave for whatever reason, she was to be given the sum of five thousand pounds. If, however, she stayed on in the service of 'my son John', she could leave at age sixty with a small pension.

Having weighed up the situation, John had decided that he would put up with the prying old trout for the next few years. At least she would be made to work hard for him if she wanted to earn the money.

'I've been preparing the food all day and it's already cooking, but I'm sure I can find a use for it. If I can't then I'll throw it in the bin,' Mrs Flannigan said, crisply.

John fumed silently. The woman had a face as long as a Lurgan spade. She knew he hated waste and was openly taunting him, but there wasn't much he could do about it. He should have rung her earlier, but with all the hassle at the factory he hadn't given it a thought. He dismissed her and made his way upstairs to have a bath. Normally he would ask her to lay out his evening suit for him but he wouldn't give her the satisfaction of knowing that she had been right in thinking that he was off gambling. He would slip out when her back was turned.

As he lay in the soft warm water, he allowed his thoughts to stray pleasantly to Mourne O'Hara. He wondered how she would react if he suggested she accompany him to the Crystal Club. He didn't suppose she had ever been to a gambling casino before, but he had an idea that she might be game for something out of the ordinary. In spite of the apparent innocence that seemed to shine out of those eyes of hers he had the feeling she wouldn't mind going out and meeting a new experience head-on. He would test her out sometime. Anyway! If his plans were to come to anything, she would need to be slowly educated as to his needs. Lowering himself further into the water, he rested his head on the edge of the bath and with a smile, allowed his imagination full rein.

CHAPTER 6

When Tara broke the news that she and Jay-Jay had set a date for the wedding, Mourne was delighted, but less so when Tara asked if she would be her bridesmaid.

'Tara, you are sure you want me? I wouldn't want to upset your other friends. I mean . . . what about May Cummings? I would—'

'I'm having May as well. Look! I know you don't exactly court the limelight, but we get on so well, and although you don't go around with my crowd, I always enjoy your company. I look on you as a very special friend, and besides, our colouring is so good together.' She laughed and punched Mourne's shoulder. 'Go on! Say yes!'

'Yes!' Mourne smiled, but as she confessed to Kitty later: 'I don't really feel at home with the idea.'

'It isn't a bit of good telling me that. You should have been more courageous and made it clear to Tara.'

'I couldn't do that,' Mourne cried. 'It would have been insulting. Tara's been very good to me. She invites me out with her and doesn't mind that I don't join in with the others – not that I have anything against them, or what they get up to, but they enjoy doing things that don't appeal to me, and Tara fits me in with her quieter expeditions. I love her to death, so I couldn't let her down.'

'Then don't moan about it.' Kitty smiled to take the censure out of the words. 'Tara has just paid you a great compliment and I think it won't do you any harm to comply. It isn't a martyr's job, after all.'

'You're right, Mam.' Mourne sighed. 'I just hope she doesn't choose some outlandish fashion for the dresses.'

'I never saw Tara as being all that stylish,' Kitty remarked.

'She's never had the money,' Mourne said. 'But when we looked round the shops that time we went to Belfast she was picking out the most bizarre styles as the ones she would have if only she was rich.'

'Ah! Well now! You could be in trouble, then,' Kitty laughed. 'Her husband's family are not short of a shilling or two, so I'm told. I'll bet he's paying for the wedding, for the Foleys haven't two pennies to rub together.'

Mourne needn't have worried. Tara confessed that she was relying heavily on her two bridesmaids to keep her right. 'I know I've a tendency for the flamboyant,' she said, 'so I want you and May to come with me to help me choose the dresses.'

Mourne sighed with relief when she related the conversation to Kitty. 'We're going into Belfast next Saturday – there's more choice there – and Tara wants to meet up with Jay-Jay and Eamon to discuss plans.'

'I take it that Eamon is going to be best man?'

'Yes! It'll be nice to see him again. I've met his fiancée once and she was friendly. I'm looking forward to meeting her again, too.'

Kitty busied herself with her cooking as her daughter left the room but when she had gone, she put down her knife and leaned thoughtfully against the sink. She was concerned about Mourne. Ever since she had been told about the circumstances of her birth she had become less communicative. It wasn't noticeable to the average person, but Kitty could read her daughter as no one else could. Mourne rarely spoke about the boys she met when she and Tara went out together; once she would have rattled on about the latest one with enthusiasm. The only time Kitty had seen anything approaching animation in her daughter's face was when she met David again. When she spoke of their trips out together, it was done with the first signs of genuine enjoyment in many a long day.

Upstairs in her bedroom, Mourne was sitting on her bed with legs crossed, staring as she often did these days at the cross above her bed. She often escaped to her room these evenings, because she suspected that her mother sensed something was wrong and she didn't want to risk a confrontation. It was the way her mother would look at her when she thought she wasn't being observed. Mourne knew there were times when the hurt that was buried inside her showed now and again, even though she put on the face that told the world everything was all right. Unfortunately, her mother always seemed to be there when she was feeling at her most vulnerable.

Father Patrick, bless him, was too busy worrying about his church, his flock and the leaking roof to notice much of what went on under his nose. His main interest when he was not saying Mass and hearing confessions was to retreat to his study and meditate or listen to his music with his milk and brandy in one hand and a cigar in the other. Not that he wasn't there for her if she needed him, but she'd have to tap him on the forehead and speak to him directly if she wanted his help. Father Patrick belonged to the school of thought that believed in the saying, 'If you look for faults you'll find them.'

Mourne rose and crossed to the window. The night was clear with a bright moon suspended among the endless stars. She stared longingly into the velvety sky and wondered, not for the first time, where her real mother was at this moment and who she was. She would give anything to know. Restlessly she returned to her bed and crept beneath the sheets. She began to cry, but determinedly wiped the tears away. She must be strong. She must remember all the good things that were in her life. It was a pointless exercise to look backward and wonder why! Why! Why!

Tomorrow she was going up to see Mr O'Rourke. She looked forward to it. She felt a kind of peace when she was with the old man and his dog, and now that the harshness had gone from the winter, in spite of the cold March winds, there was no reason why they couldn't go walking as they always did. Hanging on to that thought she finally drifted off to sleep, and was so deeply immersed in her troubled dreams she was unaware of the fact that Kitty had crept in on her way to her own bed, and was standing with her hand on heart looking down on her daughter as she stirred restlessly. She wondered, sadly, if things would ever be the same between them again. Would they ever regain that precious closeness they'd once had – for it had gone now the truth was known – and her heart was scalded by the sadness of its passing.

What Mourne loved about her monthly trips with Mr O'Rourke was that there was always something new to do. Today they had gone deep into the woods to gather sticks for the open fire. She had been well tutored, and knew which wood didn't burn well and which burned so well so that it lasted no time at all. She loved the woods, and the further in they ventured the better. There she revelled in the smell of rotting wood and the pine resin with its sharp, warm aroma.

'Leave the pine,' said O'Rourke. 'It gives off a grand smell but the sparks can land a foot away and I don't want my home burnt down around me.'

Occasionally, where the trees were thinnest, the sun cut through, its rays showing up the dancing dust. O'Malley was sniffing the air in appreciation and making darting movements towards an unseen quarry, and trying to catch the flecks as they jumped and flickered in the still weak rays of sunlight. O'Rourke had stopped to lean against a tree as he lit his brier, drawing the smoke into his lungs with evident contentment while Mourne sat beside him and idly rubbed the rough surface of a pine cone.

At last O'Malley, tongue lolling, had decided he'd had enough of the game he'd been playing and flopped down over his master's feet to rest. The stillness was broken only by the gentle rustling of the tiny creatures whose habitat they were invading. Somewhere a fox called to his mate, and overriding the sound was the drone of an aircraft circling in an invisible sky.

There was blissful peace for a long time, until Mourne tentatively said, 'Could I ask you a question, Mr O'Rourke?'

'Ask away.' O'Rourke's voice was soft and heavy with well-being so the nature of the question was all the more startling when Mourne asked it.

'Would you have any respect for a woman who abandoned her baby?'

It was a while before O'Rourke answered. Something told him that there was more behind the question than a casual inquiry and he had to be careful what he said in reply. 'It would depend entirely on the circumstances,' he said at last.

'And if the circumstances – the reasons – weren't known?'

O'Rourke took a deep puff on his pipe. 'In that instance I think I would hold judgement and perhaps give her the benefit of the doubt until bad intent was proved. Why do you ask?'

'Oh! No reason. I heard about just such an instance the other day, and my first thought was that if I was that child, I'd feel totally rejected.' Mourne hoped to God that nothing in her voice was giving her away. She rattled on for a while about children and love and relationships, while O'Rourke listened and puffed steadily on his pipe. He would rather not have such unhappy thoughts enter his consciousness in such a peaceful setting but he said nothing as the girl beside him talked. Something had set her mind worrying and it was best she let it out.

'Life's not always easy, is it, Mr O'Rourke?'

'Depends on how you view it,' said O'Rourke slowly. 'There isn't a creature on earth – and man is included in this – who hasn't hit bottom at some time, but then there are the good times to equate.'

'You've had your bad times,' said Mourne. 'Yet you seem to view it all with great forbearance. I've never seen you put out by anything.'

O'Rourke tamped out his pipe. 'Listen, young Mourne. I'll tell you how I see life. To me my life is the very tall mountain that I have to climb. I've never once considered that the climb would be an easy one – but it has to be done if I'm to reach my goal. Every so often I reach a ledge on my mountain where I can rest awhile to recover and regain my strength. These ledges allow me periods of peace from any sorrow or worry that may have beset me on my climb . . .' He paused and said, with a grin, 'I think I've reached my final ledge.'

'Then what?' Mourne had listened, fascinated but wary.

O'Rourke roared with laughter, startling the wildlife. 'Then I start on the final plunge to the abyss below where the divil waits to add me to the flames, and I pray that Himself up there will shoot out an arm and grab me by the collar and say, "Get up here O'Rourke. You're going the wrong way!"'

Mourne laughed with the old rogue, but a weight had been lifted from her.

'Time for home,' said O'Rourke, and held out his hand to assist Mourne to her feet. He settled the bundle of wood across her shoulders, arranged the straps around her armpits and pulled the rope gently to stabilize the burden before tying it round her waist so that the bundle was well supported and not pulling on her. When he had adjusted his own, larger bundle, they set off. O'Malley lolloped on ahead until he was out of sight. Now and then they caught a glimpse of him as he turned, balancing on one leg with the other paw in the air, to look back to ensure that they were still following.

They were a quarter of a mile from home when they heard the shot. O'Rourke, momentarily stunned, looked at Mourne. No one had ever before discharged a gun in this area. The rabbits and foxes lived further down the valley. While he and Mourne were looking at each other in puzzlement, another shot rang out. O'Rourke's blood chilled. His legs felt like lead weights as he stumbled forward, all the while trying to undo the bundle of wood. Panic rose in his chest, tasting of bile. Rounding the corner he came upon the field where Ben Doran's sheep normally spent the winter, but the field was empty; they'd be further down for the lambing.

Shading his eyes he scanned the field rapidly and felt a tightness in his chest as his gaze lit on the greyish form lying there. 'O'Malley!' he shouted. 'Dear God, O'Malley!' He ran and stumbled the last few yards towards the big dog, unheedful of the tears running down his face. 'Oh! Not O'Malley!' But there he lay, as though peacefully sleeping, with his eyes closed against the sun. O'Rourke knew he was dead. There was a stillness about him.

He cradled O'Malley's head in his lap, only vaguely aware of running footsteps pounding the turf. A voice above him called out, breathless with exertion.

'It's all right Bob. It's only a dog!'

O'Rourke's voice was crucifyingly sad. 'Well, O'Malley. That puts you in your place. Twelve years of magic moments. Twelve years of faithful friendship; of fidelity and companionship, of hunting and trout-tickling. Twelve years of joyousness and life, of listening to me blethering on as though you understood every blessed word – and you were only a dog, after all.'

'I'm terribly sorry!' said the voice above him. 'We thought he was a fox. I really am most terribly sorry.'

The words were spoken with an English accent. 'It's no one's fault,' said O'Rourke.

'What can we do to help?' said the man, in distress. His companion remained silent.

'Nothing! I will manage.'

'Please! Let us help you carry the old chap.'

O'Rourke stilled the gesture as the man stooped towards O'Malley. 'Don't touch him. I'll manage,' he said, and with a fair degree of difficulty and to the obvious embarrassment of the two men, he struggled to lift the big dog on to his shoulders and set off for home.

When he'd gone, Mourne walked towards the two men. 'You said you wanted to help,' she said dully. 'You can carry those two large bundles of wood to that man's home – I'll lead the way – and when we get there you'll keep out of sight and make your way home as soon as you've done.'

'We really couldn't – the dog just—'

'There isn't anything to be said.' Mourne assisted the two men in their efforts to get the bundles of wood on to their backs, then started towards the cottage. Her shoulders were hunched and her head was bent. The day which had started so well was now ruined. A thought struck her which saddened her still further. O'Rourke had toppled off his ledge and was back on his mountain again.

* * *

90

The residents of the market town of Ballycash were stunned when they heard of the death of O'Malley. He had been a part of their lives for such a long time, and so many tales had been told, with much embellishment, of the smartness of the dog and the deeds he had performed. Strangely, it wasn't the fact that he was dead that appalled them, for 'He was getting on a bit,' as Cullen remarked as he packed the shopping for a customer. It was the way of his passing that caused the anger and distress.

Barry Grant, taking time off from his emporium to have a gossip in Cullen's stores, regarded the empty chair where O'Rourke normally sat and gave a heavy sigh. 'It was not a fitting end for a dog of O'Malley's calibre,' he said.

'What the hell were those two men doing up there with guns? There's no game that far up till you get into the woods, and then there's only the small wildlife. They have to be strangers to the area,' ventured Tom Haggerty.

'Young Mourne O'Hara says she'd never seen them before and their accents weren't Irish,' said Vincent Riley.

'Bastards!' said Cullen fiercely, and then apologized to the widow McClusky for his bad manners.

'Don't apologize, Mr Cullen. You're saying aloud what we all feel. I just wonder what poor O'Rourke is going to do now. That dog was his companion and his life since his wife passed on. He must be feeling bitter this day.'

But O'Rourke wasn't bitter. 'In a strange way I'm glad it happened as it did,' he said. 'Once the shock of his passing wears off I'll be pleased that it was so merciful.' He was answering his old friend Dr Owen when he'd expressed his sorrow.

Gerry Owen had made the trip up to see O'Rourke because everyone had been concerned that he hadn't shown up at Cullen's for a week. They were worried that O'Rourke was feeling miserable and depressed about the whole business. He watched now as O'Rourke tamped his pipe, puzzled by his words.

O'Rourke gave a crooked smile. 'Why does that surprise you?'

'I know how much O'Malley meant to you. I was thinking that you'd be angry about the way it happened.'

'I was heartbroken, but not angry, when I saw him lying there. Those men didn't do it on purpose and when I thought about it, I almost felt like thanking them . . .'

'Thanking them?' cried Gerry. 'Am I hearing right?'

O'Rourke turned. 'Think about it. O'Malley was over twelve years old. He had arthritis in his back legs and though he could walk the hills with me and listen to me rambling on, and still chase a rabbit and tease the cows with his barking, he was getting old. It broke my heart sometimes when I watched him shuffle nearer to the fire because his bones were stiff and the body was not retaining enough heat. I dreaded the day when I'd watch him slowly die of old age, wondering how I could ease his suffering. Don't you see? This way my old friend went quickly and peacefully after a wonderful day in the woods with young Mourne and myself. For all the pain that's coming to me in the next few weeks because he's gone, I couldn't wish him back to a lingering, painful old age.'

Gerry nodded. O'Rourke, as usual, had his life worked out. He would deal with the situation with his usual dignity. Gerry would report back to the others that, given time alone to deal with his sorrow, O'Rourke would be sitting in his chair as usual for his weekly game of cards and a gossip as soon as he felt he had picked himself up.

Mourne spoke to Gerry anxiously, next day, as he came into the reception area to pick up the morning's notes. 'How was Mr O'Rourke when you went up to see him?'

'How did you know I'd been up to see him?'

'Mr Cullen mentioned it when I went in to get some groceries for Mam.'

'You can't scratch your ear in this town without everyone hearing about it,' Gerry marvelled, and then said, 'O'Rourke will be fine. The man has the sense many of us would give a king's ransom to possess. He takes the view that it was a humane way for O'Malley to die, taking into account the fact that he was beginning to show his age.'

Mourne nodded slowly. 'That's just how Mr O'Rourke would think,' she said, softly.

Gerry laid his hand on her shoulder. 'You know him better than any one of us who've known him all his life.'

When Mourne arrived home that evening her mother called out from the kitchen. 'There was a phone call for you about an hour ago, from John McCrory – I told him he could ring you at the surgery but he said he'd call again this evening.'

Mourne frowned. 'Did he say what he wanted?' She entered the tiny scullery where her mother was scouring a pot.

'Sure why would he? If he's going to call you tonight he'll hardly discuss the content of his call with me.'

'No! Of course not! I just wondered if he'd mentioned if it was important.'

Kitty put down the pot. 'I hope you know what you're doing, Mourne. That man has a reputation.'

'Don't look so worried, Mam,' Mourne laughed. 'I'm not fast enough for him. He's probably taking a rest from his own lifestyle to see how the other half lives.'

'Has he asked you out?' Kitty spoke bluntly. 'Only, I'd think twice about it if I were you.'

'Not yet! Not in so many words. But he paid me a lot of attention at the ball and I had the feeling he was annoyed when David arrived. I noticed he left soon after. I must say, I'm surprised he's interested enough to phone.'

'Will you go out with him if he asks?'

Mourne said, thoughtfully, 'I think so. Just as he might be curious about my lifestyle, so I'm curious about his. It might spice life up a bit.'

Kitty watched her daughter leave. Mourne was a sensible girl; she usually weighed things up. She just hoped that the glamour that went with John McCrory didn't upset the balance. Her daughter was at the age when a little excitement could undo a lifetime of teaching. She took up the pot again and began to scour furiously. She would have to trust her daughter. What the hell else could she do? She slammed the pot on to the draining-board before she wore a hole in it, as her mind went over the various possibilities of a relationship between John McCrory and her daughter.

John McCrory rang again at nine o'clock that evening. Mourne happened to be passing the phone at the time which was a relief, for Father Patrick was in the study and would have nipped out. She didn't want to have to face an inquisition.

'I wondered if you would like to have dinner with me at the Headland Hotel one evening.' John McCrory's voice, even over the telephone, had a seductive quality that made her tingle.

She hesitated. There might be complications in getting involved with him. Then Mourne chided herself. She was allowing the hints from Mam and Father Patrick to colour her instincts, and because she felt guilty about condemning him without trial she said, almost with a hint of defiance, 'Yes! I would like that!' and held the phone closer to her ear as she awaited his reaction. She heard a sigh of satisfaction and then he spoke.

'If Saturday evening is suitable, then I'll call for you at around seven-thirty. We can have a drink in the lounge bar beforehand.'

'Don't worry about collecting me!' Mourne said, hurriedly. 'I know the Headland Hotel. I could meet you in the lounge.'

'You will not. I can't have you coming in on your own. This isn't an assignation, for God's sake. It's all open and above board.'

'I didn't mean to imply—'

'I'll call for you at seven-thirty.' John's voice suddenly sounded curt. The seductive tones were now clipped and precise.

Mourne replaced the receiver. Well! That hadn't gone very well. Not only was her initial nervousness regarding the evening heightened, but she now felt embarrassed about the date altogether.

Father Patrick emerged from his study. 'Was that himself on the phone? I heard from your mam that he'd called earlier.'

Annoyed, Mourne said, 'It depends who you mean by "himself".'

'Don't bandy words, my girl. You know fine well who I mean. How many phone calls do you have from young men in one evening, that you need to sift one out to name?'

Mourne made a face. 'Yes! It was John McCrory. He wants to take me out to dinner on Saturday evening.'

'So?'

'So, I agreed, and now I'm wondering if I did the right thing.'

'It's your decision.'

'You don't mind me going to dinner with him? I thought—'

'And you thought right. I don't care much for the man. He's too fond of the high life and I wouldn't trust him with my own grandmother where money is concerned, for he'd steal the eye out of your head and laugh at the hole. But you are not my granny and I think you can take care of yourself – besides, as rogues go he isn't the worst, so you might as well cut your teeth on *him*.'

Mourne burst into laughter. She felt as though a weight had been lifted off her. 'You *really* don't mind me going out with him?'

'I didn't say that! I do mind. I don't have a lot of respect for the man, but like I said, it is all part of the learning thing and if I can't trust him, I know as sure as God is in his heaven I can trust you.' What Patrick didn't add was that he intended to make quite certain that John McCrory knew just how he felt about things.

By the time Saturday evening arrived, Mourne was so nervous she almost willed her mother to insist that she shouldn't go out. She asked

Kitty again if she was sure she didn't mind. Her mother, busy with a piece of sewing, looked at her.

'I think I can trust you to behave. Father Patrick feels likewise. Go and enjoy the evening.'

Mourne, aware that she had unwittingly offended John McCrory by saying she would meet him at the hotel, was even more nervous than she need have been and she jumped as she heard the doorbell.

She started for the door at the same time as her mother emerged from the tiny scullery. Kitty put out her hand to stay her progress. 'This is Father Patrick's house when all is said and done. I think he would like to answer the door.'

Mourne's nervousness increased. Since when had Father Patrick shifted himself from the chair to answer the door? She knew there was a reason behind this sudden move. 'I'm going to see what's happening,' she said.

'You will hold still,' Kitty said. 'Everything's being done properly. Father Patrick will ring when he's ready.'

When the bell rang in the kitchen, Mourne started. My nerves are shot to pieces, she thought.

Kitty spoke. 'They're ready for us. Now remember, Mourne. There's no need to apologize to John McCrory for our concern. If he's worth his salt then he'll understand that we're acting in your best interest.'

Jesus! She couldn't believe this. 'Why now?' Mourne said, suspiciously. 'We never went through all this palaver when I went out with Anthony Rice.'

'We know Anthony. We don't know a lot about McCrory other than that he was wild as a youth.'

'Which means you're coming in with me,' Mourne said, resignedly.

'That's right. I would like to be introduced. I know that he's lived in these parts all his life and I've seen him at a distance many times over the years, but the family's not one that has mixed much. Being wealthy and living along at Kilkeel means that they socialize out of the area, so we know little of his background – other than the reputation he's acquired since his parents died. Anyway! I think I am entitled to meet the man who's taking my girl out.'

When they entered the study, Mourne stared in surprise. Father Patrick was sitting in his chair with a sherry in his hand and John McCrory sat opposite drinking his. He stood up as Mourne and Kitty entered and shook hands politely when Mourne introduced her mam to him.

'Mr McCrory and I have been having a chat,' said Father Patrick, turning innocent blue eyes on her.

I bet you have, Mourne thought, and turned sweetly towards John. 'I'm ready to go when you are, John.'

As they drove away in the rather flashy car, Mourne stole a glance towards the window and was rewarded by a hasty swish of the curtain. She'd kill the pair of them as soon as she got home.

While they sipped their drinks in the little cocktail lounge of the Headland Hotel, they chatted; Mourne, self-consciously, and John with an air of complete ease which further rattled her. At last she blurted out: 'Look! I'm sorry about all that business at home. I don't know what got into those two—'

'I do,' John interrupted with a curious little smile. 'They were looking me over to make certain I was harmless.' He didn't mention the hidden warning he'd picked up when Father Patrick had said, ingenuously, 'Look after our girl, son. She isn't used to all the sophistication that you take for granted.'

Later, when they had made their choice for the meal, Mourne, to impress John with her knowledge, remarked that she was surprised oysters were on the menu as she understood that they shouldn't be eaten unless there was an 'r' in the month.

John looked at her in amazement before saying gently, 'That's no longer true – not since the invention of the fridge, a fact which pleases me since I adore the things.' He grinned at her. 'Anyway, we're only just into May, so I don't think we're at risk.'

Mourne reddened. 'You must think me very stupid.'

'Certainly not!'

Mourne, for the rest of the meal, allowed her companion to lead the conversation. She had been stupid, and unnecessarily so, for she should have remembered that May had arrived, if only just. Hadn't she spent every evening of the last week of April helping her mam to sew the costumes for the Queen of the May procession?

John McCrory studied her. She needed some work doing but she had definite potential. He had to play his cards carefully. Still! He was pretty nifty at playing cards. He held a good hand, and so long as David McNeill was across the water in England, he had a good chance of a full house.

After the meal they moved into the coffee lounge with its soft lighting and comfortable armchairs. Mourne settled back and glanced around her, revelling in the feeling of luxury, admiring the embossed wallpaper and envying the glamour of the women seated around the room. She could hardly believe she was dining here. She and Tara had often looked at the hotel from the outside, sighing with longing as they watched the cars disgorge those lucky people who had the means to frequent it. They had often dared each other to walk up grandly to the door, past the top-hatted figure guarding it and into the mysterious interior. Of course, neither had plucked up the courage and they had eventually wandered back on to the main street in Newcastle and dreamed over a cup of coffee in McNee's café.

Tara would be green with envy when she told her that she had dined with John McCrory. She must give her a ring. They hadn't seen much of each other just lately. Tara was still busy with the preparations for her wedding and they had only chatted on the phone once since they'd had their fittings . . .

'You haven't heard a word I've said.'

Mourne started from her reverie at John McCrory's words. 'Oh dear! I went off into a dream then. I'm sorry.' She felt the blush rise from her neck and cover her face. The man would think her a person without manners.

John McCrory hid a smile. 'That's perfectly all right. I could see you were taking in the surroundings. I did just the same when I first came here to dine. I was about nine years old then. I'm used to it now.'

If he was trying to make her feel better, he was failing. Mourne was cross at her lack of concentration – and the fact that this man had been used to luxury such as this from an early age made her feel even more inadequate. She consoled herself that wealth was not always a sign of breeding. She may not have known the luxury of dining in places like this, and she may not have the money to wear clothes worth a small ransom, but she had been brought up to be able to hold her own anywhere.

'Actually, I'm afraid my mind had gone well beyond the doors of this place. I was thinking of a friend and myself and the things we did together.'

John frowned and then smiled quickly to hide his momentary displeasure. He had no doubt that she had been thinking of David McNeill. Her eyes had gone soft and glazed as she sipped her coffee. He leaned towards her. 'I think I'd better take you home. I promised your guardian I wouldn't keep you out too late.'

Mourne looked at her watch. 'Sure it is only ten o'clock. I don't think Father Patrick was thinking I'd be back this early.'

'Are you certain? I got the impression he wanted you home as soon as the meal was down.'

'You make me out to be a real culshie. I've been out later than this and Father Patrick has not had a word to say about it. Anyway, Mam would be more the one to make a fuss.' Mourne felt destroyed at the idea that this very sophisticated man should think she had no mind of her own in such matters, or that she, at her age, had to keep dormitory hours. 'I'm sure you were mistaken. I think Father Patrick was thinking of a later time. He just meant that he didn't think I should be kept out till all hours.' Oh God! This was getting worse. Now she sounded like a child begging to be allowed a little more time up before being packed off to bed.

Satisfied, John McCrory pretended to give the matter some thought. 'Well! I'm not sure you're right about this.' He hesitated.

Mourne leaned across. 'I know what I'm talking about. If Father Patrick has a complaint to make he can make it to me and I'll set him right. Anyway! In three months' time I shall be twenty-one years old; I'll be in charge of my own actions then.' She paused, her pretty face rosy with indignation. 'I can assure you that you won't be blamed. He knows what I'm like—'

'Very well!' John broke in, with assumed reluctance. I suppose it is early. Certainly for me.'

Mourne bit her lip. 'And for me,' she said haughtily, 'I've been out much later than this and no one turned a hair.'

'If we wander along the seafront towards the other end of town, can I hold your hand?' John McCrory teased, and bit his lip to hide his desire to yawn as the girl blushed and agreed. My God! She was truly a holy innocent. He would have to spend a few evenings at his club to make up for this bore of an evening. He certainly wouldn't have considered playing pat-a-cake with this mere girl if he thought for one moment that he would be seen by anyone he knew – he'd end up a laughing-stock. He must keep reminding himself that the success of his future plans lay in making this girl fall in love with him. That she was as unsophisticated as a cheese scone was something he would have to live with. At least she was a looker, and with the right clothes and the right grooming she would do very well. He would have to tread gently, though. That interfering old buffer Father Mulligan obviously

98

had her interests at heart and no doubt looked on anyone with the name McCrory as the devil's playmate. He would have to convince the old fool that his intentions were honourable.

CHAPTER 7

John McCrory slammed the door shut with a ferocity that made it shake on its hinges. God, how he hated bossy, interfering women. To have to put up with Mrs Flannigan was the biggest thorn a man could have in his side. The woman was a lethal weapon when it came to sticking her nose in his life. He would never cease to curse his father for the wording of that bloody will.

Mrs Flannigan's muffled voice sounded from the other side of the door. 'It isn't a bit of use you throwing a tantrum, Mr John. I've made you a good substantial meal and you will eat it before you go out. I mean business here. You'll be drinking the night away and you'll need some food to line your stomach.'

'I'll be eating at the club. How many times do I have to say it!'

'That stuff you put into yourself there is of no use to man nor beast. Sure what good is chicken breast in aspic to a man of your build, now I ask you.'

John walked over to the door and pulled it open. 'How many times have I told you not to call me Mr John! And how many times do I have to tell you that I am thirty-one years old *and I do not need a nanny any longer*. You are my housekeeper. You take orders from me, now—'

'Your meal is on the table. It's not a bit of good you going on at me. Your mam and your da instructed me to take care of you – you're like a son to me after all the years I've cared for you – and I will not let you go out of this house on an empty stomach.'

John gave in. He always gave in. The woman was so determined to smother him with her cosseting he wanted to strangle her, but in the end it was easier all round if he went into the dining room and ate a few mouthfuls. The rest went to the fat fart of a dog she let run wild around the place. Christ! If anyone ever found out about his subjection to this hag he would lose face all round. There was no other way. He would have to bring forth his plans sooner than he had wished. She must go!

John McCrory adored tarty women – high-class tarty women – who didn't give a tinker's curse if he starved to death or cut his own throat. They were out for what they could get and to this end they fed his ego and did his bidding and were well rewarded for doing so. There was no commitment on either side. *He* had a beautiful, well-dressed woman on his arm when he needed her and she enjoyed a good night out. John always insisted on his women doing him credit. They might be tarts but they had to look good. To that end he was generous with his gifts of clothes and jewellery.

Aware that time was passing and that he was due to pick up Helen Moore in an hour, John took himself down to the dining room. The table could accommodate twelve at a sitting and he loathed sitting down to his meals with acres of polished wood in front of him, but Mrs Flannigan was a stickler for propriety and as with everything else, he found it simpler to comply with her wishes.

He nibbled away at the piece of steak pie set before him, knowing that the devious old witch was likely to whip in silently to ensure that he was enjoying it, but when he felt secure, he opened the door and let the fat white dog inside. Cobber, knowing the drill well now, always waited patiently for the signal. If it wasn't given then he seemed to sense that the meal was not forthcoming and would slink away into the kitchen to the less succulent fare in his bowl. Tonight his luck was in and before John could burp, the meal was disappearing down the willing gullet. He snatched the plate up before the dog had entirely finished it and booted his great arse out of the door again. Mrs Flannigan would be suspicious if there wasn't some left on the plate.

His glance, moody and still dark with annoyance, scanned the hall. The old banshee was nowhere to be seen. Before she arrived with his dessert, he grabbed his coat and ran for it, angry that he should feel unmanned – but he always did when he gave in to her. His inadequacy in dealing with her stretched back a long way to when, as a small boy, she terrorized him if he didn't do as he was told. On the other hand she had been the only one to show him any love.

He could still remember the familiar scent of her as she held him close to her bosom and sang Irish lullabies to him because his parents were never there. She had been the one to tend his wounds and she was the one who cried when they packed him off to boarding school, out of the way. He *should* love her, but he didn't. She had made him so dependent upon her that he felt only a deep resentment towards her. Perhaps if she had let go when he got older he would have had some residual feeling for her, but after his mother had died and his father ignored his existence, she had taken him even further under her wing and his dependency had increased. When he joined his father in the business, his father's contribution to building his character had consisted of barked orders and hours of mindless instruction. Now, thanks to all of them, he was a bloody emotional mess.

As soon as he entered the opulent foyer of the Crystal Club, John felt his mood change. He loved this place. It was here that he was respected, not only for his wealth, but for his expertise with the cards. Poker was his game but he was adept at any of them, be it a game of chance or one that required a large amount of skill. There was no music here, just the sound of the chips as they clicked together on the table, and the gentle rustle of cards as they left the dealers' hands. This was no place for music; it would only intrude. The mind had to be alert and incisive when decisions were made, not lulled into a state of languor.

He made his way to the poker table, acknowledging the waves and nods of his friends and acquaintances with a haughty jerk of his head. Here, he was one of the élite, he was his own man; here he could shake off his deep sense of inadequacy and show the real John McCrory. He sat down and motioned for Helen to stand beside him. She knew to be quiet and still as he took his mind off everything else but the cards in his hand. He sighed with contentment.

Later, they dined. Helen was tucking into her meal as though it was her last. She ate daintily but quickly, and as he idly observed her his thoughts wandered. He found himself speculating on what the delectable Mourne was doing at this moment and a tiny smile curved his lips. He must bring her here one evening and observe the effect on her. He had found her to be very beautiful – but cold. Her wonderful eyes had an innocence that had appealed to him and in a strange way, excited him. They had been appraising but disinterested. He was intrigued. Women never looked at him in that way. They usually gave him a signal and fell over themselves to make his further acquaintance, and the fact that she had not shown a reaction to the look of appreciation he had thrown at her had sent his blood racing. This girl, he surmised, had no real interest in men. Mourne O'Hara was definitely the girl he was looking for. He suspected she had a lot in common with girls like Helen. She had the same air of disinterest about his well-being as they had, but in her case she had that extra something they lacked – breeding. She also had what he required most. No desire for him. She might grow to like him, but instinct told him that she would never love him. That that emotion was missing had been the deciding factor for him. She was the one he would marry.

Mourne stuck her head round the door of the consulting room before showing the next patient in. Gerry Owen looked up from his notes as she gave a slight cough.

'What is it you want?' He peered at her over his glasses.

'I'd like to pop over to Cullen's stores for a minute. You're on your last patient so it's a convenient time – will that be all right?'

'Since when have you bothered to ask my permission, you article?'

'Since the last time I didn't and all hell was let loose because you were missing a set of notes.'

'Well, this is not the same thing! Surgery is finished so I'm hardly likely to make a fuss. You're just making a point here.'

Mourne didn't answer. She was concerned because Mr O'Rourke had not been seen in Cullen's for the past three Wednesdays, having sent a message to say that he would get in touch when he felt able to abide company again. Mourne understood how he must feel with the loss of O'Malley only weeks gone, but the fact that no one had heard from him was worrying. Billy Todd who fetched his groceries for him reported that he was coping, but this was no consolation. The pair of them were as thick as thieves, and Billy would cover up for O'Rourke if asked.

Tara's wedding had taken up Mourne's time and she felt guilty that she hadn't spared a thought for anything other than her role as chief bridesmaid. True, Mr O'Rourke wasn't expecting her to visit, but nevertheless she felt that her selfishness in being so caught up with her own life was reprehensible. Once the wedding was over she had then become involved with John McCrory, and somehow the days and weeks had flown past.

Mr Cullen had no further news of O'Rourke. 'Why don't you whip up and see him,' he suggested. 'Sure where would be the harm. You know how fond of you he is. I think he'd like to have you visit.'

'But he said he wanted to be alone awhile to deal with his grief. I don't want to impose,' Mourne said, doubtfully.

Jack Cullen leaned his arms on the counter and said, 'Of us all, you're the one he would most like to see. And we'd all like to know that he's well. Even though Billy Todd has assured us he is, I wouldn't be surprised if O'Rourke put him up to it so he doesn't have us worrying. I do know that he isn't eating. His bill is down on the usual amount – and that's takin' into account the fact that he hasn't had a dog to feed.'

Mourne was startled. She frowned. 'I'll go! I don't like the sound of what you've just said. Tomorrow is the day I normally go up to see him, which is why my mind started fretting.' She moved towards the door, but Cullen called her back.

'Here! Take this piece of cooked ham up to him for his tea. He's particularly partial to my cooked ham; it'll encourage him to eat.'

The next day, with some trepidation, Mourne made her way up to O'Rourke's cottage. There was no sign of life, no smoke coming from the chimney. That in itself did not alarm her, for Mr O'Rourke was a man who rarely felt the cold and it was now May and he would be using his primus stove, but it was the bleak look of emptiness that heightened her concern. There was a strong chill in the air this high up, and she shivered slightly and pulled the light half-coat she was wearing closer round her as she climbed the last stile.

The heavy door was closed. She knocked loudly. There was not a sign of him. She bit her lip, uncertain what to do next. She looked to the spot where O'Malley's outdoor bed normally sat and a sadness swept through her at the empty space. She sat down on the wall as the memories flooded back to her of their walks in the hills and the way she and Mr O'Rourke had laughed at the antics of the dog, and marvelled at the intelligence in the big eyes when he did something that he knew had delighted them. She started at the sound of barking and jumped down off the wall as a bundle of ferocity hurled itself at her.

'Down, Tarag! This is my friend.'

Mourne turned in astonishment to O'Rourke, who was smiling at her. She went towards him. 'I was worried about you. I hope you aren't cross. I just had to come and – and Jack Cullen sent you up some cooked ham.' She held up the small parcel and waited.

'Great! I'm very partial to cooked ham. We'll have a bite to eat.' O'Rourke took the small parcel and opened the door. 'I've missed our walks. I'm glad you came. I was going to leave word with Jack Cullen to tell you that I'm a bit more of a human being again.' He looked down at the dog who was now lying meekly at his feet, his tongue lolling and his nose twitching at the smell of the ham slices that his master was now unloading on to a plate.

Mourne couldn't wait any longer. 'Where did the dog come from?' she asked.

O'Rourke, placing the kettle on the top of the primus stove, turned. 'Do you remember John McCrory, the man who knocked you down when he jumped the ditch?'

'Yes?' Mourne said, but neglected to mention that she had seen him since.

'Well! About a week after O'Malley's death he arrived at my door. He came to offer his sympathy and to ask after your health. We got talking and McCrory mentioned that he knew of a dog who was to be put down as there was no one willing to take him on, and he wondered if, under the circumstances, I would see my way to having him. Of course I refused at first. I felt the man had no sensitivity in view of the fact that I had lost my best pal, but he wouldn't give way. He told me that it wouldn't be true to O'Malley if I let a good dog die for the sake of sentimentality, and that it was fate that had decreed this dog needed a home at the time of my sad loss. I wanted to throw the man out of the door for I've no great liking for him, but then I stopped. He was right! I knew it. Like he said, O'Malley would have no respect for me if I let this poor creature die because I was acting like a maudlin eejut. I told him to bring him to me, and so there he sits. He'll never replace O'Malley – no dog on earth could do that – but we need each other, and he's a certain charm about him that appeals to me.'

Mourne looked down at the dog sitting by his new master's feet. He had the same look of devotion in his eyes as O'Malley used to have when he gazed up at O'Rourke. 'Why have you called him Tarag?'

'I once knew an Irish wolfhound called that, and I thought it sounded very haughty. I had a wicked desire to call this little fellow such a name to make up for his obvious lack of breeding and size.' O'Rourke gave a huge grin and fondled the dog's ears. 'I'm growing very fond of him.'

'He obviously adores you!' Mourne observed. It always amazed her how easy Mr O'Rourke found it to train a dog. It said something for the patience and quiet authority of the man.

'He knows the hand that feeds him, more like,' said O'Rourke, modestly. 'But it has to be said that he's a quick learner. Already he can come to heel at the command and he knows not to go near Ben's sheep. I think we'll do well together.' He bent down and fondled Tarag's ear and ruffled the brown coat till it stood up. 'Like O'Malley, this fella is of no known breed. There might even be a bit of sheep in him, judging by the texture of his coat,' he laughed.

Mourne smiled. It was lovely to hear Mr O'Rourke laugh again. She watched as he got up to pour the now boiling water into the teapot. She was glad she had come. Her mind was now at rest and she had her friend back in her life again. They would walk the hills and go trout-tickling again. She said as much to Father Patrick when they were seated at the table for the evening meal.

Patrick nodded. 'You did the right thing. Sometimes I worry about the man, up there all on his own. He isn't getting any younger and one of these days he'll have to move down from the hills and into the community – like it or not.'

'He'll never do that,' Kitty remarked, slowly. 'Strangely enough, he feels nearer to his wife up there. He has time to think and remember, in the silence and the stillness of the night. Now that O'Malley is buried there he'll want to stay.'

'I've no doubt you're right! But I think that fate might take a hand. Besides, Gerry Owen isn't getting any younger. It isn't right that he should have to trek all that way – especially in winter – should the man become ill.'

'I thought David was going to take over the practice?' Mourne held her breath as she waited for Father Patrick's reply.

'It depends on whether he takes to it when he has spent his six months here. We will know soon enough. It seems that all has been settled over the water and he has tied up all the loose ends. He's been given the leave of absence and all we need is the date of his arrival to be confirmed.'

Mourne's heart leapt. The last time she had spoken to Uncle Gerry the whole issue had still been in the air due to a hiccup in finding a replacement registrar for the six-month period. Now it would appear the whole thing was on. She hid her excitement as she inquired if Father Patrick knew the week, if not the day, of David's arrival. She had a holiday coming up in late June and she hoped he would arrive while she was still working at the surgery.

'Tell me! How did you enjoy your honeymoon?' Mourne leaned back in her chair and regarded her friend Tara with a grin. They had met at a restaurant in Ballynahinch, the big market town being halfway between Belfast and Ballycash.

Tara giggled. 'You shouldn't be asking me that.'

'Oh! I didn't mean – I meant . . . how did the holiday go?'

'The holiday was great. Mind you, I've now discovered that my man is a wasteground when it comes to appreciating culture. Jay-Jay wasn't keen on Rome. He said the place was littered with ruins and that the Colosseum was an eyesore that should be knocked down so that something useful could be put in its place.' Tara turned her eyes to heaven. 'His suggestion was to build a sports centre on the spot – or a decent park, so that people could get away from all the traffic for a while – he couldn't stand the noise.' She giggled helplessly. 'I couldn't get him to cross the road till there was a long gap in the traffic.'

'Did you catch a glimpse of His Holiness?'

'Not at all! There wasn't a sign. The Swiss Guards had the place surrounded. We did visit the Vatican museum though. At that point I let Jay-Jay off the leash so he could look for a place to have a drink and a bite to eat while the rest of us did the tour of the Basilica and the Sistine Chapel. He ended up in a bar with an Englishman. From what I can gather, the pair of them moaned about the continuous diet of spaghetti they were forced – *forced*, mind you – to eat. They likened it to eating a plate of giant worms.'

'What about the rest of the tour?'

'Aw! It was great! Florence was my favourite – but Jay-Jay was happiest when we reached Venice. I couldn't haul him away from the canals. We spent a fortune sailing around in gondolas.'

Mourne listened entranced while Tara described in detail the breathtaking beauty of the buildings and their interiors. She was filled with a great desire to see them for herself, so vivid was the description. She sighed. Perhaps, one day, she too would go to Italy and do all those things.

'Which was your favourite building?'

Without hesitation Tara said, 'The Sistine Chapel! There was something about the place that struck right to the heart of me. I can't fully describe the beauty and the peace of the place.' She paused for a moment, her face lit with the memory of it all.

'But Florence was the big one for me. The buildings – the works of art – the statues . . . You must go there one day, Mourne. Nothing I've said today can paint the pictures that are still in my mind . . . you have to see it for yourself.'

They finished their coffee and rose. 'Shall we take a walk out into the countryside?' Tara glanced at her watch. 'We've an hour before lunch.'

Mourne walked along with her head bent, engrossed in her thoughts, while Tara rattled on about her new life with Jay-Jay. Since she had met John McCrory Mourne had found herself chafing at the restrictions that bordered her life. She longed to meet someone who would love her and cherish her and never leave her. Her heart fluttered and a *frisson* of fear ran through her. Could she ever trust anyone enough to accept such a commitment? She feared not. If she didn't love, there was less risk of rejection.

'You haven't heard a word I've said, Mourne O'Hara. You've gone into one of your brown studies.'

Mourne, realizing that Tara had stopped, turned back and apologized sheepishly.

'I am sorry, really I am. It was all the talk of the lovely honeymoon you had and the life you'll be having with Jay-Jay. It made me think about the state of my own life. I was wondering if I'd ever meet someone who would want to spend his life with me – there isn't a lot of choice in Ballycash.'

Tara looked at Mourne in surprise. 'What are you on about? Haven't I heard that John McCrory has his sights on you?'

'He has not! I went out for a meal with him once. I think he was at a dead end and hadn't anything more exciting on that night. He remembered me from a couple of accidental meetings and probably thought I'd fill the bill for an evening, that's all!'

'Well that isn't the story I heard. My brother belongs to the golf club and he says there was a bit of rivalry between John McCrory and Dr Owen's nephew. He says that John McCrory left the dance with a face like a thundercloud because you were dancing such a lot with the nephew, who was all over you.'

'The name is David McNeill! and he was not, as you so vulgarly put it, all over me. He was paying the normal respect he would to any old friend . . .' Mourne paused. 'Did Peter really think David was being attentive beyond the call of duty?' The idea set her nerves tingling.

'That's what it looked like, according to him.'

'You've never mentioned this before.'

'Sure why would I? As far as I was concerned there was nothing in Peter's observation – you would have told me, wouldn't you?'

Over lunch Tara spoke of her difficulty in persuading Jay-Jay that she should go out to work. They were living with his parents and Tara was finding it tough. 'His mother's very nice and we get along great, but honest to God, Mourne, the woman has a phobia for cleaning. I think she should see a psychiatrist . . .'

Mourne burst out laughing and a fat man in his overburdened chair paused in the act of putting an éclair to his mouth and stared at the pair of them. Tara giggled.

'We'll get thrown out of here,' she said, and continued: 'I swear that woman would polish my elbow if I left it in the air long enough. She definitely has a disorder of some kind – even Jay-Jay says she isn't right. I think she should see someone.'

'Will you move into a house of your own?'

'We will when Jay-Jay's da gives him the rise in pay he has promised him. Meanwhile I'd like to work to earn a bit of money; every little helps.'

'Would the da not think about giving you a job in the business?'

Tara's eyes opened wide. 'Do you know! I hadn't thought about it. That just might serve the bill. I wouldn't actually be lettin' them down by working for a stranger and at the same time I would be helping them, and there *is* a job going soon. One of the typists is leaving to have a baby.'

The rest of the lunch was eaten hurriedly so that Tara could catch her bus, which departed fifteen minutes before Mourne's. As she left, Tara called out, 'Thanks for the idea. I'll let you know if it comes off.'

Mourne strolled down the broad street unaware of what went on around her. She was only now realizing how much she had depended on Tara for friendship and companionship. She would miss her in the days that stretched ahead. She had no one to visit the coffee bar with and no one to laugh with when life threw up one of its little surprises set to amuse them. From now on her contact would be mostly by telephone with the occasional meeting. True! She had a few casual friends she'd grown up with, and she had become very close to Rena, but there was that something between Tara and herself that was precious. She sighed and ran for the bus.

Father Patrick removed his jacket and hung it neatly on the peg before going into the kitchen. His eyebrows were creased in a frown. He stood with his shoulder against the door as he watched Kitty roll out dough for the pie she was making. She looked up at him and his frown deepened. 'Have you heard the latest gossip?' he asked.

'I never take any part in gossiping. If I do hear something I keep an open mind before I pass judgement.' Kitty, having pared the pastry to

110

fit the dish, now turned to put it in the oven. Her shoulders were stiff with disapproval.

'It isn't any good you going all sanctimonious on me, Kitty – I can tell by your attitude that you know very well what gossip I'm alluding to.'

Kitty did know, but the last thing she wanted to do at this moment was discuss it with Patrick Mulligan; not when he had that stubborn look on his face. There was no use dealing with him in such a mood; he would see no one's point of view but his own. She would wait till he had eaten, or at least had a rest in his study, after which he would be more amenable.

'Away in your study and I'll bring you a cup of tea and we'll talk later. You're tired. I can see it in your face.'

'The face won't alter. I'm as tired as I always am after giving religious instruction to that class of reprobates – the state of it is no indication of my mood – nevertheless, I'll away in till later.'

When she had finished getting the evening meal ready for the table, Kitty made her way to the study. Father Patrick rose as she came in and stood by the fireplace. Kitty sighed. When he did that it meant he was going to run off at the mouth. She sat down in her usual chair and waited.

'You do realize that our girl is being linked with John McCrory?'

'Seeing as we gave her permission to go out to dinner with him I suppose it isn't surprising,' said Kitty slowly, and added, 'although I don't know how it got around so quickly.'

'She was seen walking arm in arm with him past the harbour.'

Kitty was annoyed. You couldn't swallow a fly in Ballycash without someone knowing about it and spreading the news. 'What's the problem with that? They probably went for a walk to help their dinner down. We knew they were going out for a meal.'

'I didn't give my consent willingly – I was influenced,' said Patrick. 'The man has a reputation. I would have questioned the wisdom of the whole idea, but I knew I was outnumbered.'

'Patrick Mulligan! We can't run Mourne's life for her. I'm just as concerned as you are, for I hear that he's a gambler and I am not in favour of a man who will knowingly throw money away in one of those places when there's hunger and want staring us all in the face, but Mourne is nearly twenty-one and in a few months' time we'll have no control over who she sees or what she does with her life. We can only hope that she remembers all she's been taught.' Kitty drew breath

111

after the long speech and looked at the man facing her. She appreciated all he'd done for them and knew that he was concerned for Mourne, but she felt that the situation was being blown out of all proportion.

'David will be over soon,' Patrick said reflectively. 'It'd be great if they got together. I know they like each other – perhaps things might go deeper between them.'

Kitty rose. 'I'd like nothing better, but I won't hold my breath. For all we know David might be set up already over in England. We'll just have to wait and see what happens, but whatever the outcome is, I will support my daughter.'

'Why don't you have a word with her?'

'I'll see! There may well be no need, and if we interfere at this stage she'll more than likely resent it and do something silly.' Kitty's eyes softened. Patrick Mulligan meant well, but his concern for Mourne at this time was misplaced. She knew her daughter too well to think that she would do something rash. 'Let's see what happens before we make any move.'

There was the sound of a door opening. 'Here she is. Not a word, mind.' Kitty looked sternly at Patrick who, with a shrug, sat back in his chair.

Greeting her daughter with a quick hug, Kitty said, 'I don't expect you'll want to eat if you've had a meal out, but come into the kitchen and tell me all about Tara. How is she adapting to married life?'

Mourne laughed. 'I got severely reprimanded when I asked her that, but judging by her bright eyes and the giggle, I think she's enjoying it. They had a wonderful time in Italy.' Mourne spoke over her shoulder as she wet the tea in the pot from the ever-boiling kettle. 'Do you want a cup?'

Kitty shook her head. 'I've just had one – which reminds me, hadn't you better pop your head round the door and say hello to Father Patrick? You know he'll be sulking if you don't.'

'Tara enjoyed Italy then?' she inquired when Mourne returned.

Mourne gave her all the information she had gleaned from Tara and Kitty nodded when she heard Jay-Jay's views on Rome. 'I'm not surprised,' she said. 'I got the impression he was more the practical type.'

'Tara called him a philistine,' Mourne laughed. 'But she said it fondly. She's very much in love with him.'

'And so she should be, or where was the sense in marrying the lad?'

'You think it's always a necessity to love someone to marry them?'

112

Mourne stared into her cup while she waited for the answer.

'Yes, I do!' Kitty said slowly, at last. 'Marriage is hard enough without going into it minus that advantage.'

'But surely if two people get along together they've just as much chance for a good marriage? After all, we know couples who only stay together because they have to, yet *they* were madly in love in the beginning.'

'Were they?' Kitty asked. 'Sometimes we are influenced by looks or personality and think that the essential ingredient is there. We don't look beyond the outer covering to what's beneath.'

'How on earth will I know if I'm in love?' Mourne asked. 'The whole thing's a minefield the way you tell it.'

'Give yourself time for things to develop,' Kitty advised. 'It's usually the quick off the mark marriages that seem to founder. Ask yourself if you're marrying for the right reasons.' She stood up. 'I'd better get on with my work. Anyway! I shouldn't worry about it. You've a fair share of common sense. You'll know if you're marrying the right one, but if there is the slightest doubt listen to your heart – now, will you answer that phone? It's patently obvious that our lord and master next door has no intention of shifting himself to do so.'

A few minutes later, Mourne re-entered the kitchen. 'That was John McCrory,' she said casually. 'He wants to take me out to dinner at his club. I told him I'd like to go – if that's all right with you.'

It wasn't all right with Kitty. On the one occasion they had met she hadn't taken to him, but then she was going on instinct and hearsay and that wasn't fair to him. She turned. 'If you want to go, sure I can see no reason to forbid you. You're nearly twenty-one; you don't need to ask permission.' She gave her daughter a quick hug. 'But remember what I've just said.'

'Ach Mam! I've no intention of marrying the man. I'm enjoying his company and . . .' she giggled, 'I'm delving into a life I know nothing about. It's all great practice for when I meet my prince.'

'I don't care if you marry a pauper so long as you're happy with him,' Kitty said, with a hint of caution.

Mourne laughed. 'One fine day!'

Kitty stood for a long time staring out of the little window. Perhaps Father Patrick was right. Maybe she should discuss John McCrory and his reputation with Mourne. Was she wrong in hoping that it was just a fling she was having and that she would quickly tire of his type of lifestyle? She sighed. She hoped none of them would rue the day he had knocked her daughter down while he was out riding his horse.

Mourne had arranged to visit Rena. John had asked her to dress up for the evening and she wanted to borrow the cape again.

'Not the cape,' Rena advised. 'It would be much too heavy for the occasion, particularly as the days are so much warmer now.'

'It isn't warm enough to go without something over the dress. I haven't anything else,' Mourne laughed. 'I sound like a right pauper. It's just that I don't have much cause to wear an evening dress very often, so I feel the expense of buying a new jacket wouldn't be justified.'

'You could buy a pretty shawl,' Rena mused. 'If you bought a cream-coloured one you could wear it with just about anything.'

Mourne liked the idea. 'I hadn't thought of that.'

'Where's he taking you?'

'His club. It sounds grand, doesn't it?'

Rena was pleased that Mourne was seeing a bit of life. She had wondered for some time how such an attractive girl could be content with the life she led. She spent too many hours with older people and helping out with church work. And there were times when she had a wistful look in her eyes, particularly when she was with the twins. Once, when they had been bluebelling in the woods, and the twins were up to their usual devilment, Mourne had turned to Rena and asked, 'Would you ever think of leaving the children?' Rena had been mildly shocked at the nature of the question.

'God, no! They're a pair of fiends, but they're mine and I love them. What makes you ask that?'

Mourne had shrugged. 'You hear of mothers abandoning their children. I just wondered if there was ever a justification for it.'

Rena had stared at her. 'There is never a justification for such an action, Mourne. Children are God's gift to us all.' When she had seen the stricken look in Mourne's eyes, she had wanted to cut her tongue out, for she had then remembered that Mourne was adopted. Somehow everyone tended to forget that Kitty was not Mourne's real mother.

Rena had tried hastily to retract her words. 'Mind you! There are circumstances beyond the control of us all. I'm talking here about *deliberate* abandonment, where there's only a selfish reason.' She had been relieved to see a smile appear and Mourne had said, 'Of course. I do see what you mean,' before turning away to walk towards the girls.

'How about you and I go into Newcastle on Saturday to look for a

114

shawl?' Rena said now. 'We could have tea out and take a stroll along the promenade and eye all the young men on holiday.' She smiled impishly. 'It's been a long time since I ogled another man.'

'You devious article!' Mourne laughed. 'I could use that remark as a form of blackmail if you didn't do my bidding. I'd tell your poor unsuspecting husband what a wanton of a wife he's married – you have a deal.'

That evening Mourne told Kitty of her plans. 'I understand that a long dress is preferred when ladies dine at John's club.'

'Lord save us. You *are* moving in top circles,' Kitty said. Her brow frowned, but she kept her thoughts to herself. She resolved, however, to make a few discreet inquiries; maybe Gerry knew more about the kind of place this club was.

John McCrory expertly parked the large car and hastened round to the passenger side to assist Mourne. He had deliberately parked in the general car park instead of his usual allotted place at the front. He had decided not to enter the dining room through the large gambling hall. Time enough to give her a hint of the other activities of the club when she had been lulled by the discreet lighting and the plush furnishings in the dining room – not to mention his own ability for smooth-talking.

Helen and the other girls said he could charm the birds off a tree and he intended to put his skills to good use this night. He had no illusions that Mourne O'Hara would fall in love with him. She showed little emotion when he touched her, and although she laughed with him and seemed eager to learn about life she gave the impression that she was always on the defensive. She would give him no trouble, he was certain, so long as he abided by her rules.

When they had ordered, he leaned across the table. 'What do you think of my club?'

'It's very . . . very plush?' Mourne waved her hand towards the room and smiled. 'I've no intention of pretending that I'm used to all this. I am to sophistication what an eel is to a salmon. However! I'm a quick learner and could easily find myself becoming used to such luxury.'

John was amused. 'It will be my pleasure to induct you.' He was more than happy to be seen in the company of a lovely girl like her. It hadn't escaped his notice that many eyes were straying towards their table. 'You are very beautiful,' he said.

'I have to warn you,' Mourne replied, a blush staining her cheeks,

'I don't like flattery.' But she too had been conscious of the looks that were being thrown their way, and felt a glow of satisfaction.

John McCrory was cynically aware that the looks they were getting were also because she was so unlike the usual women he had on his arm. Most were wondering what he was up to. He leaned closer. 'We might as well give them all cause to speculate. And, I might add, I really wasn't flattering you – I meant what I said.'

The wine waiter arrived at that moment and Mourne didn't have to reply. She suddenly felt uneasy. The evening was not as she had thought it would be – a quiet meal in a discreet dining room – and she became uncomfortable about the continuous scrutiny, aware that she was not up to the style of the other women. She wondered what on earth this man was doing with someone like her. It was obvious to her that the smart, sophisticated women with their expensive clothes and hairdos were more his type.

She began to relax, however, once she'd had a glass of the excellent wine and a few swallows of delicious food. John, to please her, had stopped with the fulsome compliments and was now treating her as someone who had a brain. He was a very amusing companion and the more relaxed she became, the more she realized that the evening was proving to be a success after all. It would have been difficult not to have enjoyed it, she thought, when she looked around again at the décor and the sumptuous furniture. Everything was bathed in a pink light. The napery was pink and the walls were papered in a delicate shade of the same colour. The room had been designed for the ladies, and the only concession to the male escorts was the large wine rack adorning the wall with its many bottles of expensive wines.

When they had finished their meal, John asked, 'Would you like to see the rest of the club?'

Mourne nodded and said, 'Yes! I would.'

He took her lightly by the elbow and guided her towards the door which led to the gambling hall, and watched her face carefully as she passed through. He noted the look of startled surprise as she entered the brightly lit room, such a contrast to the soft-hued one they had just left.

'This is where large sums of money are won and lost,' he murmured, adding, 'keep your eyes down till they adjust to the brightness.'

'Why does it have to be this bright?'

'One has to be able to see the cards and the croupiers have to be on the alert for cheating. This is no place for shadows. Come on! We'll have a stroll round – have you ever been to a gambling club before?'

'You must know I haven't!' Mourne blinked as she looked up at her companion and the brightness made her eyes water again. He didn't appear to be affected. He placed her arm through his and they walked around, stopping now and then to watch the games of poker in progress in the small card room.

'You'll notice that the bystanders never speak above a whisper and rarely interrupt the players. It would be more than their lives were worth if they did. These men are playing for big stakes.'

Mourne had indeed noticed. She had also taken note that the bystanders were mostly women. They strolled on and stopped at the roulette wheel. Here it was less quiet but once the wheel began to turn at speed, all conversation ceased and an air of tense anticipation took over, culminating in sighs or in wild euphoria, depending on the outcome of the individual bets. She was enthralled by the whole scene and a *frisson* of excitement passed through her as she watched. She wondered what her mam would think if she knew what she was doing at this very moment.

'I think we should be making tracks,' John said, eventually. He was satisfied with the result of his own gamble. Judging by the look on Mourne's face, the whole concept of gambling didn't disgust her. So much for her constrained upbringing by the religious mother and the fat priest. He reckoned that somewhere in her natural bloodline there had been an ancestor with a gambler's instinct. He was now more convinced than ever that he had made a good choice.

CHAPTER 8

Mourne decided to go for a walk as she had some serious thinking to do. She had been seeing a lot of John McCrory just recently, and had become aware of the change in his attitude towards her. He was behaving as though she was exclusively his and she was concerned that he might be reading into their friendship more than she was prepared to give.

Being independent by nature, a trait that drove her mother wild, she resented his assumption that she was his property. She had made it clear that she wasn't ready for commitment. He hadn't taken any notice and continued to assume that when he wasn't around, she should be waiting for him. This had been reinforced when he had phoned the parochial house and on finding that she was not there, had inquired testily of her mam if she knew where she was.

'The man acts as though you should be waiting in the wings for him to call,' Mam had said, when she related the conversation they'd had.

Mourne had never known her mam to be so annoyed when relaying a message.

'Have you given the man cause to think that you're his property?' she'd asked, her normally soft voice sharp with irritation.

Mourne sighed. She would have to do something. She didn't want to lose John's friendship, but there were times when he said something or behaved in a certain way which made her uneasy. On one such occasion he had spoken so harshly and haughtily to a waitress for having slopped a tiny drop of coffee that the poor girl had blushed a fiery red and spluttered an apology before retreating. Her annihilation had been complete when John had complained about her incompetence to the manager. Later, he had apologized ruefully to Mourne for his behaviour, but she had suspected that the apology had been made because he had seen how shocked she'd been. After that incident, he

119

had been more careful how he treated others in her presence and she had almost forgotten the incident, till now.

So engrossed was she in her thoughts, she was halfway down the wide street of Ballycash before she realized where she was. She stopped. Ahead of her she saw a man standing in front of the surgery, his hand on the door latch. Her heart lurched in her chest and she ran forward.

'David!' she called.

David McNeill turned swiftly and held his arms out as the flying figure hurtled towards him. A smile of delight lit up his face as she ran into them just as she had done as an eight-year-old, but she wasn't an eight-year-old any longer, and they laughed together as he lurched against the wall with the weight of her.

'God! Young Mourne. I forgot you'd got heavier. I was half expecting the tiny slip you once were – not that you're much bigger now,' he added hastily as he swung her round.

'Stop referring to me as "young Mourne." And what are you doing here? You aren't supposed to be arriving till Wednesday.'

'I got away earlier, so don't complain. I thought by the way you hurled yourself at me that you were glad to see me.'

'I am so, and I'm sorry I sent you crashing.' Mourne wished she hadn't acted with such impetuosity. She was embarrassed at having shown such emotion. The man would think she was chasing him.

David put the key in the door. 'I'm going in to have a look around the place.'

'Sure you spent time here not so long ago – what's changed?'

David entered the waiting room. 'For a start I'd like to know what's upstairs – there doesn't seem to be any access from down here. Perhaps you could help me?'

'There's two-bedroom accommodation with a small kitchen, a bathroom, and a reasonable-sized living room.'

'Has anyone ever lived there?'

Mourne frowned. 'I don't think so! Certainly not since I've been receptionist here. Mam would know – or why don't you ask Uncle Gerry? It's his place.'

'I intend to. Meanwhile is there a way up to it?'

'Of course there is, but the entrance is down by the side of Barry Grant's shop. The side door was shut off by a plywood wall when Uncle Gerry took over the building.' She pointed to the bunch of keys. 'You have the key there.'

120

'Then let's go investigate!'

'Why do you want to investigate? There are only empty rooms. We use some of them for storage purposes.'

They had reached the side door and David, fumbling for the right key, answered vaguely. 'I don't know what I want with them at this moment, but I do hate to see space that hasn't been put to good use.'

Mourne trailed after him as he went from room to room, and she watched his face carefully as he did so. He was frowning in concentration.

'This puts a whole new angle on my plans for the future,' he said, as he passed through into the small kitchen. 'All it needs is a bit of reorganization and this building could be utilized to its full potential. Of course it depends on whether Uncle Gerry agrees to my plans.'

'Then you do intend to take over the practice?' Mourne held her breath for his reply.

'I don't know yet,' David said, cautiously. 'I have to be certain that I'll have fulfilment. I can't give up a perfectly good job with prospects to take over a country practice unless there is more to it than delivering babies and diagnosing ills – however, the signs are there.' He grinned. 'Watch your step, young Mourne. I could be your new boss, and I'm a hard taskmaster.'

Mourne's heart skipped a beat. She must be careful she didn't get hurt. David was only interested in her as an old friend. She must keep reminding herself that to love is to be hurt. To get close to him and then find it was going nowhere would be too cruel, and a situation from which she knew she would not recover easily. One rejection in a lifetime was quite enough.

'You've gone very quiet,' David remarked. 'Doesn't the prospect of working for me appeal to you?'

Giving herself a mental shake, Mourne smiled. 'So long as you're not a known slave-driver with intentions of persecution towards your lowly staff, then I suppose I can live with the idea. Now! If you're done with me, I'll be off home. I'm due to look after the children at Devotions this evening.'

'I suppose I shall have to come to heel and attend Mass and Devotions now that I'm home. I fear I've lapsed somewhat.'

'It won't do you any harm,' Mourne said, and added, 'I'll find it a source of great amusement seeing you at Mass.' Her smile broadened even more as she watched his face change at the prospect of pursuing his religion again.

121

David groaned. 'It'll be hard to buckle down again.'

'Look at the words embroidered on the altar cloth – *Will you not spend one hour with me* – and think yourself lucky you have the freedom to worship,' Mourne said as she waved goodbye.

David, watching her go, was thoughtful. She was so young and so vulnerable. She had lived in this quiet backwater all her life and he supposed the closest contact she had to wickedness was what she read in the papers. She knew little of the sordid things that could happen. The poverty that existed here was the kind of poverty that had dignity attached to it. No one was despised for having nothing; the proud boast being that one was poor but honest. There was not the incentive to steal and commit crime to pay back society for its lack of caring, as there was elsewhere. He locked the surgery door and made his way to his car. He must put his thoughts about this girl from his mind. He was beginning to care too much. She was part of his past, and she must stay that way. Rosemary was his present and his future.

'I've got to talk to you, Mourne. Can you meet me in Ballynahinch on Saturday?' Tara's voice had a hint of panic in it.

Mourne hesitated. She had intended going into Belfast to do some shopping. She needed a couple of new dresses for the summer days ahead. She was seeing a lot of John McCrory, and he was a man who liked to have a stylish girl on his arm. The clothes she had were adequate but dated.

'Is something the matter, Tara?'

'Things couldn't be worse, girl.' Tara's voice was muffled and Mourne realized, with a shock, that she was tearful. 'I really need to talk to you. You're the only one I feel I can turn to. I'm in trouble and I need your help – I can't say too much on the phone. My mother-in-law's due back any minute.'

Without further hesitation, Mourne said, 'Never mind Ballynahinch. I was going into Belfast to do some shopping; just tell me where to meet you and I'll be there.'

'Aw, that would be great! I'll wait by Queen Victoria's statue at the city hall at two o'clock – if that's all right.' The relief in Tara's voice was evident.

'That's fine. I'll be well finished by then. I'm taking the early bus so I'll have plenty of time for shopping and a spot of lunch.'

Mourne frowned as she put down the phone. What on earth could have happened to put Tara in such a panic? She entered the large kitchen and found her mother brewing tea. 'I'm meeting Tara in Belfast on Saturday.'

Kitty turned. 'Good! I like to think that you've some company when you're down there – do you want a cup of tea?'

Mourne nodded absently. She sat down and put her chin in her hands.

Kitty handed her the cup of tea and settled herself opposite. 'And how is the bold Tara? Is she setting her mother-in-law to rights?' she asked, and smiled at her little joke.

Mourne looked up. 'I don't think she'd have the nerve. By all accounts the mother-in-law is a bit of a tartar. Tara says she's a fanatical housekeeper and they all have to stick to the rules. It gets to be very wearing. Jay-Jay has been pretty well house-trained over the years, but poor old Tara isn't the tidiest of people and she falls foul of her now and again.'

'She can't be as bad as that, surely?'

'According to Tara she's the patron saint of housewives and the family have to pay due homage to every brush and tin of wax polish in the place.' Kitty laughed at the idea and Mourne gave a little smile.

Looking closely at her daughter, Kitty remarked, 'I'm glad to see a smile. You were sittin' there with a face as long as a Lurgan spade. I wondered if it was bad news.'

'No! I was just having a think about something,' said Mourne, and rose. 'I'm away to have a bath before supper. Is there enough hot water?'

Kitty looked at the clock. 'There is if you don't go mad. I'll just have time to get the heater going again before himself arrives home.'

When Mourne came down later, her mother poked her head round the scullery door. 'You're the popular one. There were two calls for you. David rang to see if you wanted to have a wander along the promenade after supper – he'll call for you if he doesn't hear otherwise – and the other fella phoned to say he'll call for you at seven.' Kitty raised an eyebrow. 'Isn't it grand to have a choice?'

'Mam! He has a name. I know you don't care much for John but he's never done you any harm, and he deserves some respect.'

Kitty shrugged. 'You're right on both counts. I'll try to do better.' She withdrew and left her daughter to seat herself. As far as she was concerned the man was a chancer, and if it wasn't for the fact that her daughter seemed to enjoy his company she wouldn't give him the time of day. But there, she had to give the girl her head. She was sensible enough to keep it, thank God!

When her mother had gone, Mourne was thoughtful. In spite of her defence of him, she hadn't been happy at John's assumption that she would be waiting for the telephone to ring and the temptation to call him and tell him so was great, but she gave a little sigh and decided she would be cutting off her nose to spite her face if she did. At least he showed her a bit of the high life; putting up with his arrogance was a small price to pay. She left a message for him to say she had already made arrangements and would contact him again.

She was ready when David arrived, and as ever she was pleased to be going out with him. There was something very relaxing about his company.

'You're all set then young . . . sorry . . . Miss O'Hara?' he grinned, and Mourne clipped him playfully round the ear.

Kitty watched them go and wished with all her heart that the pair of them would make a go of it. Sadly, David still saw the freckle-faced child and not the grown-up lady. Maybe lightning would strike and he would realize that the girl was now a woman and would be well able to match his worldliness. She gave a rueful sigh. There would be more chance of Patrick Mulligan giving up his brandy.

Although the early holiday crowds were beginning to throng the promenade there was still room for all. Later in the season there would be a veritable crush of bodies, for the delightful miles of sandy beaches brought them here in droves, but this evening they were able to stroll along in comfort. Mourne was in seventh heaven as she walked, as David had his arm draped over her shoulder and she felt cherished. He smiled at her and gave her shoulder a little squeeze and her heart did a tap-dance in her chest.

'Would the earth shatter and the sun drop from the sky if I took you for a glass of wine?' David asked later when they had reached the halfway mark towards the station end of the mile walk from the harbour. 'The walk has given me a thirst.'

Mourne stopped. 'I don't think I'd like to be seen in one of the pubs,' she said doubtfully.

'What about Brannigan's Hotel – open to non-residents – which is as discreet as you can get. Don't tell me you haven't had the odd glass of wine when you've gone out with the occasional beau?'

'That's different. We usually dine out and the wine goes with the meal. But I haven't the nerve to go into a pub yet.'

'I've seen girls in pubs. It isn't the terrible thing it used to be; however, Brannigan's it is.' David left his arm where it was as he shepherded her across the road, unaware of the man standing on the steps of the more luxuriously appointed Headland Hotel, his dark eyes shining with fury.

Later they had an ice cream, and ambled along like a pair of urchins, licking the delicious cones and holding hands.

'I hope I don't meet anyone I know. My credibility as a doctor will have gone right down the drain,' David grinned.

'Don't act like a stuck-up article. You're no better than anyone else, David McNeill. You only have a few letters after your name,' Mourne taunted, and laughed in delight as he threatened her with the now dripping ice-cream cone.

The faint sound of music was heard in the distance and they looked at each other.

'Do you fancy a seat in the stalls to listen to the band?'

Mourne gave a mock sigh. 'A real sit-down . . . a paid-for seat?' she teased. Normally, as one of the *hoi polloi* she sat around on the sand for a free listen or on the wall running along the esplanade. Only the élite paid for the privilege of listening to the music in comfort.

'I will actually treat you to the real thing. Consider this as a true reading of my regard for you, young lady.'

Quickly they hurried on and found a seat at the back where the music wouldn't be too loud, and as they sat there, Mourne had that vague feeling that she was being observed. It always made the hair on the back of her neck rise. She turned slowly, hoping to catch sight of a face that she could recognize, but as always, there wasn't one. An oddly dressed young man was sitting astride the wall; she glanced at him curiously. His gaze passed over her with complete disinterest as he turned to stare out to sea. She sighed. Yet again her imagination had run away with her reason. She shivered and David put his arm round her shoulder.

'Are you feeling cold?'

'Not now!' she smiled. Now, she felt safe.

It had not been a good day for John McCrory. Things had started going wrong when he discovered that a whole lorry-load of canned fish had overturned on the way to Belfast. According to his driver, almost the entire stock had either been crushed or at best, the canning labels had been torn or scratched when the cardboard boxes containing them had burst open. There had seemed little point in carrying on with the journey so he'd furiously told McCarthy, the driver, to bring the lot back and those cans that had survived could be relabelled. The cans that were dented would have to be sold at a knock-down price.

As if that wasn't bad enough, he had phoned the parochial house to ask Mourne to meet him and the mother had coldly informed him that she would deliver the message when her daughter arrived home, and that no doubt she would phone him back. Mourne had done just that, but it was only to tell him that she couldn't meet him as she had already made other plans. They arranged to meet on another evening but it meant he had to reorganize his diary. The annoying thing was, he still had no date for this evening. He had toyed with the idea of giving Helen a call but decided against it. She was not on the best of terms with him anyway, as she had already heard rumours about the new woman in his life. Those wretches at the club had lost no time in letting her know and her nose had been put out of joint.

He decided to skip dinner at home and dine at the Headland. He was a regular there and not only did he get good service because of it, but there was usually someone around to have a drink with. The only bit of joy he got out of it all was seeing the horrified face of Mrs Flannigan as she contemplated the prospect of all the lovely food which she had spent hours cooking being thrown out.

John didn't enjoy the meal. He hated dining out alone anyway, but dinner had not been up to the usual standards, and while he was willing to admit that the mood he was in might have had something to do with it, he nevertheless sent for the manager and made a complaint before stalking out. When he reached the entrance the sight of Mourne O'Hara, the little scut, walking along the high street in broad daylight with David McNeill's arm thrown familiarly across her shoulders and a smile on both their faces made him grind his teeth in fury. So this was the other arrangement she had spoken of! In his mind he had thought she meant she was doing something with the church.

With hands clenched in his pockets he continued to watch as they crossed the road, laughing and chatting. One day he would pay her back for this little episode, he vowed. But he must play his cards right. He was a gambler: he knew that his winning streak – there was always one – would come to him. He could wait. The bold Mourne O'Hara had retribution coming to her. He waited till they had gone from sight before making his way to his car. The whole bloody day had been a fiasco. He might as well go to bed with a bottle of whiskey and get sozzled. That way he wouldn't fall over and hurt himself.

By the time Mourne reached the statue of Queen Victoria she was breathless with running and her feet ached with all the traipsing round the shops. She need not have hurried, Tara wasn't there – she should have remembered that her friend's timekeeping was suspect. She leaned against a wall near by and waited. Taxis and buses came and went with monotonous regularity and still no sign. She began to wonder if she had got the date wrong. She was about to go when she caught sight of the perspiring, red-faced figure tearing up the steps towards her.

'Oh God. I'm sorry I'm late. The mother-in-law insisted on me helping her change the furniture round. I didn't dare refuse. She would never stop going on about "ungrateful girls who had no thought for others" for the next week. At least.' Tara sat down beside Mourne, grateful for the rest, for she was panting heavily and her explanation came out in gasps. 'Give me a minute to catch my breath.'

'I'm in no hurry. I can get the four-thirty bus so we have plenty of time. I was just worried that I might have got the wrong day.'

'Where will we go for a bite to eat and the chat?'

'You know Belfast better than I do! I was hoping you had it all planned.' Mourne rose as Tara got to her feet. 'That wasn't much of a rest!' she said.

'I only needed to catch my breath. I ran all the way from the bus stop down Donegal Street. I'm all right now.'

'Where will we go?'

Tara thought for a minute. 'We'll go to the café we went to that day you met Eamon,' she said, with inspiration. 'It was quiet there. We can find a table well away from everyone else.'

'Fine!' Mourne followed as Tara made her way on to the pavement and then strode along beside her. 'Is what you have to discuss with me as serious as you make it seem?'

'Believe me, Mourne. We are talking major mayhem, here.' Tara rolled her eyes skywards. 'I'll tell you all when we sit down to our tea – meanwhile sharpen up that acute brain of yours ready to advise me – I am at my wits' end wondering what to do.'

The waitress had finished and was on her way back to the kitchen when Tara said tightly, 'I'm pregnant!'

Mourne nearly dropped the teapot. 'Congratulations!' she said, but she looked at her friend in puzzlement. 'Is that all?'

'That's the problem!' Tara prompted.

127

'Why? You must have known that being married and – and – well, it has always been on the cards that one day it would happen.' Mourne continued to pour the liquid into her cup.

'But not now! Not at this precise time!' Tara wailed.

'Nature has a way of not asking permission, Tara. And why not now? I expect Jay-Jay is over the moon. I don't understand . . .'

Tara took a large gulp of the scalding liquid and coughed. 'Think about it!' she wailed. 'There I will be! Stuck indoors with a child with the housewife from hell. I'll not have a minute's peace. She'll be on at me all the time about the mess the baby is making and I'll be going round the twist trying to keep us out of her way. It'll be all right for the husband and the grandfather, they can swan off to work – I'll be left tryin' to fend off a nervous breakdown and not to murder herself.'

'What has Jay-Jay got to say about it?'

Tara fiddled with her hands. 'I haven't told him.'

'I think he'll want to know.' Mourne couldn't keep the sarcasm out of her voice. She didn't want to upset Tara further, but she felt that she was behaving like a real eejut.

'I think I do know that!' Tara retaliated. 'But I need a plan before I tell him. I need to know in my mind what I'm going to suggest.'

'Why not suggest that you move out of the family home now that you're expecting a baby?'

'And what will we use for money? The father-in-law's a good man but I don't think he'll hand the business over just yet and believe me, with the price of houses as they are at the moment, I think that would be the only way we could do it.'

'Drink up your tea,' said Mourne. 'We'll take a trawl round the arcade and while you're looking at the goods, I'll do some thinking.' Mourne had an idea simmering in her head but she needed to give it some more thought before she put it to Tara.

They walked around for fifteen minutes before Mourne took Tara by the arm and led her to a seat not far from their meeting-point. 'I have an idea,' she said. 'But first tell me. How far along are you?'

Tara looked at Mourne in horror. 'You aren't . . . you are not suggesting . . .?'

'Don't insult me!' Mourne cried. She realized, to her horror, that Tara had thought she was considering an abortion. 'I need to know how far along you are so that I can judge if my plan will work.'

'You've a plan?' Tara gripped Mourne's hand. 'I'm two months gone.'

'Good! The plan is a very simple one. Tell your father-in-law first!'

'I can't do that! Jay-Jay would be devastated.'

'He won't know his father heard about it first, you eejut. Your father-in-law will keep that fact to himself.'

'So! Why should I tell him before anyone else?' asked the puzzled Tara.

'Explain to him that you're pregnant and that you're telling him first because you need his advice. Then you go on to tell him you're worried about the lack of space and privacy and the overall upheaval that having a baby will cause to all concerned in such a tiny house – you did say there are only three bedrooms?'

Tara nodded.

'I take it that your father-in-law likes his creature comforts?'

'Guards them with fervour!' Tara's eyes lit up. She could guess how the plan was shaping up.

'It's my guess that if you drop a tear and crease the brow, your father-in-law will help you find some accommodation – and keep his counsel – so that he can keep his creature comforts intact.'

'You devious, brilliant article!' Tara hugged her friend. 'Say no more! I know just what I have to do. I'll let you know the outcome.' She stood up and did a jig. 'I knew I could rely on you.' She pulled Mourne to her feet. 'I'll walk you to your bus.'

Tara was so excited now, she gabbled on and on relentlessly as they walked towards the city hall again. It was a moment or two before Mourne realized what she had been saying. She stopped. 'What about John McCrory?'

'I said I saw him with a stunning blonde girl who had on a royal-blue evening gown. I wondered if you were still seeing him these days – only you haven't mentioned him lately . . .' Her voice trailed off as she saw Mourne's face.

'Where and when did you see them?'

'Jay-Jay had to do a pick-up at the Crystal Club one night and I went along just to get away from the mother-in-law for a bit. We were waiting for the regular pick-up to come out when I saw John McCrory and this girl – both in full evening dress – and he was helping her into his sports car . . . Oh God! Have I upset you?'

'Not really! I do go out with him but it's no grand passion – he's just a friend. I just wondered if I had been set aside – not that it would matter,' she added hastily.

And it *didn't* matter, she told herself later as she lay in bed.

Nevertheless, she was a wee bit annoyed that John hadn't had the good grace to tell her he was seeing someone else. She mulled over the idea that Tara might have been mistaken but discounted it, for Tara was observant and she never missed a trick. The girl, whoever she was, was definitely on close terms with John. Thank God she *didn't* have any strong feelings for him. But then! Hadn't that been the very reason she had gone out with him – because she knew that if he did abandon her for someone else she wouldn't feel bad about it? It did present a problem, though. She had made arrangements to meet him on Saturday evening and she wasn't certain, now, that he would turn up. She wondered if she should ring him, but after further thought decided she would not. He was calling for her and she would dress to kill, and if he didn't arrive then sure where was the harm – except to her ego.

She needn't have worried. John was on the doorstep at the appointed time. Mourne stepped into the car and waited for him to seat himself before saying, 'Are we still going to the pictures?'

John, busy with the gears, said carelessly, 'Of course! Unless you've changed your mind.' Secretly, he had hoped she had. He bloody loathed sitting in the darkness watching people cavorting about on an over-bright screen. The storyline meant little to him. He preferred a bit of real-life action, but he was prepared to be a martyr for the task he had set himself. His hopes were dashed.

'I'm still happy with the arrangement,' said Mourne.

John gave her a sideways look. Something was wrong. He sensed a coldness that was alien to her. 'Have I done something to displease you?' he asked.

Mourne hesitated. There was no point in precipitating a row – there might have been nothing in what Tara had seen. Better to let events overtake her. 'Heavens no!' she smiled. She sat back calmly against the seat. She was pleased with her decision. O'Rourke would have been proud of her. 'Remember, young Mourne. When you are trolling through life there will be many times when you have to make a decision that can affect your future, so think before you leap. It's sometimes wiser to wait and let things lie fallow awhile. The world won't fall apart because you have paused for thought.'

John, in an effort to bring Mourne round, took her for a meal at the Headland – she had enjoyed herself the last time they went there, for she hadn't stopped talking about it. By the end of the evening he knew that his ploy had worked. She became more relaxed and there was warmth in her voice and in her smile as she chatted to him. Only once had she shown signs of her earlier coolness. She had suddenly asked if he had been back to the Crystal Club since they had last been there.

'Twice!' he had smiled. 'And since I needed someone to accompany me, I took my cousin with me. She's been there with me before and seems to bring me luck.' He hadn't intended to mention Helen in this manner, but he'd had a shrewd suspicion that he had been seen. He had an instinct for such things; it was why he won so often at poker. He could almost read his opponent's thoughts and he could recognize a bluff from forty paces. He was certain, now, that Mourne's earlier coolness was associated with the fact that someone had seen him with Helen.

He became more certain of it as the evening progressed and her attitude changed. His explanation had obviously set her mind at rest. She began to laugh more, and once or twice she touched his arm as she related her own experiences since they had last met. This in itself was odd. Normally she didn't encourage intimacy, and he had determined that this was an area of their relationship that would eventually have to change. He had to tread carefully, though. The last thing he wanted was to scare her off.

When they were saying goodbye at the parochial house gate he leaned over it and said, 'How would you like to spend Saturday sailing round the coast? I have a boat, anchored in the marina at Bangor, which I share with a friend. We could sail down past Donaghadee . . . past the mouth of Strangford Lough and round to Dundrum Bay, then back to Bangor for a meal at the marina . . .'

'It sounds grand!' Mourne said. 'But I've already arranged to go mountain-climbing with Mr O'Rourke and David McNeill. Perhaps another time.' Her tone had been carelessly polite and John had to hide the chagrin he felt. That bloody man!

'Yes! Of course. I'll get in touch.' Irked, he bade Mourne a hasty farewell and walked to his car.

On Saturday morning, Mourne woke to the sound of birds twittering and a lorry trundling noisily down the side road past the house. She stretched and looked at her watch and as she did so, she was aware of another sound – the sound of children crying. Alarmed, she ran to the window and drew back the curtains. The Maguire twins were sitting on the wall howling their eyes out and calling her name.

Hastily climbing into her slippers, Mourne dashed downstairs. She remembered that her mam was at Holy Communion at this hour – she went every morning without fail. She unlocked the back door and pulled it open. Cassie was the first to jump down and run towards her.

She reeled back as the little figure, immediately followed by Noreen, crashed into her. Both children sobbed loudly and Mourne, steadying herself, and unable to understand what was being said, pushed both girls gently away after a brief hug.

'For God's sake! What's the matter?'

'We couldn't wake you up. We – we – we were so frightened,' Cassie hiccuped, between sobs. Noreen began to howl again. Mourne shook them both gently.

'How can I find out what's wrong if you don't calm down and tell me? Slowly and clearly, please.' She ushered the twins into the kitchen and sat them down. 'Now then! Take a deep breath, Noreen. You're the eldest; control yourself and tell me what the matter is.'

'Mam is hurt . . . she is . . . is . . . really bad . . .' Noreen hiccuped.

Mourne held her shoulders. 'Why? Did she fall? Where is she?'

'She's on the bed and . . . and . . . she's crying . . . She . . . she told us to get you . . .'

'Let's go!' Mourne grabbed the children by the hand and ran down the road towards their house. Her heart was thumping wildly and it was only as she ran through the door and caught her nightdress on the latch in her haste, that she realized she was still in her nightclothes.

She sat the twins down on the settee and said, hurriedly, 'Sit here till I come back . . . which is your mother's bedroom?'

They pointed to another door. 'In there – at the end . . . Will Mam be all right?'

Seeing the tears start to well up again, Mourne gave them a hug. 'Of course she will. I'm here now. You just sit here and be good for me.' Once through the door, she ran towards the last door at the end of the short passage. She burst in and ran towards the bed where Rena was lying. 'Holy Mother of God!' she cried out as she looked down on Rena. Rena's eyes were closed and she was clutching her belly. Beads of perspiration sat out like raindrops on her ashen cheeks. Her eyes were closed and her face was distorted by spasms of pain. Mourne touched her and Rena's eyes flew open. 'Oh thank God!' she gasped. 'I need a doctor!'

Mourne didn't waste her breath asking further questions. She ran straight to the telephone in the hall and rang Uncle Gerry. David answered.

'David! I'm at Rena Maguire's place – Holly Cottage. It's just

132

down the road from the church on the road going towards the village of Ballyfoil. Rena is lying on her bed and is clutching her stomach in agony. Please get here as soon as possible.' Without waiting for an answer she put the phone down and ran back to Rena. David might give her a right telling-off for hanging up, but there was nothing further she could tell him, and anyway, by so doing she had conveyed to him the urgency of the situation.

Rena, her face still bathed in sweat, seemed more composed. Mourne took her hand. 'David will be here very shortly. I didn't waste time talking for there was not a thing I could tell him. Are you feeling a bit better?'

Rena shook her head. 'The pain goes now and again and comes back worse than before,' she gasped.

'Exactly where is it? David will need to know and you may not be fit to explain when he comes.'

'All over!' Rena said, and rolled around in agony as another bout hit her.

'Grab hold of my hands, Rena, and dig into them as hard as you like. It will help. I think you might have appendicitis.'

'I haven't got one . . . out . . . long ago . . . Ohhhhh!'

Hurry up, please hurry . . . Mourne thought, and was glad when the spasm ended and Rena let go of her wrist. Ruefully she rubbed it and said gently, 'I'll just pop back to make sure the twins are all right. I left them sitting on the sofa clutching each other.'

Rena nodded. 'I'll be fine for a minute – anyway the pain is there whether you're here or not. See to the girls . . .' She bit on her lip as the next wave of pain convulsed her. She had to hide it. She wanted Mourne to go to the wee'uns. God love them, they were probably paralysed with fear.

When Mourne re-entered the sitting room, she found the twins curled up together as though joined. They had fallen asleep through sheer exhaustion and were making little burpy, hiccupy sounds. Mourne's eyes softened. She had been about to ask them where their da was, but she'd ask Rena when she went back to her room. Just as she was about to go back there was the sound of a car, so she went to the door instead.

David hurried towards her. 'Any idea what has happened?' He spoke over his shoulder as he went ahead of her straight to the bedroom. She shook her head and said she had no idea.

Rena was between pains, so she was able to answer David's

133

questions as he ran his hands expertly over her stomach. He watched her face as he did so and found the centre of the pain on the left of her abdomen. As he traced his hands towards the right side, Rena tensed up again. He took her pulse and turned to Mourne.

'I think we will need an ambulance. This is more than just an appendix—'

'Which she hasn't got,' Mourne interrupted.

When Mourne had gone, David sat down on the edge of the bed. 'I'm going to give you an injection for the pain and while I am preparing it I'll ask you a question. If you can't answer then just shake or nod.'

Rena nodded, and cried out as the pain hit her again.

'Have you missed any periods?'

Rena nodded.

'How many – one? Two? Three?' Rena nodded again. 'I thought as much. I think you have an ectopic pregnancy. We need to get you into hospital. Is your husband around?'

Before Rena could answer Mourne re-entered the room. 'He'll be away at the Camogie match in Lurgan – am I right?'

Rena said, sleepily, 'Yes.'

Mourne raised her eyebrows at David.

'I've given her an injection for the pain.' He closed his case. 'She's about four months' pregnant . . . and the baby's growing in the Fallopian tube.' His mouth quivered suddenly. He had just realized that Mourne was still in her nightdress. She had only thrown her cardigan over it when she had run to the house with the twins.

She blushed. 'I've worn dresses more revealing than this,' she said defiantly, but all the same she hurried over to the door and took down Rena's dressing-gown. 'Rena won't need this till she's up and about . . . She *will* be up and about soon, won't she?' Her face clouded. She wasn't sure just how serious an ectopic pregnancy was.

'So long as there are no complications. It's the resulting damage that worries me more – there's the ambulance. Can you see to the twins? And if there is any chance of getting in touch with her husband it would be a help . . .'

Mourne gasped. 'And there's Mr O'Rourke – he'll wonder where we've got to.'

'I'm not too bothered about O'Rourke,' said David. 'If I know him, he'll wait ten minutes extra and then take off. He'll know he'll get an explanation from us sometime.'

'He might think we've had an accident – it is possible.' She moved aside to let the ambulancemen carry the stretcher out. Rena was well away. The drug had taken effect and she was sleeping like a baby.

'Forget O'Rourke! Just see to the twins until the father arrives back and meantime I'll keep you up to date with what's happening at my end.' David hurried out to his car. The ambulance had already started off.

Mourne got busy. She woke the twins up and ferried them along to the parochial house where Kitty was waiting anxiously. 'What has been going on?' she asked. 'I saw the ambulance.' She held her arms out to the twins who were clinging tearfully again to Mourne's hands.

Mourne explained.

'You poor wee things. Come over here to me. Everything will be fine. When your da comes home he'll visit your mammy and then he'll tell you I'm right. Meanwhile Mourne is going to go upstairs to her room and get into some decent clothes.' Kitty eyed Mourne's nightdress. 'Have you been out in public in that outfit?'

'Mam! I had to run like the clappers. The twins were inconsolable. The last thing I had on my mind was my mode of dress. Anyway, as I explained to David, I've worn dresses that are more revealing.'

'In the name of the Holy Ghost isn't it just as well that David is a doctor. Will you get upstairs and put something on before Father Patrick comes in.' Kitty turned to the twins. 'Will we go and get some sweeties for you? I know when I was a wee girl they were better than any medicine.'

The twins, content now that their mother was being taken care of, and having been assured by everyone that she was going to be all right, thought the idea of going along to Garrity's for sweets was a grand one. They happily strode out with Kitty, who had wiped their noses – rather roughly – and blotted their tears with a tea towel. Kitty called back over her shoulder that all was ready for the lunch and Mourne was to set two more places and run through to tell Father Patrick to push on a bit or he'd be goin' without.

Mourne was determined to do no such thing. Father Patrick might take that kind of talk from her mother, but he'd give herself a right talking-to for being so cheeky. Instead she set the pots further away from the heat and took the roast out of the oven and put it on top of the range to keep warm.

Shortly after lunch, David rang to say that his diagnosis had been correct and that Rena was now on her way to the operating theatre. He asked Mourne to leave a note for Mr Maguire for the poor man would wonder what had happened to his entire family.

Mourne gasped. David was right. Not one of them had given a thought to the reaction of the man when he came home to find his house empty and his family gone.

'I'll ring back later when I have more news,' David said, adding, 'I am going into the operating theatre with Mrs Maguire.' What he didn't mention was that things were a bit dicey at his end. Rena Maguire was a very very sick woman. Things could go either way, but one thing was certain: Rena Maguire might have difficulty conceiving again. Everything depended on the state of her Fallopian tubes and how much infection there was.

CHAPTER 9

Two weeks had gone by since Rena had been admitted to hospital. She had been very ill following her operation and the knowledge that there might be complications later had brought on a deep depression. Donal, her husband, spent much of his time at the hospital. Kitty looked after the twins when they came home from school and Mourne took over when she was finished at the surgery. It was agreed that it would be better to try and keep things as normal as possible, and to that end, the twins slept at home in their own beds and Mourne stayed with them until Donal got back from the hospital each evening.

Knowing that their mother was not going to die after all brought the twins out of the listlessness that had assailed them in the first few days after Rena's admission, and a visit to the hospital to see Mam sitting up in bed looking well further helped them back to being the rapscallions they normally were.

Visiting-time, though, had to be curtailed because of their boisterous behaviour. On the last visit Mourne noticed that while the twins were there, Rena had gone so quiet she was almost uncommunicative and it was obvious that, after the initial hugs, she couldn't cope with them. 'They are so pleased to see you getting better,' Mourne said to Rena, as the twins wrangled at the bedside.

Rena looked at them and then turned dulled eyes to Mourne. Tears started to form. Mourne hastily asked a nurse if she could take the twins away for a few minutes. The twins, thrilled at the idea of a tour of the wards to meet the other patients, set off willingly, leaving Mourne and Rena alone.

Rena dabbed her eyes. 'What is the matter with me, Mourne? I love those two to death but I can't seem to bear them near me. They'll think I don't love them. I-I-I dread them coming . . . isn't that an awful thing to confess?' Rena held her handkerchief against her mouth lest the little ones heard her crying. Mourne wheeled the portable screen towards the bed to hide them from view and took her into her arms.

'Cry away! You've not yet mourned the baby you lost. You're depressed, and no one has had the wit to tell you. They probably think that if they mentioned the word depression you might wallow in it. While I sit here you can wallow all you like. What's wrong with having a good cry and hitting the depths? It's only by knowing what it's like down there that you can appreciate what you have got to sustain you in the real world.'

Relieved at Mourne's words, Rena cried her heart out. Her eyes became red with her sorrow and her face bloated with the tears she shed. Mourne sat there silently and peeked out occasionally through the screen to make certain that the nurse and the children were out of sight. She'd be killed if the nurse came back and saw what she had wreaked. Not that she cared. Like O'Rourke had once said, 'Bottling things up never served anyone well. Sure where is the point of holding it all in and not allowing yourself to search for the compensations that are there waiting.' Well! Rena had the right to scream her head off and cry her eyes out and find release for the pain inside her.

Eventually Rena stopped and drew breath easily for the first time. She looked at Mourne sitting there by the bed, with the copper hair shining in the light from the window. 'I haven't had such a good cry for a long time. It was as though my mind had died and my body lived on past its time. Now, I feel just a little bit stronger and more able to cope. Where did you find the wisdom?' she asked.

Mourne rose. 'From Mr O'Rourke! I have no great knowledge in a lot of matters, but sometimes, just sometimes when a crisis occurs, I find the answer in something he has said to me in the past as we've walked the hills with his dog.' She smiled at Rena. 'I've been through something of the sort myself, recently. It was the advice he gave to me – I merely passed it on.'

Being busy at the surgery left Mourne little time to visit Rena often. She was home now and things looked hopeful. With visits from the district nurse and some domestic help hired by Donal, she was beginning to find her way again. Mourne reflected on the past few weeks and thought how swiftly life could change. A few weeks ago she could not have imagined how rapidly Rena would have recovered, yet here she was, only a short time later, almost back to the old Rena.

Donal had got things organized so that Rena would have fewer worries when he went back to school to prepare for the return of his pupils after the summer break. Cassie and Noreen had been threatened with extinction if they didn't behave well – not that they took a blind bit of notice – and Mourne, to avert catastrophe, sometimes took them down to the beach or along to the big park where they played on the swings and picnicked. They loved this, and Mourne found her own enjoyment in theirs.

David had settled into village life with ease, and everyone pulled together to help. He was now well entrenched as the new doctor, and while Uncle Gerry was away on holiday he had taken on Maggie Cullen for extra hours so that Mourne could take the children out of Rena's hands to give her a break.

David's ideas for the surgery update were exciting. Already he had had plans drawn by Joe Phelan, a local architect, and Uncle Gerry had gone along with them, much to everyone's surprise. It was going to cost a lot of money for the refit to be accomplished and Father Patrick, when he'd heard of the plans and how much it would cost, remarked to Kitty that he reckoned Gerry Owen was secretly taking drugs which had affected his judgement.

Kitty had her own opinions. 'Nothin' of the sort. The man is as sly as a fox. Do you not see what he is about?'

'What?'

Kitty sat down at the table and faced him. 'Don't you see? The more changes David makes, and the more of Gerry's money he spends, the more responsibility he will have towards the practice. *Which means that he will feel obliged to stay on.*'

'Ach away! The boy wouldn't be taken in by that. His argument would be that Gerry could have said no at any time.' But the more he thought about it, the more Patrick felt that there was something in what Kitty said. There was no one more devious than Gerry Owen, and he should know – he had been at the butt end of ideas spawned by that tortuous brain of his on many occasions over the years. And taking into consideration the way the man had manipulated the situation to get David over in the first place, Kitty could well be right.

'I wonder what changes he is making?'

'Ah, well! I can help you there,' said Kitty. 'Mourne has been assisting David. He uses her as a sounding-board before he puts the idea forward to Gerry. He wants to open up the upstairs and turn it into accommodation, with one of the rooms to be used for the storage of equipment and supplies.'

'What purpose will that serve? He'll be living with Gerry and there is a storeroom next to the consulting room, anyway.'

'Will you whisht and listen,' Kitty reprimanded him. She settled herself comfortably. 'Apparently, David fancies the idea of living on his own if he decides to stay. If he decides otherwise, the upstairs could be let to earn its keep. He has also decided that Gerry's consulting room is far too big – he says he would need only a quarter of the space to hold a desk and a couple of chairs, with a cabinet for the odd piece of equipment.'

Patrick nodded. 'He is right there, right enough. There are families with six children living in more cramped rooms than that one – but Gerry does like a bit of space around him. I can't see him going with that idea.'

'Didn't you hear me the first time,' Kitty said impatiently. 'Gerry has no notion of staying on – so lack of space won't matter a tap to him. Anyway!' she continued, 'Mourne says that his room will be made smaller and blocked off to provide a room for minor surgery and examinations. Next door, the old storeroom will be enlarged and set up as a treatment room for the district nurse to use so that she doesn't have to trail round to do routine dressings in people's houses. He thinks it is a terrible waste of her time.'

'Where are they going to get the room to enlarge the storeroom?'

'David says the waiting room is far too big for the number of patients who use it, so he's got Joe to pinch a bit of floor space and also to make the reception area bigger, for the place is too poky and there is no room at all for half the notes and no space for Mourne to work at.'

'Did Mourne tell you all this?'

'She did!'

'So much for confidentiality,' Patrick snorted.

'She was discussing the redistribution of a few slats of wood, plaster and floor space – not the insides of someone's anatomy. Sure where was the harm. She was so excited about the changes she had to tell someone.'

'And why not meself?'

'You are never interested in what you term "small talk", Patrick Mulligan.' Kitty scoffed. 'Anyway! I've no doubt when Gerry comes back from his holiday he'll tell you all about it and the pair of you can gas till your heart's content.'

Kitty told Mourne that evening about divulging the information to

140

Father Patrick. 'He was miffed that you hadn't mentioned any of it to him.'

Mourne's eyes rolled heavenwards. 'Sure he is never interested in gossip. Anyway, I thought Uncle Gerry would have kept him informed.'

'I don't think even Gerry knows how far David is going. He'll hit the roof when he gets the estimate.'

Mourne shrugged and rose. 'I'm away off to bed.' There had been no telephone messages for her and she was disappointed. For the past few weeks her social life had suffered, as much through her own lack of interest as by Rena's illness. She had hoped that John would have contacted her. She missed the evenings she had with him. His was a lifestyle that continued to fascinate her, and she enjoyed testing herself out when she was invited out by him. She had also hoped that he might have come back to her with the idea of sailing round the coast but – nothing. Even her trips with David had come to an end. He was caught up in the excitement of all that was going on at the surgery. They had made a new arrangement to go hill-climbing with Mr O'Rourke. At least she had that to look forward to this weekend.

As she went out of the kitchen the phone rang. She ran to it. It was John McCrory. He wanted to know if she still wanted to go sailing and would this weekend by suitable. She groaned. 'I would love to, John,' she apologized. 'But I'm going climbing with Mr O'Rourke. The last arrangement fell through because my friend was carted off to hospital and I got heavily involved. It's one of the reasons why I haven't been in touch. Could we make it the following weekend?'

'We could have done but for the fact that the long-range forecast is poor. I will phone you to arrange another time.'

Mourne sighed. She could feel his annoyance down the phone like a tangible thing. She hated upsetting anyone, and he had been particularly kind to her. She made a promise to herself that she would not let him down next time, even if it meant turning David down instead. It had not escaped her notice that John had not asked her to go out one evening.

It wasn't in John McCrory's nature to respect women. They were tolerated either for their appearance or their skills. The beautiful ones he considered as appendages to his ego; the plain ones were chosen for their skills. Mourne O'Hara fitted the first category; Mrs Flannigan the second. He discounted personality. It was of little importance in the scheme of things. Indeed, the last thing he wanted was a woman with enough personality to be a threat to him.

Were he to break down his conceptions yet further, he would place Helen and the other girls he escorted in the role of courtesans. Mourne he saw in the role of chatelaine. She would be the one to grace his table; to socialize; to bear him a son. True, she was socially naïve, but the discipline of her upbringing and the natural dignity of her bearing bode well for the training he would give her once she was his wife.

In her favour, too, was her air of detachment. She would not expect undying love nor give it. John shuddered. A cloying woman would drive him insane. It might take some doing, but he would have to convince Mourne that marrying him would be a worthwhile option. Of one thing he was certain: anyone who interfered with his plans would be ruthlessly dealt with.

His thoughts were interrupted by his arrival at the club car park, and the realization that the light rain had turned nasty and was now slashing down; he had to make a dash for the entrance.

It was annoying that Helen had refused to accompany him. She had told him straight that she was no longer available since she'd heard about the new woman he was seeing. The others she didn't mind – they were escorts – but this one was for real. It really was damned annoying. Helen was his favourite. She was always well turned out and with her blonde hair and slim wand of a figure she was a very attractive woman – she was also discreet. She knew much about his secret life but would never speak of it – not after the one time early in their acquaintance when she had opened her mouth too wide and caused him embarrassment. He'd had to teach her a painful lesson.

He gave his hat and coat to the cloakroom attendant and made his way to the bar. The room was nearly empty. It was too early for the gamesters, who had to keep their wits about them, and too late for the diners who were already sipping wine at table.

The barman, Eddie, smiled at him. 'The usual, Mr McCrory?'

John nodded. 'Make it a double. It's slashing down out there.' He took the double whiskey and downed it in one go.

A stranger sitting nearby smiled. 'You looked as if you needed that!' He held out his hand. 'Mike Boswell.'

John shook the outstretched hand. 'John McCrory!' The man was blond-haired and of slight build. His hands, cupping the glass, were white and soft with well-manicured nails. John's interest heightened. 'Are you English? I haven't seen you here before.'

'Right first time! I haven't been here before. Came over to Ireland for a long weekend to drop in on a friend, met another one, and here I am.' He spread his arms.

'Where is your friend?'

Mike Boswell grinned. 'He's playing the wheel. He is doing all right. Me? I'm cleaned out. Nothing for it, old chap . . . back on the next packet that sails. No money left. I'll have to meet up with my friend next time I come over.' He ran his gaze over John. 'You not having a gamble?'

John shook his head. 'I only do the tables if I have a beautiful woman standing behind me – for reasons I can't fathom.'

'And why not? I knew a man once who wouldn't lift his cards until he had bowed three times to the table and kissed the pack.'

'Did he win?'

'He did not! I beat the socks off him. My rabbit's foot had a stronger magic.'

John laughed. He liked this man. The evening might not be the disaster it had set out to be.

'Where does this friend of yours live? The one you're not now going to visit.'

Mike Boswell's voice was slightly slurred as he answered. 'It doesn't matter now. I haven't the time nor money left. He lives, temporarily, in a place called Ballycash.'

John's nerves jumped. 'Has he lived there long?'

'Just a few weeks. The man is insane. He has a great job in England and he has practically tossed it out of the window.'

'What is his job?'

'He's a surgeon. He just recently landed a senior registrar's post at St Angela's Hospital – a job I would give my eye teeth for – and what does he do? He takes off on a six-month sabbatical to work as a country GP. Now is that not madness?'

John hid his excitement. 'You're a doctor as well?'

Mike nodded. 'Still a junior registrar,' he said, bitterly.

'Another whiskey?' John called Eddie over. 'Two more doubles, Eddie.' He turned back to his new friend. 'Why don't we sit over on the sofa? It's a damn sight more comfortable than a bar stool. My backside is getting a kink in it.'

When they were seated, John asked, 'Why did your colleague do such a daft thing? It can't have gone down well with the bosses.'

'I told you. The man is a bloody genius as a surgeon. The bosses would lick his arse to keep him if he asked them to. As to why he did it, it's to help out his ancient uncle who is dying of an unspecified illness.'

John was startled. If the friend in question was David McNeill, then someone was lying. He knew that Gerry Owen was away living it up in foreign climes.

'So! Your friend will be sorely missed. Perhaps he has no ties and doesn't give a damn about the job and the bosses?'

'The fair Rosh-Rosh-Rosemary will miss him, that's for sure. They've been together for some time.'

'You mean – they live together?' John could hardly contain himself.

Mike grinned. 'Not in public, my dear ch-chap. But who knows what they get up to in private.'

'That close, eh?'

'Closher than that,' Mike slurred. 'They are engaged to be married old shap – er – chap.'

Satisfied with what he'd heard, John rose to leave. Mike Boswell was getting pie-eyed anyway. Christ! What a scoop to have up his sleeve. He would wait for the right moment to make use of this information.

Mike Boswell was now snoring gently. John walked quietly away. On the way home in the car he made plans. He would ring his friend across the water. Willie Tate owed him a favour. Getting him to England before the police caught up with him for embezzlement had not been easy, and the promise had been made that if John needed his help at any time he was to get in touch. The time had come – Willie was going to do a bit of snooping for him. It should be easy. He only lived a couple of miles from St Angela's. It would be no trouble to find out all he could about this Rosemary. He swore. Damn! Mike Boswell hadn't mentioned her surname.

Mourne was going through what she referred to as her 'God is good and what have I got to complain about' stage. She was well versed in the philosophy. Didn't Father Patrick ram it down her throat every time she wore a frown and moaned about the direness of life in such a sleepy, backward town?

What if she *had* been left, defenceless and unwanted, all those years ago? Things were different now. The Mourne O'Hara of today had an extended family that it was hard to fault. There was Father Patrick, whose interest in her was entire, who, with her Mam, had made certain that her body was stoked with good food and warmed by their love.

There was Uncle Gerry, who had kept her sane over the years with his down-to-earth attitude when she threw a tantrum over some minor happening in her life. Uncle Gerry, who acted as a buffer against the surfeit of care she got at times from Mam and Father Patrick.

Then there was that quiet, homespun philosopher Mr O'Rourke, who showed no interest in her past and set her right about her future. Who answered her questions without delving into why they had been asked in the first place, and who had the gift of wisdom.

And the Maguire twins, with their distorted view of the mundane, who made her laugh and remember what it was like to be a child again; through whom she had met Rena, their mother, who had since joined the band that kept Mourne O'Hara straight.

Why then did the terrible feelings of rejection and insecurity keep rising like a tidal wave from the depths to make her life seem, at times, to be beige instead of coloured, making her have to count her blessings? As O'Rourke once said to her, 'Mourne! The day you have to sit down and count your blessings, there is something going wrong with your life. Fix it!'

David had remarked on her mood as they hid their cycles in the hedge before continuing the journey on foot across the four large fields up to Mr O'Rourke's stone cottage.

'I'm not being moody!' she said. 'Can I not have a quiet moment without you thinking such a thing, David McNeill?'

'No!' David stopped and regarded her quizzically. 'This is not just a quiet moment. I noticed during surgery the other day that you wore the same look, and you were not chatting to the patients as you normally do. You sat in your little wooden box of a room and stared into space when you were not actually working – I noticed it several times as I came out to call in the next patient. You looked as if you had the cares of the world on your shoulders. It wasn't like you at all.'

Mourne scowled. 'There is nothing wrong!' She added, 'You never said anything at the time.'

'Of course not – we are all entitled to our moments of introspection. But that was last week, and you are still at it. Maybe I can help.'

Mourne gave a little smile. God! He was the last person to help. He was part of it. She was frightened that she was beginning to care too much, and seeing him every day at the surgery was becoming a sweet torture. It had brought back all the fears she had tried to bury since discovering her origins. The fears that she might love someone and

145

find herself rejected again. She couldn't bear the thought. She didn't want to feel strongly about anyone lest she lost them. 'I'll be as right as rain once I get my head cleared up there on the mountain. I always feel grand after a day out with Mr O'Rourke.' She smiled and strode ahead. The subject was closed.

O'Rourke was waiting on the loose stone wall in front of the little cottage, and as they neared he rose. Tarag immediately ran towards them, his tiny paws scudding the ground. He yelped round them like a mad thing and David knelt to scuff his ears and calm him down. 'He hasn't forgotten us then?' he called to O'Rourke.

'Not a bit of it!' O'Rourke said. 'He has the same instinct and memory for people that O'Malley had – and the same enthusiasms.' O'Rourke's voice softened as he said the name of his old friend. It had taken some time for him to be able to speak of him. He would sit for great lengths of time by the rock under which the dog lay buried. It had helped him. Tarag seemed to sense the depth of his sorrow and would lie quietly, gazing up at him till he rose, and then he was like a mad thing tearing around and barking shrilly as only a terrier could do. There was something about the bark of a terrier that put the fear of God into the other animals round about, and even the foxes had stopped coming to forage. He had started with his barking now, and O'Rourke yelled for him to whisht.

They walked three abreast along the broad path up towards the lower slopes and O'Rourke remarked to David, 'I hear tell that you are wrecking the surgery in the interests of making it more practical.'

David smiled. 'You make it sound terrible. Most of the work is done during the evening until dark, with only the odd bit of hammering during the day, and there are tarpaulins up to keep the debris away from the public.'

Mourne let out a laugh. 'He makes it sound like it was nothing, Mr O'Rourke. I can tell you that John Finnigan went in to have his bunions seen to and came out with a couple of aspirins in his hand and a request for a drink of water to down them . . . and Mrs Gerachty, who is near her time, nearly gave birth there and then when a large piece of masonry crashed to the floor the other side of the said tarpaulin.'

'It's your turn to carry the knapsack, madam,' David replied with a laugh. He threw the knapsack at her and Mourne smiled brightly as she pulled it over her shoulders. A lightness had filled her mind. She began to enjoy herself as she always did when she went on these

146

walks. Up here in the clear air with the purple, sloping mountains reaching for the sky, she always felt that things were never that bad.

Later, when they had climbed right up to the small waterfall where they stopped to eat their packed lunch, she lay back against the rock and listened to the men discussing the plans David had for the practice, and she hoped with all her heart that it meant he had already made the decision to stay, in spite of the deep inner fear that she might regret the hope.

They set off again. By now, being more experienced, O'Rourke had forged on ahead and Mourne kept pace with David who was less adept at climbing. She laughed gently as he kept losing his footing on the loose scree and then was mortified as she lost her own footing, only this time she skidded down several feet, grazing her elbows and the left side of her body quite badly.

David made his way down to her and lifted her up. She felt even more shaken as he held her close for a moment. She groaned as she felt the strength of his arms, and he, thinking she was in pain, drew her closer and spoke softly to her.

'Sit down awhile. I'll catch up with O'Rourke and let him know what has happened. We'll go back . . . you need that arm seeing to.' He kissed her lightly on the cheek and she became aware that the caress had deepened as he gently stroked the long Titian hair back from her face and looked into her eyes. She tried to pull away, but for one blissful moment he stalled her and she noticed that he suddenly looked puzzled. She made another effort to release herself and this time she succeeded. She sat down on the hard ground and leaned against a rock. 'I'll be all right here,' she said, shortly, and watched his eyes change as he said, 'Don't move. I won't be long: I expect O'Rourke has already guessed something has happened as we haven't caught him up,' and then he was gone.

It was difficult riding her bike back, but she bit her lip and tried to overcome the pain that steering the bike was causing her. The last thing she wanted was for David to know how she was hurting. The only other alternative would be to sit astride his crossbar and leave her own bike hidden, and she couldn't risk the feeling she knew she would enjoy if she was riding along with his arms stretched round her. She had planned her life. She was not going to risk being hurt. Not if she could avoid it.

The smell of wet plaster was thick as they entered the empty surgery.

147

David opened the windows to let the smell out after settling Mourne in the consulting room. He stood for a moment and breathed in the warm but fresh air from outside and tried to control the feelings that were taking hold of him. He shouldn't have held her so close. There had been no need. But suddenly, seeing the lovely eyes clouded with pain he had yielded. He had no right to. It wasn't fair to Rosemary. He groaned. Christ! What was happening here? Was he falling for Mourne? To him she was *young* Mourne; it was how he had always thought of her – the few times that he had done over the years – a cheeky little red-haired, green-eyed article with a penchant for driving him mad by following him everywhere. Even when he had returned to Ballycash after all the years away, he had not thought of her as a woman. To him she had been taller and older but still the young Mourne O'Hara of his youth. Why the hell did things have to alter? Why in God's name did he have to become aware of the soft body and the sensual feel of her? He didn't suppose she even knew that she was a sensual woman now. There was still that naïvety about her that had been there as a child.

Aware that he had left her to undress, he gave himself a mental shake and went through to the consulting room where she was sitting with her sleeve rolled up. He took a deep breath. 'I'd better have a look at your side as well—'

'My side is all right! I've had a look at it,' Mourne interrupted, hastily.

'You might think so, but that was quite a cropper you came . . . Don't worry. I would need a chaperone. I'll give Kitty a ring.'

'My side is all right!' Mourne repeated firmly. 'If I have any trouble I can always let you know. At the moment it just feels very stiff and sore, but I've had a look and there are no abrasions. My clothes helped.'

David examined the arm without another word, and when he had finished he said, 'It needs to be thoroughly cleaned. The grit has embedded itself here and there quite deeply. It will have to be taken out with tweezers.' He began to prepare a tray.

Alarmed, Mourne said, 'What do you need a syringe for?' She winced as she moved and let out a tiny groan. Her arm was now smarting pretty badly and, like her side, was beginning to stiffen up.

David continued what he was doing and spoke over his shoulder. 'I need to irrigate the abrasions before and after I remove the grit, so I want you to keep quite still. It will smart like hell but you must be still as I don't want to push the large pieces further in. Once I've got rid of the surface grit I'll give you an injection of penicillin to prevent any infection.'

'Do I really need an injection?' Mourne groaned. 'I hate injections.'

'Look here, young Mourne! Just be thankful that penicillin was discovered. This helped to save a lot of lives during the war. God knows what was in the scree. We have to be certain your arm is safe.'

Mourne winced as the first syringeful of sterile water trickled over her arm, and to cover up she said crossly, 'I wish you would stop referring to me as young Mourne. Sure I'll be twenty-one years old in a few weeks' time. I think you owe me a bit of respect, David McNeill.'

David laughed. 'You will never change. That quiet demeanour you show to the world hides a fierce temper. Am I the only one to have fathomed that out?' He was glad the moment had lightened. His heart was sore that he had to inflict pain on her, but it was necessary.

'No, you are not! I don't hide my feelings.' Mourne winced again when David took out the larger pieces of grit. She managed to stop herself from crying out but she was glad when the bandage was on and it was all over.

When Kitty saw Mourne come in with her arm bandaged she hurried to her. 'What has happened to you, child?'

'I slipped on the scree – and will you not refer to me as "child"?' said Mourne, crossly. 'I've had enough of that from David.'

'To us you are a child. Even though you're all grown-up you are still my bairn.'

'David McNeill's only ten years older than me. Why does everyone treat him as though he was my uncle?'

Kitty had to admit that Mourne had her there. 'I suppose he seems older because he has been away and seen the world, he is a doctor, and he has that air about him that says "experience" – but I do understand why you feel annoyed.' Kitty put her arms round her daughter. 'You haven't said . . . Are you all right?'

'I am fine, I told you. I slipped on some scree – that's all. David took me into the surgery and fixed me up. He gave me an injection of penicillin too, the horrible man.'

'You should thank him, you ungracious article,' Kitty admonished. 'It's as well you were climbing with a doctor and not someone from another persuasion – and where was O'Rourke when you were careering down the mountain on your backside, might I ask?'

'He had gone on. I stayed behind with David, who is to mountain climbing what I would be to surgery. The man is completely out of condition.' Mourne laughed. She didn't mention that she had climbed the mountain before with David.

Mourne had been in two minds whether to ring John McCrory and tell him she couldn't see him that day. Her arm and side, although much better, were still giving her some discomfort. It was Saturday, though, and the thought of staying home and listening to the radio while Father Patrick snored away in the den following a heavy lunch, and her mother and her clique of friends sewed their interminable dresses and knitted yet another hundred or so matinée jackets for the black babies in Africa, was not to be borne.

It was now a week since she had injured herself and the healing was almost done; it was the muscles that were giving her the problem. She hadn't realized it at the time but she had twisted herself trying to grab hold of some bracken. Another burst of laughter from the group made up her mind for her. She put the phone down and tore upstairs to get ready. She'd take a couple of aspirins with her and down them if she felt uncomfortable.

John arrived on time. They had made no plans, so as she closed the door behind her Mourne turned to him. 'What are we doing today?'

John hadn't made any decisions about what they were going to do, but he was always one for a quick turnabout and he looked down at his lovely companion and said: 'How would you like to go along to Strangford Lough and take a boat out? Later we could drive over to Bangor and I'll show you round the marina.'

'Are we still going to go out in your boat sometime?'

John nodded. 'My partner and I take it in turns – and my time starts next month. I doubt if the boat will be there today: if I know Sean, he'll be off round the coast for a run on a day like this.'

'Do you ever sail together?'

'Rarely! We have our own sets of friends and he lives in Donaghadee which is not so far from Bangor, so he tends to use the boat more than I do. However sometimes we throw a combined party on board for all our friends.'

Mourne settled further into her seat. Her side was throbbing a bit, but it was bearable; she manoeuvred into a more comfortable position and felt better. She hadn't mentioned that she had injured herself, and John hadn't noticed that she had a plaster on her arm.

Once on the boat, with the slight breeze cooling her skin, Mourne was able to forget the arm as she leaned over the side and watched the wake. She became almost mesmerized. The water was so clear she could see the marine life; fish were darting and flashing about and when John nudged her arm she looked up and saw that he was pointing to where some seals were basking in the sun. It was a wonderful trip.

Afterwards, they drove to Bangor and dined that evening at a small exclusive restaurant. His own boat was not in the marina, as John had anticipated, but it didn't matter. Mourne would see it another day when they went out in it. For the moment she was enjoying wonderful food just as she had enjoyed the equally wonderful trip along the lough. It had to be said, John McCrory knew how to entertain. There were times when she squirmed a little when he treated the staff with disregard for their feelings, and at those times she had the urge to remonstrate with him but she refrained; it was his only fault and she was a coward. With her, he was generous and kind.

Of late she had found it easier to converse with John. Now that she had been going out with him for a while she had lost her initial shyness. He didn't make her laugh, not the way David did, but then she had known David since she was a child, so they had more common experiences to recall and laugh about. With David she was at ease and her natural humour freely exerted itself. John McCrory was of a more restrained nature. His preferences, such as gambling and sailing, gave them little common ground to come together over, but she admired him for his sophistication and his ability to make her feel at ease in situations where, half the time, she didn't know what she was supposed to be doing.

Such as now! The waiter had brought them a tiny bowl with a piece of lemon floating in it. She looked at it and then at John, in amazement. He laughed.

'It's to wash your fingers in before the dessert course. It will remove the smell of fish from your hands.'

She knew she was behaving like a culshie, but she had to say it. 'I didn't have fish and if I had done, I would have used my knife and fork.'

'I had fish, though,' said John. 'It's how things are done.'

'I'll say this, John. I'm learning a lot about social etiquette from you,' Mourne laughed.

'And I will say this for you, Mourne O'Hara. You have no side and you aren't afraid to admit if you don't know what to do in a particular situation.'

'Mr O'Rourke says that if you don't know about something then you won't learn if you are too proud to ask.'

'And how is Mr O'Rourke?' John couldn't give a tinker's curse how the old man was, but Mourne was fond of him and it was going to do him no harm to inquire and sound as if he did care – no harm at all.

'He's very well. David and I went climbing to the higher Mournes with him last weekend. And by the way, the little dog you gave him has been a godsend. He has a lovely nature and Mr O'Rourke is dying about him. It was wonderful of you to think of giving him the dog so soon after O'Malley died. The rest of us would never have dared. It seemed too soon – but the trick worked. Mr O'Rourke was so busy trying to feed and care for Tarag he had less time to mope over O'Malley.'

John smiled. 'I'm glad I was of help.' Like hell he was. He had been the most surprised man in Ireland when he discovered that O'Rourke, instead of feeling devastated by the arrival of the dog, had thanked him. He had done it out of malice to pay the old bugger back for his attitude when they had their run-in up on the hills. Still! Some good had come out of it. Mourne O'Hara thought he was the Son of God for a while anyway.

'Has your man, David, made up his mind if he will stay or not?'

Mourne frowned slightly. 'He says he has not! Even though he's in the process of altering the surgery. He says nothin' will be lost if he does decide it's not for him, for the place was a wreck and would be all the better for a makeover.'

'And who is paying? It's all very well to take that line when it isn't his money going into it. His uncle is having to fork out, I suppose.'

Mourne's frown deepened. 'I – I don't know. I never thought . . . I suppose . . . I – I don't know,' she said finally. The waiter came at that moment to lead them to the lounge for coffee. Mourne was thoughtful. Surely Uncle Gerry would have come to some arrangement with David. She couldn't imagine that David would have taken advantage of the old man. He wouldn't! How could such an idea enter her head? She glanced at John as they sat down in the comfortable armchairs. He was looking at her oddly.

'There is another aspect to all this,' he said softly as he watched her face for her reaction. 'Will his fiancée be happy with the arrangement. Surely she should have a say in where she lives.'

Mourne's heart stopped. 'His – his fiancée? He hasn't got a fiancée. What on earth gave you that idea, for goodness' sake?'

Mike Boswell had given him the idea – and Willie Tate had confirmed it. The fair Rosemary was an important member of David McNeill's surgical team – or was, before he had been promoted to gynaecology registrar and she had elected to stay in general surgery. Oh! He had done a good job, had Willie. He had discovered that Rosemary and David had been engaged for quite some time and at one time had almost set a date for the wedding. When John had heard the news he had drunk half a bottle of whiskey to celebrate and cheerfully suffered the effects for two whole days afterwards.

'I'm sorry! I hadn't realized . . . you didn't know?' John fixed a suitable expression on his face and reached over to touch her hand. His expression didn't alter as Mourne, her face white with shock, retracted hers. She would pay for that, he thought. Particularly as he now knew which way the wind blew with her affections.

The evening was ruined for Mourne. She tried, after the initial shock and reaction had worn off, to make amends. It wasn't John's fault. He had just been concerned about the effect David's decision would have on his fiancée – what did he call her? – Rosaleen or Rosemary? She felt angry that David hadn't mentioned he had a fiancée.

John rose and held out his hand. 'I think I've given you a shock. I'll take you home. I expect David will have an explanation. In fact I'm sure of it. David McNeill is not a man to do anything underhand.'

Mourne, by now beginning to recover, smiled weakly. 'Of course! I'm sure you're right. I've known David a long, long time. It wouldn't be in his nature to deceive us all.' But Mourne's heart was heavy as she prepared for bed that night. What was even worse than learning about David's fiancée was the knowledge that she had no idea how she was going to cope with the situation. Should she mention that she knew or not? She was certain of one thing. She was fervently thankful that she hadn't let him see how she was beginning to care. Tears pushed beneath her eyelids. She had been right to try and stop herself loving David. Hadn't she feared, deep down in her heart, that she would suffer a rejection again? And she had been right. She must never, never love anyone. Not to love was the safest way.

Next day, after lunch, she made her way along the coast road to Annalong. She had a great need to go up to the rock where, over the past months, she had found solace; it was where she was closest to her origins. At last she had gradually begun to feel a deep sense of belonging when she sat with her back against the rock and let the stillness surrounding her enter her soul. Kitty O'Hara had made her life happy and comfortable – she loved her to death – but something kept drawing her towards the place where she had been found. Her roots were here. She desperately needed to think so.

Learning of David's perfidy had knocked her confidence. She wouldn't easily forgive him for it. She had trusted him. Just lately they had become so close. Up there on the mountain she had thought she had seen something in his eyes that made her heart jump. She had hoped she could rid herself of the fear that she would be hurt if she got too close to anyone – she desperately wanted to be free of it – but once again she had been proved right. How stupid she had been. She should know better than to let her guard slip. She would have to be more careful.

CHAPTER 10

Gerry Owen was home again. His holiday had done him the world of good. He hadn't had a holiday like it in many a year, and he was grateful to his nephew for suggesting it. He left his suitcases where they were in the hall and entered the living room where Mrs Haggerty had set a tray with a pot of tea and a warm, buttered soda farl. He could see the salt gleaming on the country butter from here. God! How he had missed the good Irish cooking. All that gourmet stuff was all right for a while, but his stomach was now refined to death. He was sure he had lost weight. The delicate nature of the food and the small portions had forced him on occasion to resort to eating in a café halfway through the day.

Hardly had he got the first mouthful down him when there was the sound of a car and a figure hurtled through the door. 'Have you enough tea in that pot for an extra cup?' David begged. 'I'm dying of thirst. It's hot out there.'

Gerry poured some tea into the cup David held in his hand. 'Have you given up work for the day, or are all your patients miraculously cured?' he asked.

'I've done my rounds and I'm going along to the surgery in a minute to write the notes up and make a few calls, but I met Mrs Haggerty and she told me you had hit home so I thought I'd drop in to welcome you.'

'And take the last drop of tea in the pot,' Gerry grinned. 'It's good to be back and to see you again. Sit down and tell me how things are going with the rebuilding. I hope the bloody racket is finished. I can't be coping with noise when I'm working. I am not a young man.'

'The worst is over,' David assured his uncle, adding, 'You're looking great. That holiday has done you the world of good. There's new life in you.'

'Have you made up your mind to stay?' Gerry asked, ignoring the compliments. 'I would hate to think I had spent all that money for nothing.'

'It won't be for nothing. The place was ready for a refit. I don't know why it wasn't done years ago. You would have been better served.' David's face sobered as he added, 'I'm still not sure.'

'But you like it here! You told me so before you shoved me off to the Continent—'

'I did not shove you . . .'

'You did! But it was a good idea all the same . . . but you told me you were enjoying working here, and I was hoping that meant you had serious intentions of staying.'

'I still have serious intentions of staying.' David put the empty cup down and leaned his elbows on his knees, his brow puckered in concentration. 'There are a few problems that I have to resolve before I finally make up my mind. You must understand that this is a major step I'm taking. I have a good career going and I have to be sure I'm not taking off down the wrong road. I'll know more when I get a reply from Downpatrick.'

'That reminds me. There's a letter for you on the hall table. I found it among the pile that was for me,' Gerry said, and waited while David fetched it.

'It's postmarked Downpatrick,' David said.

'Well! Open it then.'

David scanned the page quickly and then looked up. 'Well! This does go a long way to help,' he said. 'They have offered me a post – two days a week – to do general surgery.'

Gerry regarded his nephew curiously. 'How did you swing that?'

'When Rena Maguire went in for her op for her ectopic pregnancy I accompanied her. I was allowed to go into theatre and I got chatting to the consultant who did the op – John Keeley – and I told him I was considering taking over your practice but that I didn't want to lose my surgical skills. He mentioned that they were hard-pressed for extra hands and he wondered if I was interested in general surgery. I explained that it was my chosen field, and he said he would have a word with the superintendent. The letter says it all,' David said, exultantly.

There was a companionable silence, then Gerry spoke. 'Have you mentioned to Mourne that you're an engaged man?'

David didn't look up. He had intended to, but somehow the moment had never been right. He had left it too long to announce suddenly, 'By the way! I just forgot to mention that I am engaged to a girl called Rosemary.' He could just imagine the shock on Mourne's face. He groaned inwardly. It was going to be difficult. He wished he had taken his uncle's advice in the first place.

'It isn't fair that she doesn't know the score,' Gerry said quietly.

'You're right! She will have to be told – they all will.' David rose. 'Meanwhile I have work to do. Are you intending to take a trip to the surgery to run an eye over the work?'

'Tomorrow will do well enough, I'm tired now. I need a bit of sleep. I've got used to the idea when I was away – and it will have to be the first habit to go – but I need it now.'

'I'll take the cases up to your bedroom before I go. I'll see you this evening.'

When David got back to the surgery, Mourne was just closing the reception area. 'I'm just popping over to Cullen's for a minute,' she explained. 'Mr O'Rourke is over there playing cards with the rest of his friends and he was asking if I was all right. I'd like to let him know that I am.' Mourne avoided David's eyes.

'When you come back, could you come along into the consulting room? I want to talk to you.'

'Certainly!' Her voice was cool. David stopped halfway to the door of his room. Mourne hadn't been her usual self all morning.

'*Are* you all right?'

'Yes!' Mourne walked out. She wasn't going to let him know that she wasn't. She was determined to keep control of her emotions.

She saw Mr O'Rourke as soon as she opened the door. Tarag came rushing to meet her. She laughed. 'I should tell the hygiene people about you allowing this dog in here, Mr Cullen.' She ruffled Tarag's ears.

Jack Cullen leaned on the counter. 'Would a nice piece of cheese help you to keep it quiet?'

'No it wouldn't. I will not have you accuse me of accepting a bribe.'

O'Rourke called to her. 'I can see you've got over your fall, girl.'

'I only have a small area left unhealed.' She walked over to the group. 'Are you winning?'

'I am not! It's good to see you fit again. I hope it won't stop us going for a climb another day?'

'It won't!' Mourne looked at the others. 'You should all go climbing

157

with Mr O'Rourke. It would do you all a power of good.'

'I'd rather be crucified,' John Fallon said, turning his eyes to heaven. Everyone laughed.

When she returned to the surgery, Mourne took a deep breath, knocked on the consulting-room door and entered. David, busy writing, didn't look up as he said, 'I won't be a minute; take a seat.'

She watched him as he worked and felt a tightness in her chest as she studied him. A lock of hair was shielding his face from her. Uncle Gerry was always on at David to get his hair cut – he said he looked like a gypsy – but Mourne loved his hair. He had this habit of bending his head forward and sweeping his hair back with his hand. Of course it flopped forward again, and he would occasionally repeat the action. She was still studying him when he looked up and slammed the notes to the side of his desk. She reddened at the thought that he might have caught her watching him. To cover her embarrassment, she said quickly: 'Did you want to see me for anything important?'

David looked at her thoughtfully as he fiddled with his pen. He turned away briefly and then brought his gaze back. Suddenly she knew what he was going to tell her. His whole attitude was one of discomfort. She felt no pity for him.

'I don't quite know how to say this—'

'Are you tryin' to tell me I'm going to be sacked?' She was baiting him.

David frowned. 'You're being facetious, Mourne.'

'I was trying to lighten the moment. You look so dire.'

David took a deep breath. There was no easy way to tell her and maybe doing it here in a clinical atmosphere was not the best idea, but taking her out for a meal and then shooting her down with his announcement would be worse. He didn't know why he was worried about telling her; it wasn't as though anything had happened between them. He had managed with some success to control the errant thoughts she stirred in him and he didn't think she suspected how she affected him. His guilt lay in the fact that he had not been open with her in the first place, and he now realized that he had been wrong to keep silent.

'Mourne, I've never mentioned to anyone that I am engaged to a girl in England. Uncle Gerry said last night that I should have done.' God! It sounded so curt and sudden. He felt like a schoolboy defending a misdemeanour. He fiddled with his pen and didn't look up till she said coolly:

'I know!' Her tone was sharper than she'd intended. 'What made

158

you and Uncle Gerry feel you should mention it now?'

'We were discussing my future . . . How did you know? How *could* you know?'

'John McCrory told me he met a friend of yours at his club who mentioned it.'

David didn't know which annoyed him most. The fact that McCrory had told her, or the fact that she didn't seem to mind.

'It didn't take him long to acquaint you with the facts,' he said coldly.

Mourne rose. 'John wasn't being vindictive. He mentioned it during dinner one evening. He assumed that I already knew. It would have been nice if I could have said that I did.' She looked into David's eyes and saw hesitation and doubt. 'Why did you not mention it, David? We've been friends for years. Hearing it from someone else was hurtful.' As he listened to her he was acutely aware that the flashing green eyes were having an effect on him.

'I'm sorry! I never thought . . . London and my life there seemed light-years away as the days passed. Anyway! You and I were getting to know each other again and somehow telling you would have been an intrusion into our new-found friendship.'

Mourne turned to go. 'It wouldn't have made any difference to our friendship, David. We go back a long way. I think you could have told me, but now that I know we can put it behind us and carry on as before.' She kept her voice carefully in check.

When she returned to the reception area, she let the blackness roll over her. How could she stand in there and say it didn't matter when her heart was scalded? She wanted to scream out that it did matter to her, but that she had to work with him and she didn't want to lose his friendship. At least she still had that.

David wasn't faring any better. He stared moodily at the door for a long time after she had gone. He saw how much he had hurt her and would have given anything to be able to stop it. He wondered who this friend of his was who had told John McCrory. He rose, grabbed his case and made his way to the reception area. Mourne was sitting with her head bent over some cards that she was sorting. He put the case on the counter and leaned against the wall. She didn't look up.

'You're angry with me. You say you're not, but the very set of your shoulders tells me so.'

'Of course I'm not angry with you.' Mourne didn't look up from her task as she spoke. She was determined to hold on to her dignity.

'But I'm sorry that you didn't feel you could tell me about such an important matter – and I feel sad at the lack of trust between us. I would rather have heard such an important piece of news from you than from John McCrory.'

'Are we still friends?'

'Don't be silly, David. Why should we not be?'

'Then will you let me take you out for a meal this evening?'

'That sounds perilously like a sop rather than a genuine desire to be in my company.'

'Now you are being silly! Since when have I not enjoyed being with you?' There was a trace of anger in his voice. 'You tell me one moment that my disclosure won't make a button of difference to our friendship, then you turn a perfectly reasonable request into something underhand.' He paused. 'Who was this friend of mine who spoke to McCrory?'

Mourne sighed. 'I have no idea – and I'm sorry! You're right. I was wrong to say what I did. The fact is, I have already arranged to go out this evening.'

'With John McCrory, I suppose. You see a lot of that fella.'

Mourne's lips tightened. 'Yes! I suppose I do. I enjoy his company, but as a matter of fact I am meeting someone else.' She had no intention of enlarging on her statement. Why should he know that she was only popping down to see Rena? Let him think what he liked.

David took his case from the counter and walked away. He turned at the door and grinned suddenly. 'Our first row,' he said, and disappeared from view.

Patrick Mulligan and Kitty O'Hara sat facing each other across the kitchen table. It was one of those rare evenings when he decided to join her. The day had been hot and his study was like an oven because the windows had been closed all day to keep out the smell of animal dung and fish. It had been market day, and even now in the early evening the smell lingered. Here in the large kitchen they were able to keep the door open that looked out on to the graveyard. The smell of the flowers on the well-tended graves did much to keep the pong away from the area behind the house. He leaned back in his chair with a sigh of contentment as he watched Kitty doing her sewing. Her fingers were never still, he thought. If she wasn't cooking or cleaning, she was knitting or sewing. The woman had no life of her own, but she was a satisfied woman for all that.

160

'Do you never wish you could drop all this and go off somewhere –
on a world cruise, maybe?'

Kitty looked up in surprise. 'Are you offering?'

'Indeed I am not! Sure where would I get the money. My stipend
wouldn't take us further than the Magillicuddy Reeks in Kerry.'

'Why did you mention the Magillicuddy Reeks? Have you a secret
yen to visit them?'

'No! I just like the way the name curls round the tongue,' he
grinned. 'Are you as happy with your life as you appear, Kitty? Have
you really no wish to travel and see a bit more of the world?'

'On the money I earn? Are you mad, or what?'

'If you had the money!'

Kitty thought for a moment before laying down her sewing. 'Years
ago when my Charlie was alive we thought about going over the water
to see London. Charlie had this thing about the history of the place. He
was dyin' to see the Tower of London and the Houses of Parliament
and walk along the banks of the Thames. He wanted so much to see
Westminster Abbey and the Cathedral . . .' She stopped as the memories
washed over her. Patrick took off his glasses and set them on the table
with his newspaper.

'Why didn't you go? I'd have helped with the money,' he said
softly.

Kitty brought her mind back. 'It wasn't the money – we had that at
the time – but we wanted a baby more. We were always afraid to
break into our savings in case I got pregnant. Sadly I never did, and
there are times when I wish that Charlie could have had his dream trip.
But there, it's no use having regrets. Anyway! To answer your question.
I have never had any desire to leave here since Charlie died. I have all
I want since we got our wish and little Catherine Mourne O'Hara
arrived.'

'Speaking of Mourne! Are we doing anything for her twenty-first
birthday? I think we should mark the occasion.'

'I think we should,' Kitty agreed, 'but I'm not sure she would want
a party.'

'For why?'

'I know my daughter. She doesn't like a fuss. I think she would
probably prefer a family dinner at a good hotel.' Kitty looked thoughtful.
'Even that might prove a bit embarrassing . . . she might want to invite
that fella McCrory. I don't think that would go down well with
David.'

'Why should he care? He's just a family friend.'

'Maybe he would like to be more,' said Kitty mysteriously, and rose. 'I think the best thing to do is to leave it to Mourne. It will be her big day, after all.'

She was busy preparing the evening meal when Mourne walked in. She waited till her daughter had given her a hug. 'Father Patrick and I were just discussing what to do about your twenty-first birthday.'

Mourne blanched. 'Oh, Mam! Let's not have a fuss. Let's just have a dinner here with Uncle Gerry and David. I couldn't face all the planning and the decisions as to who came and who didn't—'

'Whisht with your gabbling. That's just what I told Father Patrick. I had a feeling you wouldn't want a big do. How about us all going out for dinner at a hotel? I'd like to enjoy the day as well, you know. I don't want to arrive at the table beetroot red with effort and no strength left to enjoy the occasion.'

'That would be great!' Mourne hugged her. 'By the way, speaking of meals. You do remember I have next week off and I'm going to stay with Tara for a few days in her new house?'

'I hadn't forgotten, but you were right to remind me. The amount of food you put into you would have been money wasted if I'd stocked up.' Kitty laughed. 'I'll be able to buy a new hat for the occasion with the money saved. How does Tara like living in Carryduff?'

'She's only been there three weeks. I don't suppose she knows herself. But the fact that she is now living this side of Belfast and can get a bus at the bottom of the road if she wants to take a trip up to see her mam, is a bonus in itself. Jay-Jay's family live on the other side of the city.' Mourne didn't mention Tara's state of euphoria when she had told her gleefully over the phone that the father-in-law had come up trumps as Mourne had said he might, and had deliberately set them up at the other side of the city so that they could have a life to themselves.

Mourne had been conducted round the house and shown every stick of furniture and every ornament. She had been asked for advice as to whether or not Tara should put primrose-yellow curtains in the back bedroom or blue ones, and should she have single beds or double? She was rattling on like a maniac.

Mourne put her hands to her ears and laughed. 'I don't mind which, I just want a cup of tea. I am dying of thirst Tara Garrity, and if you don't give me a drink soon I shall hop on the next bus back.'

Tara continued to burble on as she wet the tea and Mourne smiled and listened.

'Isn't it great that I'm only forty minutes away from Mam's place? I can't tell you how grateful I am for your advice.' Tara hastily bit into a biscuit before continuing. 'Mourne, I was so scared when I told Jay-Jay's da that I was pregnant and that I was worried about the chaos it might cause at his house . . . but he straight away said that I was to have my own place and as far away from interference as possible.'

'He knew about your problem with the mother-in-law?'

'He did! He said that she meant well and that her compulsive cleaning was an illness in itself, and he didn't think she would mind that we would have to move out because she was gettin' on a bit, and having a baby around would be a bit much.'

'He didn't think it odd that he was the first to hear the news?'

Tara put the tray on the table. 'He was so wonderful – I think he was flattered. He said that he would make it our secret. As soon as Jay-Jay announced the news he would then offer us a house.'

'How long before the baby's born? You're not very big. If I didn't know what a slim kitter you were before you got married I'd never suspect you had a baby in there,' Mourne laughed.

'I'm nearly four months gone – I'm due in December. Mam says I was the size of a baby rabbit when I was born, so it would appear that small babies run in our family. She says she was dancing on the table at Sean Rafferty's wedding when she was already six months on – which is probably why I like dancing so much,' Tara grinned.

'Are we going out today?' Mourne asked. 'It's just that I'm only here for three days so I wouldn't mind a walk round the shops.'

Tara looked at the clock. 'We can catch the three-thirty bus. We'll have tea in our usual café and then we can take a waltz round the arcades. We had better get the dishes washed – it's three o'clock now!'

'Can't we leave the dishes? Sure Jay-Jay will be home before us. He could do them.'

Tara roared with laughter. 'What Irishmen do you know that I don't?' she gasped. 'I don't know an Irishman who would set foot in the kitchen except to get himself a drink of water. Your man Jay-Jay wouldn't tie his own bootlaces if I let him get away with it. He's a darlin' man but he has the same view as all his friends. The woman's place is in the home – the man's in the workplace.'

'That was once, but this is nineteen fifty-two. Things have changed since the war. Roles have altered.'

'Somebody forgot to tell my Jay-Jay,' Tara said fondly. 'But I'd not have it any different. He is there for the big things and I don't mind being a housewife.'

They had reached the bus stop before Mourne brought the conversation back to the principle she held that a man should take his share of responsibility in the home.

'But Jay-Jay does, he'll put up shelves and help me with curtain-hanging – and he's a dab hand at gettin' in the coal. But he draws the line at things like washing-up or cooking. Jay-Jay says that a woman has her part to play by keeping the home fresh and clean and everything running smoothly, and the man goes out to earn the crust.'

'Why doesn't his attitude surprise me when I remember what you've told me about his mother and the way she spoils the men of the family?' Mourne remarked.

Tara's little face puckered. 'I like things the way they are,' she said firmly.

They rose to get off the bus as they reached the city hall and she hurried down the steps to the pavement. Mourne followed and ran to catch her up. 'Tara! I'm sorry. I really didn't mean to sound critical. Really I didn't!'

Tara stopped. 'And I'm behavin' like a sulky eejut. I know you didn't mean it personally. Jay-Jay is a good man. He helps me a lot, but like most Irishmen he guards his maleness.' She took Mourne's arm and grinned. 'You'll marry a man with plenty of money, so you won't have a problem. You'll have a servant to do it for you.'

Mourne laughed. 'I don't think so,' she said. 'But I tell you this, Tara. I will try to make whoever I marry pull his weight. I've been reading a lot just lately about the changing role of women. The war has brought liberation to the kitchen, and I'll be fighting my corner.' Their little spat forgotten, they entered the café and sat down, once more in accord with one another.

The waiter was at their table in a trice. 'What'll you have ladies – same as last time?'

The two girls looked at each other. 'Do you remember us, then?'

''Course I do. Sure I wouldn't forget two fine lookin' girls like yourselves.' He particularly hadn't forgotten the redhead with those eyes – green as the water in the lakes of Killarney. He had remembered that, for the last time he had set eyes on her he had just come back from Killarney where he had been amazed at the colour of the lakes, which he had expected to be blue. One of the guides said it was a trick of the light on that particular day, but the image had stuck and then he had met the green-eyed goddess that very same week. He gazed at her now. She was just as cool as the lakes too. He turned to her friend and raised his eyebrows.

'The same as before it is,' Tara said with a giggle.

'I don't remember what we had before,' Mourne laughed.

'Nor do I,' Tara said. 'I'm dyin' to see what it was.' They both dissolved into giggles again.

The rest of the holiday was of the same quality. They laughed and giggled and went shopping for a new dress for Mourne, who said she had an important dinner coming up and she wanted to look chic.

Tara didn't inquire who she was going with. She suspected it might have something to do with John McCrory. It was he who Tara had been hinting about when she spoke of Mourne having servants. She didn't care much for the man. Her uncle had worked for his father at the canning factory for seventeen years, and had been sacked within a week of the old man's death because he had dared to ask for more pay on behalf of his mates. It wasn't the sacking that had rankled so much, it was the unfairness of it. Her uncle had tried to explain that he was only acting as spokesman for the others, but John McCrory had turned on his heels and walked away after telling the other men the same thing would happen to them if they tried the trick again. John McCrory was the most hated employer in the area but jobs were hard to come by with all the men coming back from the war, so they had to bite their tongues and buckle under.

The girls went to the pictures to see Gene Kelly's latest film *Singin' in the Rain* and hummed the tune all the way home. Next day they took the bus to the other side of the city and visited the grounds at Stormont again and had lunch at *their* café, but their waiter with the smiling eyes was off that day and they got a sour-faced elderly woman who barked at them and ostentatiously removed the ashtray from the table when she heard Mourne ask Tara to put it elsewhere.

On the last day, to Mourne's surprise, Jay-Jay offered to take them to Donaghadee in one of the cars. They ate shellfish from a paper bag as they strolled along the shoreline and watched the white-sailed yachts and the small cruisers making their way along the coast.

'John McCrory is takin' me sailing sometime,' Mourne remarked, and was surprised by Jay-Jay's reaction.

'Are you goin' strong with that man?' he asked.

Mourne thought she must be imagining the disapproval in his voice. Why would Jay-Jay disapprove? He didn't know John. 'I don't know about going strong, but yes! I do go out with him.'

There was silence for a time, and Tara wriggled. Mourne had taken note of her discomfiture. At last Jay-Jay said, 'Do you know that he gambles?'

'Is it a sin?' asked Mourne with slight irritation.

'No! It is not. But John McCrory is big-time. He belongs to the Crystal Club and you only become a member there if you're in the money or you belong to one of the big syndicates. An awful lot of wheeler dealing goes on there.'

'That doesn't mean that John is one. I've been there with him. He seemed to be highly respected and the waiters were falling over him – a sure sign that he is a man of importance.'

Jay-Jay sat down on the harbour wall beside Mourne. 'Mourne! You need to be almost a millionaire to be able to keep your membership there. Most of the punters are once-in-a-while types, but if you say that everyone was all over him then it sounds as if he is a member. Now I ask you. Where is the money coming from? The canning factory has been doing all right but I've heard rumours that it has been in trouble lately.'

'I don't know where he gets the money – his father has probably left him some. But it has nothing to do with us. He also has a share in a boat which he keeps in the Bangor marina – he must have money to afford that,' Mourne said crisply, adding, 'I've never found John McCrory to be anything but a gentleman.'

'I'm sorry! Sure what do I know. I've never met the man and am only going on rumours,' Jay-Jay said contritely, and jumped down off the wall.

'Come on! Forget John McCrory,' said Tara quickly. 'Mourne is having a bit of a whirl with him. Nothing serious, isn't that it Mourne?'

'That's about it,' Mourne said with a tiny smile. She found John a most interesting and caring person. She couldn't think why her friends didn't like him – particularly as they had never spoken two words to him on their own admission. She shrugged off her misgivings and followed them.

When Mourne arrived home she met Father Patrick just as he was going into his study. She gave him a quick peck on the cheek and answered his question. 'Yes! I had a lovely time. I am now refreshed and ready for anything. Is Mam around?'

Patrick rolled his eyes. 'She's not only around, she's running about like a hen on a hot griddle.'

'Why?'

Patrick sighed. 'Come into the study for a bit. I'll tell you why.'

Mourne followed him and sat down on the edge of the armchair.

Patrick went straight into his explanation as he lowered himself into his chair. 'I have decided to go into semi-retirement. To that end I wrote to the Bishop who unfortunately, and in my opinion with indecent haste, accepted my decision. A new man will be arriving next week to live with us and to help me run the parish with a view to taking over.'

Mourne, trying to hide the shock that his words caused her, said, 'Had you regretted your decision? I mean, you seem to think the Bishop was a bit quick with his reply.'

'No! I haven't. But when you think that I have been writing letters to the man and his office for the past year in the hope of gettin' a few slates put on the roof and I am *still* waiting for an answer, his haste in replying to my latest request is somewhat surprising.' Patrick couldn't hide the irritation in his voice. 'I've been thinking about this for some time,' he continued. 'I am not a young man and I've found, lately, that running the parish is becoming more difficult. When Gerry decided he would retire it gave me cause to assess my own situation.'

'But you never said a word! Will this affect Mam and me?'

'No, it will not! I never said anything because I wanted to wait until I'd heard from the Bishop. I would have told you before things went further; I never expected to hear so soon *or* to have a young priest billeted on us.'

'Oh dear! Is that why Mam is flying around?'

'If the woman could wash the wallpaper she would do it. The bed-frames have been polished and the quilts battered to death out in the back patch, and the sheets are so white they look as if they have had a lick of paint.' Patrick laughed in spite of himself.

Mourne said, 'I'd better go up and see her. She's probably trying to prove to the new man what a wonderful housekeeper she is.'

'I expect so. But I doubt if things have changed all that much since my days in a seminary. We were all too busy drinkin' and having our last flings to worry about the state the tiny cells we called rooms were in, and most of us were so hung-over at times, we ate the food more for the sake of our bodies than for the taste. The man will think he's gone to heaven when he arrives here, and when he tastes Kitty's cooking he'll be certain of it. Sure she has no need to go this mad.' They both jumped and laughed as they realized that Kitty had now moved to the bedroom above their heads.

'You had better get up there. That thump means she's in my bedroom,' said Patrick. 'Tell her if she so much as moves my missal to the other side of the bedside table she is likely to be excommunicated.'

Kitty was removing fluff from under the bed when Mourne poked her head round the door. She edged her way out and stood up. 'There you are!' she said. 'I expect you've heard the latest drama. I heard himself chatting to you in the study.'

Mourne nodded. 'He thinks that you're giving yourself unnecessary work.'

'Does he? Well! No one comes to this house and has cause to say that I don't keep it up to scratch,' Kitty said firmly, and realizing that she had not greeted her daughter properly, she wiped her hands on her crossover pinny and gave her a hug. 'I needn't ask if you've enjoyed your little holiday with Tara. You look well and glowing. The tired look has gone. How is Tara?'

'I'm going to make a mug of tea,' said Mourne sternly. 'You can put that feather duster down and join me. We'll have a good crack together then, so the poor spiders have time to escape to a new home.' She went from the room before Kitty could refuse.

In spite of her outer calm, however, Mourne felt disturbed. Everything seemed to be falling apart. She had the familiar sinking feeling that she'd known over the last few months. Her life seemed to have become unstable again. For a short time she had managed to put her fears behind her, but today her insecurities had risen to the surface again.

Tara was married and living miles away. Uncle Gerry, and now Father Patrick, had given in to age. David, whom she had just got used to having around again, had socked her with the news that he was engaged . . . and John McCrory, in whose company she found some solace, was proving to be unpopular with everyone. She couldn't understand why he was regarded so ill. Was jealousy the reason? To her he had proved a godsend. He had been there for her when she was at her lowest ebb and never once had he overstepped the mark. He had shown her a life that she might otherwise have only read about in magazines, and she felt comfortable with him . . . Her thoughts were interrupted as her mam came through the door and sat down at the table.

168

'Why are you suddenly looking unhappy?' Kitty asked. 'Share those deep thoughts with me.'

Mourne said, sadly, 'I don't like change, Mam. I want everything to be the same as it has always been. I still wish I hadn't been told about being found up in the Silent Valley.'

Kitty's heart stopped. She took a gulp of the hot liquid to give her time to answer. This was the first time Mourne had come anywhere near to letting anyone know that she still felt the desperate hurt of being abandoned by her mother. She and Father Patrick had been so short-sighted. Instead of coming to terms with it, Mourne had dug a pit in her mind and buried her fear.

'I seem to be left by everyone I love – even O'Malley has gone from me!'

'Jesus! Mourne. He was a dog . . . he was accidentally killed. How can you talk like this?' Kitty put her arms around her daughter. 'You must know how much we all love you. You shouldn't think in terms of people leaving you. They're building their own lives and you are still a part of them, even if it's in the memories they store of the past. You will leave me, and this house, but I will always be there in your heart and in your memory.'

Mourne sighed and moved out of her mother's embrace. 'I'm having a fit of the blues. Take no notice.' Her mam didn't understand, she thought, it was the fear of loving someone too much and losing them that saddened her.

'How is everyone since I went off on my jaunt? Has Uncle Gerry settled back into local life after all his gallivanting?' She tried to force a little jollity into her voice.

Kitty took a sip of her tea. 'He has no option. David has carted himself off to London for the weekend so he is back in charge.'

So! David had gone over to see his fiancée. Mourne moved towards the scullery so that her mother couldn't see how the news had upset her. When she had composed herself, she turned. 'If you ask me nicely I'll give you a hand with getting supper ready,' she said brightly.

'Good girl!' Kitty rose. 'I'll just finish upstairs while you peel the taties and set the table. Are you going out this evening, by the way?'

'I'm popping down to see how Rena is. I promised her I would as soon as I got back. David tells me she is coping well.'

'Not too bad at all, not too bad at all,' Kitty agreed. 'The girl is a marvel when you consider that David said she could easily have died.'

That wasn't all that David had said. He'd had to break the news to

169

Rena that the chances of her having another child were very slim. Mourne didn't mention this to her mother. She wasn't certain if it was privileged information, but she felt that it was up to Rena to make it public if she so desired.

Rena was stretched along the settee with a drink in her hand when she arrived.

'Aren't you the lady,' Mourne laughed. 'All you need is a Pekinese by your side and you're there.'

Rena laughed. 'I'm still ordered to take things easy,' she said. 'Away and help yourself to a drink.'

'Very decadent. If Mam saw me, she'd be convinced I was on the road to ruin. As far as she's concerned, drinking is for the special occasion.'

'Sure what the eye doesn't see the heart won't grieve about.' Rena cleared her feet off the settee and made room for Mourne. 'Tell me all your news. I could do with cheering up. I see few people these days – and they only pop in for a short time.'

For the next hour they talked about Mourne's holiday and the latest village gossip before Rena said, gently, 'You're trying very hard but I can tell that your heart is not in this. Is there anything wrong?'

Mourne looked at her friend in horror. 'I have no notion of depressing you with my paltry worries, you have enough of your own. And anyway! I can assure you they are very silly when I think what you have just gone through.'

Rena smiled. 'I've come to terms with my problem. I will probably worry more if you don't get those paltry worries off your chest.'

'They're more like frustrations,' Mourne smiled.

'Then clear your mind. I'm a good listener.'

Mourne set down her drink and curled up, a tiny frown between her brows. 'I am being very silly, I know I am – but two things have happened which have upset me a little.' She paused and looked at Rena. 'Are you sure—'

'I'm sure! Fire away.'

'David has just broken the news to us that he's engaged to be married to a girl in England. She's a theatre sister at the same hospital as him. It came as a bit of a shock. I feel hurt that he kept this from us for so long.'

'Are you in love with him?'

Mourne stared down at her hands. 'He is very attractive,' she said, warily. 'I've worshipped him since I was eight years old and I've been so happy getting to know him again. I just resent – I think I am,' she whispered.

'Why don't you let him know?'

'What? I couldn't do that. Anyway, he must love this girl or he wouldn't be engaged to her.'

'There's no disputing that, but things change. Perhaps he will fall in love with you if you give him time.'

Mourne shook her head. 'He still treats me as he always did years ago when I was "young Mourne". As a matter of fact, he still calls me that. No! He loves me in a different way to the way I feel about him.'

'Give it time!' Rena insisted, laying her hand on Mourne's. 'Now, what's the other problem?'

Mourne spoke of her relationship with John and how she got the impression that he wasn't popular. 'I can't think why! He's so kind to me, and look at the way he gave Tarag to Mr O'Rourke – a gesture that no one else thought of making. I just cannot understand why he isn't liked. Mam refers to him as "that fella". It's a matter of contention between us.'

'Your mam and the others are not going out with him. If he treats you well and you enjoy his company, then where's the problem?'

Suddenly Mourne smiled. 'You have the gift of putting things into perspective, Rena. You're right. I'm the one who is going out with him and I *do* enjoy his company.'

'That's settled then. Now! How about another drink of this very fine wine?'

That night as Mourne settled down against her pillow she felt the turbulent thoughts that had been troubling her float away. Perhaps it was best if things stayed as they were between her and David. At least she couldn't lose what she'd never had. She wouldn't live with the fear of being abandoned again when love was never there in the first place.

John McCrory might never ask her to marry him, but if he did, would it be such a bad thing? Marriage to John might not transport her into seventh heaven, but she could be content. There would be no moments of uncertainty and despair if her heart was not involved. She found his dark, brooding good looks exciting, and she was in awe of his air of sophistication and his ability to stand out in any company. She respected him and was content when she was with him. What more could she ask for?

The following morning she rang John from the surgery. He sounded pleased. It was the first time she had rung him and her voice shook as she spoke. 'I thought I would give you a ring to let you know I'm back,' she said tentatively.

John laughed. 'Do you realize that this is the first time you have contacted me? Things are looking up. So far I've had to do all the running.'

'I was afraid it might seem too forward.'

John McCrory smiled to himself. She was going to be putty in his hands. 'I'm glad you got up the courage; I like you being a bit forward. I was going to ring you sometime today anyway. I'd like to take you out to dinner if you're free.'

'I have no other men waiting in line,' Mourne said. 'I would be delighted.'

How naïve the girl was. Helen would have given him the impression that she had a whole string of eligible men ready and waiting!

'I'll call for you at seven. I have a proposition I want to put to you.' The line went dead.

He had sounded so imperious. Mourne felt a tinge of resentment, then she shrugged. It was part of him. It was why she found him attractive. She wondered what kind of proposition he was going to make. She suddenly felt nervous and was glad when the first patient came to her window to take her mind off her thoughts.

CHAPTER 11

John was unusually late. Mourne became increasingly nervous as she looked in the mirror for the umpteenth time, patting and stroking her hair.

Kitty observed her daughter from her vantage-point at the table. 'There isn't much you can do with hair that is hanging straight down your back like a waterfall,' she remarked in amusement. 'If you're hoping that by stroking it you can conjure up a set of curls I should give up. There's no chance.'

Mourne scowled. 'I'm not worried about my hair, I'm just passing the time. It isn't like John to be late. I just wonder if he's coming at all.'

'He'll come, I have no doubt of that. He won't find another girl like you . . .'

Before Mourne could reply there was the sound of a horn. 'He's here,' she said, unnecessarily. She kissed her mother and hurried out.

Kitty stared thoughtfully after her. She had never seen her daughter in such a twitter over a man. What was so different about this one?

At ten o'clock Father Patrick came into the kitchen. 'I'm fed up with my own company. I've come in for a chat.'

'B'God you *are* at a dead end. You only come in to fill your stomach at this hour.' Kitty rose to get him some milk and biscuits.

'I don't want anything. I'm in to discuss this dinner for Mourne. I was wondering if she would be wanting to invite that fella McCrory.'

'She won't be inviting him. She said she would only be wanting a family party and I don't think she'll be passing it around that it is her birthday, from what I can understand.'

'She's a strange wee girl, that one.' Patrick sat down at the other side of the table and leaned across. 'Do you think there is anything in this relationship?'

Kitty sighed heavily. 'If there is, there's not much we can do about it.'

'I was hoping that David and Mourne—'

'Well! That hope has gone. I can't tell you how disappointed I was to learn of his engagement. In all the time he's been here he never once mentioned it. I wonder why?'

Patrick didn't answer. He had his own views on the matter. Eventually he said, 'David will be coming, won't he?'

'We'll ask him, of course,' said Kitty. 'I can't think of a reason why he should refuse; he's very fond of Mourne. I confess that I too had hopes that something might come of their regard for each other.' She sighed again. 'I feel sure John McCrory has designs on Mourne. It does worry me; his reputation is not good.'

'We are goin' on hearsay. For all we know the man has been maligned. If Mourne likes him then I think we can rely on her judgement.'

'Can we?' Kitty's lip curled. 'The man is like a brooding eagle with those dark eyes and that slightly hooked nose. He is a very attractive man, and has all the sophistication and the social know-how to trap a naïve young girl such as Mourne. There is something about him which bothers me.' Kitty, with a degree of agitation, rose to put the kettle on.

Patrick drummed his fingers on the table, reflecting on what Kitty had said. He too had some qualms about John McCrory, but for quite different reasons. He had heard a rumour that the canning factory was in trouble. Pigsticker Riley had told him that the orders were falling and the recent accident when all the cans had been dented had lost them that outlet, for they hadn't been able to deliver a new consignment in time. The market had gone elsewhere and stayed. Even more worrying was the rumour that McCrory was gambling heavily.

When Kitty had poured the tea and sat down, Patrick asked again: 'Do you really think Mourne is serious about this man?'

Kitty nodded. 'Serious enough,' she said and fell silent. After a few minutes she spoke again. 'Did you know that Mourne spends a lot of her free time up in the Silent Valley?'

Patrick frowned. 'No, I did not! How do you know?'

'She takes her bike and sets off with an apple and a drink and sometimes a sandwich, and doesn't return for a couple of hours.'

'What makes you think that's where she goes?'

'Because twice just lately she has had to take her bike along to have punctures mended – I suspect that the granite on the lower scree is the culprit – and I've found branches of ling trapped beneath the mudguard. That particular heather is found on the Mournes. I think she hides her bike and tramps up to the rock and just sits there.'

'Ach away, woman. You can't be sure.'

'No!' said Kitty, 'I can't be sure, but I can see no other explanation, and taking into account the fact that she has never really come to terms with what we told her, I think it's fairly likely.'

'She has never shown any sign! I thought she was doing very well.'

'You would, Patrick Mulligan. You never see further than the sermons you're preparing for Sunday. But I hear her crying in the night: I have found her just sitting with her back against the bottom bedboard gazing up at the cross that you found in the box.'

Patrick said, quietly, 'I never knew.'

'Well! There isn't any more we can do just now except support her. I wonder what she's doing now?' Kitty mused.

Mourne was at that moment gazing at John McCrory in amazement. They had walked along the promenade following dinner and to her surprise, John had gently taken her hand and smiling, said, 'I hope you don't mind?'

She didn't and said so, although her heart was pumping at the significance of it. She had been going out with John for some time now, and apart from taking her arm to assist her out of the car or to help her negotiate some obstacle, he had never shown any signs of a desire for further intimacy.

They walked along until they came to the harbour wall where they sat down to stare out to sea, and she shivered slightly as the sea breeze blew in. John glanced at her and gently drew her into the warmth of his body with his arm around her shoulders.

She stiffened slightly and he gazed down at her. 'Do you mind?'

'No-o-o . . . she said, hesitantly. 'I'm – I'm just surprised. We've never – never—'

'Perhaps it's time we did,' John smiled. He put his other arm around her and said gently, 'Just relax and enjoy the warmth.'

They had been sitting thus for some time when Mourne said, 'John! You mentioned that you had something important to ask me?'

His arms loosened. 'Yes, I have.'

'Ask away then. I am dying with curiosity.'

'Will you marry me?'

Her heart leapt so high in her chest she thought he would feel it. 'Wha-a-t?'

'You heard right!' said John, calmly. 'I want to know if you will marry me. I realize that it has come as a shock, and that you'll need time to think about it, but I hope the answer will be yes.'

'You've never shown any sign that you were this serious,' Mourne gasped.

'It's a fault of mine. I find it difficult to show emotion,' John said. 'I say this with regret. It has to do with my upbringing. But I have grown very fond of you, and I think we would do well together – unless of course there is someone else?'

Mourne slowly shook her head. 'There is no one else.' She moved from his embrace. 'I like you, John. I enjoy being with you and I find you very attractive, but marriage? Is fondness enough? I notice you didn't say "I love you"; just that you had grown fond of me.'

'I did mention that I am hopeless at such things.' He sounded so uncertain, so unlike the sophisticated man she knew, that she had to smile at him.

'I would need time. I'm very flattered.'

'I wasn't intending flattery. I am very serious.'

'I know! I didn't mean it the way it sounded. But it's a huge step to take. We haven't known each other long and, let's face it, we haven't exactly behaved like a couple of lovers, now, have we?'

'You're right,' John jumped down to stand beside her. 'It is a huge step, and I would consider you mad if you said yes straight away, in view of the fact that neither of us has fallen over the other in the delirium of love, as you pointed out. But, you know, many people who swear undying love are not always able to sustain it. We at least would start married life with no illusions – think about it.'

His words had such effect that Mourne found herself doing just that until she thought, This is crazy! Here I am, standing by this man's side considering the possibility of marriage to him, and I know I don't love him. Her mind seized up in panic. 'I would like to go home now,' she said breathlessly. 'We both have a lot of thinking to do – you might regret your impulse, for a start.'

When they had returned to the car John said, 'We have never kissed. Why don't we take the first test and try it?' When she didn't object, he took her slim body into his arms and bent his head towards her.

Mourne raised her face to his and was pleasantly surprised at the enjoyment his kiss gave her. It was soft and exploratory without being intrusive and she found herself returning it with more feeling than she anticipated.

'There! That wasn't too bad, was it?'

She shook her head. 'In fact, it was very pleasant.'

He kissed her again when they reached her house and when he had driven off, Mourne found that she was trembling. She opened the door to the annexe and made her way to her mother's room.

Every evening her mam spent time kneeling at her prie-dieu. Mourne hesitated, fearing to disturb her, but the urgency of her dilemma was too great. 'Mam?' There was no movement. Her mam was so absorbed in saying the rosary, she had not heard. Perhaps this was not the right time. She silently backed out and closed the door. It could wait till morning.

Sleep didn't come easily that night. She tossed and turned for most of it and when sleep did come eventually, it was an uneasy one. Next morning she felt drained. She should be filled with excitement; it wasn't every day one got a proposal of marriage, and certainly not from such an influential man, but instead she felt apprehensive.

As she entered the kitchen, her mother was dishing up Father Patrick's breakfast of bacon and eggs and fried soda farls. Mourne glanced hastily away. The smell of eggs and bacon was too much this morning. What with the wine she had drunk last night and the worry about how to tell the two people she most loved that she might marry John McCrory, her stomach was already feeling fragile.

Kitty looked at her daughter as she put the plate of food in front of Patrick. 'You look terrible,' she remarked. 'Could you not sleep?'

Patrick looked up from his paper. 'Your mam is right! Did you have too much to drink last night?'

Mourne glowered at the pair of them. 'Yes to the first and no to the second.' She hadn't over-imbibed – not by normal standards. She just wasn't used to drinking wine.

'You'll feel better after you get something into your stomach,' Kitty said.

Mourne groaned. 'A slice of toast, Mam. I'll take it out in the garden. I need a bit of fresh air. I'm a bit overtired, that's all.' She couldn't tell them her news at this hour. Anyway, there was no rush. First she had to make up her own mind. Where was the point in telling anyone until there was something to tell? 'I'll be going up to see Mr O'Rourke this afternoon,' she said, instead. 'I won't be in for lunch.

I'll get something to eat from Mr Cullen.' She took the toast and tea and made her way out into the strip of garden, nodding her head as her mother inquired if she would mind taking some soda farls up to O'Rourke as she had promised to bake him some fresh wheaten ones. They were his favourite.

Unfortunately it was a busy surgery that morning, and the headache that had been vaguely present when Mourne woke was now a raging migraine. She popped in between patients and asked David if he could let her have something.

David ran his gaze over her. 'God! You look white. Maybe you should go home.'

'I've a headache, that's all,' Mourne said, irritated. 'You shouldn't be encouraging your staff to mitch off.'

David frowned. 'What's got into you? Just lately you've been snapping my head off. What happened to my friend Mourne?'

'I'll go over to Mr Cullen and buy some aspirins . . .'

'Don't be silly!' David reached into the cabinet behind him. 'Here you are. If it doesn't get any better let me know.'

'It's my afternoon off – I'm going walking with Mr O'Rourke. That'll do the trick.' Mourne closed the door behind her. Her heart began to thump. David always had that effect on her. She groaned inwardly. If he had been the one to ask her to marry him, would she have hesitated? she wondered, as she settled herself behind her desk and swallowed the tablets with some water. It was an intriguing thought. She had resigned herself to the fact that she had fallen in love with him, but she was determined that she would fight against it. At least marriage to John McCrory would mean contentment. There would be no moments of ecstasy, but there would be fewer moments of uncertainty and despair such as she had known recently in her feelings for David. Knowing that David didn't return her love was painful, but this way she wouldn't run the risk of being abandoned for someone else.

A cross-looking David arrived at the hatch. She started. 'I'm sorry. Did you buzz?'

'At least six times. Look, Mourne, either you are fit to work or you are not. If you decide you are, then for heaven's sake do it properly. You were sitting there in a dream. I have visits to make this afternoon, and I would like to finish surgery on time.'

Her face reddened. David had never spoken to her like that before. She knew she deserved the reprimand but nevertheless she felt resentment.

178

Although he had kept his voice low, she knew that the two patients still waiting to be seen were aware of what was happening. Hastily she retreated to the back of the room to prepare the notes for tomorrow.

Tarag had his nose down a rabbit hole and his rear end was wiggling frantically as he tried to get further in. Mourne laughed at his antics. It was the first time today that she had felt like doing so, but her headache had gone and her spirits felt lighter as she drew in the sharp cool air travelling down from the peak of Slievenaglogh. They had climbed a fair way up the slopes and were leaning against a crag for a breather and to eat their packed lunch.

O'Rourke spoke. 'That's the first sign you've given that you're happy.'

'I have had the fiercest of headaches, and it is gone now. That and the scenery and the breeze from the mountain top has helped. It's been a dire morning.'

'Why so?'

Mourne looked into the far distance. 'One thing and another,' she said carelessly.

O'Rourke remained silent. If the girl wanted to talk to him, she would. Further questions were unnecessary.

At last, Mourne spoke. 'Mr O'Rourke, I have a problem. Could I discuss it with you?'

'I am in no hurry to move on. The day's pleasant, I am well fed . . . Tarag is employed. Tell me what you like – if I can help, I will.'

'Just as you always do!' Mourne said quietly. She threw the remains of her wheaten farl to the ground and hugged her arms to her sides. 'A man has asked me to marry him.'

O'Rourke waited. He had no notion of helping the girl along. Either she wanted to talk or she did not. He would put no pressure on her.

'John McCrory has asked me to marry him . . . I don't know what I should do.'

'You aren't asking me to make up your mind for you, are you?' O'Rourke asked. This he had not expected.

'No! Of course not. The thing is, I don't love him but I am very fond of him, and I feel that I would rather be fond of someone and happy than be madly in love with someone who might desert me and cause me pain.'

'Are you telling me that you would choose John McCrory because if he left you it wouldn't matter?'

179

'Not exactly . . . Yes, I suppose I am . . .' Mourne said ashamedly. 'That sounds bad, doesn't it.'

'It certainly sounds selfish. I must say that you surprise me. The last thing I would have said of you was that you were capable of selfishness.'

'It isn't quite like that; you see, John knows I don't love him. He isn't in love with me either, but we are very fond of each other and we get on so well together, he asked me if I might make a life with him. I am not averse to the idea, but I think my mother and Father Patrick might not be so happy about the arrangement. I don't know what to do.'

'You make your own decision. It's your life, and the mistakes you make in it and the happiness you get from it are all down to you. But have you given thought to the fact that at your age you might meet someone to fall in love with him, and that you will have destroyed your life because of this fear?'

'I have already met him and there is no hope there, I am certain of that. My fear is that if John and I marry, we may find that it isn't enough that we like each other and enjoy each other's company.'

Tarag had now got close scent of his prey and was setting up a barking session. O'Rourke moved towards him and removed him with a tap of his boot before throwing a stick down the path they had come up. Tarag, interested in the new game, charged after it and O'Rourke returned to Mourne. He leaned back against his rock and said, 'Many marriages that have been entered into without love have survived. In the Indian culture the girls don't even get to see the bridegroom until the ceremony. The parents do all the matching and the negotiating. Those marriages, for the most part, work very well.'

'God! I'd hate not to have met the man I was to marry,' Mourne said, aghast at the thought.

'Not at all. The parents match them up for their interests, their politics, their caste . . . for everything. At the time they get married the young couple find they have similar interests – their love grows from that. In our culture when a girl and a boy fall in love they don't always put any effort into finding out if they are compatible. They are bound by their great passion and are surprised to find when they eventually marry that they know very little about each other.'

Mourne said, tentatively, 'So you think it would be all right if I married John.'

'Indeed I am not saying that. I'm saying that you have as much chance of making a go of things as a couple who marry because of a wild passion. At the end of the day it has to be your decision and yours only. You should give it a lot of thought before you make your mind up. Once you have, then don't waver.'

'You're a very wise man, Mr O'Rourke. I've said this before.'

'I am not a wise man. I am a man of advanced age who has seen it all. I travelled the world in the merchant navy before I opted out,' O'Rourke laughed.

'You have the gift,' Mourne insisted, adding, 'I will give the matter more thought because I think it just might work between John and me. We get along well and I admire his sophistication and his ability to get things done – which is why he's not always popular.' Mourne's voice faltered. 'There's only one thing that bothers me. He enjoys gambling.'

O'Rourke laughed. 'What do you think the boys and I are doing round Cullen's stove? Many men like a flutter. My sweet wife hated it, but she put up with it. It isn't the worst thing in the world to have a gamble.'

Mourne wanted to tell him that John's gambling was a bit more than a game of cards round a stove or a flutter on the Derby, but she held back. As Mr O'Rourke said, the ultimate decision was hers. She only hoped that the John McCrory she knew was the real John McCrory, and not a projection of someone he wanted her to see.

The family gave her a wonderful twenty-first dinner party at the Headland Hotel. The food was superb, and Kitty had arranged for a cake that she had made herself to be brought to the table at the end of the meal, after which they repaired to the coffee lounge to a discreet corner where a bottle of brandy was resting on the table amid a pile of presents.

Her mother had bought her a pair of gloves made of the softest leather. Father Patrick had lashed out on a matching handbag. 'Chosen,' he informed her, 'by your mother on my behalf.' From Uncle Gerry she had a cheque, and from David an exquisite pair of pearl earrings. She was flushed with pleasure. The only thing to mar the evening was the unfortunate remark that Uncle Gerry made that he was certain his nephew hadn't chosen the earrings himself, for he had no taste.

Everyone laughed, but David frowned and glanced towards her. 'The assistant chose them,' he explained. 'She is in the jewellery business after all, and should know a good set of pearl earrings.' Mourne smiled.

Just before the party broke up, as they stood by the cloakroom waiting for the others, David looked into her eyes and gave a small grin. 'How does it feel to be an old lady? You do know that it's all downhill from now on?'

'That's right! Depress me,' she retorted with a laugh. He was not going to see that she had been hurt by the earring episode.

'I've enjoyed myself this evening,' David whispered. 'I wouldn't have missed it, but I would like to take you out to dinner another time – just the two of us.' There was the merest hint of a plea in his voice as he spoke.

Mourne gave another tiny laugh. 'Not a good idea, David,' she said. 'What if your fiancée should hear about it and get the wrong idea?'

David frowned. 'You're probably right. She might not understand if I should ask my friend the young Mourne O'Hara out for a meal to say thank you for the years I've known her,' he said coldly.

Mourne had to bite her lip to stop the tears forming behind her eyelids. She hadn't meant to say what she did. It had just popped out. She watched as he turned on his heel and walked out to his car with Uncle Gerry. She would have given anything to retract her stupid, senseless words.

After Mass the following morning, the twins came bounding towards Mourne. 'We have a present for you,' Noreen said excitedly.

'I wanted to tell her,' Cassie cried, and belted Noreen on the shoulder. 'Mam said I could tell her and you could hand it over.' She lunged for the parcel but Noreen was too quick, and she thrust the parcel into Mourne's hand causing Cassie, with the adroitness of the frustrated, to grab her sister by the hair.

Mourne was trying to separate them as Rena ran up. 'Can I not trust the pair of you to do anything right?' She yanked them apart and each twin glared at the other across the space. 'I declare to God He had it in for me when He saddled me with this pair,' she said, in an aside to Mourne, before saying to the twins, 'Away off and torture each other somewhere else.'

'Don't be hard on them,' Mourne laughed.

'Will you come over for tea today?' Rena asked as the two scampered off. 'That pair will be disappointed if you don't come. The invite is from them.'

'Of course I will. I'll not open my present till I arrive, either.'

182

They had reached the entrance to the church driveway and Rena stopped to call the twins. 'I was all for handing it to you when you came, but they couldn't wait. It had to be now. It's a wonder they didn't trip you up as you came back from receiving Holy Communion.' They both laughed. The girls arrived.

'Why are you laughing? Are you happy?'

'I'm coming to tea,' said Mourne. 'And I am happy.'

'Hurray!' the twins yelled, friends again, as they jumped around in a circle.

'His Holiness the Pope wouldn't get such a welcome,' Rena mouthed.

Donal, Rena's husband, arrived at that moment. 'What about the Pope?'

'Nothing!' Rena laughed. 'Mourne is coming to tea.'

Donal's face dropped. 'You didn't say, Rena. I've just arranged a round of golf with David McNeill.'

'Who needs either of you?' As Donal went off, Rena sighed and looked at Mourne. 'It's a man's world, isn't it?'

'At least he pays the rent,' Mourne laughed. 'And I've seen him do the dishes.'

Rena pretended to scowl. 'That was for show and I was ill at the time.' She looked fondly after her husband's retreating figure. 'He is a good man; I have never regretted marrying him.'

They wandered slowly along till they arrived at the parochial house gate. 'Did you know Donal long before you married him?' Mourne asked, curiously.

'Yes, I did, but I was going out with someone else. Donal kept pestering me to go out with him but I didn't like him much.' Rena laughed. 'I thought he was a bit dull. Tony McCarty was more my style. We were a pair of hell-raisers right enough. Then one day Tony suddenly broke off our relationship when he fell for a girl from Dundrum. My mother swears to this day that I married Donal on the rebound.'

'Did you?'

Rena thought for a moment. 'I suppose I did,' she said at last.

'And Tony McCarty?'

'He dumped the new girl and took off for America.' Rena moved off. 'I'll expect you around three o'clock. If it is still warm and sunny we'll have tea in the garden and maybe go down to the stream, later.'

Kitty looked up as Mourne entered the kitchen. 'We're eating in the dining room today. This kitchen is like an oven.'

'I'll put my things away and give you a hand,' said Mourne. She was about to walk away when her mam spoke again.

'I meant to ask. Was there anything special you wanted to say the other night?'

Mourne hesitated. 'Just to say goodnight, but I didn't like to disturb you.'

'That's all right then. I just wondered.'

Mourne had firmly decided that she wouldn't speak of John's proposal until she had made her own decision. There was no doubt in her mind that her mother would not take kindly to an engagement to John McCrory, and she had quickly realized as she watched her mother at prayer that night that the hour was too late to bring up the subject. She would have robbed her mother of a good night's sleep.

Mourne's silence throughout lunch was noted by Patrick. He watched her moving her food around her plate and remarked upon it. 'Does the pattern on that plate offend your eye? You look as though you're tryin' to hide it. You have chased your food from one end to the other and back again—'

Kitty intervened. 'It's a hot day. It would scald you out there. I should have done a salad – will you leave the girl be.'

'I hate salad,' Patrick said.

'I know! Which is why we're having roast beef on a day like this. No wonder Mourne can't eat it.'

Mourne smiled, relieved that she had been handed an excuse to leave. 'You are right, Mam. I just don't feel like food.'

'Well! See that you eat a bit at Rena's today. What you've eaten so far wouldn't keep a sparrow alive.'

'I will – I promise.'

When she had gone, Kitty said to Patrick, 'She had something of importance to discuss with me the other night but she changed her mind.' Kitty related the events of that evening.

'Maybe she just wanted to say goodnight,' Patrick observed.

Kitty shook her head. 'I saw her face in the mirror.'

'Why didn't you say something?'

'I was at my prayers. She'll tell me in good time, I'm certain. I think that I am not going to like what she has to say.' Kitty frowned.

'Your imagination is running away with you, woman.'

Stacking the dishes later, Kitty stopped for a moment in thought and then shook her head. Father Patrick was wrong. She knew her daughter too well. Something was bothering her and was waiting to be said, but she hadn't been able to bring herself to utter the words.

Mourne's appetite had not improved by teatime. She nibbled at the sandwiches, delicately prepared by Rena, and gratefully downed the tall glass of orangeade. The twins were now squabbling amiably some distance away and Rena was lying back in her deck-chair with her face turned to the sun.

At last, Mourne spoke. 'Rena?'

'Mmmm?'

'When Tony McCarty broke off your relationship, were you very upset?'

Rena thought for a moment. 'I felt abandoned – it was so unexpected. But I was so angry at his perfidy I hadn't time to mope. It helped that when I met Donal the following evening at a ceilidh he asked me to go out with him and this time I agreed. He didn't know that I had been dumped by Tony, mind you, as I was behaving like I had been inhaling laughing-gas.' She giggled. 'He lost his step – we were dancing the haymaker's jig at the time – and put the whole set out.'

'And you truly don't regret having married him?'

'Never!' Suddenly aware of the serious note in Mourne's voice, Rena sat up. 'This is not just a casual inquiry about my love life, is it?'

There was a long silence. Rena waited.

Mourne spoke, at last: 'John McCrory has asked me to marry him.'

'And?'

'I don't think I love him.'

'Then don't marry him. You haven't a gun at your back.'

'I want to say yes. I feel comfortable with him and there is no one else. He also doesn't expect too much of me.'

Rena frowned. 'Does he love you?'

'Not passionately. We have been very honest with each other. We enjoy each other's company and we both feel we could make a go of it.'

'God save us, Mourne, that is no basis for marriage. What if you meet someone later?'

'I have met someone, but he is already booked and I know that I won't fall in love with anyone else, so I feel that I could be happy with John . . .'

'It's still a poor substitute—'

'But you said yourself that you didn't exactly love Donal when you married him, and you have a good marriage now.'

'Mourne, love, I was already half in love with Donal by then and I hadn't realized it till we started going out together. It's true that when I married him I still wasn't sure if I was kidding myself, but I realized by the end of the honeymoon that he was the man for me . . .' Rena's eyes widened. 'David's the one, isn't he? I can see the parallel.'

'You're mistaken,' Mourne said hastily. 'David is a very old friend – besides, he's engaged to a girl across the water. She's a nurse at the hospital where he's a registrar.'

'Don't talk daft. You love him,' Rena said softly.

Tears filled Mourne's eyes. 'Yes! I do love him,' she confessed. 'But I am not going to mope. There's no chance for us – and even if there was, I wouldn't take it.'

'Why not?'

'I have this terrible irrational fear that if I love someone too much they will leave me. If things had come to a head with David, I would be forever worrying that he would one day go back to Rosemary. I don't want to take such a risk.'

'You're right! It is a completely irrational fear,' Rena said firmly. 'All this is because you were adopted. But that doesn't mean your mother abandoned you. You don't know the circumstances, Mourne. The poor girl might well be spending her own life feeling destroyed because she had to give up the baby she loved.'

'Anyway, it's all supposition. David isn't in love with me. I'm his old friend – young Mourne O'Hara – and I have no intention of giving in to my feelings. In fact, the more I discuss it, the more I convince myself that marriage with John would work.'

'He's certainly the catch of the year,' Rena said, and seeing Mourne's face cloud over she added hastily, 'Not that I'm talking about his wealth. I mean that he is the most attractive man for miles – those dark devilish eyes . . . the upright arrogance of his bearing . . . the way he speaks in that rich baritone voice . . .'

'Have you decided I may not be making a mistake after all?' Mourne asked.

'No! But I can understand how you could be tempted to make the choice. I beg you to give it more thought.'

At that moment Cassie and Noreen ran up. 'Are we going down to the brook?'

'Indeed we are,' said Mourne. 'I shall wear the beautiful voile scarf that you gave me for my birthday.'

'You'll cook in this heat, you eejut,' laughed Rena.

'No I will not. It's light and airy and even if I do, it will be worth suffering to please my two lovely friends.'

Monday morning's surgery was the busiest Mourne had ever known. Since David's arrival, the young people of Ballycash seemed to be developing odd maladies – anything from migraines to bunions that were no more than a reddened bone where the shoe rubbed. Mourne was all for telling them that they were to stop wasting time and filling up the surgery list unnecessarily, but David with good humour remarked that things would settle down. 'Trust me!' he said to Mourne when, on a particularly bad day, she found herself with a waiting room full of giggling girls.

It didn't help that the second phase of building had begun and there wasn't enough room to swing a kitten, much less a cat. David had been forced to move into a smaller 'nurses' room' which had been constructed by stealing a few more feet from the already reduced area of the waiting room. In the interests of confidentiality, all the notes and lists had to be stored in reception. Mourne was swamped by extra filing cabinets and was constantly irritated at having to squeeze into almost inaccessible places to find things.

Even David, the most easy-going of individuals, could be heard hammering on the wall to communicate his displeasure when the workmen were too noisy. Mourne had to convey to them on one occasion the reminder that the rule was that they deal only with 'the quiet bits' while surgery was in progress, and that Dr McNeill would be obliged if they could stick to the contract.

'What quiet bits? There are no quiet bits when you're knocking down walls,' Billy Toner, the gaffer, snapped. 'Dr McNeill will have to put up with it – he started it all in the first place.'

Which was only the truth, Mourne thought, trying to rub her headache away. She leaned out of the small opening that led into the waiting room and apologized to the patients still waiting to be seen.

Most of them laughed. 'Don't apologize, Mourne,' said Dan Donnelly. 'I speak on behalf of us all when I say that this is better than watching our lousy team playing Camogie, and certainly beats the pictures for there hasn't been a good film for weeks.'

'You're all mad,' said Mourne, shaking her head.

'I disagree!' ventured old Biff Kennedy. 'I am a sick man. I could do without this racket.' To prove his point he lifted his stick and struck the wall a few hefty blows and shouted for the racket to stop.

The consulting-room door flew open and David appeared. 'I'm trying to take someone's blood pressure. Who's making that row?'

'I am!' said Biff. 'I'm here to be cured and I'm likely to be farting off with a nervous breakdown instead.'

'They're only sanding down the walls, for God's sake. You made more noise with your stick than the workmen.' David began to laugh as he realized the incongruity of it all, and the whole room joined in. He crossed to Mourne. 'They would never believe this in England,' he said.

Mourne said, 'That lot out there should be seeing a psychiatrist. They think it's an absolute gas sitting there with all the to-ing and fro-ing. Old Biff is the only one to complain.' She giggled and realized that her headache had miraculously disappeared.

'Old Biff was always a cantankerous bugger. I remember him from my youth,' David grinned. 'Still! This won't get the baby bathed or Mrs Kelly's blood pressure measured.'

The phone rang. It was Uncle Gerry. He was doing all the outside visits. 'Will you tell David I have just arranged for Mrs Haley to be admitted to Downpatrick?'

'I will. David said if you rang in could I ask you to pop in and look at Mrs Downey on the Bryansford Road? She rang in this morning to say that her catheter is leaking. We can't raise the district nurse. She's away on her rounds.'

'Wise woman! Judging by the racket coming over this phone, I think I'm well out of it myself.'

Mourne put the phone down. Dan Donnelly was at the opening. She leaned on the counter top. 'What can I do for you, Dan?'

'You could send old Biff in next. He's driving us mad.'

'If you don't mind losing your turn. You're due in next.'

'Not at all. Things are so hep here I think we've forgotten why we came in the first place,' Dan grinned.

'I think you're all fit for the madhouse, myself,' Mourne observed. 'They would never put up with this across the water.'

'Sure they think we are all as mad as hatters in Ireland. We're only living up to expectations.'

Dan crossed the room. 'You're next on the list, you old cod!' he said to Biff.

When they had all gone David phoned in and asked for a cup of tea. 'Put the phone through to my office and join me.'

188

Mourne's heart flipped. 'Was there anything special? I have a mountain of filing to do,' she said.

'Do as the boss tells you,' David put the phone down.

'I hope you will change your mind and come out to dinner with me one evening,' he said later, as they sipped their tea. He stared at Mourne's head as she bent over her cup, making a big deal out of removing a piece of fluff from the rim. He hoped to God he hadn't ruined the rapport that existed between them, but he knew he had come perilously close by telling her so baldly about Rosemary. It had seemed the best way to do it at the time, but the more he thought about it the more he realized that the situation had been badly handled. He waited now for her reply.

'That would not be a good idea, David,' Mourne said. Her heart was pounding in her chest as she slowly lifted her head. 'I don't think that John would be too happy about me going anywhere with you – even as an old friend.'

David frowned. 'Why should John McCrory mind? You aren't married to him.'

Mourne drew a slow, shuddering breath and rose. To steady her nerves, she gathered the now empty cups from the desk and cradled them in her arms. She looked into David's eyes – those grey, long-lashed eyes that were always kind and affectionate when he looked at her – and said with a calm that she had dredged up from her innermost being, 'Not yet! But he proposed to me over a week ago and is waiting for my answer.'

David stared back into her eyes. His face was still, his eyes dull as he said, 'And?'

'I'm seeing him tonight. I am going to accept.'

CHAPTER 12

In October, David returned to St Angela's. There were six months to go before his contract ended. Gerry and Mourne had accompanied him to the airport to see him off.

As Mourne watched his retreating figure, a grey cloud descended on her thoughts. That terrible feeling of being abandoned hit her again. Why when she felt such love for someone did she get this feeling? Every sinew, every nerve, every part of her body longed to have his arms round her and those eyes looking down into hers as they had done that day by the river when they had gone fishing with Mr O'Rourke.

She had been frightened by the exchange, then. It happened too soon following the revelation that she had been left up there in the Silent Valley by her mother. Her whole instinct had been to respond. God knows her body was willing her to do so, but her mind had warned her against being hurt further and had caused her to stiffen and pull away. She knew that David had sensed her withdrawal by the puzzled hurt in his eyes. There had been times since when she had felt the invisible pull again, when they stood too close or some affectionate banter had passed between them, but David had diffused the situation, making her feel he had lost interest. She clung to Uncle Gerry's arm as his nephew turned to wave one last time. He pulled her close to him and patted her hand.

'Sure he'll be back in six months to plague the life out of us again: the hammering and banging will start upstairs when the builders begin to rip the rooms apart and we will want to throttle him. It is but a respite – nothing has changed.'

Mourne smiled weakly to hide the sadness within her. Things *had* changed, she thought. They had changed the day she had told David of her plans to marry John McCrory. It had just been a coolness of manner at first, but as the weeks passed she had felt the gulf between them widen. David had only once, since then, accompanied her up to Mr O'Rourke's cottage and that was to bid him goodbye.

To others they appeared as close as ever; they smiled and responded to each other like the friends they were, but Mourne could detect the hurt in his eyes when John McCrory's name came up. This surprised her as he had given no indication that he minded when she had told him of her plans. He had merely looked up slowly from the notes he had been studying and said, evenly, 'Congratulations! I'm sure you know what you're doing – I had no idea things were that serious between you.'

His attitude had stung. David had become such an important part of her life lately, and she felt he could have shown a bit more interest. His voice had remained quite even as he went on to remark that he hoped marriage to John McCrory didn't mean that she would be leaving the practice.

'I can't see John wanting his wife working – can you?' she had responded icily, as she left the room.

Her mother had taken the news badly and Father Patrick had grunted and said, enigmatically, 'Each to his own,' before walking from the room. The clear disapproval only served to strengthen Mourne's resolve. 'Think what you like,' she said. 'John is my choice – we understand each other.'

Kitty watched her daughter's soft mouth stiffen in defiance. She knew that she had to tread warily. In spite of her normally gentle manner, Mourne could now and then show a temper that would frighten the divil from his den. When she was angry she was unbiddable. She had been so even as a child, but Kitty had her ways of deflecting the anger and usually managed to avert disaster.

'Take no notice,' she said, soothingly. 'He had high hopes for you and David. It was a great disappointment when we heard about his engagement to the English girl.'

Mourne's eyes hardened. 'I haven't accepted John on the rebound,' she said.

'I feel happier for hearing that.' Kitty smiled. She put her hand on Mourne's. 'It wouldn't be any good pretending that John McCrory would be my choice for you – I don't understand the man for a start – but I know you are a sensible girl and if you have chosen to marry him then I will accept that.' She paused and frowned. 'I have to say, Mourne, I cannot like the man. He is good-looking and he has an air

192

about him, but I cannot find myself taking to him at all. I would be doing us both an injustice if I pretended otherwise, but I will try to get along with him. It's unfair to judge swiftly.'

Mourne had hugged her mam. 'I haven't done this on the spur of the moment. I knew that accepting John's proposal wouldn't go down well, but I really do care for him and I hope things will work out for us both.'

Kitty smiled but her heart felt cold. The words Mourne uttered had given her no comfort. Not once had her daughter mentioned the word love, and her demeanour was not that of a woman who had just spoken about the man she was going to marry. It was more like a business arrangement. She sighed. There was little she could do but hope that her girl really did know what she was about. Marriage was for ever. It would be a terrible waste if she and John McCrory found that they were not suited.

Of late, Mourne had been spending more and more time up in the Silent Valley. She would sit by the big rock and let the serenity and peace of the place enter her heart and soul. Here in the place where no birds sang and where there wasn't even the whisper of a leaf to disturb the silence, she felt happy. It was said that all the birds had flown during the building of the reservoir in the 1920s, frightened by the noise of the excavating machinery as it dug into the solid rock.

Today she laid her bag on the granite-strewn surface and lay back against the huge boulder and closed her eyes, shivering slightly as the October chill penetrated her thick jumper. She moved around to a less exposed position and as she did so, she felt that now familiar sensation of not being alone; firmly she put the feeling aside. She had come to believe it was all in her imagination.

Mourne had stopped mentioning her fear to John. He tended to dismiss it as nonsense, and remarked once with a peculiar little smile that he hoped he wasn't marrying a girl who was prone to strange thoughts like poor Mary Potter who insisted she saw ghosts and had many times heard the screech of the banshee.

She frowned. She should be thinking of John and the forthcoming wedding, but she found her thoughts were filled by David. She wondered what he was doing now, at this moment. Was he with Rosemary? Was he giving any thought to the people he had left behind in Ballycash? Did he miss their walks with Mr O'Rourke? Mourne buried her head in her arms and the tears came rushing. Suddenly, all the fears and

193

tensions of the past few months overcame her. The self-control she had managed to sustain was gone and she wept for the life she desired with David but couldn't have.

After a time, she resolutely dried her eyes and taking out her sandwiches, she half-heartedly bit into one. The past was gone. She would now try to make a success of her marriage and find contentment with John. He wasn't expecting a relationship filled with love and passion. They both understood each other. This marriage would work . . . it had to. She would make it work.

Conversation that evening was all about the wedding day, which was now drawing closer. Kitty was worried that there wouldn't be enough food. 'You know what it'll be like. The whole village will be expecting to come to the church and for a bite to eat in the hall afterwards.'

Mourne gasped. 'Mam! This is supposed to be a quiet wedding. John will be furious if you invite the entire village for the wedding lunch.'

'The arrangements will stand,' said Kitty firmly. John had so far shown little interest in any of it.

'I will have to warn him.'

Kitty frowned. 'Has he no family he wants to invite? I can't believe the only people he is inviting are the best man and two other friends with their girlfriends.'

'He has distant relatives. He doesn't see them and sees no reason why they should come. I think he has not kept in touch with them since his parents died.'

Kitty shrugged. 'Well! It's different for you, and he will have to understand.'

Father Patrick raised his head from his paper and grinned. 'Has he any idea that the pair of scallywags you have chosen as bridesmaids are likely to banjax the whole affair, given half the chance?'

Mourne laughed. 'Rena has them under control. They have been threatened that if they so much as put one foot wrong or say anything untoward, they will be banished to their aunt Sarah's for a whole week. Believe me! That is deterrent enough. According to Donal, Rena's sister is a real stickler for etiquette and the twins – being the pair they are – usually come back home like a pair of wild birds let out of a cage. Everything that is breakable or precious is put out of sight until they calm down.'

'You can't help liking them,' Kitty said, laughing at the picture

194

painted, but Patrick scowled. 'I want no trouble. I don't trust those articles. I saw the way they were acting when they were trying on the dresses. I thought the cloth would be ripped the way they were waltzing about.'

'It was excitement. They'll behave – you'll see. Rena has promised to shackle their legs together beneath the dresses if necessary.' Mourne rose. 'I'm away to give Tara a ring.'

Tara's baby was due shortly, and she was hoping it would arrive in time so that she could attend the wedding dressed to kill, but the signs were that she wouldn't make it. The phone call confirmed it.

'Not a bloody sign,' Tara laughed. 'I've tried jumping up and down, I've tried hot baths . . . what haven't I tried? I'll be there looking like a barrel let loose. You'll have to make sure that Dr Owen is there just in case, as well.'

'You take the limelight away from me and you're for it,' Mourne laughed.

On the way to her bedroom she met Father Dougan, the young priest who had come to live with them. He grabbed her by the arm.

'Is himself in there?' He nodded towards the kitchen.

Mourne grinned. 'Yes! And you are in trouble for not turning up for the meal. He says you are not going to treat the place as if it was a seminary.'

Cahal Dougan groaned. 'I got caught up with some friends and they insisted I go for a bite to eat. I haven't seen them for weeks, not since I arrived here – it seemed churlish to refuse.'

'You can tell that to Father Patrick,' Mourne laughed. 'I heard him rise from his chair, so he is on his way to the study.'

'Where are you off to? Could you not stay and give me support?'

'Certainly not! I'm off to meet John.' She smiled to herself as she watched Cahal go into the kitchen to meet his fate.

On Saturday John took Mourne to see her future home. There was a slight drizzle as they arrived for lunch. Mrs Flannigan his housekeeper met them at the door and immediately fussed about the state of John's soaking-wet hair.

'Would you stop this!' John said, irritably. 'I got wet getting my wedding suit out of the boot of the car. I will not die of pneumonia for the sake of a bit of rain.' He introduced Mourne to her and walked on.

Mourne felt intimidated by the diminutive housekeeper as she stared into the strange brooding eyes. She had heard tales of how possessive she was about John – she had practically reared him. She fussed round him now, and ran to get him a drink of whiskey to warm his stomach and glared at Mourne as though his soaking had been her fault.

John, on the other hand, treated the housekeeper with such a lack of respect Mourne found herself feeling pity for the woman. She was appalled by John's attitude as he complained that the potatoes were not the fluffy balls of flour he liked.

'I hate this glutinous brand of potatoes,' he said. 'You know I like them bursting open with the insides looking all white and fluffy.'

'I thought these would look better as we have a visitor,' Mrs Flannigan said with meek apology.

'And why have you not boiled them in their skins? You silly woman.'

Mourne was astounded at the interchange. A row over a few potatoes?

'Please!' she said, placatingly. 'I'm impressed by the way Mrs Flannigan has catered for us. The meal looks wonderful.' She glanced at Mrs Flannigan and was unnerved to find her glaring at her. 'I – I – I'm sure it will all taste grand,' she faltered.

Mrs Flannigan said 'Hmmph' and left the room.

'She goes!' said John, with a sideways look at Mourne. 'As soon as we are married she is *out*.'

'But John—'

'*Out*.' John's eyes darkened. 'I've been waiting for years for an excuse to get rid of that woman – she drives me to drink. But because of a clause in my father's will I have to keep her in employment until she reaches retirement age – or I marry. You will never be accepted by her, Mourne. She'll make your life hell.'

John's mood had only slightly lightened as he left her at her gate, and Mourne turned off the lights and made her way across to the annexe feeling very troubled. She had seen a side of John she hadn't known existed. The wedding was only two weeks away and already she was wondering if she should have fought more against such an early date. It had been John's idea to have the wedding in November. She had wanted a spring wedding when the flowers would be coming into bloom and the whole atmosphere was uplifting and optimistic.

'Why so soon?' she'd gasped. 'We've only been engaged a short time ... besides, I think November is rather a depressing month.'

John had said coaxingly that he couldn't wait so long, and why not brighten up an otherwise dark month by having a bright and joyful wedding? She had relented, and it was true that the preparations had been enough to keep her excited and interested when normally in November there was all the damp weather and wearisome treks under umbrellas and long lists of Christmas presents to be bought. They could buy their presents on their honeymoon in warm sunshine, as they were going to the Riviera. They were hiring a car in Cannes and driving along to Monte Carlo.

Kitty watched as Mourne wandered among the guests and a lump rose in her throat at the beauty of her. Her dress was of cream parchment silk satin in the latest ballerina length and her russet hair, shining and straight, was coiled in a chignon beneath a matching satin pillbox hat with a short fluff of tulle netting. Her face was animated as she laughed and conversed. John, by her side, spoke little, and Kitty was aware that many of those present were in awe of him.

It hadn't helped that John's friends had all arrived in morning suits and the girls on their arms were dressed to kill in couture clothes, and that they mingled only briefly and now stood in their own group looking a trifle superior. If it hadn't been for Mourne's constant tour round the hall to laugh and chat, things could have been sticky. It was fortunate that Gerry and Donal Maguire were also doing the rounds so that no one was neglected. Kitty sighed. It was all a bit stiff and formal. She moved from her temporary retreat, settled a smile on her lips and rejoined the groups.

Mourne was at her side in an instant. 'How do you think it's going?' she asked anxiously.

'I think everyone is enjoying themselves. I don't think it bothers anyone too much that John's friends are being a bit standoffish. After all, they don't know a soul. They're outnumbered.'

'They could have tried harder all the same,' Mourne said.

Kitty squeezed her arm. 'I wouldn't worry a tap. Everyone came to see you. They couldn't give a tinker's curse about those who are not willing to join in.'

'Weren't the twins perfect!' Mourne said. She felt a little better for having chatted to her mother. She had been sorely disappointed on two counts before she even got to the altar and somehow her mood had only slightly lightened since. The first disappointment had occurred when David had sent a telegram of congratulations and regretted he couldn't attend due to pressure of work, and then to cap it, Tara's baby had decided to arrive just a few hours before the ceremony. She missed them both, but felt particularly hurt by David's defection.

197

The twins ran up to her at that moment and she turned with a smile and hugged them both. Kitty left them to it and walked over to a group of her friends. She had seen the sudden darkening of her daughter's eyes and she frowned. God! She hoped Mourne had done the right thing. Try as she would she couldn't take to John McCrory, but she couldn't let Mourne down. He had been her choice and Kitty had to abide by it.

'We're glad we didn't go to your funeral after all,' Cassie said seriously to Mourne.

Noreen nodded vigorously. 'It's been more fun being a bridesmaid,' she contributed.

'You aren't meant to enjoy a funeral,' Mourne laughed, but the twins had skipped away. John joined her.

'How long before we can go?' he asked.

Mourne frowned at her new husband. 'Is it that bad?'

Realizing he had said the wrong thing, John took her arm and held it to his side and whispered, 'I can't wait to get you alone.'

By the time they reached their hotel in Cannes, Mourne could hardly stand for exhaustion. Their plane had been delayed, the day had been long and the airport lounge so crowded they'd had difficulty finding somewhere to sit. All the comfortable sofas had been taken and they had ended up sitting upright in bucket seats with their luggage crushed around them. None of which helped John's mood. He hated conditions like these and showed little tolerance.

'Is everyone mad? What a time of year to be going on holiday,' he'd grumbled.

Mourne gave a tired smile. It was typical of John. Already she was getting to know how his mind worked. 'Maybe, like us, they are off on honeymoon,' she'd quipped.

'I see a good few of them are taking the children,' he'd replied sourly.

Mourne didn't bother to answer. John, she had discovered, had no sense of humour.

She looked round the hotel room. It was sumptuously furnished; John had spared no expense. She noticed the two beds and felt a twinge of thankfulness that they would not be sleeping together just yet. That was the moment she dreaded. She had very little idea of what was expected of her, and although she was prepared to be a wife in every sense of the word, she felt too tired and exhausted from travelling

198

to be able to contend with yet one more new experience. She sank down on to the bed, grateful for its soft comfort.

John said, 'You look worn out. I'm going out to arrange the hired car. Why don't you try and have a nap before dinner.'

Mourne grimaced. 'I don't really want anything to eat. Would you mind dining alone just this once, please?'

'Of course not! You get your head down. I'll probably go out after I've eaten so don't wait up. We can catch up tomorrow. You'll feel better once we set off along the coast.' He dropped a light kiss on her lips and smiled, more to himself than to his wife. Things couldn't be better. He had wondered how he would get out of having to do his conjugal duty; he was grateful that his wife had presented him with an excuse.

As the door closed behind him he sighed with relief and with a new skip to his step made his way to the dining room. He was starving, and had every intention of enjoying a good meal and downing a bottle of equally good wine.

Later, when he had seated himself behind the wheel of the hired car, he slipped the young man who had dealt with him a couple of notes. It was still only ten o'clock. This was the Continent – the night was still young. His French was pretty basic. 'Is there a casino here?' he asked.

The young man shrugged. 'Non.'

John slipped more notes into his hand. 'Private game?'

The man gave a smile. 'Oui. I know of several. Wait here.' He hurried into the showroom and reappeared with a slip of paper. 'Here is the address of one.'

John thanked him and drove off. He smiled. Mourne was so tired she wouldn't rouse till morning. He had the night to himself.

When John had left the room, Mourne lay back against the pillow and read a little but she soon felt her eyes begin to droop. She craved sleep but needed to freshen up, so she sat up and gazed out of the window at the view for a while before going to the bathroom where she showered and changed into her nightdress.

Feeling refreshed, she lifted the book and began to read again. She had no idea of the moment when her mind and body gave up but she suddenly felt that delicious languor steal upon her once more and soon there was the blessed oblivion of sleep.

At first she lay quietly, the only movement being that she made to shift into a more comfortable position as she dreamt. But her dreams, which at first were gentle and happy, suddenly became dark and dangerous. She fought to wake up from the nightmare she was in. Some malignant force was pinning her down. She was gasping for breath, and she found herself trying to emerge from the terrible trauma that was filling her mind, but her tiredness was so great it continued to hold her in limbo. She cried out for her mam as a searing pain ran through her body and she arched in desperation as she tried to dredge up the will to waken.

When she finally managed to drag herself from the darkness she wished she had not. She found that her arms were pinned back against the pillow and John was hovering above her, his dark head thrown back, his neck taut, and his eyes closed as he thrust into her again and again. 'No! No! Not this way! Oh God, not like this!' She tried to push him off but he was too heavy. The final lunge was so forceful that she had to clench her teeth hard to stifle the scream that was soaring up from deep within her.

Suddenly the weight fell from her body and she lay there, relief flooding her. It was over. She attempted to raise herself, but her insides felt so sore that just to move made it worse. She tried to speak but the words wouldn't form. For a long time she lay there, tears running down her cheeks as she fought the nausea that rose in her throat. John, having rolled off her, was lying with his eyes closed. Her mind could not take in the enormity of the situation and she lay there wondering if it really was just a terrible nightmare and she was still in that twilight area between sleep and waking. John could not have done this to her. She took deep shuddering breaths to try and control the feeling of sickness and at last she managed to crawl to the bathroom and start the shower running. Her nightdress and her body were soiled, and she needed so desperately to cleanse herself.

It proved to be a painful exercise. She felt as though she had waded through a thousand thorn bushes, but at last she had finished and she made her way into the bedroom and lay down on the other bed. John was still sleeping soundly; the smell of alcohol was heavy in the room. It was the longest, saddest night of her life. At last, filled with despair, she took a small pair of nail scissors from her bag and spent the next few hours slowly and systematically cutting her beautiful satin nightdress into hundreds of tiny scraps.

Next morning she dressed and put on a small amount of make-up to hide her bloated eyes and her pallor. In the mirror she could see the figure of her new husband. Asleep he looked somehow younger and more vulnerable. She could see in him the little boy he once was, and her heart twisted as she recalled the previous night. In sleep he had lost that air of brooding sophistication he normally wore. The eyebrows were no longer arched in that superior way he had and his mouth, now drooping slightly, looked soft and young. She had to wake him. They couldn't stay poised like this for ever as though they were in a tableau.

She shook him until his eyes reluctantly opened. He stared up at her, uncomprehendingly at first, and then as he began to focus she could see awareness dawn.

'You'd better get dressed or we'll be late for breakfast.' She knew her voice was coming out like an actress speaking her lines badly. There was no lift to it. She was about to move away when John grabbed hold of her wrist. She tried to take it away.

'We have to talk!' he said. 'Last night I was drunk. I—'

'We can talk later,' Mourne said, tonelessly. 'I'm going down to breakfast.'

'Frig breakfast. I need to explain about last night. Anyway! I'm not hungry.'

Mourne's eyebrows rose. 'I am!' was all she said.

John shot out of bed. 'Let me explain—'

'Believe me!' said Mourne quietly. 'Any explanation you have will be received with more understanding if I have food in me.'

'I could do with some strong black coffee when I think about it.' John threw a clean shirt on and went into the bathroom to freshen up.

Mourne waited, surprised at the calmness that had now settled on her. Nothing anyone did to her ever again would affect her as much as this. The moon could fall out of the sky and she wouldn't care. Her regard for John McCrory had died a sorry death last night.

John drank the first cup of coffee without drawing breath. His mouth felt foul. He poured himself another cup and sipped it more slowly this time. As he sipped, he watched his wife eat a hearty breakfast. The sight alarmed him. She should be sitting there feeling distraught – not eating as though the world's food output was diminishing and she had to get a store in while she had the chance. He sensed the deep anger in her. It was like a live thing surrounding them both, and the fact that she spoke so calmly and without so much as an inflection in tone told him that he was going to need more than an explanation to build his bridges again.

They were driving along the coast on their way to Nice before he brought up the subject again. After breakfast, Mourne had again

201

refused to discuss things. 'I am so hurt and dismayed and – and *angry* I would end up shouting, and I don't intend that the guests in this hotel will enjoy a sideshow – the walls are not so thick they would keep the secret.'

'Can we discuss last night, now?' he asked as they drove along. Better to get it over, he thought. By the time they arrived at their hotel in Nice he wanted things to be resolved. His plans had not included rows over something so trivial as sex. Served him right for marrying a girl who had been brought up in the sterile surroundings of a parochial house with a doddery priest and a prissy mother.

Mourne, staring straight ahead, said quietly, 'When we stop for our picnic lunch would be better.' She needed some more time to get her mind round this. It helped that she was the piper who was calling the tune, but she knew it was a small advantage. Once John stopped feeling guilty he could wrap her into a parcel and tie the string. She had to get herself organized to combat his superior skills in dodging the issue.

At around two o'clock they stopped by a deserted cove. The sand was hot and white and Mourne was glad to climb on to the one large rock there. She organized the food which the hotel staff had packed for them and before John could utter a word she handed him his portion and said, 'This is as good a place as any for a talk – but we'll eat first. It's Father Patrick's theory that you should never row on an empty stomach for you won't feel like eating afterwards.'

John glared. 'We are going to row then?'

'I don't know how we can escape it. It's hardly likely that we'll be falling all over each other like a pair of lovebirds.'

When they had finished their meal, Mourne neatly disposed of the debris into a paper bag and threw some leftovers to the birds, before sitting against the rock with her arms clasped around her knees. John, busily drifting sand with his foot, didn't look at her. Her coldness alarmed him. Anyone else would have erupted – guests or no guests – but it was not this girl's way. In the name of Jesus, what had got into him? It was true that he'd had a lot to drink, which was unusual, for he normally never drank to excess as he liked to be in control at all times – but the extra amount couldn't account for the euphoria that had come over him when he had won all that money. He had, he remembered vaguely, developed a headache and someone had given him a tablet to ease it. Perhaps it had worked against the alcohol? Certainly his mood had become wilder after this and he vaguely

202

remembered driving back to the hotel in an erratic manner.

Seeing Mourne lying there with her nightdress up around her middle and exposing that lovely body had filled him with a desire he couldn't control. Without rational thought he had undressed and reached for her . . .

'I'm ready to hear what you have to say.' Mourne's voice broke his reverie. Suddenly the whole scene came back and tears started behind her lids. *Hell*! She was not going to give in. Her sanity lay in keeping control.

'I don't know how it happened. I did have a lot to drink and – and – seeing you lying there I . . .'

It was useless. Her control snapped. She turned to him in fury. Her anger was all the greater because she had been trying so determinedly to keep calm. But how could she keep calm when her new husband had virtually raped her? 'Where was the need for what you did?' she cried. 'Merciful God! I am your wife. You could have wakened me up – or better still you could have had a cold shower.'

John's eyes locked on hers. 'Remember that you *are* my wife,' he shouted back. 'I don't know why I'm being made out to be a bastard. It's what husbands and wives do, for Christ's sake.' Suddenly he stopped seeing himself as being on the defensive. He had given her a good toss. Did it matter if she had been half asleep? His only sorrow now was that he didn't remember the whole of it.

Mourne shot to her feet. 'You aren't even sorry for what you did,' she gasped. Lifting the wicker basket from the ground she threw it at him, hitting him on the side of the face. 'You culshie! The veneer of sophistication wore off last night. You are nothing but a culshie!'

John grabbed her by the wrists. 'You listen to me! You are my wife. I have a right to make love to you. It's what marriage is all about. You'd better believe that there will be more of the same. I want a son, and by Christ you will give me one.'

Mourne's face whitened. Suddenly everything fell apart. She could keep up the pretence no longer. She slumped down against the rock and buried her head in her arms. The tears were scalding her. She had made a dreadful mistake. This man had no respect for her, or for any woman – his manner was but a thin layer of refinement that hid the beast that he was. Others had sussed him out. She had been blinded by his urbanity. There was nothing she could do. She could never let anyone know the awful mistake she had made. From now on her life would be one big cover-up.

John lowered himself down beside her. 'I know you don't believe me, but I really am sorry. I had too much to drink. If I could undo everything that happened last night I would.' And it was true. The last thing he needed was a wife who would fight to keep him out of her bed. He certainly had a lot of work to do to get things back as they had been.

'It needn't have been that way – that's what hurts. I was a virgin and I was willing to give myself to you – but it was all so violent. You didn't make love to me. You had sex with me – just as you would with some tart from a whore-house.'

'Let me make it up to you. Give me a second chance.' The silly girl would never know how much it had cost him to make such an appeal. He didn't give a toss for her feelings. He had only exercised his rights. He'd just gone the wrong way about it. It had been no fault of his. The shites who spiked his drink were to blame. How could he help himself, anyway, when she had been lying there like a harlot with her nightdress around her neck? A man like himself was not built of stone.

By the time they reached Monte Carlo where they were to spend the final week of their honeymoon, they were both behaving in a more civilized manner. John was being a perfect gentleman. He oozed care and contrition and was blatantly pandering to her.

Mourne had at first retained her icy manner until she realized that John was being clever. She was the one who was still causing tension. He, on the other hand, had spoiled her with presents and deferred to her every whim. In Nice he had insisted on buying her some new clothes. She had demurred, until he explained that he would be taking her to places where she would need an evening dress, so she gave in. She only had the one she'd bought for the golf club ball and as John pointed out, she couldn't keep turning up to functions in the same dress.

The chosen dress was of pale blue satin, slightly off the shoulder but not so low as to cause her embarrassment. After studying her reflection in the mirror she had turned to John, however, and said stiffly, 'I wouldn't wish to embarrass you by looking as though I had never been to the opera or visited a nightclub, so I will accept the dress, but I would rather you didn't feel it was necessary to buy me so many presents.'

John had looked evenly at her. 'You run the risk of sounding churlish. I want to make amends. Don't begrudge me.'

'I don't wish to sound churlish, but I would prefer that we take things one step at a time.' He was trying his best, but though she felt calmer and the soreness had gone from her body, the mental scars remained. No doubt she would forgive him in time: his explanation that he had been slipped a tablet following copious amounts of alcohol had a ring of truth about it – but she wouldn't be rushed.

It had been John's suggestion that he would ring ahead and book separate rooms, but Mourne had been adamant that it would not be necessary. 'We have single beds – that will suffice. It is enough that you have allowed me the rest of the holiday to restore my self-respect—'

'Forgive me,' John interrupted, with a frown. 'You sound like a teacher reprimanding a student. I would appreciate it if you could be a little less stiff and formal. Can't you forget the whole bloody mess for a few days and enjoy what's left of the hon— holiday?'

From that moment they had found a way of dealing with each other. Mourne no longer lay stiffly in her single bed wondering if he would keep his word, and John kept the seething cauldron that was in him under control. Things would change as soon as they got home, but for now he would behave like a gentleman.

'I would like to go to the Casino tonight.'

They had been in Monte Carlo for three days now, and Mourne was standing on the pretty little balcony overlooking the square below when John made his request. She reluctantly tore her gaze away. 'I'm not very keen on the Casino,' she said. 'Do you need me? I only stand by your shoulder when you are playing and I find it so boring. I would rather like to stroll down by the harbour and look at the yachts.' She was fascinated by the flotilla of handsome boats gently rising and falling on the blue water, and had already spent a delightful morning on her own just watching the activities as John slept following a late night at the tables. She had managed to persuade him to go alone but she had a sinking feeling that he wouldn't let her off again. She was right.

'I lost heavily last night,' he said. 'And I am certain it was because you weren't there by my side – I need to recoup my losses.'

'What difference can my being there make?' Mourne asked, in surprise.

John couldn't tell her that he only got lucky if he had a beautiful woman standing by his side – any woman – so he arched his eyebrows and gave her a thin smile.

Mourne groaned inwardly. She loathed the Casino with its bright lights and subdued noise and the sense of drama dominating the big room. She hadn't felt such a powerful tension when she had visited the Crystal Club and she had enjoyed her evening there, but the Casino here was thick with it.

'I let you choose what we do during the day. Surely you could bend a little when I ask you to spend an evening with me at the Casino?' John said.

'Yes, of course – I'll come!'

John smiled as he left the room. His mother had always said he could manipulate the devil for his own purposes.

Mourne, standing by John's side, rubbed her ankle with her other foot. She had secretly removed her shoes and was trying to ease the ache in her legs. John had decided to play the wheel tonight and she had been standing here for two hours listening to the croupier saying, 'Messieurs et Mesdames, place your bets s'il vous plaît.' Her eyes were tiring under the bright light overhead and her back was breaking with the effort of standing straight. Now and then she stole a look at John's face but she couldn't tell whether he was winning or losing, so impassive was his expression. She gave an involuntary sigh of weariness. John looked up and frowned, but said nothing.

At last, after another hour and to her relief, he scooped his chips towards him. He pushed a coloured chip towards the croupier and, taking her arm, ushered her towards the grilled window shielding the cashier. She waited while he cashed his chips and when he returned he smiled. 'I think we should celebrate. We'll have dinner out tomorrow evening – I know an excellent restaurant.'

'You won then?'

'Of course!' John grinned. 'I told you I would if you stood with me.'

'Did you win much?' Mourne didn't really care how much he had won but she felt obliged to ask. He looked so pleased she knew it had to be more than usual.

'Twenty-two thousand pounds.'

She stopped dead. 'How much?'

He repeated the figure.

Mourne's face whitened. 'What if you had lost your stake?'

'It would have caused problems, but I didn't – so let's celebrate. We'll go for a drink—'

'Not tonight,' she begged. 'I'm dead on my feet.'

John forced a smile and shrugged. 'All right. It would have been a nice end to a perfect evening but I know you've been standing a long time, which I appreciate, so tomorrow evening the night will be yours.'

She was grateful. 'Thanks!' she said.

'You go on up to bed – I'm too tense to sleep. I might stroll down to the harbour and have a glass of wine and unwind a bit.'

Mourne hesitated.

'Don't worry, I won't repeat my recent mistake.' John's lip twisted as he watched her go. Her hair had taken on a new vibrancy in the moonlight. It looked glorious sweeping straight and shiny over the satin dress. For a split second, a deep regret engulfed him that a lovely girl like Mourne could not tug at his heart. He waited till she had passed through the large glass doors and then walked away.

Later, as he sat alone at a table outside a tiny bistro, deep in thought, he reflected on his behaviour. It was true that he had scant regard for the women whom he simply used when he needed sex, but he was truly at a loss to explain his actions on that first night of his honeymoon. He was convinced that the tablet he had been given by the men he had played cards with was a drug of some sort – although he had no idea why they had done what they did. He had been effectively cleaned out, so it wasn't for the money. He frowned. They knew he was on his honeymoon. Perhaps they had done it in the knowledge that it was likely to enhance sexual desire? The bastards.

John slapped his glass down heavily on the table, causing the other patrons to glance towards him. He rose from the patio and strode towards the harbour wall. The setting was idyllic: white moonlit sands . . . expensive yachts, the muted sound of laughter and music coming from one of them . . . the soft air and the shushing of rippling waves against the sides of the boats . . . He slammed his hand down hard on the wall and didn't feel the pain, he was so angry.

His mother and that bloody housekeeper of his were to blame for what he had become. His father was not entirely innocent either, but he had at least shown him some affection. Unfortunately it had been replaced in later years by a stern, uncompromising attitude, so that the love he had felt for him had turned to resentment. His mother had neglected him disgracefully. She had left him to the care of the overwhelming Mrs Flannigan while she led her shallow, carefree life.

She had never kissed him . . . never actually held him in her arms or swung him up towards her. The most he ever got was a kiss planted on a glove and transferred with a casual smile to his cheek. Only once had he been held close. The day had been hot, and they were walking to the large gates at the end of the drive when he had fallen over and cut himself rather badly; she had rushed to him and picked him up before calling for Mrs Flannigan. If he closed his eyes he could still recall the potency of her expensive perfume mingled with the smell of perspiration which lightly beaded her neck. The contact had been minimal, and she had called at once for Mrs Flannigan to take *the child* to the house and clean him up, and if necessary call the doctor.

Mrs Flannigan, to compensate for his mother's evident disinterest, had smothered him with love, which served only to alienate him as the years passed. He could never decide which had rankled most. The deprivation he had suffered through his mother's inability to show love, or the overwhelming affection he had received from a servant. He knew only that over the years he had developed a dislike of women, and he now used them just as his mother and her housekeeper had used him – for their own ends.

At least he had warned Mourne that he was not passionate and loving, and had been relieved that she had been unconcerned. His suspicion that she was in love with David McNeill had been confirmed the night of the golf club dance, and having decided that the virginal girl with the emerald eyes and rich auburn hair was the woman to bear his son, he had made up his mind to destroy any chance McNeill might have. The only question was how to go about it.

It had seemed like a gift from the gods when he had run into that cahoun of a doctor at the Crystal Club, who had given him the chance he had been looking for. He had made good use of the information garnered. Now he had things just the way he had planned. He had a woman who expected nothing from him that she was not prepared to give herself. Like the good Catholic wife she was, she would submit to his sexual advances. It was bloody unfortunate that he had blotted the character-reading he had given her, but he had managed to retrieve it and with time she would forget. So long as she produced the son he so desperately needed, she would have no more problems from him.

The noise of roistering males charging along the quiet road startled him. He jumped off the wall and made his way back to the hotel.

CHAPTER 13

It was the first week in April. David was due to return very soon. Gerry and Father Patrick were sitting in Patrick's study discussing his arrival.

'That fellow-me-lad had everything worked out well for himself,' Gerry observed.

Patrick smiled. 'How so?'

Gerry scowled. 'Who's the one sitting here with ear problems? I've spent the last four months dodging falling plaster when I go up to the storeroom, and I declare to God I may well be missing a diagnosis for the thumping and banging that's been going on.'

'Away on with you, Gerry.' Patrick rose to pour some brandy into Gerry's glass. 'You could sight a midge up on Slieve Donard peak. What you don't hear you see. There isn't a sign or symptom that would escape detection.'

Gerry took a sip. 'I'm gettin' on, Patrick. The medicine that David practises is in another league altogether. He'll be a great asset to the practice – did you know that he'll be doing minor surgery?'

'Aye! you said.'

'You'll be able to have those warty tags removed from your back,' Gerry said, mischievously.

'My tags and I have grown old together. Divil the hand will touch them, however skilled.'

Gerry leaned back in his chair. 'Ah well! The offer stands if you change your mind. Have you seen anything of Mourne lately?'

Patrick frowned. 'She came past last week. I didn't think she looked well. She had a painful bruise on her face . . .'

'Why didn't she come and see me? Did she say how she got it?'

'Aye! She fell off a chair when she was trying to reach the top of the kitchen dresser. She hit the side as she fell.'

'Why didn't she come to the surgery?' Gerry repeated.

'It looked worse than it was, so she said – and by the time we saw her it was beginning to fade.'

Kitty came in at that moment. 'What's fading?'

'The bruise on Mourne's face. Gerry was asking how she was.'

Kitty put the tray down on the table. She handed Patrick his warm milk and Gerry his cup of coffee before answering. 'Mourne says she's doing fine.' She looked from Patrick to Gerry. 'Mind you! If you believed all you were told you would eat all you see. I'm not entirely convinced.'

'Why not?' Gerry asked.

Patrick said, 'She assured me she was as happy as a sandboy.'

Kitty shook her head. 'Trust a mother's intuition. I saw a wistful look in her eyes when I turned round. She was looking round the kitchen as though she wanted to commit it to memory. When she realized I had turned to look at her she became all chirpy and babbled on about nothing.'

'Perhaps you were imagining things,' Gerry suggested.

'Not a bit! I know the girl inside and out, and ever since she was given that Morris Minor by John when they arrived back from their honeymoon, she has racketed about in it visiting everyone – and she looks tired. Since John insisted she gave up her job at the surgery she has been tackling the housework with only that young girl he hired after he fired Mrs Flannigan. She says the house is falling to rack and ruin and needs a complete overhaul.'

'The man is made of money. She has only to ask,' Gerry said.

Kitty shrugged. She had her own theories about that. Mourne had let slip once that John McCrory was still enjoying a flutter. Kitty had a suspicion that John's 'flutters' involved more money than the ordinary gambler. 'There have been rumours flying around for some time that the canning factory is in trouble,' was all she said.

'My left eye,' Patrick scoffed. 'He sacked a few troublemakers and they've spread a few malicious tales.'

Kitty rose. 'We may never know the truth – Mourne is very loyal. The best we can do is to be here for her if she needs us.' She paused at the door. 'By the way, there was a telephone call from Father Dougan. He says he will be a day earlier getting back as the conference finished early.'

The two men looked at each other when she had gone. 'Do you think Kitty's suspicions have any real foundation?' asked Gerry worriedly.

Patrick nodded. 'That girl is the linchpin of Kitty's life. Kitty knows more than she has let on.' He frowned. 'We can only wait.'

Mourne had heard that David was back. She knew they would have to meet some time, in view of the fact that the families continued to dine at each other's houses. But she was putting off the inevitable for as long as she could. It helped that she now lived in Kilkeel, and when she did visit Ballycash, it was during surgery times and she could whip past in her little car.

She often called to see Rena and the twins when she visited her mam, but she rarely went walking in the hills and on the mountain with O'Rourke. She had only been twice since her marriage and when John heard about it he had told her furiously that she now had a position to keep up, and walking the hills with a man who dressed shabbily and lived in a hut on the side of a mountain was no way to be going on. He was in business, and it did him no good for it to be known that his wife was carting around the countryside with a man who was one step up from a tramp.

She had been astonished at his words. He who had been so kind as to bring Tarag to the old man to help him through his sorrow. To hear such a thing coming from him had been a shock.

'You weren't being kind and thoughtful,' she had challenged him. 'You saw it as a means of impressing me! How could you be so devious?'

John hadn't denied it.

'How many more lies have you lived?' He was a stranger. Mourne thought, I do not know this man. 'How long did you think you could hoodwink me before I discovered the real you?'

John had shrugged. 'Long enough for my purposes. You were the only woman I could tolerate. I made no secret of the fact that I was not a romantic – just as you made it clear by your own actions that you were no more in love with me than I was with you. We've used each other. I wanted a son – you wanted to settle down to compensate for your precious David already being on the slippery slope to marriage himself. Don't tell me different. I read the signs and I made my move. We will do well together, but only if there is a clear understanding between us.'

He had looked sternly at her before continuing. 'I don't ask much of you. I leave you alone for most of the time, and on the rare occasions when I do make love to you I disregard the fact that you are so passive

211

it is like making love to a log.' His lips twisted in a bitter smile. 'I made a mistake on our honeymoon and I am being punished still. Just remember that I don't keep you short of anything, so the least you can do is deal fairly with me when I make this request.'

It was the longest speech Mourne had ever heard him make. Since her wedding, she had discovered that John used conversation not as an art form, but to charm some poor soul into giving him what he was after – or to issue orders. She had been so angry at his assessment of Mr O'Rourke she had found herself pacing the floor, turning on her heel and marching back again with her arms hugging her body.

'You will not stop me from seeing a man who has shown me nothing but kindness; who has been there for me when I needed advice and a ready ear; who has not a bad word to say about anyone, not even you; and who till my dying day will be treated with respect by me.'

She had been amazed at her own temerity. Until now she had been a quiescent wife, resigned to living in a certain uneasy harmony with a man she didn't love but whom she had initially admired. She had tolerated the late nights and the gambling sessions with his friends in the great hall below, standing silently up in the gallery outside her bedroom and looking down on them as they caroused and drank and gambled. He had pointed out that she had known he was no angel. She had no illusions about his feelings for her, but she had thought in view of his kindness to Mr O'Rourke that he held some sympathy for the old man. Her normally placid nature had turned to fury and she had surprised even herself when he had spoken of the old man with such disdain. She had waited with bated breath for his reaction and was chilled when he had turned on his heel and walked away without another word, leaving her to take a deep breath to stop herself shaking.

A few weeks after her altercation with John she contacted Mr O'Rourke and made arrangements to visit. She missed her old friend sorely, and as she walked out to her car she felt light-hearted for the first time in days. The only shadow on her horizon was the fear of meeting David. He had been back home for two weeks now, and according to her mother was as popular as ever. Uncle Gerry was now in semi-retirement and looking forward to finishing altogether once David was settled.

Mourne was so busy with her thoughts that she hadn't realized she had reached the centre of the broad street in Ballycash. She hastily slowed down. Tom Nolan, the local constable, was dead set against drivers who didn't keep to the speed limit in the middle of the town. She suddenly caught sight of Rena and the twins coming out of a shop and slowed to a stop. 'Hello Rena! Hello twins!' she called out. Cassie and Noreen dashed towards the car followed more slowly by Rena.

'How are you all?' Mourne was delighted to see them.

'We're fine!' the twins said in unison, and Rena and Mourne laughed.

'I don't know how they do it,' Rena said, as she put her bag of groceries down on the ground. 'They always seem to know what each is going to say.'

'Can we have a ride in your car, Mourne?' Cassie begged.

'Please!' Noreen added.

Mourne looked at Rena. 'Can they?'

Rena looked skywards. 'Don't ask daft questions. I'd give my right arm for a few minutes to myself. I'm going in to buy a new dress and these two will have the shop in uproar. Are you sure you can spare the time?'

'I'm off to see Mr O'Rourke. He won't be going anywhere till I arrive. I'll drive these two around the area for a bit – take your time. If you aren't here waiting when I get back in fifteen minutes, I'll take them into Hannah's bakery for a drink and a cake.' Mourne waved and set off, the twins, at the first sign of assent, already having jumped gleefully into the back.

'Where are you taking us, Mourne?' asked Noreen.

'Along the top road, over the bridge towards Paddy's brae, round past McBurney's farm to look at the bull and then back along the brook road to where we started. Is that all right?'

Mourne could see the twins nodding vigorously in the rear-view mirror and smiled. They were easily pleased.

They had completed half the journey before Cassie spoke. 'Have you found your sparkle yet?'

Mourne grated the gears harshly as she drove up the hill towards the farm. She stared into the mirror at the twins. She couldn't think of an answer. What had Cassie heard? She remained silent.

'What's a sparkle?' Noreen asked.

'Do you really not know?' Cassie's voice held contempt for her sister's lack.

'I heard Mam tell Da that Mourne had lost her sparkle lately,' said Noreen, 'but I forgot to ask what it was. I bet you don't know either. You think you're great, so you tell me what it is.'

'It's a necklace – so there.' Cassie shot the tip of her tongue out at her sister.

'Is she right, Mourne?' Noreen asked.

'Yes!' Mourne said. 'That's just what it is – and I haven't found it yet.' Her voice trembled slightly as she spoke. She would have to be more careful how she conducted herself. It would be awful if her mam noticed her mood change. It worried her that Rena had, although Rena was more observant than most.

Rena was waiting for them. The twins tumbled out and ran into her arms.

'You enjoyed the ride then.' Rena gave a grateful smile towards Mourne.

'It was great!' said the twins. 'But Mourne hasn't found her sparkle yet!'

Rena looked at Mourne in alarm. 'Jesus! What have you been saying?'

Mourne gave a little smile. 'They think I've lost a necklace. I told them I haven't found it yet.'

'I'm sorry.'

'Don't give it another thought. I'll come and see you soon.' Mourne waved and drove off.

When she reached the point where she had to leave the car, she frowned. There was a black car already there. She found another spot and set off across the fields to O'Rourke's cottage. Her thoughts were still on what Cassie had said. Obviously Rena and Donal had been discussing her when the twins had been near by. It concerned her that her mildly unhappy state – and it was only mild – had been so obvious. On the whole John treated her well. It was when he'd had a bad night at the gaming tables or had taken on too much drink that he became a bit aggressive, but she had learned to recognize the signs now and things had improved. He hadn't hit her for weeks. She must be more careful. God! she really must. No one must know. She had made a terrible mistake and would have to live with it. It had been her decision to marry John – no one had held a gun at her back, as Rena had once said.

O'Rourke was standing outside his cottage, shading his eyes with his large hand. 'Sorry I'm late,' she called, and frowned as she noticed that O'Rourke's right foot was heavily bandaged. 'What's happened to your foot?'

'I was cutting wood for the winter and dropped the hatchet. We didn't have time to contact you to save you a trip.'

'We?' Mourne waited with bated breath.

David walked out of the cottage. 'Hello, young Mourne.'

Mourne's throat went dry.

'He-hello David.' She stood as though rooted.

O'Rourke hobbled into the house, calling over his shoulder. 'I'm away in to take the weight off this foot. You two take a walk and get re-acquainted.'

David lifted his eyebrows in inquiry. 'Mourne?'

Mourne swallowed. 'Yes – er – that would be nice.' David took her arm. 'You must think I'm a right eejut,' she said, as they strolled along. 'It was just such a shock to see you there. Will O'Rourke's foot be all right? I do hope so.' God! She was babbling.

'Right as rain,' David assured her. 'Fortunately it was the blunt end of the axe that hit his foot. It shouldn't be too long before he can walk the hills again.' They had stopped by the granite overhang about half a mile from the cottage, and David leaned against it.

Mourne, aware of his scrutiny, blushed. She turned her back to him and stared down towards the valley. Her heart was bounding in her chest and the tears were so near the surface she was afraid to move a muscle. He looked so dear and so kind. His eyes, grey and gentle, were doing things to her heart that they had no right to do. She could hardly bear his nearness. She sat down on the dry grassy mound and waited.

David continued looking at her, his gaze travelling over every inch of her young form. He wondered if she had any idea how much he loved her. God knows, when he was last home he had tried to keep her from seeing, but on one or two occasions he thought he had failed. One of those times had been on the riverbank on that wonderful trip with O'Rourke when they had watched in fascination as the big man tickled the trout. He recalled the magical moment when he'd touched her and he'd wondered—

Mourne spoke, interrupting his thoughts. 'How are you, David?'

'Bearing up,' he said, slowly.

'And your fiancée? I thought you'd be married by now.'

'I've only been away six months.'

'Long enough to get married,' Mourne rejoined. Her courage was coming back. She was in control of her emotions once more, and she

215

was quietly proud of the way she kept her voice even and only slightly interested.

'There won't be a wedding.' David spoke slowly and softly, his eyes watching for her reaction.

Mourne felt a quickening in her breast as she gave a gasp. 'Why?'

'I realized that I would be selling Rosemary short if I went through with it. You see, I fell in love with someone else.'

There was such a heavy, prolonged silence, Mourne was convinced the man by her side would hear the sound of her heart beating seven bells out of her chest. She moved away. He followed.

'Aren't you going to ask who it is?'

Mourne paled. She wasn't ready for a confrontation like this. Although she had managed to stabilize her breathing and her heartbeat, she knew that one word of love from David would finish her.

'It really isn't any of my business,' she said shakily.

'Oh, but it is!' David pulled her towards him.

'Please! Don't! I can't bear it!' Suddenly she burst into tears and bowed her head as David hugged her to him. Oh, how she had longed to have him put his arms round her and hold her! But she had to be strong. The only way she could keep her sanity living with a man she didn't love was to keep up the pretence that there was nothing between her and David. She pushed him away. 'I must get back!'

David grabbed her arm. 'This has got to be said. Even though it is too late, I think we need to get things straight between us. If we had recognized this feeling and confessed it in the first place our lives would not now be in the parlous state they are.' He drew his hand across her wet cheek. 'I felt I owed loyalty to Rosemary so I tried to fight the feelings I had for you. I thought that if I kept you at a distance, my infatuation – for that was what I thought it was – would pass. I was racked with guilt; Rosemary had done nothing to deserve being jilted—'

'Please! Stop!' Mourne said pitifully. 'I can cope if I don't give in to all this. It is too cruel to have you say all this to me now, when it's too late . . .'

David grabbed her shoulders and turned her to face him. 'If you loved me, why did you accept John McCrory? For God's sake, Mourne, why?'

Trying desperately to get control, she detached herself from his hold and faced him. 'I'll tell you why!' she said. 'When I discovered that I had been abandoned as a newborn infant, something in me died.

216

I vowed that I would never put myself in the position of being rejected ever again. When you came back into my life and I found myself falling in love with you, and that this time it was a hundred times more deep than the childish crush I had on you all those years ago—'

'Why couldn't you have been honest with me? There were occasions when I almost confessed that I had fallen in love with *you*, but you became so distant suddenly, I held back from telling you.' David's voice was rough.

'I was scared; scared that if I cared for someone too much I would be hurt all over again.' Mourne shuddered. 'I would rather go without love than face those terrible feelings I had the first time. Then I met John. He was fun to be with and for a time I felt secure again. You see! John was honest with me. He told me that he didn't love me but that he liked being with me. When he told me about Rosemary I was devastated, and I decided then that if he ever proposed to me I would accept . . .'

'Without love?' David cried.

'Yes! Because if ever John left me for someone else I knew it wouldn't hurt, and if it wasn't a marriage based on love, at least we were compatible.'

'I never knew how deeply you felt about your birth mother.'

'I told you – up there on the mountain.'

David shook his head. 'I didn't realize – I'm sorry.'

'It's too late for us. Go back and marry Rosemary . . .' Mourne stifled a sob.

David shook his head. 'I'm afraid that wouldn't work. Apart from the fact that I love—'

'I don't want to hear.'

'That I love you,' David carried on. 'I want to stay here in Ballycash, and Rosemary would never leave London for a small village at the back end of the world. Even if she changed her mind, I'm afraid it's too late. I couldn't marry her.'

'It has all gone terribly wrong, hasn't it?'

David nodded and gave a bitter sigh. 'We have got to come to terms with the situation and try to get on with our lives the best we can. There will be dinner parties with our folk and there will be Christmas and other occasions. We can't pretend we won't meet . . .' They looked into each other's eyes.

Suddenly Mourne was in his arms. She knew the battle was lost the moment those dear eyes looked into hers. Her heart might break later, but just now, as she felt his lips search for hers, she lost all sense. Nothing could come of it, but at least they had this moment to treasure. The bitter sweetness of it just added to the joy that flooded her as the kiss went on, stopping only when David, with a groan, said, 'God, I love you!' before bringing his lips down on hers again.

When they drew apart at last, David said, shakily, 'I have to get back. I have a clinic this evening. Gerry has the evening off.'

It was when he spoke the words in an almost normal voice that Mourne knew the hardest time was now just beginning. She had to meet him and greet him as a friend, knowing that inside her whole being would be crying out for him. She bit her lip as she looked at him.

David took her hand. 'I know how you're feeling,' he said sadly, and she knew that he did, because his expression mirrored hers.

Eddy Coleman knocked on the glass pane and waited. His heart was in his mouth, for John McCrory had been knocking off workers at the rate of knots lately to save on overheads. He wondered if his turn had come. Eddy had been upgraded to manager fairly recently and, if he was honest, he would have to admit that his right hand didn't know what his left was doing. He was a mechanic, for Christ's sake. He knew machines – not how to manage a bloody factory. He had only been promoted because his salary would be less than Callum Brown's, his predecessor's. The carrot had been that when things improved, his salary would be increased.

Against his better judgement he had accepted the position. He had a family to support and obviously John McCrory thought he was capable enough. However, his position since his promotion had been a right shite of a situation. The men were disgusted that he had so readily stepped into Callum Brown's shoes, thereby causing his young family hardship. It had been no use trying to explain that someone had to do it for John McCrory, being the right bastard he was, was more than likely to sack him if he didn't accept, and he too had a family who had to be dressed and fed—

'Come in!'

Eddy opened the door and entered. John McCrory had a scowl on his face that would have intimidated a greater man, and Eddy felt his insides curl up.

'The output in the factory is diminishing. What the hell is happening out there, Coleman?'

'We haven't enough packers, Mr McCrory,' Eddy explained. 'You turned a lot off to save money—'

'Mind how you speak to me, man. I turned them off because the business was slack. I don't intend to pay workers when there is no work. It isn't a question of economizing – I will have them back when the orders pick up. I have some good contacts and my salesmen are out there doing their job.'

Eddy's lip curled, but he hid his feelings well. Did this eejut of a man think they were all daft just because they hadn't been born into the favoured classes? If Callum Brown was behind that desk where this clunkhead was now sitting, sales would be well up. The bloody profits, instead of being ploughed back in to upgrade equipment and organization, were either being poured down this erk's throat or passed across the roulette table in wads of notes. Old Simon McCrory might have been the hardest man on earth to work for, his standards were so high, but by the good God he had the place up and running on oiled wheels. An upturned lorry-load of cans and a lost order would have been but a blip. The situation would have been turned around to advantage. His son was not only a lousy boss, he was also a cahoun.

'Get those orders moving. I don't care if you have to put a hand to them yourself, just get them out on time. If I lose any orders because of your incompetence you will be fired. Now get out there and do the job.'

John slammed his hand down on to his desk in frustration as Eddy Coleman went out. He had done the wrong thing by getting rid of Brown. The man had been a good manager and the men respected him. But where needs must the devil drives a hard bargain, and unfortunately the firm was in difficulties and money had to be saved – and Brown commanded double the salary of Coleman. Well! It was too late now. He was not going to eat crow in front of that lot on the factory floor.

It would help if he could recoup some of his losses at the table. Just lately he had been on a losing streak. All he needed was a break. He could have done it too, if that bloody new bank manager had given him the loan he'd asked for. He tapped his fingers on the desk. He'd done it in Monte Carlo and he could do it again – he knew he could. He was feeling lucky. Unfortunately, he had foolishly spent the money he'd won on a new boat. He could have managed with the old one, but the temptation to have his own boat and not have to share had been too great – particularly as the money had been a bonus.

By the end of the day he still hadn't solved his problem. He glanced at his watch: it was late. The factory had closed down two hours ago, but the thought of going home to his unwilling statue of a wife was too much. He would go to the hotel and have dinner and a few jars. He wouldn't bother to ring Mourne – she would know by now that he wasn't coming home. That was another area in which he had made a bad error. Had he known that Mourne O'Hara was completely disinterested in the physical side of marriage, he wouldn't have bothered to court her. Her poise and her cool manner were what had attracted him, and he realized now that this should have set warning bells ringing. Things might have been different had she presented him with a son, but in spite of his allocated once-weekly session, she had shown no sign of breeding. Something would have to be done about the situation. He should never have agreed to her terms, but at the time he had been riddled with remorse because of his own behaviour. His face darkened. It was time she learned that as a dutiful wife she should please him when he requested it. He would show her that he was master in his own home.

Mourne was only mildly annoyed when John didn't arrive home. She was irritated because she had prepared a meal for him and had she known he wouldn't be home, she wouldn't have bothered to cook. A sandwich would have sufficed, for the day and evening had been hot for late May. Besides, after all the house-cleaning she had done with Annie she was exhausted. Annie had complained about the amount of work she had to get through to keep the large house looking reasonable and Mourne, in an effort to stop her giving notice, had said she would help her. If John knew that she did so he would be very angry indeed. John had very firm rules about the mistress and servant relationship, which was fine for him – he wouldn't be the one to have to cope alone with a house as big as a small castle and falling apart at the seams.

Mourne hated this house. It had a sinister feel to it, and when she stood up in the minstrel gallery to look down on the cavernous hall with its dark panelling, she sensed the unhappiness of the past. She was always careful when she stepped out of her room just off the gallery for she suspected that the banister was rotten, although the dark paint and polish might hide its secret.

Bored, she trailed downstairs to the smaller sitting room, and as she passed the telephone in the hall she lifted the receiver on impulse and rang Tara. She sorely missed Tara. She had seen her only once since she had returned from her honeymoon and she had a great desire to meet up with her and laugh again at foolish things.

Jay-Jay answered the phone. 'Hello stranger!' he laughed. 'We wondered if you had died in your sleep. How are you?'

'I'm doing great! and yourself?'

'I'm on the verge of divorce. I'm going to cite irreconcilable differences,' he laughed, adding, 'Whatever I say or do – she differs with it.'

'God Almighty! For a split second I believed you.'

'Ach away. Sure Tara and the baby would never cope – and besides,' he paused, 'here's herself. I'll let her tell you.'

'You couldn't believe a word that man says,' Tara's infectious giggle sounded over the phone. 'It's about time you gave me a ring, girl. You haven't seen your godson for a while.'

'There are two ends to a telephone,' Mourne laughed. 'How is wee Thomas? And what's new with you? I'm dying to see you. We must meet.'

'That would be great and it couldn't be a better time,' Tara said. 'Jay-Jay has to take a fare up to Newcastle the day after tomorrow. He wouldn't mind dropping me off. Would that be all right with you?'

'Can you make it for lunch?'

'Free lunch? Of course I can,' Tara giggled. 'Throw in a ride in your new car and we have a deal.'

They talked for a long time. Tara rattled on about life with a baby and how her ma-in-law spoilt the devil out of him, and how he was already showing signs of being a wow with women. When she put the phone down Mourne smiled. Her mood had lightened. She was going to see her friend and hear the latest great news she'd hinted about. She switched off the lights and went up to her bedroom again. She'd read for a while and hope that John wouldn't come in the worse for drink and in a bad mood from losing at the club, which is where he probably was.

Her luck was out. John came barging into her room well after midnight and shook her roughly awake. 'I have shomething I w-wish to shay to you, ice maiden. Wake up and lishen.'

Mourne's heart pumped. He must have taken on a right load. Even when he had taken more than usual he never slurred his words. John was acutely aware of his dignity. He could be arrogant and rude in drink, but she had never seen him slurring and lurching all over the place as he was doing now. She struggled awake and tried to take

221

control of the situation. John was now lying across the bed, making an attempt to get up again.

'John,' Mourne said soothingly. 'Whatever it is, it can wait till morning. You are tired now. I'll help you to bed.' She could feel her voice trembling as she spoke and took a deep breath to steady it. He mustn't know that he was alarming her. He enjoyed seeing her at a disadvantage.

John lurched upright, and swaying unsteadily, looked down at her. 'I will have my shay,' he insisted.

Mourne sighed. 'Say what you have to, John, so that I can get back to sleep.'

'I am going to have my marital rights. You will not deny me entry to your bedroom at any time – understand?'

'I understand. Now let me help you to your room.' Fearful that he would insist on his marital rights at this late hour, she held his arm and tried to get out of bed.

'From now on this will be *our* room,' John said, and staggered.

A shudder ran through her. He'll have forgotten all this by tomorrow morning, she thought hopefully. She climbed from the bed, and as she did so John fell across it again and began to snore. She sighed with relief, and then smiled as an idea struck her. Going round to the other side of the bed, she lifted his legs up on to it and proceeded to undress him. It wasn't easy because he was a heavy man, but she managed at last to get his clothes off so that he lay stark naked. Then she slipped out quietly. Before he woke in the morning she would be lying beside him. He was so stocious drunk he would never remember how he got there, and hopefully he would assume he'd had his wicked way with her.

Mourne ran to the door as she saw Tara's figure halfway up the drive. For the first time in weeks she'd had something to look forward to and she wore a huge smile as she called out, 'Where's my godson?'

Tara said, 'You'll see him another day. He's with his doting granny. I had no intention of refusing her offer, seeing as I don't often get away on my own. I want this day to be ours because I haven't seen you since the christening – we've a lot of talking to do.'

Mourne gave her a tight hug. 'I was going to make us lunch, but I changed my mind. You and I are going to drive to Strangford Lough and spend the day there and dine at the new hotel – my treat. We'll talk the hind legs off a donkey between the pair of us.'

Later, over lunch, Tara told Mourne her news. 'I'm pregnant again.'

222

Mourne gasped. 'What age will Thomas be when the new baby arrives?'

'He'll be a year old. Sure he could be walking by then, and believe me his granny will never be away from our place. She'll be a great help.'

Mourne looked at Tara in surprise. 'Things are better between you and your mother-in-law, then?'

'Now that Jay-Jay and I have our own place we get on great guns. It was mostly her obsessiveness and her perpetual house-cleaning that was the problem. Once we were out of the house I found I liked her more and since Thomas was born she's been great.' Tara laid down her knife and fork and leaned back. Mourne was looking a bit thin. Never a large person at the best of times, she now looked waiflike. 'Are you on a diet or what?' she asked. 'There isn't anything of you. Are you happy?'

Mourne smiled. 'I'm happy enough.'

'What do you mean, enough?'

'I mean that considering I wasn't deeply, madly, truly in love with John I am happy. We both knew it wasn't a love-match made in heaven – if you remember, you advised me against it.'

Tara nodded. 'I suppose so,' she said, reluctantly. 'But somehow you've lost your old sparkle. I can't help feeling a bit worried about you.'

God! There was that phrase again. She must be going around looking unwittingly sour, Mourne thought. 'John and I are trying for a baby,' she said brightly.

'So far without luck,' Tara said. 'Or you'd be sitting there with a big grin on your face.'

'I was always yards behind you. My time will come, and I'll end up outsmarting you all by having triplets.'

'Just hope Himself up there hasn't heard that remark,' Tara giggled. 'Having one at a time is hard enough – I wouldn't speak to Jay-Jay for an hour after the birth. I told him I blamed him for all the agony I went through and swore I'd castrate him if he touched me again.'

She was silent for a moment. 'I hoped you might fall for David McNeill,' she said softly.

'Things don't always go the way you want them,' Mourne said quickly, hoping she had managed to hide her pain. Where was the use letting the world know that she was desperately wishing she could turn the clock back?

223

Tara's shoulders lifted and she laughed lightly. 'You can't say you haven't married well. The man is made of money, the factory must be making a mint. Jay-Jay is really envious that your husband can spend so much time at the Crystal Club when all *he* can do is drop his clients off in the car park.'

Mourne hid her concern. She hadn't realized how much time John did spend at the club – obviously more than she had reckoned – and then there were all the evenings he spent down in the hall playing poker with his friends. She frowned, and then seeing Tara look at her she said quickly, 'I don't feel like dessert. How about you?'

'You aren't doing me out of my pudding,' Tara laughed. 'I'm eating for two. I want the jam sponge – you can sit and watch.'

Mourne raised her hand discreetly for the waiter.

After lunch they strolled round the lough, enjoying sightings of waterfowl and admiring the white-sailed yachts silently breasting through the water.

'I hear that in the future there are going to be great changes here,' said Tara. 'I hope it doesn't become too much of an attraction. I think once the tourists start to overrun the place, the wildlife will suffer.'

They found a quiet spot and lay down on the soft grass. After a time, Mourne rose and strolled down towards the water's edge where there was a cooling breeze, as Tara drifted off to sleep in the pleasant warmth of the sun. Gazing dreamily across the gently rippling expanse she wondered what David was doing at this moment – and where he was doing it.

She continued to stare, but now her gaze was unseeing as her mind went over the events of the past few days. She hugged her knees closely to her and buried her face in her folded arms. She had been too hasty. She had lost the man she loved and would spend the rest of her days deeply regretting it. If only John hadn't changed so much in the short time they had been married, she might have learned to respect him and maybe a kind of love would have been born of that respect; but he had changed, and she knew that she would never now be able to love him. She relived in her mind the moment when David had taken her in his arms and kissed her, and now, as her body responded to her thoughts, she felt the tears sting her eyelids. It was at that moment that Tara called out to her. She hastily wiped her eyes and rose.

They were halfway home before Tara said, tentatively, 'Will John be home when we get back?'

Mourne shook her head. 'I'm lucky if he gets back in time for a meal. He seems to spend more time at the factory these days than he does at home.'

'Do you mind?'

Mourne kept her eyes on the road and her voice calm as she replied, 'I mind in as much as I wasted a lot of food in the early days; now I wait for him to come in before I cook.' She laughed lightly. 'He gets a bit annoyed sometimes, especially when he's hungry, but I've made a stand. I told him that there was no reason why he couldn't phone if he was going to be late. We had a right barney of a row about it, to tell you the truth. I told him that if we didn't come to terms with each other – and soon – I would leave.'

'What! You mean divorce him?'

'No! Merciful God, His Holiness the Pope would have something to say about that. I meant I would go home to my mother.'

'Sure the Pope would never know,' Tara giggled.

'Father Patrick as his local representative would.' They dissolved into peals of laughter. 'Look! We shouldn't joke about such things,' Mourne said, and wiped her eyes. 'If we carry on like this we'll have an accident.' She felt buoyant. Tara had that effect on her. They laughed about the most inconsequential things, and both knew that this was one of them. The idea of a Catholic girl ever contemplating such a step was so steeped in the realms of fantasy, it was a laughable matter.

'I do miss you,' said Tara. 'I have no one to laugh with. The mother-in-law sees life in black and white and Jay-Jay thinks that girls giggle too much, so I tend to laugh about more practical things with him.'

'Come on! Jay-Jay has a great sense of humour,' Mourne scoffed.

'I know he does,' Tara said, 'but you and I laugh at the daftest things, and I always feel happier after one of our silly sessions.'

They turned into the driveway and saw Jay-Jay's taxi. 'There's the man himself, God love him,' Tara said fondly, and Mourne felt a stab of envy at the tenderness of her voice.

Jay-Jay turned down her invitation to come in for a cup of tea. They had to get back. He was due to pick up his client shortly. 'After all!' Jay-Jay grinned. 'The poor man is paying for my wife's trip. It's hardly fair to keep him waiting for the return journey.'

The phone was ringing when Mourne entered the hall. It was John. He wouldn't be home for dinner. He was not going to the club. He had a crucial appointment with a man who was interested in investing in the business, and they would be dining in Newcastle. Mourne smiled in amusement. The altercation she'd had with John had done some good after all.

'Have you any idea what time you will be home?'

'No!' he replied reprovingly. 'It's enough that I'm ringing to let you know. I have no intention of stating times and dates—'

'I didn't mean . . . I just thought that if you were going to be late, I would go and see Mam.'

'Fine!' said John. 'Give her my fond regards.'

Mourne recognized the sarcasm in his tone and put the phone down with an angry thump, before lifting it again and ringing the parochial house.

Father Dougan answered the phone. Mourne asked if her mother was there.

'She isn't! But the boss is,' said Cahal Dougan, and Mourne laughed.

'I'll speak to him, then.' She waited whilst Cahal found Father Patrick.

'Hello Mourne. What can I do for you? Your mam is out at this moment.'

'I wondered if I could come over for supper – John won't be home till late, and I thought it would be nice to see you both as it's been a while.'

There was a pause. 'We're going to Gerry's for dinner. Why don't we meet you there?'

'I can't invite myself to Uncle Gerry's just like that,' Mourne gasped.

'Talk sense. He's one of the family. He would be delighted to see you. He was going on about it the other day. He says he hasn't seen anything of you since you got married except for a brief visit before David arrived back. I'll have no nonsense. We don't see much of you as it is – and as you well know, Mrs Haggerty makes enough to feed the forty thousand. Away and get ready and we'll meet you there – I'll let Gerry know.'

The phone went dead. Mourne smiled. He'd put the phone down so that she wouldn't have time to argue the toss. She wondered if David would be there. God! Maybe she should ring back and cancel. How could she sit opposite him at the table and eat and speak as though nothing had happened between them? She put out her hand towards the phone, then drew it back. She wanted to see him again even if it broke her heart in pieces just to look at him. Just seeing him, although it would be exquisite torture, would be enough to see her through the following months.

CHAPTER 14

It was their wedding anniversary. Mourne didn't suppose that John had even remembered. She fingered the card she had ready on her knee, but seeing his face and realizing that he was in one of his usual breakfast-time moods, she hesitated. If he hadn't remembered he'd be embarrassed, and with the mood he was in . . . she slowly lowered the card to the floor beneath the table.

'Has the post arrived yet?' John looked at her over the top of his newspaper. Reading at table was a bad habit of his, his excuse being that it was the only time he could find to read the paper. He waited for her reply.

'I'll just check.' She rose and walked from the kitchen. They rarely used the big dining room, for when they were first married, John had informed her that now Mrs Flannigan had gone he would prefer it if they ate in the large kitchen unless they were entertaining. He had, he said, 'spent enough time seated at that enormous table like a bloody orphan.'

John McCrory watched his wife reflectively as she left the room. Over the last few months his relationship with her had deteriorated. In spite of both their efforts in the early days to try and put the past behind them, he now knew that no matter how hard they worked, they would never be able to do it. His behaviour on the first night of their honeymoon loomed like a spectre over them.

For the first few weeks following their return things had looked hopeful. He had kept his promise and didn't make too many demands on her, and she had kept her bargain that they would try for a child. It had been a farce. Finding himself making love to a woman who lay there like a lump of wood, he had treated her roughly to activate some feeling and grew incensed when, after the sex, she rose and went to the bathroom where he suspected she scrubbed herself clean. He frowned, and covered his face with his hands. He was an absolute shite.

The truth was, he had made a mistake. The fact that the young Mourne O'Hara had a beauty unsurpassed by anyone he had ever met was no consolation for the utterness of her respectability. She would never understand his world or the standards he lived by. He should have married Helen Moore. She understood him and had never complained when he had treated her roughly. She had known just how to handle him. When he'd lost a lot of money or his father was driving him crazy, she would quietly stay out of harm's way and give him time to recover from his despondency.

It had been easier for her, of course. She had her own place, while Mourne was living in the same house as him, and, large though it was, they were still thrown together at mealtimes. Just lately his behaviour had been worse than usual because of the pressure placed on him by the appalling state of the factory. If he didn't find some finance soon he would be bankrupt. He blamed Harry Cosgrove as much as anyone. All that wining and dining Harry at the Headland Hotel had cost him a bloody fortune six months ago, and nothing had come of it because Harry had taken advice from his bank and decided against investing.

He'd had to sell his boat to cover immediate bills, but the two thousand pounds he had held back to try and make some money with at the tables had been eaten up in a matter of a few throws of the dice. How he had held on this long he didn't know. His father's name must count for something . . .

His thoughts were interrupted by the return of Mourne. 'The post hasn't come yet.'

'It's taken you a long enough time to come to that conclusion,' said John churlishly, and thought, Christ! Can I not give the woman a break?

Mourne reseated herself and poured some tea. 'I thought I saw the gate opening and I waited to see if it was the postman,' she replied evenly. She didn't want an argument. It had been a bad summer for arguments between them. Some of the time she had managed to turn the tide, but not often. When John was in one of his belligerent moods it was very difficult to change the course of it and she always came off second-best. She sighed with relief when he had gone and the tension in her muscles eased.

Thinking back, there had been good times in the early months of her marriage when she could understand why she had been attracted to him, for at his best John could charm the birds from the trees. But those days had long gone and she found herself wishing they had lasted: the John who had courted her and given her cause to think that marriage to him would be safe and happy had disappeared; and in his place was an alien.

Taking the large tray from the sideboard she began to pile the crockery on to it. The other worrying thing was that lately she'd started getting the feeling again that she was being watched. Twice in the past month she had turned round swiftly only to find a perfectly normal-looking stranger walking along minding his own business. Sometimes she had wondered fearfully if she was going a bit peculiar.

She still visited her rock, where she sat for ages enjoying the feeling of belonging the area gave her. Sometimes, on a really beautiful day when she had eaten her picnic lunch, she would fall asleep. Curiously, it was on one of those occasions that she had suddenly started awake, absolutely certain there was someone there. She had scrambled to her feet, felt a momentary dizziness, and leaned against the rock till it had passed. She looked around but could see no one. Her imagination was running riot – it must be. Then she'd caught sight of the flowers – a small bunch of wild flowers. She was certain they hadn't been there when she'd fallen asleep. Hastily gathering up her bag and with heart thumping, she hightailed it down the mountain.

She hadn't been there since the weather had changed. This November was particularly severe, and on several days recently there had been a covering of snow on the ground. On really cold days she stayed in the house and hated it. She longed for the time when she had been working at the surgery and the days had passed busily and pleasantly. To keep herself occupied, she had begun helping with the housework until John had discovered she was doing it and had been very angry. He had given her a lecture on it being her duty as his wife to keep up his standing and not be working with his servant when he was paying her to do the job. He had heard Bobby Anderson, one of his workers, remarking what a lovely person the boss's wife was. 'Always willing to give young Derry's sister a hand with the housework when it got too much for the young girl.'

Mourne had nearly wilted under his fury but she held on. 'It seems such a small sin, to help out,' she'd said quietly. 'The house is so large and the dust gathers so quickly. Could we not find some help for the poor girl, then?'

John had flown into a temper and told her to leave the hiring and firing and the decisions to him. She had been amazed at the strength of his anger over such a small matter, and wondered if it was just the tip of the iceberg. Was there something more beneath, and was John using this small incident to dispel a deeper, more harrowing worry? She wished he would discuss things with her. She was sure that just talking to someone about it would help.

The news that Tara had given birth to a girl went some way to easing the tedium of her life. Jay-Jay had phoned her as soon as he got back from the hospital and she promised that she would visit. 'What are you going to call her?'

'Clodagh.'

'That's nice. Tell Tara I'll be down soon. Do you know when she'll be going home?'

'I think she'll be in for a while. There were a few complications.'

'Such as what? She is going to be all right, isn't she?'

'Oh aye!' Jay-Jay said hurriedly. 'Her blood pressure is very low. She lost a lot of blood. They just want to keep an eye on her for a few days.'

'Will she be allowed visitors? Perhaps I could pop down tomorrow – or is that too soon?'

'That would be grand. I'll tell her you're coming. It'll cheer her up no end.'

Mourne drove down the following afternoon with an armful of flowers, an enormous box of chocolates and a matinée jacket for the baby. She stole up to the bed to find Tara asleep. She laid the gifts down and waited. Tara looked deathly pale. A blood drip was attached to her arm and the delicate skin beneath her eyes was dark. Mourne tentatively put out her hand and gently took Tara's blue-veined one into her own. She looks so fragile and tiny, she thought, so unlike the robust girl she normally was. Tara hadn't looked so weak after her first baby, but then, Mourne hadn't visited quite so soon after Thomas's birth.

When Tara dragged herself awake she smiled wanly at Mourne. 'It's just lovely to see you. I've been feeling so down.'

'I suspect that's because you're lying there with only half your volume of blood, you silly kitter,' Mourne laughed. 'I'll do all the talking for a change. You can give that voice of yours a rest.' She lifted the presents and laid them on the bed. 'I bought the matinée coat some time ago. It's just as well you had a Clodagh,' she giggled. 'It looks too girlish for a boy – I like the name, by the way.'

'It's my grandmother's name,' Tara whispered, faintly.

'I hope you aren't intending to have a baby every year,' Mourne teased. 'You'll end up like the McGowans up at home. They've just had their sixteenth.'

Tara turned her eyes up. 'Give me the strength to resist,' she murmured.

A nurse came along at that moment to inspect the drip. 'You seem to be cheering Mrs Garrity up,' she said, with a smile to Mourne. 'Don't overtax her, though,' she whispered as she left. 'She's still very weak.'

Mourne nodded and looked towards Tara, who had closed her eyes. She stood up and touched her shoulder gently. 'I think you've had enough of me for one day—'

'Please! Don't go yet,' Tara pleaded. 'I love you being here. You just talk to me and I promise I'll just listen.'

She fell asleep, however, in the middle of a tale about the Maguire twins, so Mourne slipped quietly away. She met the sister of the ward on her way out.

'Sister! Could I ask you if Mrs Garrity is all right? She doesn't seem to have much energy – I mean, after her first baby she was full of bounce.'

'It was a hard birth and the baby was large. She'll be fine. Once she has had another pint of blood she'll pick up – have you seen the baby?'

Mourne shook her head.

'Come along! She's in the nursery.'

When she saw Clodagh, Mourne gasped.

'Now you can see why Mrs Garrity is feeling so weak. The baby was a nine-pounder!' Sister Bell laughed. 'Next time you see your friend she'll be full of it all, don't you worry.' She patted Mourne's shoulder and accompanied her to the door.

Mourne saw precious little of her husband these days; when she did it was usually for social reasons, such as the meal they had just had with Kitty and Father Patrick when John, for most of the time, spent the evening staring into the middle distance and answering only when directly spoken to. Father Patrick, with a shrug towards Kitty and Mourne, had given up the ghost and excused himself.

Mourne, in an effort to regularize the situation, said to her mother, 'John has a lot on his mind at the moment. He has some problems at the factory.' She had laid her hand on his and was astonished when, with a look of sheer anger, he had yanked it away, stood up, and said frostily: 'Don't patronize me. My business is not for public discussion. Get your coat; I think it is time we went home.'

Kitty, horrified, said, 'Mourne wasn't intending to discuss your business problems, son. She was just—'

'She was excusing my lack of conversation, which was unnecessary. I admit I haven't been in the best of humours, but I've done nothing that rates an apology. I was quiet and clearly not feeling sociable – that is all. If you'll excuse us, we will be going. Thank you for the meal. Please say goodbye to Father Mulligan.'

On the way home Mourne was subjected to a tirade against her audacity in saying what she did. She was silent. John had his head now, and judging by the copious amounts of wine and brandy he had drunk it was best to let him get on with it. He was in a very dangerous mood altogether.

Not without some misgivings she went on up to her bedroom, leaving him to help himself to some more brandy. There was not a bit of use her reminding him that he'd already drunk rather a lot. Once before when he had been drinking with his friends she had gently suggested that he be careful, and he had pushed her rudely towards the stairs telling her to prepare herself for him, and meanwhile to let him decide when he'd had enough. She could still remember her humiliation as she'd climbed the stairs to the shadowed corner in the minstrel gallery and listened to the lewd comments of her husband's guests.

She had been in bed some time when the door burst open, startling her into drowsy wakefulness. John stood by the door swaying, with a glass still in his hand: 'I am very angry with you, you little bitch. You made me loo-look foolish to-n-night. I was going to teash you a leshon, but I have a better idea. I'll take back the frigging engagement ring you no longer wear. I have a good use for it.'

Mourne watched fearfully as he stumbled towards her dressing-table and began to yank the drawers open. She climbed out of bed. He was too drunk to be aware of what he was doing. She might be able to persuade him to wait till morning to find what he was searching for. As she drew level with him he thrust his arm out, accidentally landing a blow across her cheek; she felt his ring cut her. She stumbled and grabbed the window ledge. 'Please John!' she begged. 'Whatever it is you're looking for it can wait till morning.' She straightened. He had found the jewel box he'd bought her when they had chosen her engagement ring.

Watching her carefully, John opened it and took out a velvet-covered box. She didn't shift her gaze. He had to admire her. He knew she was scared but she stood there, framed by the window, with that glorious hair hanging loose and those frightened emerald green eyes staring straight at him with haughty disdain. Suddenly he felt an urge to take that proud form and bend it to his will – but first he had to put the ring safely in his pocket.

As he opened the box he continued to look towards her. 'Stay just where you are,' he said, his voice slurring. 'I've had enough of you. I need to clear my debts and I will be selling this ring. You'll get another one – if you behave – once I am on my feet again. You don't know the extent of my problems, do you? You stupid girl. You only care about meeting your friends and swanning around in the car I bought you. It didn't mat-matter that I was having a hard b-bloody time of it. Well! Now it's your turn to help me out . . .' John swept his gaze to the tiny box in his hand and his eyes bulged when he saw the emerald ring sitting cosily in its velvet bed. His hands shook as he drew the ring out.

'Jesus! Where did you get this?' He took a step towards her. Mourne took one towards him. 'Please John – oh, please don't take my ring. It was my mother's ring. It's the only thing I have of hers.'

Wrathfully he thrust her away from him with such force that she fell against the wooden headboard. She cried out as the pain shot through her eye. Uncaring, John continued to examine his find. This ring must be worth a bloody fortune – enough to set him on his feet again. Kitty O'Hara had never owned a ring like this. 'What do you mean – the only thing you have of your mother's? Where would Kitty O'Hara get a ring that's worth a small ransom? There's a man in this somewhere. You've been two-timing me, you trollop!' He became further incensed with rage.

A vision of her in another man's arms came to him. That bloody McNeill had given her this! All the time she'd been charming him with her beauty and her proud manner and her air of chastity, she had been dallying with her doctor boyfriend. His head was bursting with fury as he lunged at her. Women had always got the better of him. His bloody mother, Mrs Flannigan – and now this one. All reason fled as he began hitting her about the head and body.

Terrified, Mourne crouched on the floor as the blows rained down

235

and then, with a pleading gesture, she threw up her arms. It was at that moment that she felt a terrible pain in her ribs as he kicked her. She collapsed on the floor, and as she lost consciousness she heard the bedroom door bang shut.

She cried out as she felt herself being moved. So great was the pain it jolted her into awareness. She looked into a pair of grey eyes and tried to shake herself further awake, but she gasped as the pain hit her again.

'I think you've cracked your ribs.' The voice was gentle.

She tried to focus on the face above her but had to close her eyes again. The effort was beyond her. 'Who are you? What has happened?' she whispered with difficulty.

'Never mind who I am just for the moment. You must listen to me carefully – very carefully. Please listen!'

Mourne opened her eyes again. Through a mist of pain she saw a youngish man bending over her, a concerned look on his face. It was a darkly tanned face. She felt no fear. 'My husband – it was an accident – he – he – where is he?' she whispered.

Once she had been positioned comfortably the pain in her ribs had eased, but Mourne took slow even breaths so as to avoid further discomfort. She knew enough about medicine to know that she should keep her ribcage as still as possible. 'Go on!' she whispered.

'Don't move when you hear what I have to say. It is more important that you follow my instructions – do you understand?'

Mourne nodded. Instinct told her that she was not going to like what she was about to hear.

'I'm afraid your husband is dead!' The young man held her arms close to her body lest she injure herself further as she cried out.

Tears formed behind her lids and began to run down her cheeks.

'Your husband locked you in and had just put the key in his pocket when I arrived,' the man went on. 'We fought. He fell against the banister rail, and it gave way under the weight of his body. He fell to the hall below – he died instantly, believe me . . .'

The poor girl had fainted. The stranger gently loosened her arms and made his way to the bathroom for a wet flannel. It was imperative that she understand the dilemma he was in. He brought the flannel back and placed it on her forehead.

Mourne came to as the icy water ran down her neck. Stricken, she gazed up at the stranger. 'Why? Who are you – what are you saying?'

236

'My name is Fingal. I was standing in the grounds outside when I saw what was happening through the window – the curtains weren't drawn. I climbed up a drainpipe and through an open window to try and help . . . your husband lunged at me . . . I threw a punch in defence and he fell heavily against the rail . . .'

Mourne nodded and the tears fell rapidly now. 'I kept telling him the rail in the gallery was rotten,' she cried. 'Go on!'

'It was an accident – you must believe me.' He spoke anxiously. 'Now! Here is what you must do. Are you listening?'

Mourne nodded.

'I am going to lock you in again . . .'

'Again?'

'Your husband locked you in – I took the key from his pocket. We haven't much time – *please* don't talk, just listen,' Fingal pleaded. 'When I've gone I want you to ring Dr David and tell him that you've been locked in and are afraid that your husband has had an accident. Ask him to get here as soon as possible – got that?'

Mourne nodded and winced as the pain in her ribs worsened. 'You'll have to put the telephone near – I can't move.'

Fingal shook his head. 'You will have to reach it. You'll have to get to the chair by the table where it is and sit there. If it's lying beside you then the question will be asked, how?'

'Can you help me?'

Fingal nodded. 'But remember! You got there slowly and painfully – I know you don't understand why we're doing all this, but trust me – please. I'll get in touch with you as soon as the police have been—'

'The police?'

'Dr David will explain. You just do as I say. As far as everyone is concerned, you have been beaten and locked up and you don't know what happened next because you passed out.' Fingal, holding her arms closely to her side again, helped her to the table a few feet away. 'One more thing,' he said as she lifted the phone. 'In three weeks' time to the very day, I will meet you and Dr David up by the rock in the Silent Valley at three o'clock in the afternoon.' He left her gasping with pain as she dialled David's number.

When the phone rang David had just climbed into bed. He sighed. It had been one hell of a day. He could do without a night call. He threw back the bedclothes and went to answer it.

Mourne's voice came over the line and his heart beat fast. She was

237

in trouble. He could hear her sob as she spoke and every now and again she would give a gasp as though in pain.

'Mourne, you'll have to slow down, you aren't making any sense. What do you mean you are locked in your bedroom – where's John? Why are you grunting?' His heart nearly stopped as he listened to her halted and garbled explanation.

'Please come quickly, David,' Mourne pleaded. 'John has had an accident. I – I – he's dead but I'm not supposed to know . . .'

'I'll be there as soon as I can. Meanwhile you had better ring the police – no, wait! I'll ring them. I'm on my way.'

He raced into his bedroom, hurriedly threw on some clothes and dashed to his car, setting off at a right lick. His mind was racing to keep pace with what Mourne had said on the phone. She was hurt. He could tell by the way she gasped as she tried to explain – something about being locked in and John being dead – but she wasn't supposed to know . . . He must get to her. The police would already be there. The station was only a mile from John's place – funny how he could never think of it as Mourne's house. God! He was babbling. He was, he also realized, racing very fast along the narrow coast road. He slowed a little. Better to arrive late than not at all. In fact he arrived just as a police car drew up at the front door.

The constable, a big burly man, waited for him. 'You are the doctor who called?'

David nodded and answered, 'Mrs McCrory rang me. She sounded very confused.'

They went up the steps together. A younger policeman, who had already reached the door, turned to them. 'It's locked, sir. Shall I go round the back?'

David said, 'No need. Mrs McCrory told me where the spare key is hidden for emergencies.' He went down the steps again and lifted the heavy stone ball from its shallow pit on the right-hand plinth guarding the steps. The key was just where Mourne had said it would be. He opened the door.

It was the sergeant who saw the body first. 'My good God! Something's badly wrong here. Constable! Get on the phone and get the doctor here at the double.'

'I'm a doctor!' David said, staring in horror at John McCrory.

'I'm sorry. I mean our own police doctor. I don't think we need to certify him dead – it's pretty obvious he is – but for post-mortem and legal purposes we will need our own man.' He glanced up towards the

238

minstrel gallery. 'Looks as if he either fell or was pushed from up there.'

David raced towards the stairs. 'Mrs McCrory is locked in her bedroom. I suspect you will find the key in the dead man's pocket, Sergeant.'

Sergeant Murphy nodded to the young constable. 'Go carefully, mind. I don't want anything disturbed.' He followed David upstairs.

'Is Mrs McCrory all right?'

'She says she is, but I think she's in shock. It might be better to leave any questions till later, Sergeant.'

''Fraid you'll have to leave that one to me. I can't let things lie fallow. The trail could go cold.'

Pompous old git, David thought, and said aloud, 'Of course! You have your job to do. But Mrs McCrory won't be able to tell you much about the fall, having been locked in by her husband. I must examine her. I understand she's been hurt.' Anxious to reach Mourne, David grabbed the key from the young constable and unlocked the door.

She was half lying, half sitting by the table with the telephone on the floor beside her. Her marble-white face crumpled as David approached. 'Oh David! What is happening?'

'Everything is under control,' he said, his voice shaking. All the places where she had been hit were darkening into bruises. Her left eye was closing. Her breathing was shallow, and when he gently touched her to help her up she gave a cry of pain. 'Have you hurt your ribs?' he asked, feeling gently along her chest wall.

Mourne nodded. 'I – I fell against the table when I was trying to reach the telephone,' she lied.

David didn't believe her for one minute. The ribs would have had to be those of an elderly woman to sustain fractures by just falling against a table. Catching the plea in her eyes, however, he went along with her story. He turned towards the sergeant. 'I think we'd better get Mrs McCrory along to Downpatrick. She's broken her ribs – and I think she needs to have that eye looked at.'

Sergeant Murphy agreed. 'If I could just ask you a few questions first, Mrs McCrory . . .'

'Of course!' Mourne said. 'Could – could Dr McNeill stay?'

Sergeant Murphy nodded. 'Just tell me quickly what happened as far as you know.'

Mourne told him of the row she'd had with her husband. 'He'd had too much to drink, and when he gets in that state he tends to lose control a bit,' she said.

'You call that a bit?' Sergeant Murphy looked at the bruising and snorted, but he listened carefully as she told her story.

'So you say he lost his temper because you didn't want him to take your engagement ring and *accidentally* knocked you over when you tried to take it back?'

Mourne nodded. 'It was something that blew up suddenly and – and ended tragically,' she whispered.

'And how do you know it ended tragically?' asked Sergeant Murphy, suspiciously.

'I told her that John had fallen over the balcony,' David said quickly. 'It seemed better coming from me. I am a friend of both.'

'Is that so,' Sergeant Murphy looked straight at David. 'Perhaps you could see to Mrs McCrory and leave us to do our job. You'd better take her to the hospital, and when she's feeling more the thing I'll have another word.'

There hadn't been such excitement and drama in the sleepy town since the big fight on the twelfth of July ten years ago, when Padraig McConnell had knocked the living daylights out of one of the Loyal Sons of Ulster and the whole town had gone berserk. It had ended with a fair number of both sides being up before the magistrate the same week. However it was agreed by all that this situation was more serious, and there was a feeling of awe that such a dreadful accident should happen so suddenly to a young man in his prime. Rumours were flying round that John McCrory had tried to kill his wife.

The courtroom was filled on the day of the inquest, and when after two hours it was established that McCrory had turned violent when he was stocious drunk and having locked his young wife in the bedroom had fallen from the balcony, there were a few sighs of disappointment. The verdict lacked the drama of the earlier rumour.

It was agreed that John McCrory may have backed towards the balcony rail in order to give a final kick at the door, and the balcony had given way. 'We will never know the truth of it,' said Mr Pearson, the magistrate. 'I have no option but to record this man's death as accidental.'

Kitty put her arms round Mourne as they left the courtroom. She was worried by her daughter's pallor. 'Home to a mug of strong tea,' she said quietly. 'It's all over now. You must look forward to the future.'

In the car on the way home Mourne sat with her head against the cool glass. It was such a relief to know that all the events of the past two weeks were coming to an end. She didn't know what she would have done without the support of David and her family, and she was thankful that they would be with her when the funeral took place in two days' time. Once it was over, she would be able to sit down and remember the good times she'd had with John and try to forget the pain and horror of that dreadful night. It was terrible to think what the drink could do to a man.

They were on their way up to the Silent Valley to rendezvous with the man who had helped her when David spoke. 'You really don't know why we're going to meet this young man?'

Mourne stopped. 'David! I would have said.' She looked at him. I've never met him before. I told you all that happened that night. I've no more idea than you have as to why he asked us both to meet him.'

They walked on in silence until they reached the big boulder. There was no sign of the young man. David looked at his watch. 'Dead on time,' he remarked. 'Now! Where is the mystery man?'

'I'm here!' They both jumped at the suddenness of his appearance. 'I was squatting on the other side of the boulder,' he explained.

David took control. 'It would seem that you have the advantage over us,' he said. 'You know who we are – perhaps you could tell us who you are and why we are here?'

'My name is Fingal.' He looked at Mourne. 'I am your uncle.'

Mourne paled as she and David looked at each other in disbelief. 'My uncle?' she cried. 'I don't understand—'

'My caravan is only ten minutes away. I think we—'

'Your caravan! You live in a caravan?'

Fingal nodded. 'I am a Rom – most people call us Romany gypsies – but Romany is actually the language of our people.' Fingal repeated his invitation. 'My caravan is further down the valley. I think it would be more comfortable for us to sit down over a mug of tea for I have much to tell you – the time has come for the truth to be told.'

Mourne was about to speak again when David touched her arm. 'Fingal will give us the answers.'

They were amazed when they saw the interior of Fingal's home. It was tastefully furnished and curtained. Hand-embroidered cushions lay scattered along the settee and a display cabinet above was filled with various items of delicately beautiful Waterford crystal. The main room was large and airy and surprisingly comfortable.

David raised his eyebrows at Mourne as Fingal busied himself in the tiny kitchen, and when he placed the mugs of hot liquid on the table before them, David said with a smile that he had never been in a caravan before and was surprised how spacious and comfortable it was.

'A Romany caravan is renowned for its comforts. We live like royalty compared to some,' Fingal explained. 'Those who live in a caravan to travel the countryside are classed as tinkers and gypsies. We are neither. My parents were tribe leaders of a very proud race.' He turned to Mourne. 'Under normal circumstances you would have been treated as a Rom princess.'

'Really!' said Mourne nervously, adding, 'You – you said that you were my uncle.'

Fingal nodded. 'I'll start at the beginning and tell you the whole story. It will be simpler that way. Stop me if I say something you don't understand.'

They listened as he began to tell them of a young life that had ended all those years ago and of one that had just begun.

'My sister Marianna and I were twins,' Fingal began. 'When our parents died suddenly in an accident we were just twelve years old and part of a tribe that travelled the country making and selling artefacts and taking on work where we could. Marianna and I continued that life.'

'But you were only children,' Mourne gasped. 'Who looked after you?'

Fingal smiled. 'In the Rom culture you are a man at twelve. I drove the caravan – it was horse-drawn then – and Marianna took care of the woman's work. We were happy enough. We did all the things our parents taught us and we managed very well. Being with the tribe was a comfort.' He stopped for a moment and a look of pain crossed his face. 'I took care of Marianna. I have a gift for carving and the things I made sold well. We were not rich but we survived comfortably.'

Mourne felt her heart go out to him, but mingled with her compassion was a feeling of joy. He was her own flesh and blood. Suddenly she had a real family. She was not just an unknown baby who had been taken on by Kitty and Charlie O'Hara. She had a past! However painful this story might turn out to be, she knew that her life was changed for ever.

'For the next two years,' Fingal continued, 'we were inseparable.

At those times when things seemed bleak we were there for each other against the world. Then Marianna met a young man and fell deeply in love. She was nearly fifteen by this time; a tall lass with hair and eyes the colour of your own – you are the image of her . . .' Fingal's voice faltered. 'The young man she fell in love with was the eighteen-year-old son of an aristocratic landowner. They were besotted with each other. I found out about their affair only when Marianna told me that she wanted to run away with him. I tried to reason with her, but they were both so in love they couldn't see the folly of it.'

Fingal rose and went into the kitchen again. He returned with the large teapot which he placed on the table and told them to help themselves, but Mourne shook her head.

'Go on!' she begged.

'I did a terrible thing,' Fingal said, his face stiff with the horror of his memories.

Mourne laid her hand on his. 'Whatever you did, I'm certain you did it with the best of intentions.'

'Over the years I have tried to tell myself that, but I cannot rid myself of my guilt. If it hadn't been for my interference my sister might still be alive today.' His voice broke. He hadn't delved so deeply into the past for many years and he was finding it hard to go on, but this girl had every right to know of her origins.

'You see! I feared for what might happen to Marianna if they carried out her plan to elope.'

'Would it have been so awful? I mean . . . if they loved each other . . .'

'Marianna would have been banished from the tribe,' Fingal said. 'No one would be allowed to help her if the relationship broke down – as I was certain it eventually would through the interference of outside forces. I couldn't let that happen. She was not yet fifteen. She wouldn't have survived . . .'

'So what did you do?'

'I told Phillip's parents about the romance and their reaction was dramatic. They were horrified that their only son and heir was in love with a common gypsy girl and their immediate plan was to bundle him off to England as soon as possible. That night, I discovered later, was the one and only time they made love. Phillip stole out of the house to say goodbye and promised Marianna that one day he would come for her. In their desperation they forgot everyone and everything and gave no thought to the consequences of their actions.'

243

David put his arms round Mourne as they waited for Fingal to continue.

'When the elders of the tribe learned of the circumstances they held a meeting with the result that we were both banished. We now had to fend for ourselves. We were not yet fifteen – the future was frightening. It was even more frightening when we discovered that Marianna was going to have a baby . . .'

'But if the tribe didn't know that my mother was expecting me, why did they banish you both?' Mourne asked.

'We were banished because Marianna had slept with a man who was not of our race. Unfortunately she had confessed her indiscretion to an old woman of the tribe, in a moment of deep unhappiness, and old Gorza felt it her duty to inform the elders.'

'Could you not have found help?'

Fingal smiled bitterly. 'From where? Who would want to get involved in the problems of a gypsy family? No! I decided that when the time came we would manage. I had seen children born many times – there was no secret about the ritual. We went our way and over the following months we did all right together. We managed.'

'Why didn't you sell the ring?'

'Never! That ring was given in love. Phillip stole out in the early hours of the morning to give Marianna that ring and swear his undying love, and she made me promise not to try and find him; she loved him too much to get between him and his parents. She felt that, being young, he would get over her and he had his life to get on with. She treasured the ring even more when she discovered that Phillip's grandmother had given the ring to him for his future bride. By giving it to her he had as good as told her that this was his desire.'

'Why did you never get in touch with him? Why was I placed in a cardboard box like a discarded doll? Abandoned there on the mountain!' A cry of anguish broke from Mourne and she buried her face in David's shoulder.

Fingal gazed at her in horror. 'You were no such thing! That was the day Marianna felt the pains start. You were not due for another four weeks and we were not prepared. There was no time to get help. She gave birth to you in our caravan but it all went wrong. Oh Christ! It all went wrong.' Fingal buried his head in his hands. Mourne stretched her hand towards him but David gently drew it back and shook his head. Eventually, Fingal lifted his head and continued.

'The baby – you – came too quickly. I didn't know what to do. I cut the cord but I couldn't stop the bleeding. I tried everything. I was too frightened to leave Marianna because I knew that by the time I got back she would be dead anyway, and she begged me not to leave, so I cuddled her in my arms till she died. She made me promise that I would find you a good home so that you would have a chance in life. After I buried her there on the mountain I wrote the note and raced down the mountain to Father Mulligan. I put the ring in the box with you, together with the cross which I had recently made for your arrival, and I guarded you till the priest came.'

'What about you? What did you do after – after . . .?'

'I travelled around the country alone for years, but I always kept track of you. I know everything about you. I was at your first Holy Communion. I was there, at the back of the church, when you were confirmed, and I was at your wedding.'

'It was you! I could never understand why so many times over the years I had the feeling that there was someone following me – yet I could never catch you.' Mourne spoke quietly as the truth dawned.

Fingal nodded. 'Mostly it was during the winter months. During the summer I would come back occasionally. I had this sixth sense about you. I knew for instance that you were seeing John McCrory and I wasn't happy. I was cut to the quick when you decided to marry him. I hoped at one time that you two . . .' He shrugged. 'That man was no good. I was very uneasy that night for some reason, and I had an urge to go to the house. The urge was so strong that I knew something was going to happen. When he drove up I could see that he was tipsy, so I waited in the garden.'

'But how do you feel these things?' Mourne asked.

'I'm a gypsy. I told you – we have the sixth sense. I knew all about the debts he owed to his gaming club and that his factory was going to the wall. The man was burdened with trouble and it was only a matter of time before he snapped. That night I watched your window and when I saw you fall twice I knew he was beating you. I didn't know about the ring till I went to get the key out of his pocket.'

'None of it matters now,' Mourne said. A surge of pure happiness shot through her. She had not been abandoned after all, and all these years her uncle had been looking after her interests. 'Was – was my mother able to hold me?' she asked hopefully.

'Your mother held you to her, and no child was looked at with more love. She was so caught up stroking your hands and kissing your eyelashes she didn't know that she was bleeding to death. You were in

245

her arms as she quietly passed away.' Fingal could no longer hold back his tortured thoughts. 'If only I could believe that I was not to blame. I loved her so much. She was the other half of me.' He cried.

David, who hadn't spoken in all that time, spoke now. 'You have nothing to reproach yourself with. Think of it. There was never a chance of that young man and your sister ever being together, and the events leading up to Mourne's birth were a separate issue. You had to do what you did. You weren't to know how things would turn out. Don't destroy yourself any more.'

Fingal, ashamed of this show of weakness, straightened. 'I'll be all right.'

'Do you live alone?'

'I've been with Angelina for the past ten years,' he said, proudly.

Mourne sighed happily. 'A few short weeks ago I still thought I had been abandoned, and now I have not only an uncle but a new aunt as well.' She suddenly leaned across the table and kissed Fingal and then frowned. 'Mam – what about Mam?'

'You must tell her, of course,' said David.

Fingal stared at David and sighed. 'You're right. She should be told.'

David rose. 'We must go back.'

'You will both keep in touch?' Fingal pleaded.

Mourne hugged him. 'I have no intention of losing my new family. Mam would be the first to agree. Besides,' a note of sadness crept into her voice, 'I would like to visit my mother's grave.'

'Of course you must.'

David put his hand on Fingal's shoulder. 'We'll take it one step at a time, but I have a feeling that everything is going to be fine from now on.'

They were halfway down the hill before he took Mourne in his arms. All the time they had been in the caravan he'd had to take strong measures to control himself, but now he held the slight body to him.

She gazed up at him. 'Will you kiss me on my home ground?' she asked.

'You bold article.' David laughed softly as he brought his mouth down on hers.

'I've always loved the mountain,' she sighed later. 'Particularly the Silent Valley – the valley where no birds sing. One day they might all come back again, but one thing is certain. I am on my ledge and off the hard path of life for a time.'

David looked puzzled. 'Where did you get that from?'

'A wise man called O'Rourke told me about it,' she said laughingly as together they strode on down the mountain towards Ballycash and home.